C000082231

BURNING ACHE

STEELE RIDGE: THE KINGSTONS

ADRIENNE GIORDANO

STEELE RIDGE
www.SteeleRidgeSeries.com

TEAM STEELE RIDGE

Edited by Gina Bernal

Copyedited by Martha Trachtenberg

Cover Design by Killion Group, Inc.

Author Photo by Debora Giordano

Copyright © 2019 Adrienne Giordano

ALL RIGHTS RESERVED

No part of this text may be reproduced, transmitted, downloaded, decompiled, reverse engineered, or stored in or introduced into any information storage and retrieval system, in any form or by any means, whether electronic or mechanical, now known or hereinafter invented—except in the case of brief quotations—without permission in writing from Steele Ridge Publishing.

This is a work of fiction. Names, characters, places, and incidents either are the product of the author's imagination or are used fictitiously, and any resemblance to actual persons, living or dead, business establishments, events or locales is entirely coincidental.

Print Edition, September 2019, ISBN: 978-1-948075-34-3

Digital Edition, September 2019, ISBN: 978-1-948075-33-6

For more information contact: adrienne@steeleridgepublishing.com

ALSO BY ADRIENNE GIORDANO

PRIVATE PROTECTORS SERIES

Romantic suspense

Risking Trust

Man Law

A Just Deception

Negotiating Point

Relentless Pursuit

Opposing Forces

HARLEQUIN INTRIGUES

Romantic suspense

The Prosecutor

The Defender

The Marshal

The Detective

The Rebel

JUSTIFIABLE CAUSE SERIES

Romantic suspense novellas

The Chase

The Evasion

The Capture

LUCIE RIZZO SERIES

Mysteries

Dog Collar Crime

Knocked Off

Limbo

Boosted

Whacked

Cooked

Incognito

CASINO FORTUNA SERIES

Romantic suspense

Deadly Odds

JUSTICE SERIES w/MISTY EVANS

Romantic suspense

Stealing Justice

Cheating Justice

Holiday Justice

Exposing Justice

Undercover Justice

Protecting Justice

Missing Justice

Defending Justice

STEELE RIDGE SERIES

Romantic suspense collaboration with Kelsey Browning & Tracey Devlyn

The BEGINNING

Going HARD

Living FAST

BOOKS AVAILABLE BY KELSEY BROWNING

NOVELLAS

Sexy contemporary romance

Amazed by You

Love So Sweet

BOOKS AVAILABLE BY TRACEY DEVLYN

NEXUS SERIES

Historical romantic suspense

A Lady's Revenge

Checkmate, My Lord

A Lady's Secret Weapon

Latymer

Shev

BONES & GEMSTONES SERIES

Historical romantic mystery

Night Storm

TEA TIME SHORTS & NOVELLAS

Sweet historical romance

His Secret Desire

STEELE RIDGE CHARACTERS

The Steeles

Britt Steele - Eldest Steele sibling. Construction worker who has a passion for the environment and head of Steele-Shepherd Wildlife Research Center.

Miranda "Randi" Shepherd - Owner of Blues, Brews and Books aka Triple B and Britt Steele's love interest.

Grif Steele - Steele sibling. Works as a sports agent and Steele Ridge's city manager.

Carlie Beth Parrish - Steele Ridge's only blacksmith and Grif Steele's love interest.

Reid Steele - Steele sibling. Former Green Beret and head of Steele Ridge Training Academy.

Brynne Whitfield - Owner of La Belle Style boutique in Steele Ridge and love interest of Reid Steele.

Mikayla "Micki" Steele - Steele sibling and Jonah's twin. Master hacker.

Gage Barber - Injured Green Beret and Reid Steele's close friend who comes to Steele Ridge to help run the training center. Love interest of Micki Steele.

Jonah Steele - Steele sibling and Micki's twin. Video game mogul and former owner of the billion-dollar company, Steele Trap. Responsible for saving the town of Steele Ridge, formerly known as Canyon Ridge.

Tessa Martin - Former in-house psychologist at Steele Trap and Jonah Steele's love interest.

Evie Steele - Youngest Steele sibling. Travel nurse.

Derek "Deke" Conrad - Commander of SONR (Special Operations for Natural Resources) group and love interest of Evie Steele.

Joan Steele - Mother of the six Steele siblings.

Eddy Steele - Father of the six Steele siblings.

BURNING ACHE

STEELE RIDGE: THE KINGSTONS

ADRIENNE GIORDANO

STEELE RIDGE
www.SteeleRidgeSeries.com

1

I'M IN HELL.

It's not so much the fact that I'm about to blow a man away. I can live with that. He's a piece of shit. The world is better off without him.

The raging inferno inside me comes from knowing that, once I dispose of him, there will be more. Plenty more. And not just the twelve on my list.

But I can't get too far ahead of myself. I have to stay present and focus on the now. That's what the live-your-best-life fanatics say.

A car door slams, snapping my attention back to the street. The only break in darkness emanates from the stingy streetlamps dotted between parkway trees and the occasional blast of headlights coming down the block.

I've tucked myself behind two bushes, hell if I know what they are, but they're squat and round, and sit on the edge of this asshole's property. The neighboring home's garage on my right gives me cover from that angle. All in all, an excellent spot from which to kill a man.

And there he is. I've watched him for two weeks now.

Following him around, getting his routine—or lack thereof —down. This is my process. Observe, learn, act.

I'll give this one credit; he's no dummy. He varies his pattern, leaving and returning home at different times each day. One thing is for sure. He has no job. Scum like him don't need jobs. They rely on criminal activity to pay bills. By the looks of his home, a neat two-story, business must be decent. Most of his kind live in rundown shacks in crappy neighborhoods where kids kill each other purely on instinct.

My only regret is his two children. Well, I assume they're his. I saw the mother leaving with them two days ago, baby carrier in one hand and the toddler's tiny hand in the other. She, at least, has a job. A nail salon five miles away.

I followed her, too.

From what I can tell, she handles most of the family duties. Daycare, groceries, play dates. All her. Which I have to believe will be a good thing, since I'm about to make her children fatherless.

I hope those kids are sleeping. I don't want them freaked out by the resulting chaos.

The overcast sky obscures even a hint of moonlight. It has to be close to midnight.

Almost time.

I inhale, drawing the cool February air into my lungs. I should be in my bed right now, fireplace roaring. Instead, I'm watching Roy Jackson move down the sidewalk, his steps quick but not rushed.

He knows.

As a high-ranking gang member, any day could be his last. He never dawdles. No lingering or staying outside too long, particularly in the darkness.

Could be dangerous.

He knows.

I inhale again and moist winter air settles me. Focuses the mind. A car hooks a left onto the quiet street—*dammit*—and I duck back behind the bush. Based on his stride, I have about a five-second window. If this car doesn't get a move on, my shot is blown.

The driver hits the gas and speeds down the block, clearly exceeding the twenty-five-mile-per-hour speed limit. Where's a cop when you need one?

No cops tonight. Not for speeders and not for Roy Jackson.

The soft slap of rubber—his sneakers—against the wet pavement reaches me. He's close.

I peek out again and there he is. Twenty yards away.

I lift my weapon, line my shot to center mass, and hold my breath for half a second before slowly releasing it. My finger slides over the trigger, but there's a slight resistance. Is it me or the gun? Maybe both.

He's close.

Fifteen yards out. I'm ready.

I squeeze the trigger. *Ping.* Again. *Ping, ping.* A silencer muffles the shots enough that no one will be jerked from their bed or the late-night talk shows. Roy Jackson drops, his body bucking, then crumpling to the pavement. In the darkness, I can't see his face. *That's a damned shame.*

I shove the weapon into my gym bag and check my surroundings for nosey neighbors. Nothing.

Quickly, I hop out from behind the bush and walk—*don't run*—down the street, my steps, like Roy Jackson's, not rushed. Just another pedestrian out for a midnight stroll.

Another one off the list, is all I can think.

2

CLIENTS, MANY TIMES, WERE LIKE HEMORRHOIDS.

A real pain in the ass.

Waylon stood in front of a two-foot-square safe that a ninety-year-old man could crack open with a few whacks of his cane.

"What's wrong with it?" Walker asked.

The man had to be kidding. This would be why Way insisted on doing home visits before agreeing to build or modify any weapon.

He pointed at the square floor safe and faced his middle-aged, highly educated, yet completely dumbass client. "Mr. Walker, all due respect, you can't expect me to supply you with a semiautomatic AR-15 if this is the safe you intend to store it in. It's not even big enough to hold that weapon."

Walker obviously thought he could phone in this home visit. Maybe he figured his money and big shot CEO title would allow him to schmooze his way through it. Way had seen it all. Guys like Walker expected Way to see a safe—any safe—and be satisfied that he'd covered his ass on selling a semiautomatic, center-fire rifle with a telescoping scope to a complete amateur.

Not happening.

Way lifted his clipboard, made notes regarding the exact safe Walker needed to purchase—that sucker wasn't cheap —and handed the form over.

Walker's mouth dipped at the corners. "What's this?"

"My recommendations."

"Yeah, yeah. Fine." Walker folded the note, stuck it in the back pocket of fancy jeans like the ones Way's cousin Grif might wear.

Way? He was a simple Levi's guy. What did he need with jeans that cost $150?

"When can you get me the gun?" Walker asked.

People. Way stifled a sigh. "Not until you get the safe I recommended."

The older man's eyes narrowed. "Look, son."

And, yeah, he hated that lame-ass tactic. The one that made the person you were talking to feel like the younger, stupider version of humanity in the room.

"I'm not your son. If you want a custom rifle, customizations that will, in my mind, make it an assault weapon, I need assurances from you, along with your signature on my contract that says you'll have safeguards in place to avoid that weapon getting into the wrong hands. Or on the black market."

Walker puffed up his chest. "What are you accusing me of?"

Tactic number two: feigning insult. Way had only been in the gunsmith business since leaving the Marines a year earlier, but he'd heard enough excuses from clients to know how these things typically went. And Walker didn't disappoint when it came to the Bullshit Olympics.

"I'm not accusing you of anything, sir. I'm making my position clear. You can either follow my recommendations or find someone else to sell you a rifle."

"I guess that's what I'll do, then."

So be it. The guy was a total pain in the ass, and they hadn't even started on specs yet. All Way knew was Walker had gotten his number from another client. At which point he'd outlined what he considered fairly simple terms all customers must agree to.

Home visit.

Necessary security.

Gun safety classes.

Signed, legally binding contract.

Way was a gun guy. Always had been. Not a hunter, because he just didn't see the allure of shooting an animal. Unless, of course, that animal wanted to eat him. Then all bets were off.

But hunting? Not his thing. He'd rather head out on his motorcycle for a few hours. Or a month. Whatever it took to clear his mind, keep his family out of his business, and give himself some space.

When his schedule didn't permit road trips, he turned to guns. Buying them, customizing them. *Shooting* them. Politics aside, he enjoyed getting out on a range, sucking in fresh air, and dialing in to the singular focus of hitting a target at one thousand yards.

Some people had shrinks. Way had motorcycles and target practice.

Welcome to America. The finest nation in the world, where citizens got to choose their method of relaxation.

After this visit with Walker, he might need both the bike and target practice. A two-fer.

He left the house, a five-thousand-square-foot colonial

midway between Steele Ridge and Asheville, and hopped in his SUV, tossing the clipboard on the seat beside him.

Damn this wasted morning.

Still, it reinforced his belief that he needed to meet prospective gun owners. Get a feel for them and how they intended to use the weapon they wanted him to build or modify.

Way did both.

For certain people.

To date, he'd done work for forty clients. All since he'd returned to Steele Ridge after ten years in the military, the last six as a recon Marine.

He scooped his cell phone from the cup holder. The screen lit up revealing—*one, two-three*—six messages.

Six.

He tapped over to voice mail and skimmed the list. Two from his mother, one from his older brother Cash, two from big sis Maggie, and one from baby sister Riley.

All these calls in the thirty minutes he'd been in Walker's home.

He dropped the phone into his cup holder and blew air through his lips. So much for a quiet ride back to Steele Ridge. Now he'd spend the whole time returning these calls. If he didn't, they'd keep calling, asking where he was and why he wasn't getting in touch. And then, if he didn't respond, one of them would "drop by" his workshop for some manufactured reason that would make it appear like a legit visit when really they wanted to know why he wasn't returning calls.

God forbid he should be working.

He loved them. Endlessly. They were funny and nuts and so insanely loyal that sometimes he wondered how the fuck he got so lucky. His family was the sole reason he'd moved back to Steele Ridge.

With all that loyalty came living in a fish bowl and for a guy who'd spent the majority of his life entertaining himself, the attention wore on him. His crew didn't understand his need for quiet and space and he'd begun to wonder if moving back had been his first mistake.

Too late now.

He fired the SUV's engine and drove off the perfectly paved street with its perfect homes and even more perfect landscaping.

Sorry folks, not buying it.

As a man who liked to study people, he always pondered what might be buried under all the pretty.

Something he wouldn't have to worry about with Walker, if their meeting was any indication, because he'd probably never hear from the guy again.

No problem there.

He didn't need the headache.

Forty minutes later, after a quick stop to drop off cleaning supplies at the animal shelter, he pulled into his driveway, bypassed the house, a ranch with a wraparound porch he liked to sit on at night, and drove straight back to the barn he'd remodeled into a work space.

The barn's glossy red paint glowed under streaming sunlight. As much as he'd hated his mother's idea, he had to give her props for talking him into it. He'd gone with a basic white for the house and the red gave the yard a nice pop of color. Classic and clean. Just how he liked things.

He parked next to Sam's BMW and walked to the side of

the building, where she'd hung a welcome sign on the solid pine door.

A welcome sign.

He liked the small touches, but really? He was a damned gunsmith. What did he need a welcome sign for?

Sam Tucker, sister to his future brother-in-law, was his office manager/accountant/girl wonder. Before she'd come into his life, his office and finances were a mess. Accounting software? Invoices? Receivables? What was that? He just deposited checks people handed him into his account.

When business had grown to a level where his tax guy told him handshake deals weren't advised, Way had gone searching for a bookkeeper. His sister Maggie suggested Sam and here they were.

He pushed open the door and found Sam at her over-sized L-shaped desk. She'd added a few framed photos of Steele Ridge landmarks to the walls, but as yet, the large open area consisted of engineered hardwood and...well... Sam and her desk.

"Hey."

"Hi." She stopped typing and smiled up at him. "I'm glad you're back. I'm heading into town to meet Jay for lunch."

Her brother had taken a job as the quarterback of the local pro football team so he could stay close to Maggie.

Love. Wasn't that sweet?

She held up a folder. "These are checks. If you'll sign them, I'll stop by the bank on my way home tonight."

"Sure thing."

"Thank you. And, Way?"

He held up a hand. "Don't ask."

She laughed. The sultry hum of it filled the open space and made him realize he'd spent the last few months, his mother and sisters aside, avoiding females. A growing business meant no time for relationships. Or the responsibilities that came with them.

"I'm asking," she said. "Based on your reaction, I'll assume you haven't called him."

"I will."

"Today."

He sighed. "Financial planners give me hives."

"I realize that, but as of this morning you have $378,000 sitting in your checking account. Call him and make the appointment. Jay loves him. Believe me, he's been through a few investment guys. This one has made him a small fortune."

"Compared to Jay, I'm small potatoes. What does this guy want with me?"

"Um, your money? You've made over half a million dollars in a year. If you keep this up, your small potatoes will grow. And grow. And grow."

Complications.

He hated complications.

"I'll call him."

"Before I get back."

He laughed. "Jeez, you're pushy."

"Yes. I am."

She retrieved her purse—some fancy thing with two intertwined G's on the front—while he looked at the checks. Six of them. He fingered through them and noted the amounts. Thirty-two thousand dollars. That's what she'd handed him.

Jesus, the money was rolling in. Something that should have made him ecstatic. Yeah, he was happy about the safety having a war chest allowed him, but small businesses, like women, took time and responsibility.

And he sure as hell didn't want to be locked down.

He flipped the folder closed. "Thank you. For everything."

"You're welcome. How'd the visit go with Walker?"

"Eh, not feeling it."

"Really?"

"Yeah. You should see what he planned on using as a gun safe. An AR wouldn't even *fit* in that thing."

"Huh. So, no-go on that one?"

"Doubtful."

"Well, you may not have time for him anyway. We had a call this morning from Mrs. Sumter. Her father's birthday is coming up. She's thinking a handgun."

Mrs. Sumter had already purchased two weapons for her father, a gun enthusiast and hunter. The previous projects were a rifle and a .38. Both had been a shit-ton of fun to build. On the .38, having no idea what constituted a decent gun, Mrs. Sumter had green-lighted most of Way's recommendations and he'd basically built the old guy his dream weapon. Ambidextrous safeties, front and rear night sights, ergonomic grips, the works.

As fun as another project for the Sumters might be, he wouldn't mind putting her off for a week or two and hitting the road on his bike. With Walker being a bust, his schedule had a nice little break in it. A break that would allow him to straddle his Roadmaster and head south. Atlanta, maybe. Or Nashville. Explore Smokey Mountain National Park on the way. Do a little camping and hiking for a few days. Then there was Cades Cove, that sweet little eleven-mile loop dotted with historic buildings and mountain scenery.

Yeah. The more he thought about it, Nashville might be the spot this time.

"I'll call her," he said. "I'll need a couple weeks before I can start that one."

Sam blinked at him, her blue eyes vacant. His office manager, a workhorse to her core, was clearly confused. She knew his schedule better than he did. And he didn't have any projects on the books that would keep him from starting the Sumter project ASAP.

He jerked a thumb toward the door. "I'm, uh, gonna hit the road for a week. Or two."

When she blinked at him again, he reconsidered his word choice. "Maybe ten days. Not long."

"Oh." She nodded. "Sorry. I didn't realize you were leaving."

He laughed. "Neither did I. I figured I'd be doing this Walker thing, but since that's not going anywhere—at least not until he gets the right damned safe—I might as well take off. If you want, you can take some vacation time or whatever."

She thought about that. "Maybe. A few days at least. If you want, I could work on finishing this reception area."

Sam, in her infinite rich girl wisdom, noted that visitors paying ridiculous amounts for custom weapons might want to see more than a desk and a few framed photos. She'd suggested an oak reception desk, sofas, and a wood wall—whatever the hell that was—as a focal point.

His cousin Britt, a contractor, had agreed to do the wall and woodwork, and Sam had picked out the furniture, including the custom-built reception desk. Knowing her taste, Way didn't doubt the room would be freaking gorgeous. He just couldn't wrap his mind around the thirty grand it would cost.

Then again, Sam was about to deposit that much into his account.

"Yeah," he said. "Go ahead."

Why not?

Even if every step felt more like a big-boy decision and less of an I'm-gonna-hit-the-road one.

3

THERE WAS A REASON THIS MEETING WAS TAKING PLACE outside the office. When a gal worked for the CIA, off-site chats generally meant one thing.

Secrets.

Really good ones.

Roni sipped her iced tea and eyed Karl Quigley across the table. As the CIA's associate deputy director of administration, Karl was, in short, her boss. Well, her boss's boss's boss.

Around them, the busy restaurant came alive with chatter, tuxedo-shirted scuttling waiters, and busboys hustling to change soiled tablecloths. All of it a bit too fancy for Roni's taste, but she'd heard the pasta was to die for, so she'd indulge the big shots on their choice of venue.

She set her iced tea down and ran her hands over the napkin in her lap, drying the moisture transferred from her glass. "We're waiting on Don Harding?"

Karl nodded. "We are."

As older men went, Karl rocked the short, salt-and-pepper hair look. Throw in a tailored suit and pocket square and his tall, broad build was one to notice. Roni supposed he knew that, because he made no effort to shrink away from appreciative glances from women. On the contrary, Karl went all in with a flashing smile and even a few hellos as they'd entered the restaurant.

Whatever they'd be discussing at this meeting might be a secret, but it wasn't enough of a secret that they had to hide.

Interesting.

"I'm guessing if I was in trouble, this meeting would be happening at Langley."

The corner of his mouth lifted into a rueful smile. Karl liked her directness. He'd told her as much when they'd first met months earlier. In his position, he didn't have time or patience for games. Good thing, because Roni Fenwick hated both.

Her tendency to be blunt, along with her background as a former FBI special agent, ticked all kinds of boxes—investigator, check, mind-fucker, check—when it came to being an education and training specialist, aka psych-trainer for the CIA.

"You're not in trouble," he said. "The opposite in fact."

Oh.

Boy.

Out of her peripheral vision, she caught movement to her left. Don Harding, head of the agency's science and development department, strode toward them. He wore a no-nonsense black suit, crisp white shirt and light gray tie and his short hair, as usual, was gelled into place.

In opposition to Karl, he could be any regular businessman on his lunch break. Don might not have had the swagger or all-out attention-grabbing presence, but there was something there she couldn't quite nail down. In her short stint with the CIA, she'd met Don three times and had failed to get comfortable in his presence. Then again, God knew she needed a whole lot more time to vet someone's character.

He slid into the chair to Roni's left. "Good afternoon."

"Hi," she said, straightening just a bit. The man had that effect on her.

He set his briefcase on the floor, then retrieved a folder. "Sorry I'm late."

Karl lifted one shoulder. "We ordered for you. I have a meeting at two. I got you pasta."

Whether Don found that irritating or not would remain a mystery. He simply nodded and faced Roni.

"Let me get straight to it."

Exactly how she liked it. "Please do."

"We need your help on something."

"Of course."

He handed her the folder. "Don't open it here."

Oh.

Boy.

Secrets, secrets, secrets. A burst of excitement puckered her skin.

Don pointed at the folder. "There's information in that folder regarding a shooting in North Carolina. A gang member."

"Okay. And what does the a—" She stopped, checked herself while glancing at a passing customer. "What do *we* want with a dead gangbanger?"

"It's not about him."

Don's gaze snapped up and he cleared his throat. Their

waiter approached and set plates of steaming food in front of them.

Karl picked up his fork, waved it at her. "The rigatoni is homemade. I'm sure you'll like it."

"I'm sure. But I'm confused about this case."

"It's the bullet," Don said.

The bullet. Now the CIA was chasing bullets instead of bad guys? What the hell was this about?

Obviously sensing her confusion, Don swallowed a mouthful of food before leaning in. "You'll see it in the photos, but the bullet disintegrated on impact."

Frangible ammo—or soft rounds—were designed to break apart upon impact and were often used in the military for close quarters combat training.

The fact that one of these rounds wound up in a gang-banger shouldn't have the CIA on red alert. The local PD maybe, but the CIA? No.

Which, Roni guessed, was exactly why this little secret meeting might be happening.

"All right," she said. "And what?"

Don gave her a hard look. As if no one ever dared to question him. She'd irritated him. Big deal. Wouldn't be the first time she'd crossed lines. *Welcome to my world, pal.*

"And," he said, his voice carrying the gravelly sharpness of anger with a side of sarcasm, "we're testing a particular frangible bullet. It's made with acid. Once it hits flesh it basically vaporizes."

Whoa.

If the man wanted her interest, he had it. She leaned in. "Are you telling me the bullets you're testing are what killed this gangbanger?"

"Now she's getting it," Karl said.

Don hit him with that same hard look he'd given her a

minute ago. That sucker should have vaporized him better than one of the acid-filled bullets.

"What does this have to do with me?"

"The victim is a member of the Street Dragons."

This just got curiouser and curiouser. Six months ago, before the death of ATF agent Jeff Ambrose, he and Roni worked on a joint task force investigating cigarette smuggling. As an undercover agent for the ATF, Jeff spent his days cozying up to the owners of a distribution plant at the heart of the investigation. While he worked undercover, Roni, his FBI counterpart at the time, did the legwork, trying to prove who was hiding unreported cigarettes and where. According to Jeff, cigarettes were disappearing somewhere between the manufacturer and the distributor, more than likely being hidden to avoid paying federal income tax. Cases and cases of cigarettes allegedly being sold on the black market. Tax free.

And that added up to big bucks for either the manufacturer or the distributor. Maybe both.

At the time, the working theory had been that the Street Dragons were dealing these illegal cigarettes as a way to raise money for other nefarious activities. The thought of her deceased friend left Roni's gut churning. She set her fork down, focused on keeping her mind on the meeting. And not on the unsolved murder of a federal agent and friend. "The task force was shut down after Jeff's death. I'm out of the loop."

"Well, we need you back in."

"Why?"

"You have a friendship with Maggie Kingston."

Maggie, a county sheriff, had designed a plan to plug the funnel of illegal cigarette sales in her jurisdiction, only to have the feds horn in on it when she'd asked for their help.

Every member of that task force respected Maggie, but they also knew who called the shots. And it wasn't her.

"What does this bullet have to do with Maggie?"

Don met her gaze. "Her brother designed it."

Give Don credit for knowing how to deliver a drop-the-mic line. He'd shocked Roni twice so far and, with her history, that wasn't easy to do.

Maggie's brother. *What was his name?* Not Cash. He worked for the fire department.

The Marine. Had to be. Maggie had often talked about him—Way,— if Roni remembered correctly. He'd been a recon Marine and was now back home, building a gunsmith business.

And somehow, more than likely through his military contacts, he appeared to be designing ammunition for the CIA.

Roni flicked a gaze to Karl, then to Don. "You want me to investigate my friend's *brother*?"

The balls.

The two men exchanged a look before Karl jerked his chin at her. "We need to make sure he's not double-dipping and selling this design on the street."

Please. The agency employed some of the most experienced operatives in the world. They sure as hell didn't need her. "And there's no other way to figure this out? Really? How do you know one of those bullets didn't get out of Langley?"

"They didn't," Don said.

"You're sure?"

Don cocked his head. "Positive. We had a hundred. Twenty have been test-fired and we have all eighty left."

Slowly, Don lifted his napkin, wiped his hands, then set it neatly in his lap again. "Roni, your work on the task force gives you an obvious in." He pointed at the folder. "You know the Dragons are part of the smuggling investigation."

There wasn't a member of law enforcement within fifty miles that didn't think the Dragons were responsible for Jeff's murder. They simply didn't know why. Was his cover blown? Did he make a deal for cigarettes that went bad?

Who knew?

Roni shook her head. "Last I checked, the Dragons were twenty-thousand strong in this country. There's no proof this guy was even involved in our cigarette smuggling scheme."

"But the link is there," Don said. "You can use that to get inside. Talk to the sheriff, tell her you heard about this case." He circled a hand. "Act like you're wondering if this guy had something to do with...with Jeff."

At the mention of Jeff's name, a man whose acquaintance brought her to this table, they all made eye contact.

"Ask her about the bullet," Don continued. "See if she knows anything."

Dammit. Roni took a second, processed the information, broke it down into smaller, manageable pieces.

She and Maggie had both been hit hard by Jeff's death. They were both angry and wanting justice, so it wouldn't be out of the realm for Roni to be doing a little side work on their friend's case that had gone colder than a freezer.

Karl pushed his plate away and gently set his napkin on the table. "You seem to be under the impression this is a voluntary assignment. Let me clarify. It's not. Consider it an order. You *will* talk to this sheriff—what's her name again?"

Great. He didn't even know the players.

"Maggie," Roni said. "Maggie Kingston. She's the Haywood County sheriff. And a damned good one."

Karl waved a hand, dismissing Roni in a not-so-subtle

way. "Talk to her. See what you can find. I'll deal with why you'll be out of the office for a few days."

"And if I get there and Maggie doesn't know anything?"

"You're a smart woman," Karl said. "Do what you need to. And don't fuck with me. I've ruined the lives of people more powerful than you."

4

By 9:00 the next morning, Roni sat in the rental she'd picked up at the airport and drummed her fingers on the steering wheel. Leaving DC had been the last thing she'd wanted to do. Particularly because it meant not exactly lying, but misleading her friend. And Roni didn't have many of those. Her own fault, given the whole lack of trust thing.

A girl with a drug-addicted mother and dead father didn't exactly have faith in the staying power of relationships. She'd spent the majority of her life isolating herself from the possibility of heartbreak. In her experience, if she didn't get close to people, the opportunity for disappointment decreased dramatically.

And just yards in front of her, behind the door of a squat one-story building, one of her few friends was about to get bulldozed.

Well, maybe not. All Roni needed to do was march in, show Maggie the photos of the dead gangbanger, and ask her about them. They'd have a conversation and Roni would leave. Head back to DC, where she'd inform dickheads Karl Quigley and Don Harding that Maggie knew nothing.

About anything.

End of story.

At which point, she'd probably be shown out of Langley, thereby kissing her career down the toilet.

Drama, drama, drama. Leave it to her with the fatalist thinking.

Roni twisted her lips and concentrated on the glass front door emblazoned with Maggie's name and *Haywood County Sheriff* in thick block letters. A conversation.

That's all it had to be.

She flipped her hair back and pushed open the car door. Time to go to work.

She strode to the door, straightening her leather jacket as she went. *Just a conversation.*

Inside, Maggie's assistant, Shari, sat at the reception desk. Back in the task force days, Roni had met Shari a few times, but mostly spoke on the phone with the woman when trying to track down Maggie.

Still, upon seeing Roni enter, Shari's eyes popped wide. "Well, hello there, Roni," she said. "How nice to see you."

"Hi, Shari. Sorry to barge in, but I was in the area. Thought I'd say hi." She pointed down the hallway. "Is she in?"

"She is. Hang on, I'll let her know you're here."

Shari disappeared down the hallway, stepping into Maggie's office. A minute later, Maggie appeared. She barreled toward Roni in a uniform that wasn't just pressed, but pristine. Maggie always did pride herself on her professional appearance. As usual, she'd pulled her honey-blond hair into a ponytail that swung as she walked. That was Maggie, all polished energy.

A blast of guilt slammed Roni. She should ditch this plan. Just tell Maggie she was back for a quick visit and stopped in to say hello. No murdered gangbanger. No covert investigation into West Waylon Kingston, a man talented enough to build bullets that didn't just decimate people, but ate their organs.

Before Roni could bolt, Maggie was on her, wrapping her in a hug that was both awkward and funny considering Maggie had a good five inches on Roni's 5'4" stature.

For a second, the physical contact set her on edge. But this was Maggie, a woman with whom she'd shared meals and long talks about the perils and sexism surrounding women in law enforcement. Sisters in crime. That was them. And Maggie, Roni felt sure, probably made an awesome sister.

The nipping came again, that constant reminder that she had no family—not one blood relative—in her life. Sure, she tried to make up for it with her college friend Cassidy's family, but down deep the crater of emptiness couldn't be filled.

And, God knew, she'd only managed one long-term relationship with a man in the last six years. If eleven months could even be considered long-term. That alliance, like most in Roni's life, ended when things started to get...cozy.

Roni didn't do cozy. Cozy meant comfort and comfort meant suffering when it ended.

Ah, screw it. Roni wrapped her arms around her friend and gave a good squeeze. "Maggie. So good to see you."

Maggie stepped back, her face lit with excitement. "Girl, you are a sight. I was literally just thinking about you last night. And then Jay came in and distracted me."

Fully aware of Maggie's assistant moving past them on her way back to her desk, Roni leaned in. "I bet he distracted you."

When a woman's boyfriend was named the sexiest

athlete by a major sports magazine, there was a lot to be distracted by.

Maggie let out a laugh that made Roni smile. Girlfriends. This is what it was supposed to be.

Jerking her head, Maggie started walking. "I honestly can't believe you're here. Come to my office. Shari, hold my calls, please."

"You got it, boss."

Roni followed Maggie down the short corridor to her office. Upon taking over as sheriff, she had immediately given the crumbling office a facelift complete with new tiled floors and light beige walls that warmed the place up.

Once in the office, Maggie closed the door and gestured Roni to a chair. "This is a great surprise. What are you doing here?"

Roni took a seat, sliding her hands over her jeans and then folding them in her lap. "I took a few days off. Figured I'd see Cass and her family. And you. I miss our chats after the task force meetings."

As the only two women on the task force, they'd bonded over working with an all-male staff.

"I know. I miss you, too. The only other woman on that damned task force and you abandoned me."

"Hey, I'm sorry. But, you know, when my country called..."

Maggie waved it off. "Listen, if a certain hunky quarterback hadn't come into my life, I'd probably be in some faraway FBI field office about now."

Last year, Maggie had been accepted into the FBI's training academy—apparently a lifelong dream—but when Jayson, Maggie's boyfriend, moved to North Carolina to play football, she'd decided to bow out of the academy invitation and stay put.

Near the love of her life.

Something Roni couldn't fathom, mostly because she'd never felt that strongly about a man, but it wasn't her place to question her friend's sanity.

So far, Maggie didn't seem to regret it. And, yeah, a tiny stab of jealousy prompted another reminder of the lack of intimacy in Roni's life. No family, no hot boyfriend to give up a career for. Nothing but her and the life she'd built. Which, considering she'd come from the foster system, wasn't a bad life. At all. It was just...lacking.

And most of the time, she was okay with that. Emotional, chaos-inducing entanglements?

She'd pass, thanks.

They spent the next few minutes catching up about life in the CIA, the training Roni had been through, and the last few months in general. When the updates finished, Roni sat back, contemplating how the hell to segue into the assignment she'd been sent to complete.

She needed to just do it. Put it out there and be as honest as she could be without spilling any CIA secrets. And without dragging her friend into an investigation. By the end of this, Roni wanted plausible deniability for Maggie. The room for her to say she knew nothing about Roni being in Steele Ridge on behalf of the CIA.

"Listen, Mags, this isn't just a social call."

Maggie cocked her head. "Oh?"

"Obviously, I love seeing you, but I wanted to get your take on something. A case. A murder in your county. I think it might have something to do with Jeff."

"If it's the gang shooting, that's exactly why I was thinking about you last night."

Of course Maggie was aware of it. Between being sheriff

and her work on the task force, it was a no-brainer that she'd be in the know.

"Yeah. I can't stop thinking about it. I mean, on the task force we were investigating the Dragons. And Jeff's case has never been solved."

"I know. Something is bugging me. Gang members die every day, right? We have three thousand Dragon members in North Carolina. The chances of it being a link to Jeff are beyond small."

"But something's weird."

"Exactly. I'm not dismissing it, but unless we find some link to Jeff..." Maggie shrugged.

Roni took that as a go-sign. "Is it your case?"

"No. Local PD is handling it. I've been briefed, though."

Roni reached into her tote bag and held up the file Don and Karl had given her. "Have you seen the photos? The autopsy report? The frangible bullet?"

Maggie's head dipped forward. "You've seen all that? How?" The shock and confusion in her eyes sent another bout of guilt raging.

Roni could easily string together a good story about wanting justice for Jeff—and she most certainly did—but it felt...wrong. Deceptive and...slimy.

She wouldn't use a good man as an excuse. She'd never considered herself a stellar person. Lord knew, Roni didn't have the upbringing to learn certain lessons, but one thing she wouldn't be, not even for the CIA, was disloyal.

She waved the folder. "Yes, I've seen them. That frangible bullet has to worry you. It terrifies me. Most of them don't eat away like that. This? This is more than that, Maggie."

After ten seconds of staring, Maggie shook her head. "I know. I met with the homicide detective last night. As I said, it's not my case, but it's in my county and they wanted to brief me. I've never seen anything like that."

"Me neither."

Maggie eyed her. "Does the CIA somehow have skin in this?"

And there it was. The direct question Roni dreaded. Damn Karl for putting her in this position.

Maggie was her friend. A good friend and a solid sheriff. But if her brother was selling these bullets on the street, the agency needed to know. Tipping Maggie off meant tipping Way off, and that Roni wouldn't do.

Not when people were dying from these bullets.

But she didn't have to lie to Maggie. Roni set the folder on the edge of Maggie's desk and tapped it. "Could this guy be part of Jeff's cigarette smuggling investigation?"

Again, Maggie shrugged. "I don't know. I'll have to look back through all my notes. I have two giant banker's boxes in storage. I can dig them out and start going through them. There's a bigger problem, though."

Bigger than a flesh-eating bullet? "What's that?"

"After the homicide guy left last night, I was curious about the bullet. I ran what we know through NIBIN."

The National Integrated Ballistic Information network, better known as NIBIN, was basically the DNA database for firearms and bullets.

"And?"

"This is the fourth case involving one of these frangible bullets. Two were in South Carolina. When you walked in, I was trying to find my brother. I want to see if he can tell me what the hell we're dealing with here."

WHEN SAM KNOCKED ON THE OPEN DOOR TO WAY'S

workshop, he looked up from the nine-millimeter sitting on the table in front of him. His cousin Reid wanted the scope checked and Way had decided to swap the whole thing out for a new, more advanced model. Give his cousin, a fellow gun enthusiast, an upgrade.

Good breeding firmly in place, Sam stood in the doorway waiting to be invited in. At some point, he'd break her of that habit. Unless he said he didn't want to be bugged, Way didn't want to always be telling her to come in.

He didn't hold out too much hope. Time and again he'd told her to ditch the dress slacks, fancy button-down shirt, and high heels. They were in a goddamn barn, not some city high-rise. Blue bloods. An interesting batch.

"Door's open," he said. "Come on in."

"Good morning. Sorry to interrupt, but Maggie left a message. She's looking for you." Sam held up a small stack of papers. "Here are the month-end reports."

Reports, excellent. He'd rather take a bullet in the eye than spend two hours reading financials. But Sam took pride in getting his finances straightened out, so he'd be a good soldier and review it all. "Thanks. Anything I should be aware of?"

"Nothing out of the ordinary. Healthy profits. You're doing much better on controlling your expenses."

"Considering I have you nagging the hell out of me, are you surprised?"

"Ha. You'll thank me one day."

"I thank you today. You're doing a great job. What did Mags want?"

"She didn't say. Just asked that you call her. She said she tried your cell, too."

His sister must have something on her mind if she was hunting him down via Sam. On his way into the workshop, he'd tossed his phone and keys on the desk by the door. Had he even turned the thing on this morning?

He waved at the handgun on the worktable. "I was working."

She laughed. "I swear, you might be the only person I know who actually shuts the phone off. You don't just turn the ringer down, you go all the way."

"The way I see it, nothing I do is so important that people can't wait an hour. Or two. If it's an emergency, my family knows where to find me."

And if he didn't return Maggie's call within the hour, no doubt one of them would show up bringing muffins or bagels or some other breakfast item that would serve as an excuse for hunting him down. Plus, these people weren't dumb. They knew he wouldn't be the douchebag who gave them crap about interrupting his day when they brought gifts.

His own personal snake pit.

"Waylon!"

Ha. Point made.

His sister's voice bellowed from the outer office. The *reception* area. "Back here."

Maggie appeared in the doorway, spotted Sam, and smiled. "Hiya."

"I just gave him your message," Sam said on her way to the door. "I'll leave you guys alone."

And *hello* to the petite brunette following Maggie. The woman had sculpted cheekbones and an exotic look straight off a magazine cover, but she wasn't some skinny waif. This one had a rack absolutely made for showing off. Something she did amazingly well in the stretchy tank top under her unzipped jacket. The skin-tight jeans only accentuated her curvy figure, and Way's mind went straight to peeling every stitch of clothing from her.

Maggie pointed at Way. "I called and texted you."

The woman behind Maggie met his gaze and her full lips slid into a crooked smile. Oh, yeah, she knew the effect she had on men.

Pig that he was, he fell right in line. And didn't even care that he'd been predictable. That's what a stunner she was.

He shifted to Maggie. "Phone's off. I was working."

"Unbelievable."

He shrugged. "Some of us aren't sheriffs and don't need to check our phones constantly."

"Hello," Sam said to the hot brunette as she passed. "I'm Sam."

The brunette stuck her hand out. "Roni Fenwick. Nice to meet you. I'm a friend of Maggie's. She's spoken highly of you."

Sam gave Maggie an appreciative nod. The two of them were interesting. At times, Way sensed Sam didn't like sharing her brother with Maggie. With their father out of the picture, Jay had become the male figure in Sam's life. In true Maggie fashion, his sister had figured out a way to keep peace. For Jay's sake, she'd said.

On her way out, Sam pointed at a folder on the desk beside the door. "Are these the checks?"

"Yes, ma'am. All signed."

"Excellent."

"Look at you," Maggie said, sarcasm dripping. "An in *and* an outbox. You turning corporate on me, little brother?"

"I'm working on him." This from Sam, who closed the door behind her.

"She's killing me," Way said.

"She's running your business."

"Isn't it the same thing?"

They both laughed, but the brunette kept a straight face. Zero reaction. Not even a forced one that'd include her in the joke.

Maggie stepped closer, leading the brunette into his workspace. Whoever the hell she was, Maggie had a comfort level with her. Her outfit didn't exactly scream law enforcement, but he'd run enough recon missions to know that might be the point. She might be undercover for the sheriff's department.

Or some other agency.

He took a second to study the worry lines cracking the skin between his sister's eyebrows. Her job? Loaded with headaches. Not just the criminal kind.

In town the other day, he'd found her breaking up a smackdown between two residents arguing over the cigarette smoke ordinance. Exactly how far was ten feet from the building?

Being the literal sort, Maggie had pulled out a tape measure and showed them.

Whatever her salary was, it didn't come close to covering that bullshit.

Yet, she seemed happy and for that, he was grateful. She made him nuts half the time, but Way loved her. "Sorry I missed your calls," he said.

"It's all right. It wasn't an emergency. But I'll reiterate that you shouldn't turn your phone off. There's a million reasons not to. What if you fall off that motorcycle and wind up in a ditch? How would we find you?"

His sister. The cop. "Mags?"

"What?"

"When's the last time I fell off my bike?"

She gave him a hateful glare. "It was an *example*. Not a judgment on your riding skills."

"I'll think about it. Now what's up?"

He knew her. She liked to be up in everyone's business. If he didn't get her off this track, she'd come up with a list of things that endangered his life. Then he'd have to march down to the B and start doing shots of whisky.

She set her hand on the brunette's forearm. "This is Roni. We served on a joint task force together."

Task Force. Definitely law enforcement.

He held his hand to Roni. "Way Kingston."

"I know," she said. "A pleasure."

She slid her hand into his, gave a solid shake, and pulled back. All business this one.

"I need your opinion on something," Maggie said. "A shooting."

He leaned against the worktable and folded his arms. Given his knowledge of weaponry, folks asking questions or hiring him to consult wasn't unusual. Maggie was no slouch when it came to guns, though. If she needed his input, it had to be something juicy. He eyed Roni for a second. Clearly, she was involved, otherwise his sister wouldn't have brought her along. "All right. Whatcha got?"

She held up her phone. "Photos. But it's Vegas rules. Technically, it's not my case. I shouldn't even be showing you."

"But?"

"It's in my jurisdiction and could impact me."

He'd been involved in plenty of top-secret missions. He understood the necessity of keeping one's mouth shut.

He glanced at Roni. "And you're involved in this how?"

Maggie knew he'd never go on record with an active case unless he understood who the players were. When it came to weapons, Way knew better than to string his ass on a line in front of strangers. All he needed to do was make a comment—on an apparently high-level case—have Roni-the-hot-brunette misinterpret what he said and before he knew it, his reputation was toast.

Roni met his gaze. "Let's just say Maggie and I have a mutual interest in this case."

No kidding. "Yeah. I get that. But I don't know you and I generally don't trust people I don't know."

"Your sister knows me. Is that not enough?"

Good one. She knew it, too, because she grinned at him. A spark of respect ignited. Ballsy women didn't scare him. Particularly ones in male-dominated professions.

"Way," Maggie said, "please. Trust *me* on this one."

He trusted her. No doubt. Wouldn't stop him from making calls as soon as Roni took her fine little ass out of his workshop.

He drew his gaze from the firecracker and jerked his chin at Maggie. "Show me."

"Two nights ago—Sunday—a gang member got shot. Three to the chest with frangible ammo. The wound is...weird."

"Weird how?"

She held the phone up so he could see it. "This is an autopsy photo."

Not only did his sister understand his ability to keep a secret, she knew he'd ceased being squeamish over gory dead body photos. He'd seen far too many limbs blown off to not have fallen numb to it all. Twisted, for sure, but emotional survival meant compartmentalizing.

A lot.

Maggie pointed to the screen while Roni looked on. "Here's the entry wound."

"Is the slug still in him?"

"No."

"Exit wound?"

"No. Not even any fragments. All the bullet left is a hollow cavity. How the hell does *that* happen?"

Shit. A vision of the ham he'd practiced on filled his mind. He peered down at the photo. Jesus, he knew what could create a hole like that.

Acid.

No way. Nuh-uh.

Unless he got screwed.

"Also," Maggie said, "there's bits of plastic in the area around the wound."

Oh, goddammit.

Screwed.

Way couldn't look at her. His sister was a human lie detector.

Instead he cut his eyes to Roni and her locked-on, but vacant stare. Head cocked, her features remained neutral. No studious pursed lips or sucked-in cheeks.

Totally bland.

Who the fuck did she work for? After they left, he'd get with Maggie, let his sister know he didn't like being ambushed.

"Way?"

He shook it off and took a second to line up his thoughts. No exit wound, hollow cavity, bits of plastic.

Tricky business here. If he said nothing, went with total denial, Mags would call bullshit. Not that he knew all about every form of ammunition, but she'd expect him, with his background, to have an idea what that bad boy was made of.

Shaking his head, he forced himself to meet Maggie's eye. Damn those eyes. "You've got frangible ammo."

"That, we know."

"This is different. There's something inside the bullet that makes it eat away like that."

Not altogether a lie.

"Like what?" Roni asked. "Acid or something?"

Maggie's mouth dipped to a frown. "Can you put liquid into a bullet?"

I sure can. "Yeah, there's a way."

Again, not a lie.

"How?"

Roni finally moved, shifting her weight and looking straight at him with brown eyes so dark he wasn't sure what went on behind them. This chick unnerved him. Slowly, Way rubbed his forehead as he focused on the photo, on the effects of the bullet he'd designed. Seeing it now, for the first time on human flesh, made his chest seize.

He'd known the ammunition was a game-changer in the spec ops world, where men and women fought wars civilians never knew about. Which made a bullet designed to disintegrate a valuable tool.

No slug, no evidence.

How the hell his design got to the street, he didn't know.

Maggie's shoulders dropped. "Darn. I was hoping you'd know where something like this came from."

Oh, he knew.

The dead last thing he'd do was drag his sister into it and put her square in the crosshairs of the government. He'd keep this to himself.

At least until he figured out who fucked him.

5

When the associate deputy director of administration called, Roni answered. Even if it meant standing in Way Kingston's driveway and shooing Maggie off.

Business, Roni told her while quickly moving out of earshot. Being a smart cookie, Maggie didn't question it, said her goodbyes, and drove off.

"Good morning, sir," Roni said into the phone.

"I expect daily updates."

Karl's voice blared through the phone, his tone firm and gruff enough to get Roni's back up.

"Daily updates are not a problem. In fact, I'd just finished meeting with Maggie Kingston when your call came in."

For now, she'd leave Way out of it. Coming to his place of business might have been pushing it. Much too in-your-face for an investigation supposedly on the down-low, but she'd had an opportunity to meet him and jumped at it.

Plus, it took Maggie out of the middle. With the connection to Way established, Roni would feel free to contact him on her own. Whether he liked it or not.

The man wasn't stupid. She sensed it in his questioning.

By now, he was probably scouring the Internet for intel on her. If the roles were reversed, that's what she'd do. Plus, he had cousins Maggie had mentioned, who could hack just about any system.

Lucky for Roni, her CIA status wouldn't be easy to find.

"You used discretion, I presume," Karl said.

"Of course, sir."

"Good. Keep it that way. Check in tomorrow. Get us something on Waylon Kingston."

The line went dead and she checked the screen.

Lord, she'd been at this less than twenty-four hours. Was she Wonder Woman now? Still staring at the phone, she let out a frustrated laugh. Had to love the suits. Guys who more than likely never investigated a sore toe, never mind a murder, and they wanted answers lickety-split.

They expected her to compromise a friendship in service of the agency.

Not happening.

After the lack of meaningful relationships in Roni's life, she considered every friend a cherished one. If the CIA wanted her to risk that, they'd have to give her rock-solid reasons. And so far, they hadn't done so.

She peered at the SUV parked mere steps away in front of the barn. Glancing around, she spotted a security camera mounted at the edge of the barn's roof. Way obviously took preventative measures in case someone intended on breaking into his space and helping themselves to whatever weaponry he kept stored inside.

Eh. She'd work around it. She tapped at her phone's screen again, pretending to check it while she wandered a few steps closer to the SUV. If anyone inside were watching, they'd see a woman casually checking her phone while absently pacing the driveway.

Still staring down at her phone, when she got close enough to the SUV, she leaned one hip against it, made a show of scrolling through her texts. A bird chirped—thank you very much—and she peered up into a sunlit sky. The little guy flew away so Roni helped herself to a look inside the truck. On the rear seat was a box of plastic lined pads used for potty training puppies. Maybe Way had a dog.

Except, with the pads was a bag of cat litter. And two giant-sized bags of dog food.

"Who are you?"

She snapped her head right and found Way, all long legs and broad-shouldered confidence, striding toward her. He wasn't jacked with muscle, but his fitted T-shirt indicated the lean tightness of his body. And the way he moved? That catlike quickness fired something in her. Something primal and urgent. *Ooohhh-eee this might be fun.*

"Well, hello." Still leaning on the SUV, she tucked her phone into her back pocket and gave him a sassy smile. "I believe we just met, but in case your memory has failed, I'm Roni Fenwick."

He returned the sassy smile.

Oh, yes, this would be fun.

Three feet from her, he stopped and folded his arms across his chest. "I know your name. It doesn't tell me who you are. And why you're snooping in my truck."

"You have pets?"

"No. Donations for the shelter. I'll ask again. Who are you?"

Didn't *that* just take some of the wind from her sails. Here she wanted to find dirt on him and the guy was nice enough to donate supplies to a shelter. Damn him.

"I'm Maggie's friend. As she said, we were on a task force together."

"'Were' being the key word. You a fed?"

Tricky question. Technically, yes, she was a fed. Not the kind he was thinking, though.

"At the time, I was FBI."

"And?"

"And what?"

"Why are you here?"

She kept her gaze on him, considering how much to share. "We had a friend who was murdered in the line. I'm trying to figure out what happened to him. This gang member dying may have something to do with that."

"Why?"

"Our friend was investigating a member of the Street Dragons. It's a long shot, but the victim Maggie showed you might have something to do with our friend's death."

"Lotta gang members in the world. It's a stretch."

She shrugged. "Maybe. Maybe not. Plenty of cases have been solved by following a hunch."

He took one step closer. "Who are you?"

Again with this? *Dammit.* The man was good. She hit him with another smile, this time dragging her gaze over his body as she took a step closer.

When all else failed, Roni wasn't above using every tool at her disposal. She'd become immune to men's hungry gazes at fifteen.

Distracting Way Kingston with her tits didn't make her a whore. It made her good at her job. "I'm Roni Fenwick."

Way tilted his head, leaned his upper body close enough that she felt his minty breath against her ear. "When I call my military buddy at State, what will he tell me about Roni Fenwick?"

Whoa. The State Department. Way above her pay grade. Good for him.

He might be bluffing, backing her into a corner to evaluate her reaction.

Too bad for him she'd been pushed into many corners in her life.

She tilted her head up, mimicking his stance. "Make that call, Way, and find out. See what you can dig up."

Eyeing her, he stepped back. "There are two things that piss me off."

"Do tell."

"People that lie and people that fuck with me or my family. I don't know you. I sure as hell don't trust you. And I gotta wonder why, if you and Maggie are such good friends, I've never heard your name."

Touché. As much as she hated to admit it, she wasn't bulletproof. The fact that Maggie had never mentioned Roni did, indeed, sting.

Bravo, Waylon.

Except, to this day, Operation Smokeshop wasn't intended to be public knowledge.

"Maybe," Roni said, "she didn't want to compromise an operation. Did you think of that, hotshot?"

He let out a hearty laugh. An honest-to-God amusement-filled bark that left her equal parts annoyed and intrigued. She loved a man unafraid of verbal swordplay, but she didn't want to stand here wasting precious time. "Is something funny?"

"You," he said. "You've got balls, lady."

"You bet I do. Rock-solid ones. You don't intimidate me. Let's get that straight."

"Message received. You still haven't told me who you are. Which makes you one hell of a spin doctor."

Again, she shrugged. "I'm a girl trying to figure out who killed her friend. That's all you need to know."

Finally, he retreated, opening up the space around her as he walked around the front of the SUV, opened the door, and stepped onto the foot rail, staring at her over the roof. "I doubt that. I doubt that very much."

WAY STORMED UP THE DRIVEWAY TO THE STEELE RIDGE training center and parked in front of the building between his cousin Reid's pickup and Micki's Prius. He'd called her twenty minutes ago, requesting a favor, which they both knew meant some sort of hacking project.

His cousin, the computer nerd, knew how to crack shit better than anyone the government had on staff.

He hopped out of the Tahoe, hit the lock button out of habit, and headed to the door, where he tapped the newly installed buzzer. In the last year, after multiple crazy incidents, security around the property had become a priority.

Way peered up at the camera mounted over the door and waved. A second later, a *bzzzz-bzzzz* preceded the *thunk* of the disengaging lock.

The U-shaped reception desk within the glass-walled lobby sat empty. Reid had recently hired Nancy Wilkins, a stay-at-home mom looking for part-time hours, to man the desk when he had a training class in residence. Given the quiet, Way assumed it was an off week for training.

Beyond the reception area, he hooked a right and pushed through the stairwell door, taking the steps two at a time to the second floor. After returning to Steele Ridge from a stint in Vegas, Micki now taught a cyber warfare class.

The training center. Family affair.

"Hey," Way said when he strode into Micki's office.

Facing the window, she stood behind one of those variable height desks in her signature black skinny jeans. Her shaggy shoulder-length dark hair, the Chuck Taylors on her feet, and a white graphic T-shirt with the pi symbol completed Micki's edgy badass look.

She closed the browser on her laptop and lowered the desk while eyeing him over her shoulder. A whirring sound filled the office as the desk made its descent. "Hello, cuz."

"Thanks for letting me barge in."

"Anytime. It's quiet around here, and Gage is in California so I'm trying to stay busy. What's up?"

"I'm not sure."

She snorted. "Why does that answer always mean trouble?"

"It's probably nothing."

"Then why are you here?"

Good point. "I need a favor."

"What am I hacking into?"

"I'm sorry to ask."

"No you're not. I'm not sorry either. This sounds like it'll be good. And might give me something to brag to Jonah about. Always happy to one-up my brother."

"You two are obnoxious with this hacking competition."

"I know. But's it's fun. We're about even on who has the most requests." She pointed at one of her guest chairs across the glass table she used as another desk and dropped into her own chair. "Sit and tell me what you need. If I can help, I will."

"Two things. A woman named Roni Fenwick. I need to know who she is."

Micki jotted a note. "That should be easy enough. Is she a criminal?"

"I don't think so. I think she's a fed. Maybe undercover or something. Full disclosure, she's a friend of Maggie's. They just stopped by my place."

"And you're not asking Maggie?"

"I don't want her involved. Yet. Something about this Roni rubs me wrong. If she checks out, no foul, and Maggie's friendship stays intact."

Micki gave him the raised-eyebrow look that indicated he might be nuts. "And the second thing?"

"Can you get into case files at the Waynesville PD?"

Micki let out a whistle. "Wow," she said. "Talk about burying the lede. You don't mess around."

What the hell was he doing? Asking his cousin to risk herself by breaking any number of computer fraud laws. Hacking a police department's system no less.

Way couldn't let her do it. He pushed out of his chair. "Forget it. I don't know what the hell I was thinking."

"You were thinking you were out of your depth and couldn't do it yourself."

"I'll find another way."

Micki sighed. "Way, don't be stupid. Sit down."

"Sorry?"

"You don't ask for help unless it's important. Are you in trouble?"

Was he? He didn't even know. He scrubbed a hand over his face. "Like I said, it's probably nothing."

"But you need to be sure."

"Yeah. It's...sensitive."

He paused. Not only was he asking his cousin to break the law, he expected her to keep silent.

She shook her head and smirked. "I have secrets on a good number of United States senators that I'll never talk about. Not even to Gage. It's my own personal security blanket that keeps a certain scumbag in Vegas out of my hair. I *know* how to stay quiet. Tell me what's going on and I'll get you whatever I can find."

Damn, she'd let him off the hook. "Thanks. Until I figure this out, I don't want anyone knowing."

"Understood."

"There's a case Waynesville PD is working on."

"What's the connection to you?"

"The bullets."

"Un-hunh."

Yeah. His cousin wasn't stupid. A gunsmith had just marched into her office looking for information about ammunition used in a murder.

Way rolled a hand. "Can you get me intel on the case? And maybe see if there are any similar ones."

"It depends. Are you in danger?"

"No. I just need to know."

"Why?"

He cocked his head. "If I could tell you, don't you think I would?"

"I suppose. You're sure you're not in danger?"

"No danger."

That he knew of.

"Okay. If you're lying to me, I'll kill you myself." She picked up her pen again. "What are we looking for?"

"Gunshot wounds, frangible ammunition, possibly center mass."

"Well, gee, that'll narrow it down."

"The bullet leaves a hollow cavity. No exit wound. There will be bits of plastic in the body, but no slug."

Micki pulled a face. "What the fudge? No slug?"

"No slug. Don't ask me questions. Please. It's better that way. Just get me the cases."

. . .

MICKI KICKED HIM OUT.

His pacing made her nuts, so she pointed him toward the door and literally booted him on the ass. Now he'd have to wait.

Dammit.

Way checked the dashboard clock. Ninety minutes. That's how much time he'd managed to kill stopping by Reid's office and talking him into firing off a few rounds from the weapon he'd modified for him. From there, he'd driven twenty miles to the discount store, loaded up on various toiletries, and dropped them off at the post office for their homeless shelter drive.

He liked doing stuff like that. Helping those in need. His family broke his stones about it constantly, because it wasn't unusual to see him hauling around cases of toilet paper or food for the animal shelter. Somehow, all those donations didn't seem enough. Never enough.

He drove up his driveway, bypassing the house on his way to the barn, and parked in his usual spot next to Sam's BMW. Normalcy. Just another day.

Stay busy.

That's what he'd do. Because, holy hell, if that was his damned bullet...

Jesus, he could be pulled into a mess.

Way ran one hand over his face, then stared at the white trim on the barn doors. Options were plentiful, but he'd have to sit tight until Micki gave him whatever intel she found.

Still, what were the chances someone else had designed the same bullet and eliminated a gangbanger barely sixty miles away?

Stay busy. All this thinking, for a man who didn't like thinking, gave him hives. He shoved the car door open and strode around his Tahoe to the side entrance. Inside, Sam sat at her desk. When he entered, she peered at him over the rim of funky black glasses that probably cost more than his mortgage payment.

"You're back," she said.

"I am."

"Getting ready to head out?"

"Head out?"

She drew her eyebrows together and narrowed her eyes like his mother often did when trying to figure him out. Well, guess what? He didn't need to be psychoanalyzed. Or have his goddamned mind read. That shit didn't fly.

"You said you were hitting the road for a couple of weeks. If you can wait an hour, I'll have some orders for you to sign off on and we'll be good until you get back."

Hitting the road. Yeah, he'd like to do that right fucking now. Forget about all this nonsense. This was the part of running a business he hated. All Way wanted was to build guns. The responsibility that came with it was massive. He got it. Understood it just fine. What he never wanted, ever, was for one of his weapons—or ammunition—to wind up in the wrong hands and destroy a life. Multiple lives.

Fuck. Me.

"I may hold off on the trip."

"Why?"

How the hell was he supposed to answer this one? *Gee, Sam, I may have designed a devastating bullet that is now killing civilians.* "Something came up."

Before she peppered him with questions, he jerked a thumb toward his workshop. "I'll be inside."

Some would call him a coward. Maybe he was. He sure

as hell wasn't gonna stand around and be interrogated by his assistant.

"Way?"

He stopped, let out a silent breath before turning. "Yeah?"

"Are you all right?"

Oh, hell no. They weren't doing this. He held up a hand. "I'm good."

He pushed through the door to his workshop, where his leather jacket hung on the wall-mounted coat hook. His mom had bought it for him five years ago and it now had the comfortable, lived-in softness he liked. His mother might not have been around much when he was young, but she knew the way to her son's heart. He tossed his truck keys and wallet on the table-turned-desk next to the inbox Maggie gave him crap about.

When he'd bought the house, he'd found the square hickory table in the attic. Nothing fancy. Only solid, sturdy wood that didn't deserve a trash heap. He gave it a good sanding and sealing and relocated it to his workspace.

On his way to the safe, he passed the three-tiered metal filing cabinet containing his alphabetized client files. Before Sam, he'd toss the files in there as he completed each job. Hell, back then he didn't expect to sustain a business. He figured he'd make a little side money while he figured out exactly what his career of choice would be.

After the first project, he tossed the file in the drawer. Then the second, the third. Fourth, fifth, and, whoopsie, out of room in the drawer. Before long, he'd filled all three drawers and had zero organization. That's when Maggie suggested Sam.

When Way reached the wall safe, he entered the code and placed his thumb against the security pad. He grabbed his laptop from the top shelf and carried it to the oversized worktable he kept free of clutter. A man needed a clean slate to work. His philosophy anyway.

He eyeballed the extra laptop he used to keep encrypted notes on certain items. Like frangible ammunition that virtually disintegrated when it reached its target. No muss, no fuss in terms of ballistics. No slug meant no tracing the weapon.

A minute later, Sam entered, her high heels clicking against the tile and distracting the hell out of him.

Focus here.

"I've got them," she said.

Squaring up, he turned and faced her as she approached. "What?"

"The orders I told you about." She held up a folder. "Here they are."

Orders. Right. He took the folder from her. "Thank you."

"Sure." She pointed at the laptop. "Is there anything I can help with?"

"I'm good," he said. "I'm checking my notes on a project."

She glanced at the laptop, then back to him. "I keep a copy, also, if you need help."

The only help he needed right now was someone to tell him his damned bullet didn't wind up in a dead gangbanger. He didn't know the guy and had no use for violent street gangs, but that ammo should not have killed Roy Jackson.

Or any other civilian.

Sickness overcame him, burning straight through the lining of his stomach. Was this what it felt like when that acid hit flesh?

He drew in a hard breath, concentrated on not losing his shit in front of his assistant. Way needed to be left alone to figure out what the hell his next move should be. Alone, he could deal with this.

Except...Sam. Right in front of him. In his space. "Sam, you don't have *these* notes. *I'm* the only one who has them. And now I need a damned minute."

The minute the words flew from his mouth, guilt slammed him.

Shit.

She looked at him with big, round, and extremely wounded eyes.

"Wow," she said. "Excuse me for wanting to help."

She spun away and marched toward the door. *Dammit.* This is what he hated about relationships. Intimate or otherwise. His family liked to harass him about being the emperor of his own world, but in his mighty kingdom of one he didn't have to deal with people in his goddamned business all the time. Questioning him, analyzing him. And leaving him with guilt when he disappointed them.

All the donations he could conjure wouldn't solve that problem. "Sam, I'm sorry." He held up his hands. "I shouldn't have gotten up in your grill. No excuse. It'll never happen again."

Narrowing her eyes, she pursed her lips. "Apology accepted. I was only trying to help."

"Hey, guys."

They both looked over at the doorway where Micki stood, a large envelope in hand.

She'd found something. Otherwise, she'd have called or e-mailed him the file. Whatever this was, his cousin decided it warranted an in-person delivery.

And that probably wasn't a good sign.

"Hey," Way said as Micki strode into his workshop.

She slid a glance at Sam. "Hi, Sam."

"Hi. This is a surprise." Sam held her hand out. "Can I hang your jacket for you?"

"No. Thanks. I won't be long." Micki came back to Way. "I, um, have those reports you were interested in."

This wouldn't be good. He faced Sam. "Can you give us a second?"

Right now, he didn't know a lot. What he did know was that he didn't want Sam in on this conversation.

"Certainly," she said. "Let me know if you need something."

She left the room, closing the door behind her. Way waved Micki over to the worktable. "That was fast."

"I hit on a good file."

Slapping the folder down, she flipped it open and retrieved what looked like an autopsy photo. She set the photo on the table. Beside that, she placed a typewritten report...and then another three.

"I found three other cases."

His head lopped forward. "Three?"

"Yes. All within two hundred miles of us. I was able to grab these photos and the ballistics reports from the lab along with some case notes."

Way picked up one of the reports, skimmed it. Large caliber bullet, no exit wound, hollow cavity.

Crap.

Next report. No exit wound, bits of plastic.

Crap, crap.

Next report. Center mass, massive internal damage, frangible ammo.

Micki slid the last photo—the same one Maggie had shared— and another report in front of him.

"This is the Waynesville case you asked me about. Roy Jackson. He's an area leader for the Dragons."

"Were the other cases gang members?"

"Yes. Not the same gang, though. It's all in the reports. Maybe it's a turf war or something, but they're all different gangs. Two were in South Carolina. One was a motorcycle gang. Two in North Carolina."

What the hell? All four shot with the same ammo and yet they were all different gangs. "The only connection is these guys were all affiliated with a gang of some sort."

"So it seems." Micki held up a finger. "I found one interesting thing."

As she was a former employee of a fixer, if Micki thought a case was interesting, it had to be damned fascinating to the average Joe. "What's that?"

She skimmed the report from the Roy Jackson case. "Here." She pointed to a paragraph midway down the page. "Read this. It says ATF was investigating Roy Jackson for cigarette smuggling."

"So? He's in a gang. They resort to illegal activity, and I

gotta believe it's fairly easy for gangs to buy cigarettes in low-tax states and then sell them in higher tax states. Or on the black market. They'd make huge profits."

"Exactly. But if you'd read this, like I asked, you'd know that there was an entire task force made up of multiple agencies."

"Maggie told me about a task force. It's how she met Roni Fenwick."

"The Jackson report mentions an ATF agent. Past tense. I was curious, so I did a search on his name. He was murdered six months ago."

That had to be the guy Maggie and Roni knew. Now they were getting somewhere. "Were there any details on the dead agent?"

Micki shrugged. "I couldn't get into any of the files on him. All I found was an obit." She tapped the file. "It's in here. I'll keep working on it, but it might take some time to crack the ATF's system."

Ya think? So much for the guilt over having her break computer fraud laws. Somehow this thing had escalated to her hacking the ATF.

"If the agent was undercover," he said, "they may not put a lot in a report. Which agency ran this task force?"

"You're not gonna be happy."

What else was new? The whole damned thing made him unhappy. "Who was it?"

"It appears to be the brainchild of the Haywood County Sheriff's Department."

Fuck. Me.

Way knew his sister was involved, but running it? "Come on! *Maggie* was in charge of this thing?"

Not only was the ammo he designed possibly being used

to murder civilians, his sister might have led a goddamned investigation involving one of the dead guys.

He needed to get his head together on this. Figure out what to do. Go to Maggie, spill it all, and see what she knew. Except, as good at her job as she was, this was over her head. She had zero experience with frangible ammunition—or dangerous covert agencies.

Focus. Work the problem. He held up a finger. "How did Maggie get involved?"

"I don't know. All it says is she created the task force to combat illegal cigarette sales within the county. You should talk to her. If she finds out your bullets are somehow linked to this, she'll rip you."

Blindsiding his sister wouldn't be the smartest thing he'd ever done. But if these were his bullets, they had bigger problems than Maggie being pissed at him.

Next issue. "What about Fenwick? Supposedly, she was on the task force."

Micki tapped the folder. "It's all in there. Work and family history. Anything I can find. Mother was a drug addict who walked out. Her dad raised her until she was eight."

"He left, too?"

"No. Cancer. He died and she went into foster care. She's one of the lucky ones. Made her way to college. She has a master's in psychology and became a federal agent. Five months ago she left the Bureau."

"Why?"

"Couldn't find that."

"So, what's she doing now?"

"She's putting that degree to work as a psych trainer. For the CIA."

．　．　．

THE SECOND MICKI LEFT THE WORKSHOP, WAY DUG HIS CELL from his front pocket, dropped onto the barstool, and hoped to all hell Clay Bartles picked up. He needed his old Marine buddy to talk him off a goddamned ledge.

"Hey," Clay said, his voice huffy. Out of breath.

"Bad time?"

"No. It's good. Late lunch. Just finished a run. What's up?"

Did he have a week?

"This is gonna sound nuts."

"Based on the shit I hear every day, you got nothin'."

After leaving the Marines two years earlier, Clay had landed a job at the State Department as an aide to an aide to someone in the secretary of state's office. Who the hell knew the kind of crap he dealt with on any given day? Clay's boss, though, was former CIA and, through him, Way had made a contact. A contact that led him straight to the science and development department at the CIA.

Where one hundred of his extremely deadly bullets were being tested.

"Good point. Is this a secure line?"

"Uh-oh. Let me call you back in a sec."

Way disconnected, tapping his foot until his phone screen lit up with a number marked private. He punched the button. "Is this you?"

"Yeah," Clay said. "We're good. Talk to me."

"Have you heard anything about that frangible ammo I designed?"

"Far as I know, it's still being tested. Why?"

"There was a shooting in the area the other night. My sister came to me this morning with autopsy photos. The bullet ripped the guy apart and disintegrated."

"And what? You're thinking the CIA is running tests on live humans?"

"No. I'm thinking my bullets got outside CIA walls."

"No chance."

He couldn't know that. "You sure someone didn't pocket one of 'em?"

"Yeah. I'm sure. Do you know what it would take to get one of those out of Langley? It'd be damned near impossible. Anyone would be stupid to try it. With the procedures they have in place, they'd get caught fast. No chance."

"Then maybe the design got out?"

"Or maybe someone else developed a similar bullet. Look, Way, you're good, but who's to say some other gun-geek didn't come up with this?"

"I thought of that. But, seriously? What are the chances that someone in this area designed the exact same bullet? Between the plunger inside, the plastic capsule, the acid, it took me months to get that design right."

All in all, he'd done a helluva job.

Now that design had made its way to the street. Despite what the public thought, the CIA did occasionally operate on US soil. What Way didn't get was how they'd be connected to Maggie's cigarette smuggling case and a bunch of gang members.

Clay sighed. "I don't know, Way. But I'm telling you, there's no chance this trails back to Langley. No way. It's gotta be a freak coincidence. And you don't wanna start making noise about it. The agency will deny it and you'll be ruined. You'll blow this deal."

"It's not about the money."

But it sure as hell was about Roni Fenwick, a CIA employee and former member of Maggie's task force, showing up. He wouldn't mention that intel to Clay. Otherwise, it'd lead to a whole bunch of questions Way didn't necessarily have answers to.

"I know it's not about the money, but how do you think it'll go over if the public thinks the fucking CIA lets secret weapons out of its control? How's that sound for national security? Russia would love that."

Screwed. That's what he was. "My ammo might be killing civilians, and I'm supposed to do nothing?"

The silence across the phone line was met with a sigh from Clay. "All right. Just, stand down for a day or two. Let me see what I can find out. How many samples did you send?"

"One hundred. Exactly."

With material like that, a responsible man didn't lose count.

"I'll see where science and development is at on it."

That's all Way could ask. "Thanks. All I need to know is whether they have all hundred accounted for."

It wouldn't explain how Roy Jackson came to be shredded by a similar bullet, but if Clay could confirm the CIA still had all of Way's samples, he'd be off the hook.

7

Tonight's target is none other than Chad Hopkins III. A young man of twenty-four whose rap sheet is longer than my leg. As I sit in the car—a Honda I stole while en route to Chad's girlfriend's house—I ponder how a kid goes from the eighth-grade honor roll to climbing the ranks of a street gang.

Heroin.

That's how. I warn people of the brutality of that drug. One use. That's all it takes before your body craves it like a starving man craves a tomahawk steak.

Tsk-tsk-tsk. Chad managed to get clean while on a six-month jail stint, but after four years of being a junkie, he'd established himself as a thug. A menace who would rape your daughter in front of you if you didn't hand over whatever he demanded.

Yes, I've done my research. Chad is no angel.

And he's next on my list.

A sharp metallic taste fills my mouth. I swallow a couple of times and do some deep breathing to rein in the adrenaline flooding my system.

The street is eerily lacking pedestrian and vehicle traffic, and I use the quiet to focus myself. In this neighborhood, being out after dark means several things: You work late, you're up to no good, or you're crazy.

The cops won't even come here at night. That's how rough it is. Shootings? No big deal.

That's the kind of animal I'm dealing with. And this quiet? Too spooky. Too ripe for danger I'm anxious to leave behind.

Chad has been inside over two hours. He'll be leaving soon, I'm sure. The girlfriend has work in the morning and, in the weeks I've been trailing him, Chad has yet to stay over. People really should pay attention to their own routines and how vulnerable those routines make them. Even the criminals sometimes lose sight of it.

I let out a sigh, hoping Chad doesn't intend on making me wait too long. Between Roy and Chad, it's been a busy few weeks of surveillance and my body is feeling the effects. Fatigue pinches my shoulders to the point where any amount of stretching is useless. I need a good night's sleep. Maybe ten.

But the list is long and there's no rest for the weary.

I check the time on my phone: 10:35. Getting close. I hit the window button and breathe in the blast of fresh air. It's a cool night. Barely fifty degrees. Never a fan of the cold, I raise the window again, leaving only a few inches of space at the top.

"Come on, Chad. Hurry it up."

I check the door again. Nothing.

Soon.

Beside me is the trusty Colt .45. A larger weapon than I'd like for this job, but the gun has to be big to hold the acid-filled bullet. Stroke of genius, that.

A flash of light catches my eye and I swing my head left to see the front door open across the street. Once again, that nasty metallic taste fills my mouth. *This is it.* Lucky me, there's a fire hydrant smack-dab in front of the house. What are the odds I'd have an unobstructed view? Talk about a sign from God.

I hit the window button again, letting that cool air fill my lungs as I lift the weapon. The weight of it, the absolute power seeps through my hand. My system roars and I breathe in, hold it for a second, and then exhale.

Calm.

That's what I need right now. One shot. That's all I'll get. One shot. Then I'll pull away, ditch the car, and disappear.

Easy.

It takes less than a second for Chad to step onto the porch. He turns back to offer a good-night kiss to the young woman in the doorway. Young love.

How very sweet.

The pause at the door gives me time to line up my shot. *Too low.* I make the necessary adjustment and wait for him to turn around. To give me a clear shot.

The kiss drags on and my pulse kicks up. *Come on. Make it snappy.*

"Christ sakes," I mutter, once again grateful for the quiet street.

The porn-movie-worthy kiss finally ends and I silently thank whatever god available. Short on patience, I'm ready to be done. I need sleep and a hot shower. Not necessarily in that order.

Chad turns. *Perfect.* I give the trigger a gentle squeeze and watch as Chad Hopkins III jerks backward and drops.

Mission complete.

.   .   .

THE *BRRRNNGG* OF RONI'S PHONE DRAGGED HER—KICKING AND screaming—from a dream about Waylon Kingston in nothing but a pair of broken-in jeans. Even his feet were bare and that, for whatever odd reason, made Roni's more-than-ready body hum.

Damn, that was a good dream.

She cracked her eyes open. The sun slanted through the gauzy curtains in her suite at Tasky's B&B, a giant farmhouse with quite possibly the softest bed she'd ever slept in.

She slapped her eyes closed again. What the hell time was it?

Still propped on her side, she reached to the nightstand, smacking her hand around until landing on the phone.

She pried her eyes open again, blinking into focus on Karl Quigley's name.

A quick glance at the ancient bedside clock indicated it was 6:05 a.m.

The man was insane.

Before the call dropped, she cleared her throat, practiced a few quick hellos, and tapped the screen. "Hello? This is Roni."

"We've got another one."

Well, good morning to you, too, sir.

"Sorry?"

"Get the fuck out of bed and turn on the news. Another gang shooting. Same bullet. Where are you on Kingston?"

She bolted to a sitting position.

Aside from dreams about Way being shirtless?

And barefoot.

Nowhere. That's where she was. She'd only arrived in town yesterday. How much did he expect from her in one day?

"Sir—"

"Forget the 'sir' bullshit. Get your ass out of bed and find out who he's selling those bullets to. They're not coming out of Langley. All are accounted for on our end."

And that automatically meant Way Kingston was selling them? Really? With the smarts of the CIA's S&D department, what was to stop one of their people from copying the design?

"And we're sure we don't have leakage with the design?"

A few seconds of silence ensued. "Fenwick, you want me to go to the deputy director and tell her someone has betrayed us and is selling a top-secret design we're testing?"

Well, no. She didn't want that, but the possibility existed.

"Of course not, sir. But—"

"No buts, Fenwick. This is not coming from inside Langley. I don't care what it takes, get me something solid on Kingston."

"I'm trying—"

"Don't try, do. Or don't come back."

Click.

What the? She checked the phone screen and grunted.

Once again, he'd hung up on her. That alone irritated her. Never mind the mandate to make Way Kingston a scapegoat.

If he was guilty of selling that frangible design, yes, he should wind up in a cell. Acid in a bullet? Horrific. That kind of weaponry had no place in the general public.

She wasn't even convinced it had a place in the spec ops world. Not because there weren't situations that called for wiping the evidence trail clean, but for the very reason she was in Steele Ridge.

The damned bullet had landed in the hands of a psycho. And now, she had a top-level CIA executive pressuring her for results.

Well, he'd get those results.

Roni style.

She threw the covers back and headed for the en-suite bathroom.

Time to pay a visit to Way Kingston and push his buttons.

WAY STOOD IN HIS WORKSHOP, HIS FAVORITE "GO AHEAD. Make my day." mug in hand. On the wall-mounted television, Shelly Radcliffe, the local station's morning anchor, had just announced a breaking news story.

Another gang shooting.

He slammed the mug on the table, sending hot coffee splashing over the rim and scalding his fingers. *Goddammit.* He shook his hand, then rubbed it dry against his jeans while his heart slammed.

Don't panic.

No room for panic. He was an operator and understood the nuances of certain high-pressure situations.

Gang shootings around Asheville weren't uncommon. Still, something nagged at him.

He punched the power button with more force than necessary before tossing the remote against the table. It clattered against the wood, smacking at his already stretched nerves.

Unlocking his phone, he hit Maggie's name and waited. If he got voice mail, he'd run into town and find her. Way didn't have the time or patience to wait on his sister's call. With her crazy job, she could be tied up for hours and, well, right now, he needed her. The fine citizens of Haywood County would have to wait.

"Hi, Way. What's up?"

Thank you, sweet baby Jesus. Even if she had used her get-to-the-point voice, she'd picked up.

He'd oblige and make this quick. "Hey. Saw the news. Another gang shooting last night."

"Yes. It's not my jurisdiction, but it's too close."

She had no fucking idea. "Wondering about that case you showed me yesterday. Was this—"

"The same bullet?" Maggie finished for him. "No autopsy report yet."

"Jesus."

"Way?"

"Yeah?"

"Why are you asking me about this?" On her laziest day his sister loved crawling straight up his ass and nosing into his business. Asking about this case? Forget it. She'd be relentless.

"You're the one who came to me with autopsy photos. Now there's another gang shooting. Why *wouldn't* I ask?"

"Maybe because it doesn't involve you."

But she didn't have a problem involving him yesterday. When *she* wanted *his* help. Wasn't that a pisser? "Fine," he said. "Next time you want my help, I'll remember I shouldn't follow up. That you're the only one allowed to ask questions. Consider me schooled."

A soft laugh sounded from her end. "You're spinning this on me? Really? Classic, Waylon."

Way pinched the bridge of his nose. He'd sure blown this conversation to hell and back. A long silence drifted between them. Nothing unusual when it came to Maggie. Over the years, they'd fallen into a routine. She'd needle him and he'd shut her down. What was it about him that took issue with Maggie's nosiness when everyone else in his family let it slide?

Maggie's concern. That's what they all called it. A nicer way of saying meddling.

And this right here was the reason the military called to him. He loved his family, missed them horribly while overseas. But he didn't need them constantly on him. Asking questions. Giving opinions.

Maggie was an ace at all that.

"I don't want to fight with you," she said.

He closed his eyes, rolled his shoulders to release the tension that crept up on him. *Relax. Relax and focus.* "Neither do I, Mags. It was a question. That's all."

"And you're sure you don't have any information on this? I mean, I know you fiddle with all kinds of weapons and bullets."

Relentless.

He had to laugh. Good old Mags.

"Forget I called. Okay? Sorry to bug you."

"You didn't bug me. And you know I can't give out information."

He was all too aware of his sister's high professional standards. He couldn't blame her. If she leaked info and it impacted a case, criminals could walk free on technicalities.

Still, this one damned time, he'd like an answer.

"I'll talk to you later," he said.

"Come on, Way. Don't be like that."

"Like what? Irritated because it's okay for you to pump me for information, but not for me to do it?"

For a few seconds, she remained silent. "You're right. I'm sorry."

Oh, that had to hurt. "Wait? What?"

She laughed. "Oh my God. You're such a bastard."

"Hang on while I scrape my jaw off the floor."

"Whatever. Jerk. Dinner at Mom's tonight. What are you bringing?"

Shit. The regular family dinner smackdown when everyone brought a dish and voted on a winner. As far as cooking went, he did okay. He'd inherited his dad's curiosity about herbs and spices and trying new twists on dishes.

However, he'd forgotten about dinner tonight and hadn't put a lick of thought into what he might bring. And he knew, right down to his boots, that Maggie got help from Jay, who'd taken cooking lessons from a trained chef.

How was that fair?

"No idea. I'll come up with something."

Because if he showed up empty-handed, he'd never hear the end of it.

"Okay. And, Way? It appears so."

"What?"

"The answer to your bullet question. It appears so. You didn't hear it from me."

A sudden silence filled the phone line.

"Mags?"

Nothing. Call ended.

He replayed the conversation, pinning down his original question. Was it the same type of bullet? That's what he'd asked.

It appears so.

It might as well have been napalm dropping on him.

Shit, shit, shit.

Someone was walking around killing gang members with his damned bullets. How the fuck?

The agency. Someone must have leaked the design. Or worse, if one of the bullets was outside the agency, it could have been reverse engineered. Any experienced gunsmith could copy the design.

He ticked back over the number of bullets he'd made. A hundred even. All of them sent to Langley for testing.

Clay. Way needed to connect again. See if he'd checked on the initial order. And if all were accounted for.

His stomach flipped. If he'd had breakfast, it would be all over the damned floor. Even thinking about those bullets on the street made his gut heave.

The workshop door flew open, banging against the desk. Roni Fenwick barged in, glaring so hard it should have blown him through the wall.

She wore another tight tank top, this one with an unbuttoned flannel shirt over it. The shirt flapped open as she stormed toward him, and her hair bounced right along with that tremendous rack of hers.

It took everything he had not to step back, to put space between himself and super storm Roni. At the same time, all that crazy energy fired something in him and...

He wanted her. Hard and fast.

"Talk to me," she said.

He wanted to do a whole lot more than talk. "Uh...Come again?"

She stopped a foot from him, her dark eyes sharper than a laser scope. "Let's quit fucking around, shall we?"

Or maybe they should *start* fucking around? Jeez, she'd twisted his mind. He gave his head a hard shake, tried to focus on the fact that she was, apparently, upset.

They'd get to whatever had riled her in a sec. Now that she'd arrived, he had a few questions.

He crossed his arms, met her hard stare. "Great idea, *Roni*. We'll start with you leaving the Bureau and moving to the CIA." Her right eyebrow quirked. Surprised her with that one. Good. "And speaking of, why is the agency suddenly at my door when a bunch of lowlifes are getting picked off with a goddamn bullet I designed? What the fuck happened? The agency lost track of a few?"

She might have been blindsided, but she sure as shit wasn't backing off. "Oh, hell, no. They're all right where they should be. All one hundred."

She knew the number. *Crap.* The agency, she'd just inadvertently confirmed, had sent her to check him out. Which meant they didn't know what the hell was going on either.

He leaned in a little, tipping his upper body a bit closer. "Then you've got a double agent inside Langley who reverse engineered them."

"Or you sold the design."

Bull*shit*. This woman. Absolutely maddening. He could lose his mind, go on about a government agency failing to protect his idea for ammunition that could change the spy world. But that's what she wanted. He ticked back to his conversation with Micki. Roni Fenwick, psych trainer for the CIA. A bona fide headshrinker.

Way stepped closer. "Watch it, lady. My military career speaks for itself. The things I've done for this country, you will never touch. So don't come in here making accusations. I'm not the one who screwed this up."

"You're insulted?"

"Honey, I'm more than insulted. I'm fucking horrified. You should be thanking me for the shit I've done to protect you and your freedom. If you can't do that, then get out."

For a solid five seconds she didn't move. Just stood there, her gaze hot on his. What the hell? Had he actually done it? Left the little spitfire speechless?

Somehow, it didn't make him feel good. In fact, he hated it.

Finally she nodded. "Okay."

Okay? What did that mean? "I don't see you moving."

"Oh, I'm not leaving. There's too much at stake, and I've got one pain in the ass associate deputy director of administration nipping at me."

He thought for a second. In the months he'd been working with the agency, he'd brushed up on the top-level guys. Just in case. "Quigley? What the hell does he have to do with this?"

"Technically, he's my boss. My boss's boss's boss really." She waved a hand. "Not that it matters."

What. *The fuck?*

Everything mattered right now. Perfect time to remind himself what she did for a living.

"Is this some kind of mind game? Something you head-shrinkers do to keep people on their toes?"

"No. Well, it was at first. Now it's not."

"Oh. Goody."

"I think you might be telling the truth. About the bullets. I see it in your body language. The way you nearly ripped my head off when I accused you of selling the design and questioned your patriotism. Plus, you're Maggie's brother."

"What does that have to do with anything?"

She poked him in the chest. "I like Maggie. I'd go as far as to say I trust her, which, if you knew me at all, is basically a miracle."

"Are you nuts?"

"I might be. But I'm sane enough to have checked you out. You think I'd come in here without background? You've had an exemplary military career. You come from a good family. Your finances check out—congratulations, by the way, for taking your talent to another level."

Nuts. The woman was straight up nuts. But, with Clay not calling him back, she might be his intel source with the agency.

He backed up a step, a quick time-out to organize his thoughts. He needed to know what she knew. "You're not the only one with contacts. I know you're a psych trainer, which is a totally different department from science and development. What I don't know is why you're here and what you have to do with my bullets."

Three, maybe four seconds passed. The mouthy brunette who'd stormed into his workspace stood, shoulders back, spine ramrod straight, and chin tilted in defiance.

Then it hit him. "Maggie," he said. "You used my sister to get to me."

STALLING.

That's all Roni was doing. Worse, they both knew it. Her silence only proved it. But what the hell was a girl to do when her plan crumbled into a million bitty pieces? From the second Way had revealed his knowledge of her CIA connection, she'd been bested. Her stint with the FBI wouldn't be hard to find, but he'd basically rolled out her résumé. In record time.

Damn, he was good.

Now he leaned in, getting right in her face, where the soapy, clean smell of a fresh shower flooded her system and sparked...something. The full force of her dream—and the vision of a shirtless Way—came back to her. She inched closer, wanting all that heat and male energy.

He tilted his head, bringing his lips to her ear, skimming her skin, and sending another shot of zinging energy straight to her nipples.

Way Kingston.

Major sexy.

"I don't like people using my family," he whispered.

The words hit her like a wrecking ball, shattering her. She was no angel when it came to her job. Yes, she lied and used people if justice required it.

But her friends?

Never. She didn't have enough of them to risk the loss.

From the start of this assignment, she'd made sure she didn't lie to Maggie. Maybe Roni hadn't been forthcoming on certain things, but...

Oh, hell. A lie by omission was still a lie.

She shook her head. Blurring lines. Never good.

She stepped back, setting her hand on his chest, gently forcing Way back and out of her space. "I didn't *use* Maggie."

"Sure you did. You're here aren't you?"

Damn him. "I'll give you that. But everything I said about Maggie is true. We worked together, we're friends—and, believe me, there are only a handful of people I say that about. Not telling her was as much to protect her as anything. If this thing goes sideways, I don't want her implicated. By the time it's over, she'll be able to truthfully say she knew nothing about the CIA operating on US soil."

"At least you have a conscience."

"When it comes to people I care about, you know it."

He stood for a few long seconds, his lips slightly puckered and—mmm, mmm, mmm—she desperately itched to touch them. Just run the tips of her fingers over his skin.

But the way he looked at her. The steady, suspicious gaze that hid unspoken questions.

What was going on with him?

More than anger, more than mistrust. This was...pain.

And people in pain, she couldn't handle. She'd had too much of it herself. "Are you all right?"

He spun away, walked to his worktable and settled on a stool, shaking his head. "Goddamn headshrinkers."

Inquiring about his well-being made her a head-shrinker? "All I asked is if you were all right. Forgive me for giving a shit."

"Please. Now you *care* about me? What the hell am I supposed to think? You used my sister to get to me and then spewed some crap about your dead friend. You expect me to not wonder about your motives?"

"People are dying. And it appears it's by a bullet you designed. I've been tasked with figuring out how that happened. There's not a manual on this type of investigation."

"I didn't sell that design. And since you're bent on finding the truth, newsflash, babe, Langley doesn't have the specs. Until they buy them, those details stay locked in my safe."

Terrific. *If it looks like a duck...* One of her foster mothers used to say that all the time and, until this day, she had never completely experienced the truth of it. "So you're the only one who has the specs?"

"Yes."

"And you expect the CIA to believe this is a coincidence?"

"Not on your life. I've put a ton of time into this project. Having those murders crop up within miles of me? It's gotta be my design. It didn't come from me, though. Someone at Langley screwed me."

"The test bullets are accounted for. If you're the only one with the specs, how did you get screwed?"

"Have you seen all the test bullets?"

"No. Some have been fired."

"Then I guess there's no way to really know if one got out."

True.

He folded his arms and studied her for a second. "You think I'm lying."

"I'm not sure what I think about ninety percent of this. I don't think you leaked that design, though. It's a start."

"At least we're getting somewhere. Are you gonna tell me what you know?" He stepped forward again, crowding her space. Smart man that he was, he sensed he'd unnerved her the last time he tried it.

Well, lust or no lust, Roni wouldn't be that easy again. She lifted her chin.

"This is my ass on the line," he said. "I have information I can share. Help me figure it out."

A partnership. Might not be a bad idea. She already knew he had one or more excellent contacts. "Some of it's classified."

"Fine. Don't tell me that stuff. Chances are, I can get it on my own. I already got the related cases."

Whatever the CIA had thought of Way Kingston, they'd underestimated him. "You identified the related cases? How?"

He grinned. "You show me yours and I'll show you mine."

Oh, he was a sassy one.

She might have to fuck him. Literally, not figuratively.

Once again, her nipples got hard. Thank goodness for padded bras, because her body sure wasn't doing her any favors. "You want to be partners?"

He lifted one shoulder. "Call it whatever you want. But if we pool our intel, we might figure out who's blowing people away with my bullets."

8

CRAZY AS IT WAS, RONI WALKED BACK TO HER RENTAL AND popped the trunk to retrieve the file Karl and Don had given her.

Talk about going off-script. If either one of them knew she'd just outed the CIA's Way Kingston investigation, she'd undoubtedly be fired. No explanation necessary.

Now that she'd done it, the next logical step would be to gather info and see where it led.

While outside, she grabbed the two shopping bags filled with dog and cat food she'd picked up the day before. Being a busy, single woman living in a high-rise didn't make her an ideal candidate for the dog she'd always wanted, but she could follow Way's lead and make donations to shelters. Why she'd never thought of it before eluded her, but now she'd become a regular donor.

Plus, it might score her some points with Way. Loosen him up a bit.

She set the bags on the ground and closed the trunk, double-checking that it had latched since she'd stored her nine-millimeter in there for safekeeping. The crunch of tires on gravel drew her gaze to the spiffy BMW she'd seen the day before.

Way's assistant. *Sam*. Might as well cuddle up in case she needed her at some point.

Bags in hand, Roni paused at her front bumper while Sam parked in the same spot as yesterday.

Sam, all tall, elegant blonde, slid from the car and slung her Fendi tote over her shoulder. That tote probably cost more than Roni made in a week. Besides, all that finery would be wasted on her. She barely carried a purse most days, opting for her vintage leather messenger bag.

"Good morning," Sam said.

"Good morning."

"You and my boss are at it early today."

They sure were. "Something like that." Roni smiled. "He's already inside."

"He usually beats me here. Unless he's out of town." She gestured to the bags. "Do you need help there?"

"I've got it. Thanks. Does that happen a lot? Way out of town?"

Sam shrugged. "I wouldn't say a lot. He likes his road trips." She pointed to the corner of the barn, at a bulky motorcycle with storage compartments on the back. "I like to joke that the motorcycle is my job security."

Road trips. A slight niggling crept up Roni's neck. Hadn't she read that two of the murders had been in South Carolina?

Sam started toward the door while Roni's mind exploded with questions. Could Way be playing her, the one who'd survived the foster care system by learning how not to be fooled?

No chance. She'd sense it. If not from her experience,

from her training. Nothing about Waylon Kingston indicated deception.

But—God—she'd never had naughty fantasies about a suspect before. Particularly when that suspect was the brother of a close friend.

Roni paused at the door when Sam swung it open, holding it for her. She glanced down at the folder tucked under her arm. All that classified info she'd just agreed to share. She should turn around. Walk away and forget this. Tell Don and Karl she'd been compromised.

She peered through the door.

Four victims so far. If she turned tail, chances were whoever had that bullet design would kill again.

And that, she couldn't let happen.

WAY TOOK THE TWO FILLED SHOPPING BAGS FROM RONI AND set them near the door. "Thanks. You didn't have to do that."

"I wanted to. I don't have a dog, yet, but I can help out. Let me know if there's anything else they need and I'll pick it up."

A woman after his own heart. He'd been toying with the idea of a dog, but dogs needed tending and big ones didn't fit in the custom carriers made for motorcycles.

And he wanted a big guy. A shepherd he could teach to play frisbee. Eventually. "There's a wish list online. I'll give you the website, but they always need paper towels. And bleach."

Putting the idea of pets out of his mind, Way cleared a large area on his worktable and grabbed a second stool from the opposite side. Shelter supplies or not, if Roni thought he'd give her intel without her doing the same, she'd be wrong.

Colossally wrong. Did he respect her for taking the time to shop for the shelter? Hell, yeah. But she could also be fucking with his mind and ten years as a recon Marine hadn't resulted in an idiot who let a pair of nice tits and dog food distract him.

From his front pocket, his phone rang. Shep. He'd call him back. He set the phone on the table, went back to Roni, and pointed to the stool. "Have a seat."

"Do you need to deal with that call?"

"No. It's my brother." His phone whistled. "That would be him texting me."

Just in case, he tapped the screen and skimmed the message telling him to call back. Nothing urgent.

"A call and a text. You can call him. I don't mind."

"It's nothing urgent. I'll turn the ringer down because this is when the fun begins."

"Fun?"

"Yep. Since Shep didn't connect, my mother or Maggie will also call."

Roni let out a soft snort. At least someone found it funny.

"Do they do that often?"

"Every damned day. I'm not married or in a relationship, so they apparently have to be in constant contact. Makes me nuts."

"Well, the psychologist in me would advise you to speak to them about your boundaries. You're running a business. If it's not an emergency, they should respect that and allow you the opportunity to complete your workday and then call them back."

Huh. Boundaries. Had he ever even told them the calls were out of hand? He thought about it. No. Never once had he told them to back off. He ran his palms up his forehead, then banged himself on the skull. "I created this monster. I should have nixed it from the get-go."

"It's hard. At first it probably seemed like they were being nice and then you don't want to look like a jerk by telling them to stop. Then the behavior continues and sometimes gets worse, but there's still that underlying guilt so you let it continue. It's a vicious cycle."

Wow. She'd just nailed his entire family dynamic. "You are scary good at this shit."

"I do try. Anyway." She slapped a manila folder down, slid onto the stool, and swiveled to face him. "Talk to them. Keep it short, friendly, and to the point. They'll understand."

"I'll do that. Thank you."

"You're welcome."

They sat staring at each other for a few seconds, which, truth be told, he didn't much mind. Beautiful women, especially cunning ones, had never been a problem for him.

Twisted fucker that he was, he got high on the brutal mental workout. He'd sit here all day and look at her.

The first to flinch loses. That was his motto.

Which might be hers, too, since they sat—and sat and sat—while the *thump-thump-thump* of his pulse drowned out any sound.

Oh, oh, oh, he'd love to touch her. Run his fingers through her hair, over her face, down her neck to...other places.

And then her full lips spread into a slow, sexy smile that left his pulse hammering for completely different reasons.

"Clearly," she said, "one of us has to give in."

"Clearly."

"You're kinda maddening."

He grinned. "Thank you."

That made her laugh, a slow, throaty sound that Way

wanted to hear more of. Man-oh-man, he liked the sound of it.

"I know we're supposed to be all serious here, but gotta say, your laugh is killer. Feel free to do it more."

She raised one eyebrow, giving him a definite you-must-be-stoned look. He leaned forward, tapped her nose lightly. "I'm not playing you. Just say thank you."

At that she nodded. "All right. Thank you." She set her hand on the folder in front of her. "Now, back to work. I'll show you what I have and I trust you'll stick to our deal and do the same."

And lookie here. She flinched first. Way should have been doing mental backflips over the win. He'd taken a tough, headstrong woman down a notch.

Somehow it left him...flat.

"I'll make you a deal," he said.

"You're full of deals today."

"Honey, I've barely started." He picked up the envelope containing everything Micki had gathered and held it to her. "In the spirit of partnership, how about we do it together? You read mine while I read yours."

Roni did the same with her folder. "Excellent idea."

Flipping open the folder, he found a sheet of notebook paper on top. The handwriting, a mix of print and cursive, filled the entire page with bulleted notes. The first murder —at least the first they'd connected to his ammo design— occurred four and a half months ago. Two months after he'd sent the first batch of bullets to the CIA. All these months, he'd been waiting on an answer from Langley. No clue what the holdup was, he'd assumed it was government bureau-cracy at work.

He homed in on the name Jeff Ambrose—the dead ATF agent. "Talk to me about Ambrose."

"What do you want to know?"

"My sister included him on this task force. I know Maggie. My guess is she handpicked all of you. And Maggie thinks every decision damned near to death."

"She's thorough, for sure."

"She's a pain in the ass."

Roni's full-on laugh sent his mind, once again, straight to the gutter. But, hey, he was a guy and she was a damned fine-looking woman with a porn-star worthy laugh.

"Well," Roni said, "pain in the ass or not, she put together a hell of a team. Jeff was a good man. Undercover work came naturally—"

"A good liar."

"I don't know that I'd say that, but he knew how to play a shady guy."

"What was he working on when he died?"

"An informant turned us on to a distributor. The informant didn't have any hard evidence, but he'd heard on the street that the distributor and manufacturer were making side deals on cigarettes to avoid paying taxes."

"They must have been stashing the cigarettes."

"Exactly. We'd established a cover for Jeff as a convenience store owner. He started buying small quantities at wholesale from the distributor and then kept increasing his order. It took six months for him to cozy up enough to ask the guy if he'd consider doing a side deal."

"What kind of deal?"

"Jeff would sell the cigarettes on the black market—i.e., tax-free—and give the guy a share of the profit. After a week, the guy came back saying he wanted in. We were a few months into him making these black-market deals and getting chummy with the distributor when he got killed."

"Chummy how?"

"Socializing, fishing weekends, tooling around in the guy's Maserati."

Way let out a low whistle. "And you're sure Jeff was clean?"

Roni gave him a pissy look. "Squeaky. Our personal accounts were monitored monthly. If he was on the take, he did a bang-up job of hiding it."

Hiding money overseas didn't take a rocket scientist. "How did the actual operation work?"

"We leased a warehouse to store the cigarettes he bought."

"Where'd the money come from to buy?"

"Maggie worked it out. I assume from asset forfeitures. When a drug dealer gets busted, any assets used during the commission of a crime are seized."

Way nodded. "They sell the assets and use the money to fund undercover ops?"

"Basically. This is when things started getting hairy. Originally, the members of the task force were supposed to be resources only. You know, helping with admin functions and such. As Jeff became more involved and the scope of the operation grew, ATF got antsy. I wouldn't be surprised if the ATF and FBI helped finance the whole thing. My boss was suddenly a whole lot more involved, wanting regular updates."

"They hijacked my sister's task force."

"Not openly, but we all understood what was going on."

Fuckers. Maggie worked her ass off and she got screwed. Typical bureaucratic bullshit. Way rolled one hand. "So Ambrose tucks in with this distributor and what? How does he get killed?"

"We still don't know for sure, but he'd gotten pretty entrenched. The more comfortable the players became, the more Jeff heard. Wiretaps and surveillance indicated certain, shall we say, unsavory-looking guys showing up at the distributor every week. Gang members—the Street Dragons."

Way pointed at his notes in front of Roni. "I saw a motorcycle gang in the intel I came across."

"Correct. There were also other individuals of interest. Not necessarily gangs. One guy owned a smoke shop on an Indian reservation. Jeff was murdered before he'd gathered enough evidence."

Roni lifted one hand. "We don't know if his cover was blown or what. Right after that, the operation got shut down."

"All right, so how does this tie back to my bullets?"

"It doesn't. Well, not in the literal sense. The only connection is the murdered Street Dragons guy. It was enough of a link that the CIA suits wanted me to leverage my relationship with Maggie to get an introduction to you."

"And here you are."

"Here I am. Trying to figure out how your bullets got into"—she held up one of the pages from Micki's report —"various gang members. Two of whom are out of state."

Way moved to the wall where he'd hung a whiteboard for noting project details. He snapped a picture of it so he'd have a copy and then erased the data.

"Give me the victims' names?"

Roni read off the names, including Chad Hopkins III, the latest victim. Way added them to the board.

"Um." Roni used her pen to point to his phone. "Your screen just lit up."

He walked back to the table and spotted his mother's photo on his phone's screen. *Here we go.*

"Like I said. My mother."

He shot her a quick text letting her know he was in a meeting and that he'd return all calls later.

There. The first step in Operation Boundaries. He set the phone back down and gave Roni a winning smile. "I told her I'd call later."

"Good for you."

"Let's see if it works." He went back to the whiteboard and picked up the marker again. "We know the first shooting was Randy Millner. That was mid-September."

"According to this report, yes."

"And the second one was November."

"Yes."

Way marked the date on the board. "And then we have one in January."

"Wow, good memory."

With his ass on the line? Damned straight. He tapped the marker against the board. "He's the motorcycle gang member." Way stepped back for a wider view. "We had murders in September, November, and January. And now Jackson and Hopkins within a few days of each other."

Roni checked the notes in front of her again. "Yes. Our suspect is escalating."

"You think it's a serial killer?"

She shrugged. "Don't know yet. But he definitely has a pattern. Frangible ammo and gang members of some sort."

"All the shots were center mass." Way jotted a note on the board. "I need the autopsy reports of all these cases."

"Why?"

"I'm gonna guess the shot was taken at a distance. At least a short distance."

Roni pointed at him. "Which would mean some level of firearms skill."

"Bingo. Your average gangbanger isn't trained with a

weapon. They don't prepare for wind or gravity or spindrift." He waved the marker. "They're amateurs."

"All right. And we know"—she reached over to where Way left her file and rifled through pages—"that the shootings started after you sent the first batch of bullets to Langley."

"Yeah."

Way shoved the cap on the marker and tossed it on the worktable. "I don't care what your boss says, someone inside Langley swiped one of my bullets. We need to find out who. Let's go."

"Where?"

"If you can call your boss and get Chad Hopkins's address, we're gonna pay a visit. See if anyone knows why or how he wound up with one of my bullets in him."

9

CHAD HOPKINS'S NEIGHBORHOOD COULD BE FEATURED ON America's Worst Neighborhoods.

That's all Way could think as he navigated his SUV down a street littered with trash and dead trees and broken-down vehicles.

Way drove past one home with boarded-up windows and a padlocked front door. Compared to this he'd grown up in fantasyland. Something, no matter how much his family hovered, he was grateful for.

Given it was a school day, the block was devoid of kids, but Way tried to imagine a bunch of seven-year-olds running and playing on these mean streets. Damn. Not an easy thought.

"Crack house," Roni said.

From the driver's seat, Way looked over at her. "What?"

She pointed to the boarded home. "I think that's a crack house. It looks abandoned, but if we popped that padlock, we'd probably find needles all over the place."

"And kids play on the sidewalk."

"Yep. Reminds me of one of my foster homes."

Way gawked. "Wait. You *lived* in a place like this?"

"The Martins. I was thirteen and spent four months with them before being moved."

"Why'd you get moved?"

"Oh, I did that on purpose. With that neighborhood, I couldn't stand it. I may have had a roof over my head, but walking home from school while dodging stray bullets wasn't the life my father would have wanted for me."

She peered out the window and Way took the hint that she wasn't interested in continuing the conversation. She had lived a wild life.

Alone and battling constant change with different families—and shitty neighborhoods. Wow. He couldn't fathom it.

"You're a strong woman, Roni Fenwick."

From the corner of his eye, he saw her give up on the window and turn back to him, so he glanced over. "I mean that," he said. "It couldn't have been easy."

"Thank you. I like to think I learned a lot."

Way turned right at the corner. Two teenagers who should have been in school stood on the sidewalk watching as Way and Roni cruised by. The taller kid's gaze, even from the distance, locked on to the SUV and Way sensed something in his eyes. Something desperate and lonely.

Needy.

The streets did that to kids. He'd seen enough of it in the military to know kids between the ages of twelve and seventeen, when faced with rough neighborhoods, had a high risk of winding up in some form of criminal life.

Way shook his head. "This is a brutal way for these kids to live."

"Sure is."

The GPS lady's voice announced their destination.

"Third house up," Roni said.

Way pulled to the curb and studied the two-story brick home with the small front porch. Grading on a curve, this home could be considered above average. Meaning no broken windows or crumbling facades. Chipped trim paint and sagging gutters were the worst of it.

A man appeared at the front screen door, peering out at them. No doubt, someone—maybe one of the teenagers—had alerted him to the vehicle at the curb.

Based on the other cars parked on the street and in the short driveways, a newer model SUV would bring attention that came with outsiders.

"So much for staying low-key," Way said.

"Not in this neighborhood. Places like this, they know who belongs."

"For the record. I thought about coming alone, but figured you'd rip me one if I tried."

"You figured right." She reached to the floorboard, retrieved her nine-millimeter from her briefcase. "I'm not about to let you treat me like a damsel in distress."

He offered up a smile. "You scare me too much for that."

Way slid his own handgun from the steering column holster. He tucked the weapon into his waist holster. "You ready?

"Definitely. You do the talking. My experience is, they'll be more forthcoming with a man. I'll hang back. Sound good?"

Why not? He'd never had a problem making conversation. "Sure. You watch my six. Something about those two on the corner isn't sitting right."

Before exiting the vehicle, Roni adjusted her waist holster, slid her gun home and draped her shirt over it in a way that kept the weapon hidden but easily accessible.

She met Way on the sidewalk where a hunk of cement had cracked and broken off, revealing the dirt beneath. If she caught a boot heel in there, she'd snap an ankle.

He grabbed her elbow, guiding her around the hole. "Watch that."

She moved left, bumping him slightly. Her breast made contact with his side and—*yow*—all that soft lush skin shouldn't be the thing on his mind right now.

Totally not his fault, but the jolt of heat storming him was definitely a problem. Roni-the-firecracker had a way of charging the space around her.

He kinda liked it.

The man behind the screen door continued to eye them. As they approached, Way kept his head on a swivel. Half-dead bush, far-east corner. Bare branches left no room for hiding.

A deep growl sounded. West side. In the neighbor's yard, a large dog peered through a rusty chain-link fence, baring his teeth at the unwanted visitors.

The gate was closed, the latch down, so Way cut his gaze back to the front porch where the man kicked the ancient aluminum door open, banging against the brick. The guy wore a ripped sweatshirt and tattered cargo jeans. His greasy blond hair was pushed back away from his face and Way guessed his age at around thirty.

Thirty going on eighty with the way he lumbered through that door.

Way inhaled, taking in the heavy odor of burning wood and rubber. Someone was burning something somewhere. He exhaled, releasing the bitter taste.

"Help you?" the man asked.

When they were ten feet from the porch, the dog's growl escalated to a bark. Too close. Even with the dog locked behind the fence, he didn't see a need to get him riled up. That bad boy was big enough to leap straight over that thing.

Way halted, holding his arm out to block Roni from going any farther. "Is this the Hopkins home?"

"You a cop?"

"No."

The man jerked his chin at Roni. "What about her?"

"No."

"Then whaddya want?"

"My name is Way Kingston." He jerked a thumb at Roni. "This is Roni. We're sorry about Chad. We have questions about his...death. You a relative?"

The man nodded. "His brother. Cody. I'm the oldest. You gave me your names, but if you're not cops, what the fuck do you care about my brother?"

A young girl—maybe four years old—appeared at the doorway, her curly blond hair sticking up in all directions. She clutched a tattered blanket to her chest while sucking mightily on her thumb.

She studied Way and Roni for a long few seconds, then removed the thumb from her mouth. "Can I have chocolate milk?"

The man swung around. "Stay inside," he said, his voice gentle, but firm. "I'll get the milk in a minute. Close that door."

Whoever this guy thought they were, he didn't want the kid anywhere near them. Then again, in this neighborhood, the residents probably spent most of their time in the back of the house.

Away from the street and possible drive-by shootings.

The girl disappeared inside.

"Cute kid," Way said. "Yours?"

"You ask a lot of questions."

Way shrugged. "Making conversation."

"Dude, I'm gonna ask you one more time. If you're not cops, who the fuck are you?"

Behind Way, Roni cleared her throat. Probably his cue to not fuck this up. He held his hands up. "We're looking into some murders."

"Investigators?"

"Sort of. We think Chad's murder is connected to others in the last few months. Have the cops given you any details about Chad's shooting?"

The guy snorted. "They don't come around here too much. They asked the typical stuff. Who'd want to hurt him, blah, blah. What kind of *connection* you looking at?"

"Your brother was killed with a particular type of bullet. I have an interest in that bullet."

From Roni's right, the squeak of an engine belt sounded and the dog started in again. Barking and growling at the activity.

Way glanced back at Roni, checking the street. An Oldsmobile—late nineties model—with rims that cost five times the worth of the car pulled behind Way's SUV.

"Company," Roni said.

Two men exited the Oldsmobile, both wearing hoodies. One wore dark wash jeans and the other basketball shorts. They could have been any two American teenagers, but their cocky struts and hard-edged, lean faces said otherwise.

Life on the streets.

If he were a betting man, he'd lay a hundred on both of them carrying an assortment of weapons. Baggy hoodies made for excellent concealment.

"What's this?" the shorter guy said to the blond man.

"They're here about Chad."

The kid in the basketball shorts gave Roni the once-over, pausing way too long in the chest area, and most definitely tripped Way's trigger.

That look? He didn't like it.

Not one bit.

He should have done this alone. Dealt with her wrath afterward.

"Cops?" Basketball shorts asked.

"No," Cody said. "Go inside."

"Then you should get the fuck out," the kid said, his hard gaze still on Roni. "Unless," he grabbed his crotch, "I can do anything for you."

Yeah. Here we go. The minute these fuckers got out of that car, Way knew they'd be a problem.

"Shut up, Reggie," Cody told him.

Roni took that moment to shift sideways, brushing her shirt tail slightly away and revealing her .38. "Not interested," she said to Reggie. "Now back off."

And, ooh, he didn't like that. He gritted his teeth as his face flushed with color. Way kept his arms loose at his sides, his right hand close enough to snap his weapon up.

Reggie's arm moved and—gun!

Shit.

Simultaneously, Roni and Way drew their weapons, pointed them at Reggie.

"Okay," Way said, keeping his weapon steady. "Everybody chill."

Reggie jerked a giant .45 at Way, then back to Roni. His aim, if he was even aiming, was somewhere around her collarbone. *Amateur.* Could be good. Could be bad.

"What do you say now, bitch?"

"Goddammit, Reggie," Cody said. "Put that thing away. You want the cops showing up?"

Way stepped sideways, shifting toward Roni. If he could get close enough, he'd slide right in front of her. "Lower that weapon, Reggie, and nobody gets hurt."

"Reggie!" Cody hollered, his voice snapping like a pissed-off gator. "You dumbass. Cut the shit."

Then Cody entered Way's field of vision. He swung the weapon, but Cody stormed straight to Reggie. In one swift move, he grabbed the back of the hoodie, threw Reggie to the ground and whipped the gun from his hand.

For emphasis, he smacked the kid on the back of the head and the *pfft* nearly made Way chuckle.

"Nobody disrespects me on my property," Reggie hollered from the ground.

Cody shook his head. "First of all, it's not your property. I'm letting your loser ass live here. Now you and this other idiot go inside while I talk to these people."

Roni shot Way a raised-eyebrow look. "I like this guy," she said.

"Sorry, ma'am," he said. "My little brother's manners are shitty."

"No problem," she said. "Thanks for handling him before it got ugly."

With Reggie disarmed, Roni tucked her weapon back in the holster while Cody walked back to the porch and set the gun down.

In the first-floor window, the little girl stood there watching the whole fucked-up scene.

Well, damn.

"Great," Cody said. "She saw that."

"I'm sorry," Roni said. "I didn't realize she was there."

He let out a heavy sigh and lowered himself to the top step, his body seeming to cave under its own weight. "Not your fault my brother's a stupid fuck.

You're pretty good with that thing. You sure you're not a cop?"

Roni met Way's gaze. Before leaving the car, they'd decided this was his show.

"She's former FBI."

"Huh." Cody looked back at her. "No shit?"

She smiled. "No shit."

Making use of Cody's wonder over the female FBI agent, Way took a step closer. "Look, Cody. We're not here to cause trouble. Like I said, I have an interest in the bullet used in Chad's murder."

"Why?"

"Can't say. Any idea who may have killed your brother?"

Cody blew air through his lips. "Who the hell knows? That kid was into all kinds of stuff. Our mother passed six years ago. Single mom trying to control three boys? She didn't stand a chance, man."

"Your father's out of the picture?"

"Prison. After my mother died, I moved in here with my wife. Trying to keep these two clean. Reggie is the youngest. Chad's twenty-three. *Was* twenty-three."

"I'm sorry."

"Me too. He had all the brains in the world." He gestured to the road. "These streets are a bitch, though. And now I got my daughter to worry about. I'll lose my mind if she winds up in trouble. It's fucking survival here, man. Chad was a good student. Honor roll until he got to high school. Then he started with the drugs and it was over."

He shook his head, let out a sigh and looked down at his feet, shuffling them against the brick. *Shuffle-shuffle. Shuffle-shuffle.*

Way gave him a second. Grief, like these mean streets,

was a bitch, too. No matter what kind of trouble Chad Hopkins got into, he was still loved.

An idea circled in Way's mind, looping and looping, but not fully forming. He glanced back at Roni, who held his gaze, then gave a subtle jerk of her chin. Clearly, she wanted him moving on, so he went back to Cody.

"What about Reggie?"

Shuffle-shuffle. "He smokes a little weed, but he's into boosting cars and running with the Dragons. He'll get caught one day. Nothing I can do about it anymore. Damn, these boys."

"What about Chad? You think you'll find out who did it?"

Cody shrugged. "The street'll eventually talk and Reggie'll hear about it. He can't keep his nose out of anything. Just like Chad."

The kid appeared in the window again and Way's thoughts finally stopped spinning. If he could help this guy get his family out of this shit hole... "I'll make you a deal," he said, his eyes still on the little girl.

Cody let out another frustrated snort. "I'm not big on deals. I tend to get screwed."

Way shook his head. "Not this time. Here's the deal: You pass on any info about Chad's murder. If it leads to me finding out who's messing with these bullets, I'll set up a trust for your kid. Get her into one of the private schools in the area. That work?"

The man cocked his head, stared at Way with narrowed eyes that screamed of mistrust.

Cody needed a push. A reason to buy in. "I want information," Way said. "That information is worth a lot to me and keeping your daughter out of trouble is worth a lot to you. It's a win-win scenario."

Ten minutes later, after pounding out the details of Way's offer, Roni and Way climbed back into the Tahoe.

"That was quite an offer you made."

Roni snapped her seatbelt on and hit him with a direct gaze. He'd play this off. No problem. "Not really. He has something I need. I gave him incentive."

Roni laughed. "Oh, okay. Incentive. Great. Do you even know what private school costs? You didn't have to go that far."

"Says who?" He fired the engine, then waved a hand. "Look around. Kids are living in this. Is it any wonder Reggie turned out the way he did?"

"You can't fix them all. Believe me."

"Never said I wanted to. I see this and it makes me realize how lucky I was. My mom worked hard. She wasn't around a lot, but we always had food in our bellies and discipline. I grew up in paradise compared to these kids. That little girl is young. I can't get her out of this neighborhood, but a better school gives her a shot. And if I can help, I'm all in."

"You are something else."

He pulled from the curb, using it as an excuse not to look at her. Really, he didn't want to discuss this. All he could think about was that little girl in the window and how it could have been Roni.

Roni had found a way out. This little girl deserved that same shot. "I'll take that as a compliment."

"As you should. Just be ready in case they start feeding you bogus information."

"If it's shitty intel, he gets nothing."

"I guess we'll see."

"I guess we will."

WEST WAYLON KINGSTON IS TURNING OUT TO BE A NUISANCE.

I'm sitting in my crappy rental, parked down the street from a place called Blues, Brews, and Books, a quasi-bar, restaurant, and coffee shop located in small-town Steele Ridge. It's my first visit and as I pretend to fiddle on my iPad, just another stranger passing through, I keep my eye on Kingston's black Tahoe parked three cars down in front of a boutique.

This town is...quaint. Something you'd see in a tourism magazine with freshly painted storefronts, vintage and recently renovated brick buildings, and gleaming street-lamps that remind me of a Dickens novel.

I can see why folks live here. There's a peacefulness to the place that stems from belonging to something far greater than oneself. A sense of connection.

I despise it with a fury that tears my gut apart and burns straight through to my skin, eating at my flesh.

Anger does that. Erodes the insides until there's nothing left but the rubble of a failed existence.

Steele Ridge, is a fucking fairytale-esque mirage that transfixes folks, fools them into false security and happy-ever-afters. I'd like to stand in the middle of this cute little town and tell every one of these idiots that life, in and of itself, sucks.

It sucks and then you die.

Deal with it.

Something I'm now doing. With my mission slowly spinning from my control, reconnaissance on Way Kingston, a man I don't need nosing around in my business, takes priority.

Fifteen minutes ago, Mr. Kingston walked into the coffee shop and has yet to exit. Whether he's met someone or not, I can't know and I'm not about to walk in there and check.

My early peek at the comings and goings of Kingston indicates he has a surprising partner in one Veronica Fenwick. Between the two of them, their combined skills are a problem.

Unfortunately for them, I've spent a career slicing and dicing issues bigger than them. I glance at the seat beside me and my briefcase containing my Colt .45.

Whatever I need to do today, I'm ready for it.

It would be a shame really. Two do-gooders in the world shouldn't be a bad thing. But I can't have them jeopardizing my mission. No matter how innocent Kingston and Fenwick are, public safety comes first. If they keep digging around, they'll blow this whole thing.

I'll chalk them up to collateral damage. A loss suffered in pursuit of justice. It happens.

The mission is the mission.

Movement from the coffee shop catches my eye. Kingston. An older woman on the street stops him and he pauses, smiling down at her.

From what I've gathered, he's a loner, but a good Southern boy, always willing to lend a hand to a neighbor or an animal in need. Good for him.

Collateral damage.

He breaks away from the woman, hops into his SUV, and backs out of his parking space heading away from me. I give him a thirty-second head start, then back out of my own spot.

His years in the military give him above-average evasion skills and in this fantasyland of a small town, strangers don't stay strangers for long.

I shift the car to drive and lightly press the gas, hanging back a good distance as he turns left off of Main Street.

Ahead of me, he cruises along, drawing me past ranches and craftsman-style homes, some with gleaming porches. Others show their age and despite sagging gutters hold a certain charm inherent with older communities.

In a different time, I'd have loved this town.

Kingston's brake lights flash and—tsk-tsk—he does a rolling stop onto Elm Street. His sister the sheriff wouldn't appreciate his lack of respect for the stop sign.

The streets are quiet so I ease onto my brake, slowing enough to give him plenty of room. The farther he gets from town, the more opportunities I have to eliminate him. My pulse echoes in my ears and I inhale deeply, forcing my body to navigate the adrenaline rush.

At the corner, I peer to my right where Kingston pulls into a parking lot. The Forever Home animal shelter. From what I've gathered, this is his favorite of the places he provides support for.

He never visits with the animals. Only drops off supplies.

Do-gooder.

Collateral damage.

I let out a sigh and turn left. Killing a man in front of an animal shelter is beneath me. Even I can see that.

Way Kingston has earned himself another day.

For now.

11

FAMILY DINNERS, TO RONI, MEANT KEEPING HER MOUTH SHUT and clearing her plate. That's how it worked in the foster system. You were thankful for the slop on your plate because the alternative, being on the street and turning tricks for meals, wasn't a good option.

That changed in college when a friend had invited her over and she'd been comfortable enough to become a regular.

All those dinners prepared her socially to the point where she no longer feared family gatherings. Even when it wasn't her family.

When Maggie had called two hours ago to invite Roni to her parents' for the evening, Roni knew enough to expect good company and an even better meal.

Now, she rode shotgun as Maggie swung into the driveway of a large farmhouse that lit up a dark sky. Porch and interior lighting offered a nonverbal welcome and Roni rested her head back, mourning the loss of her own child-hood home.

Someday, she'd have a place like that again.

Maggie parked behind a black Range Rover and pointed.

"Jay is here. You'll get to meet him finally. Roni, I swear, he's so hot I go up in flames every time he looks at me."

Maggie. Had to love her honesty. "I guess that makes you a lucky girl."

"It sure does." She pushed the engine button and scooped her keys from the center console. "I'm glad you accepted my invitation."

Of course she had. Any extra time spent with Way would only help her cause. And looking at the man certainly never hurt. Where she stood with this case, she couldn't quite figure. They'd spent the morning tearing apart notes, comparing facts, and building timelines. They'd wound up with a lack of aha moments, but after reviewing all that evidence, she had no doubt the shootings were connected by Way's bullet design.

Either that, or someone had gotten really lucky and designed the same frangible ammo.

Which she doubted.

All she knew was that when she checked in with Karl an hour ago, she'd left out the part about spending the morning sharing notes with Way and visiting Chad Hopkins's brother.

Maggie slid out of the vehicle and they strode along the brick-paved walk to the front door. "Be warned, my family is a little nuts."

"Ha. I grew up in the system. They can't be any more nuts than what I've seen."

"True. Just to be clear, they're not dysfunctional nuts. They're wacky. These dinners get so competitive, it's frightening. No one dares bring subpar food. Way is the unpredictable one. We never know what he'll whip up."

"Really?"

"He inherited my father's palate. I swear, they put together the kookiest ingredients and somehow it's always fantastic. He drives me insane."

Good looking, smart, and balls of steel. On paper, he might be Roni's perfect mate.

Another place, another time.

As they walked, Roni leaned sideways, bumping Mags. "He's your brother. From what I've heard, they're supposed to be challenging. He seems...nice."

Maggie nodded. "He's a good guy. An enigma." She laughed. "I'm always trying to get inside his head and he never lets me." She paused at the base of the porch and set one hand on the white railing that gleamed under the porch light. "I'll tell you, though, I'm a little jealous of his life. He comes and goes as he pleases."

"I saw his motorcycle earlier."

"Yep. He'll take off on that thing for weeks at a time."

"Weeks?"

"Thus, why I'm jealous."

The front door opened. In the doorway stood a tall man with dark blond hair and a close-cropped beard. Even without the chiseled muscles hiding under a long-sleeved pullover, Roni recognized the famous Jayson Tucker. The man's face had been on just about every gossip magazine circulating. Roni had only ever seen him on television or in photos, and she dared say the man was better looking in person.

And way more formidable.

"My girl," he said, smiling at Maggie. "You're late."

"I know."

She climbed the stairs and hit Jayson with a liplock that fired Roni's cheeks. Her? Embarrassed? Since when?

Maybe since she'd been lusting over Maggie's brother.

Maggie broke away from the kiss and leaned into Jay, resting her head on his chest in a gesture so soft and sweet a piece of Roni's rock-hard heart broke off. Would she ever experience that bond? That deep-seated, unconditional love?

If she got lucky—and found a way to lighten up—she would. In her own defense, after her father, her opportunities to love and be loved always came with conditions. For years, fear and mistrust left her wary of opening up. And all that baggage made it easy to sabotage relationships.

"Roni, this is Jay. The absolute love of my life."

Jay flashed a movie-star smile and kissed the top of Maggie's head.

"Lord," Roni said, "you guys really do want me to die of envy."

She climbed the porch stairs and stepped inside, holding her hand out to Jay. "It's great to finally meet you. Maggie talks about you all the time. It's just too damned bad you don't have a brother."

"Yeah, sorry. It's just me and Sam."

"Mags?" A man yelled from inside. "Hurry up!"

Jay jerked his chin. "Cash skipped lunch. Major crab so far. Plus, he made a cheese appetizer that won't hold up if not eaten at the perfect temperature."

"Good. Then we'll stall."

At that, Roni snorted. "Isn't that cheating?"

"Remind me to tell you about his overuse of bacon. *Then* we'll talk cheating."

"And let's not forget the time he had Micki hack into my security system and spy on us to make sure I wasn't doing the cooking."

Roni gawked. "No way."

Maggie let out a low whistle. "I have never seen Jay so mad. I seriously thought he'd kill my brother."

Jay laughed and shook his head. "Competition is one thing. Invading my privacy is another. He's lucky I understand motivated competitors."

"God," Roni said. "He's sweet, rich, and he cooks. Someone shoot me."

At that, Maggie let out a laugh. "You're too funny."

"Finally!" The same male voice thundered the second Maggie stepped into the kitchen. "She's here. Everybody dig in. Use the pumpernickel for dipping. This is freaking amazing."

"Hang on," Maggie said, clearly intent on stalling. "Before you start stuffing your faces, I brought a guest. This is my friend Roni."

Maggie stepped sideways and gave Roni the full view of a large kitchen filled with—*one, two, three*—eight people. All of whose hands stopped midway to a plate of sliced bread while a chorus of "Hi, Roni" sounded.

Two dogs, one of which looked to be a retriever puppy, scrambled toward her, leaping at her feet. The border collie stood back and eyeballed the scene.

"Off, Charley," Maggie said. "Nicksie, go. Beat it."

An older woman, light-haired and wearing jeans and a periwinkle cashmere sweater, approached. She held out her hand. "I'm Sandy, Margaret's mother. Welcome to our home."

Roni shook her hand. "Thank you, ma'am."

"Margaret, do the introductions while I get your dad. He's getting the fire pit ready. We thought we'd have dessert outside."

Dessert around the fire pit. They really were a modern day Brady Bunch.

As instructed, Maggie handled introductions while Roni noted different characteristics of each family member. Riley with the funky glasses. Cash with the big shoulders. Coen with the crystal green eyes.

As a kid moving from foster home to foster home, the trick had served her in helping to remember names.

Rising from the table, a man with shaggy brown hair nodded. The golden retriever at his feet peered up at Roni with soft brown eyes and she instantly wanted to curl into him.

"Hello," the shaggy-haired guy said. "Your tank top is very tight. I like it."

A round of sighs filled the room and heat swarmed Roni's cheeks as she fought the urge to button her over shirt.

"Shep!" A horrified Maggie turned to Roni. "This is my brother, Shep. I should have warned you about his *lack* of *filter.*"

Across the kitchen, Way leaned against the counter and shook his head while his gaze locked on hers. If she wasn't mistaken, Shep wasn't the only one who appreciated her tank top.

"Joss is gone one day," Way said, "and already he's flirting. Well, Shep-style flirting, anyway."

Shep's mouth dipped to a frown and the look in his eyes, that glassy veil of confusion, nearly broke Roni's heart.

"Sorry," he said. "I—"

Roni held up her hand. "No apology necessary. Thank you for the compliment."

Clearly approving her response, Way nodded. "Nice. Now eat before you miss out on this supposedly spectacular cheese concoction."

"Call it whatever you want," Cash said. "I'm winning this time."

Roni moved farther into the room, joining Way by the counter just as Mrs. Kingston returned from outside.

"Way," Maggie said, "what'd you bring tonight?"

"Oddly enough, I went with a cheese dish as well. Reggiano hashbrowns."

"Bastard," Maggie muttered.

"Margaret!"

Eyes wide, she turned to Jay. "Did I say that out loud?"

"Sure did, babe," he said.

Maggie held up two hands. "Sorry, Mom. But I'm going to reiterate my request to handicap this event. Way is better than all of us in the kitchen. If I can't use Jay for help, we should somehow limit Way."

Wow. These people didn't mess around when it came to food.

Way leaned right, bumping Roni's shoulder. "She's mad because the only time she won is when Jay cooked. We busted her."

"That may have been the best rack of lamb I ever made," Jay said.

Riley dug a fresh slice of pumpernickel into the cheese dip. "That's how we knew *she* didn't cook it."

At that, everyone—including Maggie—broke out in laughter. This was family. Good-hearted teasing and all.

The kitchen door opened once again and in stepped an older man. "Hello." He held his hand out. "I'm Ross Kingston. Welcome."

"Thank you, sir. It's an honor. You have an amazing daughter."

Mr. Kingston's chest puffed up, his pride clearly evident. He peered over at Maggie with a bright smile. "We're awfully proud of her."

"Blah, blah," Cash said. "Can we eat? Starving here."

Mrs. Kingston waved her hands. "Everyone inside. Maggie, put Roni in Joss's spot."

Way leaned over again, dipping his head closer. "You're between me and Shep. I'll save you from his horrendous flirting."

Before they got to the table, a cell phone rang, immediately followed by a second one.

"And here we go," Mrs. Kingston said.

"Sorry, Mom." Maggie and Cash both dug for their phones.

"Really?" Mrs. Kingston said. "We can't get through one dinner?"

Maggie poked at her screen, then rolled her bottom lip out. "Afraid not. Move it, Cash. It's a SWAT call."

In less than three seconds, the two of them were hustling to the door. Maggie met Roni's eye and snapped her fingers.

"Go," Roni said. "I'll Uber."

"No you won't," Way said. "I'll get you home after we eat."

"There," Mrs. Kingston waved her to the dining room. "It's all settled."

Alrighty then. Apparently, even without Maggie, the one who'd brought her to this shindig, Roni was staying. She looked up at Way. "Thank you."

For a few quick seconds, he held her gaze and oh, oh, oh, she could get lost there. She held her breath, let her body take some pleasure from a man's eyes on her in a way that, for the first time in a long time, she welcomed.

"Keep me updated."

The sound of Jay's voice broke the spell and Roni looked away, folding her arms to give her something to do with her hands before she decided to put them all over Way. Lord, had anyone noticed her staring?

"I will," Maggie said. "Love you all. Let me know who wins."

Then they were gone and the Kingston clan went about their business of consuming a meal fit for royalty.

This, Roni would enjoy.

AFTER HELPING WITH DINNER DISHES, RONI WAS ORDERED OUT of the kitchen to the fire pit, where the men argued over just how high the flames should soar.

Men. So very simple, yet so complicated.

In case the group had what Roni liked to think of as reserved seats, she waited to see where everyone landed and then chose one of the vacant chairs. Like most things for a girl without a family, she'd grown accustomed to not having a place. As a kid, it bothered her, left her in tears, half the time. Once she'd hit her preteen years, she'd hardened to it. Learned to squash those feelings. God knew they weren't serving her.

Now, after dinner with the Kingstons, that old longing roared back. She'd missed so much.

Don't go there.

Roni stared at the fire, letting the heat warm her as evening air chilled her cheeks. She folded her arms, wishing she'd worn more than a cotton button-down over the tank top Shep had admired.

Beside her, Way reached and grabbed a colorful Mexican blanket from the stack sitting on a side table.

He handed it to her and pointed. "Put that over you. It gets cold out here."

"Thank you."

Mrs. Kingston exited the house carrying a giant tray of desserts. Behind her, Riley supplied another tray with a carafe and mugs. "Dutch coffee, people. I think I've got you all beat with this one."

Even the beverages were competition-worthy in this group. Funny group.

Mrs. Kingston pointed at the blanket on Roni's lap. "You wrap that around you now. Waylon brought those home from one of his road trips. He always brings us something."

"Arizona," he said. "They're handmade."

Roni rubbed her cheek against the thick wool. "It's so soft."

"The trick with those," Way said, "is washing them a lot. When you buy them, they're stiff. Kinda scratchy."

His mother dropped into the chair next to Mr. Kingston. "He's right. I think I washed them a dozen times before I set them out."

"Well," Roni said, snuggling under the blanket. "This one is perfect now."

Mugs of steaming coffee were handed around, followed by cake that looked like yellow cake with something swirled through it. Marble cake?

"Mom made it," Way said, his voice even, yet somehow conveying...something.

"It's probably not good," Shep said.

Mrs. Kingston sighed and everyone fell into loud laughter that lingered in the night air. Something inside Roni burst open and—oh, no—she held her breath, fighting against an old pressure that built in her chest.

These people.

Every one them shared a wicked and witty tongue, yet they never got mad. Never got insulted by the intense level of competition and critiques of their food and the playful poking.

I never had that.

In all the homes Roni had been in, everything was judged. If she moved her fork wrong, she'd be disciplined. When it came to foster homes, even the most well-meaning folks felt it was their duty to mold her, to make her into something worthwhile. As if she hadn't left her father's home worthy.

After her father, nothing ever felt right or easy. For ten years she'd been...stifled.

The Kingstons? They allowed flaws.

Maybe even encouraged them.

Lost in her thoughts, Roni stayed quiet, breathing through the emotional upheaval that one night in the Kingston home brought. She watched the fire's flames lick and dance and focused on the occasional crackle of wood.

Country living.

She'd never experienced it before. Not with vast, open land and blackness for acres upon acres. Backyard fires, for her, meant nosey neighbors peeping at her.

This? No perverted neighbors.

She rested her head back and closed her eyes. Took a few seconds to enjoy the tranquility and the musky, languorous scent of burning wood. In the distance, a wolf howled, maybe one of the red wolves that Roni had heard about.

The sound should have terrified her, but somehow, it lulled her further into a Zen state.

Country living.

Yes, indeed.

12

Awake, Roni Fenwick was a sexy, brain-scrambling force.

Asleep? Total knockout.

Way stood beside the Adirondack chair she'd curled into and debated whether to let her sleep. She'd only been out maybe fifteen minutes, but as time passed and the fire died down, she might catch a chill that wouldn't leave her for hours.

Another blanket maybe.

He checked his watch. Almost 9:00.

"Waylon," his mother called from the back door, "what are you doing?"

He swung back, held his finger to his lips. "She's sleeping," he half whispered.

"Well, don't stand there, put another blanket on her before she catches her death."

His mother. The former executive accustomed to ordering people around. In his youth, she'd spent a lot of time traveling and they all got used to her absences. Now retired, she wanted to make up for lost time.

He couldn't blame her. Changing the norm took time, though, and he struggled with it. In his teenage years, his mother was gone, his older siblings were off doing their own thing, and Dad was busy with Shep. Way had spent most of his time on his own. *Now* his mother wanted to be a helicopter parent?

Before he took a step, she disappeared back inside to finish stowing leftovers and settle in with Dad in front of the television. All these years.

One place.

One person.

The weight of it settled on him. Could he do it? Be tied down like that? Same routine day in and day out?

He couldn't see it. Marriage meant sharing space and pressure to know what he was doing all the time. His family alone taught him he wasn't good at either of those things.

In short, he'd suck at being a husband.

Roni shifted in her chair and let out a long sigh that sent Way's mind reeling. He'd spent the majority of the day with her, fighting the urge to stare. To touch.

After he'd dropped her off at Mrs. Tasky's B&B, a vision of her lush little body filled his mind. Her breasts. Her curvy ass.

Then there was the taunting, smart mouth of hers.

With Roni, life would never be boring.

God bless the man who married her. He'd need all kinds of luck, patience, and stamina.

Way squatted down, studied the soft angle of her cheek, the gentle slope of her mouth.

Stunning.

One touch. That's all he wanted. As if sensing him, her eyes popped open. She flinched, jerking backward.

Whoa. He held his hands up when a zoned-out terror

sparked in her gaze. When a woman had that kind of reaction, there was a reason.

Which pissed him off. Left him wondering who did what to tough little Roni Fenwick that made her so jumpy.

"You're okay," he said. "You fell asleep."

She blinked at him. *Blink-blink. Blink-blink.*

In his military days, he'd known better than to sneak up on a sleeping teammate. Now? That life seemed so far behind, his instincts had gone soft.

She slapped her hand over her chest and glanced at the empty chairs around the fire. "Where is everyone?"

"Everyone left. My folks are inside."

"I fell asleep?"

"You did. Out cold. It's not unusual around here. Between the food and"—he turned back, looked at the old farmhouse—"this house, my parents know how to make the place comfortable."

Her blanket slipped and he grabbed hold of it, lifting it up and tucking it around her, his hands sliding over her hips as he went.

"You're lucky," she said. "I never had this growing up."

Pity that. His family wasn't perfect, but they were always there. "I know."

"You know?"

"I checked you out. Sorry. When I did my research on the shootings and your work history, I got some personal stuff, too. I needed to know who you were. What you wanted with my sister."

He waited for her to rail on him, to spew about invading her privacy, blah, blah, blah.

Not a word.

Just a curious stare.

"What did you find out?"

Throbbing in his knees drew him upright. He needed to stretch his legs, but standing over her didn't exactly create a cozy environment for talking. And he needed to know what made this woman tick.

He dragged the empty chair beside him closer and lowered himself into it. "I know that your mother walked out on you and your dad died when you were young. Too young. That had to be hard." He shook his head. "Actually, I can't imagine. Makes me appreciate what I have. Especially after meeting the Hopkins family today."

As a kid, Way might have been left on his own a lot, but he'd never felt neglected. Lonely, sure. Neglected, never. His parents, although busy with Shep, always provided for him.

"How did you get all that? Wait." She snapped her fingers. "Your contact at Justice? The one you mentioned when we were in your driveway yesterday?"

"No. Not him. Someone else. She's a hacker. She's good, too."

"If she can crack a government database, that's an understatement. And, yes, it was hard losing my father. The foster system wasn't the easiest to navigate, but I managed. I think I missed my dad so much that everything else seemed unimportant. I always told myself nothing could be worse than my father dying. And I was right."

"I'm sorry. That had to be...bad."

She lifted one shoulder. "There's a numbness that sets in after trauma. At least for me. I measured everything against losing my dad. The grandpa that stared at my chest when I was fourteen? Eh, maybe a two on the scale. As long as the perv didn't touch me, I kept it in perspective."

"Jesus! You were a kid."

"I was a kid used to being on my own. Big difference. I know that sounds unbelievable."

In a weird way, he got that. More from the atrocities he saw at war than from anything he'd experienced in childhood. He had a way of creating small boxes in his mind where he stored all the things he didn't want to experience. The deaths of friends. The old guy in Guam he kept promising that damned pair of glasses to. The kids with their limbs blown off. All his disappointments got locked away.

"I don't think it's unbelievable. I think I actually understand. Partially anyway."

She laughed. "Then you're just as screwed up as me."

"I don't think we're screwed up. I think we've learned to cope."

In the fire pit, a log crackled and broke in half, sending sparks flying.

He shrugged. "I mean, when you see things no person should have to, you figure out how to emotionally manage it. In the military, I had no problem going to the chaplain or the shrink for that."

"Good for you. A lot of men wouldn't."

"My problem was the stuff I didn't see coming. That's the shit that rocked me."

She looked over at him with those brown eyes that had a way of dissecting anything in their path. "Like what?"

He leaned sideways, studied her lips. "You trying to head-shrink me?"

At that she smiled. "Maybe."

Most would deny it. Roni? Total wild card. "Dang, you fascinate me."

She glanced back at the fire and rested her head against the chair. "I only asked a question. I want to know what it is that 'rocks' you. Consider it an occupational safeguard. If we're working together, I need to know."

No one could accuse her of being dim-witted. "You're good," he said. "We both know it has nothing to do with working together. You just like rummaging around in my head."

She laughed and the sound echoed beyond the yard, making him smile despite the fact that he did not, repeat, did not, want to be having this conversation.

"Come on, Way. Give me one example of something that rocked you. There's no judgment. I promise. Look at it this way, you know all my secrets. It's only fair."

She had a point there. He stretched his legs in front of him and watched the dying flames flick the air. What piece of himself should he fork over? How personal would he be willing to get?

The event itself wasn't a hard one to come up with, considering he thought about it every day. Did he want to share it with her? With anyone, really?

Talking about it, freeing it from his damned mind might help. Another log cracked in half, sending more sparks into the air.

A nice night, a beautiful woman he sorta liked. Why not? "All right. There's one thing that stands out. An old guy in Guam. He owned this little café I'd stop at for coffee and a pastry. He made the best *siopao* I've had."

"*Siopao?*"

"It's basically a steamed bun with meat filling. So good. I can still taste them." He waved the thought away. "Anyway, he didn't have enough room inside for tables, but he had a few on the sidewalk. I'd sit out there and he'd come talk to me. Nice old guy. No family. He'd been an only child and the few cousins he'd had all died. He needed glasses, but couldn't afford them."

"Oh, that makes me sad. Things we see as so basic and he couldn't have them."

"I know. But I remembered one of the guys had found a pair of reading glasses on the ground while on a mission. For whatever reason, he picked them up and held on to them. I figured I'd bring them to the café owner. See if they helped."

"And did they?"

Way stayed quiet for a second, his pulse kicking like an angry mule. He shifted in his chair, leaning forward to rest his elbows on his knees. Refusing to look at her, he stared into the dying fire.

"Way?"

He cleared his throat. "Yeah. Sorry. Thinking. I kept forgetting to bring them to him. I'd walk in there, see him struggling to read something and get pissed at myself."

"He wasn't your responsibility."

"Yeah, but I could have helped."

"We can all say that at times. What happened?"

Damn, this was the hard part. The part that ate him alive. "I finally remembered. I was so fucking relieved and headed into town. I got there and the café was closed. First time ever I remembered that happening. I went to the shop next door and the owner told me the old man had died."

"Oh, my God."

From the corner of his eye, he spotted her sitting up, shifting toward him, but he ignored her. Kept his gaze straight ahead. "He collapsed the night before. I never gave him the goddamn glasses."

She touched him. Just set her hand on his forearm and

squeezed. Not hard, but enough that it sparked insane energy .

"Oh, Way. I'm so sorry."

"I didn't really know him."

"But you liked him."

"I did. And I owed him those glasses. All he wanted was to be able to see, and I could've helped."

"Hang on. You know he probably wasn't mad about the glasses, right?"

Way shook that off. "It's not about the glasses."

"What's it about, then?"

Here we go. He turned his head. The glow of the flames lit her dark eyes and man, oh, man, he could get lost in them. "I didn't do what I was supposed to and that old man died. It was irresponsible."

There. Said it. All his donations, every goddamned good thing he did, couldn't wipe that away.

And now, his design, those frangible bullets were killing civilians.

His design.

His bullets.

Talk about irresponsible.

A few long seconds passed while he sat there, letting himself get lost in her deep brown eyes and praying she wouldn't speak. Just keep fucking silent and not want to talk.

She'd asked for something that rocked him and he'd told her. Now, every ounce of regret he possessed roared at him. That old man dying changed his life. Made him take stock. All the being alone he craved, the old man had. But then he died. Alone.

And Way sure as hell didn't want that. So he came home to Steele Ridge and his family that called and texted him constantly. No middle ground. Either alone or everyone up his ass. Hell, even Shep, now that he had Joss, got more privacy than Way.

"I see," Roni said. "Can I offer an opinion?"

So much for keeping quiet. "Somehow I think you will anyway."

"You *do* know me."

They shared a laugh and, damn, that felt good. To just sit around this fire and let Roni's laugh bring him from a black hole threatening to swallow him.

"Go ahead," he said. "Let me have it."

"I think, intellectually, you understand that not giving him the glasses didn't cause his death."

"Of course."

"But somewhere in your heart, where grief and anger and fear come together, you feel like his life would have been different if you'd done it."

Of course. He held his hands. "I know it would have. That's the point."

"Yes, but the glasses wouldn't have saved him. The reality is, he may have been nearsighted and the glasses fit someone farsighted. The *glasses,* Way, may not have even helped him. And all this time you've been dealing with this guilt. I hate that for you, I really do."

The glasses may not have worked.

He sat back in the chair, looked off into the blackness beyond the yard, where only twinkling stars and what looked like a plane dotted flashes of light across the sky.

"Way?"

"I'm...listening."

"Ha. A man who listens? I should marry you."

He peered back at her. The dimming fire threw a magical glow over her stunning face. *Be careful what you ask for, honey.* Everything about this woman—her ballsy attitude, her willingness to offer support, her street smarts—stirred something in him. Dug down deep and forced him to acknowledge what he'd been missing.

Companionship.

Intimacy.

Getting laid was easy. Intimacy? Not so much. The minute he started talking, women wanted more. As if talking was a free pass to a lifelong commitment.

Right now, sitting with Roni Fenwick, something told him she'd never be that woman.

And he wanted her.

What the hell? He might be losing his mind. He'd seen enough of Roni to know she wouldn't be easy. With her skills, she might be the queen of the mind fuck, and he wanted more of her?

Yeah. He did.

He leaned sideways over the arm of the chair, focused on her lips, then looked her straight in the eye.

"I'm not ready for marriage. I'd sure love to kiss you, though."

A flirty smile drifted across those luscious lips. "It was a joke."

Even as she said it, she moved closer, her gaze hot on his. Everything about her body language said yes, but he hadn't heard her agree. And he wanted that. To hear her say it. In his thirty years, he'd never pushed himself on a woman before and he sure as shit wouldn't start now.

Barely an inch from her, he backed away and she narrowed her eyes. "What?" she asked.

"You didn't say it."

"Say what?"

"Yes. I wanna hear you say you want me to kiss you."

"Ah. A man of honor."

"You bet that fine little ass of yours. Tell me yes."

"Yes."

He kissed her. A full-on assault of lips and tongue and—holy shit, the woman was a firecracker. But the arm of the damned chair made things seriously difficult. He wanted that gone. Wanted her next to him. Against him.

Skin on skin.

Visions of her naked on his bed flashed and he leaned farther over the arm of the chair, sliding his hand over her cheek. She let out a soft moan as her tongue played tag with his and the bulge in his pants became painful.

God, he was on fire. And it had nothing to do with the burning logs in front of them. All this came from under his skin.

Frying from the inside out.

She lifted her hand to the back of his head, holding him there. One thing was for damn sure; he wasn't the only one on fire.

The *thunk* of the last log brought his mind to attention. And away from the raging hard-on that pressed against his jeans.

In his mother's yard.

What the fuck was he doing?

Way eased back an inch and dragged his thumb along her jaw. Her soft hum didn't help reduce the pressure in his pants.

"I knew it," he said.

"What?"

"I knew if I touched you, I'd be toast."

HE WASN'T THE ONLY ONE FEELING TOASTY.

Lordy, the man's hands, all calloused and warm, brought

Roni's extremely dormant libido roaring to life. The flames in the fire pit were nothing compared to the heat Way whipped up.

If she could crawl into his lap, she'd do it. Just settle in and hold him for the next twelve hours. Maybe longer.

That was saying something for a girl who'd spent the last twenty-four years battling the urge to get close to a man.

She hadn't sat on a man's lap since her father passed, and she sure as hell wouldn't start now. Not with Way Kingston, someone caught smack in the middle of a CIA investigation.

But, wow. She wanted him.

Sex.

That's all this was. Sex and lust.

Had nothing to do with the story he'd just told her. Or his loyalty to his sister.

Sex and lust.

That's it, Veronica. She'd keep telling herself that.

She dropped another kiss on his lips, this one a playful smack.

"Toast," she said. "That's rather extreme, no?"

He laughed, all deep and throaty. Her nipples didn't just harden, they waved a white flag.

Sorry, girls. Business to transact here.

"Extreme or not," he said, "it is what it is."

Her gaze still locked on his, she rested her head against the back of her chair. "I like you."

"Well, since you just sucked my face off, I suppose that's good."

"Actually, it's not. I don't want to like you. Not when we're in the middle of an agency investigation. And not when I live in DC and can't just pop over every time I want my hands on you."

He shrugged. "There's this thing called an airplane."

"So every time one of us wants a booty call, we need a plane?"

The only noise was another wolf howling in the distance. Way's lack of response wasn't a shock. Roni, with all her faults, knew exactly how to back a man off. Particularly one like Way Kingston, who she knew from her research didn't like to be tied down. The quintessential rambling man off on his motorcycle for weeks at a time.

A not-so-casual reference to an ongoing relationship was enough to make him turn tail. And yet, disappointment settled on her. Why? Why? Why?

Because everything she'd said was true. She did like him. A lot.

Sex and lust.

That's what she needed to focus on. The voice in her head, the one that sat, waiting patiently for her to get too close, snickered.

Silly girl. You know nobody ever stays.

It was true. People came and went. To date, her longest standing relationship had been with Cassidy—Cass—and her family. She'd known them twelve years now. That alone felt like a miracle.

Way leaned his elbows on his chair's armrests. "You think you're slick, don't you?"

Not by a long shot, pal. "I'm sorry?"

"I know what you're doing."

"What am I doing?"

"You think dropping that hint-bomb about commuting from DC will scare the shit out of me."

Bam. She stiffened, her whole body just...frozen. She broke eye contact and watched the last of the wood in the fire burn.

Roni knew certain tricks to insulate herself, to stay alone, safe from life's unexpected twists.

It worked for her. Kept her emotionally controlled and thoroughly lacking disappointment. If a girl didn't get too close, nothing bad would happen.

After her history, did she really believe that garbage?

Worse, she'd become an emotionally bankrupt, thirty-two-year-old woman trying to annihilate whatever this was with Way before it even started.

Because he terrified her.

In the short time she'd known him, he had sparked something in her she didn't want to fight.

She closed her eyes for a second, breathed in the fading scent of burning wood and pondered the heat of that kiss. And the...want.

She wanted him. Or maybe she wanted the dream of him. A good guy who'd stick around. Forever.

"If my sneaky plan was to scare you," she said, "you don't look very spooked."

He blew her a kiss. "Sweetheart, you definitely terrify me. And it has nothing to do with your job. I have no interest in long-term relationships. Marriage, for me, means stuck inside my life. Caught up in routines and expectations. My life is my own. The emperor of the Kingdom of Way."

What did *that* mean? "I'm sorry?"

"It's a joke in my family. They call me the emperor of my kingdom of one."

"Ah. We're both loners, then."

"Yeah. Normally, I'd be gone by now. And I sure as hell wouldn't have told you about Guam."

"And, yet, you're still here."

"I am."

"Why?"

He stood, held his hand out to her. "Because for whatever reason, when it comes to you, I have no interest in being predictable."

Oh, this man.

Trouble. With a capital T.

13

On the drive back to Mrs. Tasky's, Roni sat in the passenger seat of Way's Tahoe peering out at Steele Ridge's quaint downtown. The ornate streetlamps seemed straight out of a Rockwell painting.

"Answer me one question," Way said as he turned off of Main Street.

After the conversation they'd just had, she wasn't sure how much more she could take. All this honesty was too damned hard. "I'll try."

"How does an FBI agent become a psych trainer for the CIA?"

Easily. Painfully so. "Aside from my masters in psychology, I spent ten years in foster care, being shuttled from home to home, never getting too comfortable. Bad shit happens when you're comfortable. Throw in a slice of abandonment issues and PTSD from my dad dying, and I'm insanely good at distancing myself from people enough to really screw with them."

Yes, that did just come out of my mouth.

When all else failed to scare a man off, why shouldn't she resort to sounding crazy?

Way jerked his head. "Good to know."

"Hey, you asked."

"I did. How'd you get the job? I don't think they post these positions on recruitment sites."

She thought back to the party Jeff had invited her to last summer. "I met my boss at a cookout. It was actually Jeff's—my ATF friend who died—party. Maggie was there, too. Every year he threw a Fourth of July party at his mom's place."

"Hang on a second. You met your boss from the CIA at a barbecue?"

"Hey, government employees have friends. Jeff's mom is a retired NSA analyst. Her list of contacts reads like a who's who of the spec ops world. NSA, CIA, SEALs. Absolutely awe-inspiring."

Roni wouldn't mention the SEAL she'd met at the same party and dated for a month afterward. In bed, they were pure combustion. Outside of that, between the two of them, they harbored too much pain. Neither was ready for the emotional rubble and she chalked it up as another failed attempt at a relationship.

"And you got a job out of it."

"I did. Jeff introduced me to some friends of his and his mother's. One of them wound up being a friend of my boss."

He clucked his tongue and made a left. Gone were the adorable streetlamps. Now, only porch lights from quaint bungalows illuminated the street.

The darkness, combined with silence, set her nerves crackling.

When a man like Way Kingston went quiet, there were

reasons. And she suspected she wouldn't like them. "What are you thinking, Way?"

"Not sure. It's interesting that you were invited to a party that was basically a who's who of DC. Add to that your ATF friend investigating a certain gang, one of whose members is now dead from a bullet I more than likely designed."

"You think *Jeff* knew about your bullets because he had acquaintances at Langley?"

Way glanced over at her, then turned back to the road. "Could be. You said this party was over the summer?"

"Yes. July."

"I'd already sent the first batch of bullets to Langley. They wanted modifications, so I sent them a few more."

Ugh. Roni didn't want to go there. "You think someone at that party knew about the bullets and maybe made some kind of deal with Jeff?" She shook her head. "No. He was a straight-up guy."

"He could've been the middle man. Connected the shooter with whoever stole the design."

"I don't want to believe that."

Way pulled to the curb in front of Tasky's and parked before turning to Roni. "Yeah, I get that. I'm probably wrong. If I am, I'll be the first to admit it. But let's look into it. We'll disprove it and move on."

Oh, she'd make sure he admitted it. No one accused her friends of being traitors. "Okay. I'll go along. For now. I suppose you want the list of who was at that party."

He nodded. "That's exactly what I want."

"You want me to call his mother and just ask for the invitation list? That might be awkward."

"Nah. We'll hack his e-mail."

· · ·

THE NEXT AFTERNOON, WHILE MICKI TOOK THE LEAD IN HER competition with Jonah by attempting to hack Ambrose's e-mail, Way and Roni decided on a trip to see Bernadette Ambrose, Jeff's mother. Why not see if she might offer up any intel. And with the sun shining, it wasn't a bad day for a ride with a beautiful woman.

First, he had a delivery to make. Otherwise, he'd have suggested they take his motorcycle. That would've been fun.

On the way out of town he stopped at the animal shelter to drop off the supplies he and Roni had purchased. He drove into the rear lot, parking near the back door so they could unload.

He hit the buzzer, then went back to the Tahoe and lifted the rear hatch. Thirty seconds later, LuAnn, the shelter's director, swung the door open with—*ah shit*—a puppy in hand.

She greeted him with a sly smile and a snuggle for the pup. Totally wrong on so many levels. This would be why he never went inside. Puppies were too friggin' cute.

She held up the puppy, giving Way a full view of its long legs and giant paws—oh man. He'd be a big one for sure. And a fucking brindle to boot.

Was she serious right now?

The pup's head was solid black with a long patch of white stretching from his jaw all the way down his chest. His ears were the killer. Big and floppy and sitting crossed on top of his head. Probably deciding whether they wanted to stand up.

This shit? Totally unfair.

He poked a finger at LuAnn. "Dirty pool, Lu."

"Isn't it though?"

She rubbed her nose against the puppy's snout, receiving a lick for her troubles. Affectionate little sucker.

I'm screwed.

He didn't have to be, though. He just wouldn't look. Keep his eyes averted and thoughts on his task.

Sort of like with Roni. At that, he let out a frustrated laugh.

The passenger door of his SUV opened and Roni slid out. "What's happening?"

Way hauled her donation from the cargo area. "This is LuAnn, the shelter director. She's got a puppy. Trying to get me to take him home."

And then the whole thing went to hell with Roni rushing toward LuAnn and puckering her lips, making kissing and cooing noises and, holy smokes, forget the puppy, Way wanted those kisses all to himself.

Ignore them. That's all he'd do.

"The cart is right inside there," LuAnn said as Way went by her muttering about the unfairness of life.

"This is quite the haul," Lu said, passing the pup off to Roni. "Those wee-wee pads'll come in handy with this little guy. In case you're interested, there are two of them. This is Hugo. His brother is Boss. I already put a call in to Maggie to see if she wants one for her K-9 unit. Seeing as these babies'll grow up to be big and strong."

Shit.

As usual, the cart sat in the small alcove just inside the door. He wheeled it back outside and cut a sidelong glance at Roni, holding the puppy up for his viewing nightmare.

Stay strong. That's all he needed to do. "What the hell kind of dog is that anyway?"

"No idea," Lu said. "We think he's part black lab, part border collie. We got them from a shelter in Louisiana."

"Oh my God." Roni accepted a few licks from Hugo. "He's so darned cute. His paws are huge!"

Dammit, dammit, dammit. He couldn't look. If he did, it'd be over. Between his wicked thoughts about Roni and now the dog, seeing the two together would wreck him.

Still, if he was here to get a dog, which he wasn't, this would be the perfect one. By the size of those paws, he'd be a sturdy beast Way could train to do all sorts of cool stuff. And his Steele cousins had all that property a big dog would love to run through.

Dammit.

Dammit.

Dammit.

Not looking.

He needed to keep moving and get the fuck outta here. He loaded the last box on the cart, shut the Tahoe's rear hatch, and, ignoring LuAnn, wheeled everything inside. "I'm not taking that puppy."

"Well, that's a shame, seeing as I know you like the big boys. Of course, he'll be here if you change your mind. Maybe Maggie'll want both."

Way stormed by her, giving her a backward wave. "The shopping bags are from Roni. I'll bring you another load next week. Let me know if there's anything you need."

"Thank you, Waylon."

"Dirty pool, LuAnn!"

He hopped into the SUV, fired it up, and drummed his fingers on the steering wheel while sneaking a peek in the sideview mirror. Roni and Hugo bumping noses.

Someone needed to put a bullet in his brain. Boom-boom. A double-tap right to the forehead.

He looked away, staring straight ahead at the dumpster. A much safer view by far.

Finally, the passenger door opened and Roni boosted herself into the seat.

Wasting no time, he pulled out of the lot as she fastened her seat belt.

"I think you should take that puppy," she said.

Ha. "No."

"Why?"

"I like my freedom. Puppies need attention."

"Not that much. He can hang out with you in your workshop."

"And when I want to go out on my bike for a few days?"

She turned sideways, adjusting the seat belt so it didn't rub against her neck. "You know the family that drives you crazy? They'd probably be willing to help. I think Maggie would love it. Especially if she decides to take one. They can play together."

"If she takes it for the K-9 unit, it'll live with the handler."

"Okay, smartass, what if Maggie decides she wants a pet? Forget K-9."

He could see it. Just to screw him, Maggie would adopt one of those damned dogs. "I can't."

"I think you want to."

He made a right, heading toward the highway. The sun blinded him and he smacked the visor down. "What'll happen is, the first time I want to blow out of town, the dog'll look at me like I'm abandoning him and I'm not dealing with that. I don't want to resent him for loving me."

And, wow. What. The. *Fuck?* "Wow," he said. "I can't believe I said that."

"Don't be embarrassed."

He was way more than embarrassed. He was fucking mortified. "That sounded bad."

"It sounded honest." She held up two hands. "I don't know you well enough so this is just an opinion, but I think this is stemming from your frustrations with your family. I think you're afraid you'll fall in love with the puppy and then feel bad when he frustrates you. News flash, Way. He's a puppy. Puppies frustrate everyone. It doesn't mean you don't love him. It's that vicious cycle we talked about. You shouldn't have to feel guilty about living your life. That's all I'm saying."

He glanced over at her, blew out a breath, and went back to the road. Total headshrinker. How the hell did she get all of that from one conversation? "It's not guilt. Not totally."

"Resentment. That's what you said."

Fuck me. He shouldn't have said a word. Now, she sat there, psychoanalyzing him because that's what shrinks did. And playing it back in his head it all sounded...lame. Like he was some selfish prick who only thought about himself. Maybe he was. He didn't know.

What he knew for sure, for whatever reason, was that he didn't want Roni thinking that of him. *I'm so screwed.* "It's not like it sounds. I'm not—" He shook his head. "I don't know. All I know is I was on my own a lot as a kid. My mom was working and my dad had Shep to worry about. Then Riley came along and I was the classic middle kid. Maggie and Cash were doing their own thing with their high-school friends, so it was up to me to stay out of trouble and keep busy. And I did. It was fine. I wasn't being an asshole about it. I did what I needed to and stayed out of everyone's way." He gripped the steering wheel tighter with his right hand and propped his other elbow on the door, tapping his fingers. "It's ironic to me that back then nobody had time for me and now they're up my ass all the time. That's all. It's frustrating and, yeah, I resent it a little."

"Well, who could blame you? It's not fair. They conditioned you to be one way as an adolescent and then changed the rules. I think you should talk to them. Be honest. Let them know all this. If talking to all of them is overwhelming, pick one person."

"One? Ha. Good luck with that. It's a committee atmosphere."

"Too bad. Pick an ambassador who will carry the message to the others. Let them know it's killing you and you don't want to feel this resentment."

She reached across, wrapped one hand around his arm and—dang it—why did she have to touch him.

"They love you," she continued. "They'll want you to be happy. And if you've never told them the constant checking up on you drives you crazy, they don't know they're doing anything wrong."

Well, day-am.

He took the onramp to the highway and hit the gas. "I never thought of it like that. The whole conditioning part."

"You're caught up in that cycle. Let it go. Talk to them, give them an opportunity to correct it, and you'll all be much happier."

He let out a huff. "Sounds simple enough. Wondering why I didn't think of it."

"Again, it sometimes takes an outsider to see it."

The road just ahead was clear of vehicles so he stole a quick look at her. Tough Roni Fenwick with her dark, sultry eyes and full lips that made him want to do all sorts of fun things with them. Fascinating woman. "Thank you. That... helps. It felt good to get it out of my system."

"You're welcome. Glad I could help."

"Now all I have to do is pick an ambassador."

That would take some thought. Maybe Cash. Or Maggie? He didn't know.

He'd take some time and mull it over. At least he had a

plan. One Ms. Roni Fenwick had given him. He didn't want to like her. Not one bit. But she was so damned easy to talk to.

And that was a problem.

NINETY MINUTES LATER, WAY PULLED TO THE GATE BLOCKING the entrance to the community Bernadette Ambrose called home. According to its website, Moreland Lake offered over one hundred acres of mountain lake where residents hiked, camped, and enjoyed any number of water activities.

Home costs in this particular community started at a cool one million. *Heck of a place to retire.*

He tapped the radio off, silencing Jason Aldean, and lowered his window. After he gave the guard his and Roni's names, they waited for him to make a call, and—*boom*—in like Flynn, as his mother liked to say.

Cruising along the lakefront road, he glanced at the gorgeous woman next to him and beyond her, out the window, the sparkling water, and the blue sky. It all felt...good.

He held his breath a second, then eased it out as he took it all in. Forced himself to be present in this one moment of peace.

Dang. How the hell did this complicated situation make him feel...what? Content?

Whatever it was, it was different.

He went back to the road, navigating as it curved around the lake. The cooler temps today kept kayakers away, but he imagined in another month the lake would be littered with residents enjoying a day on the water.

I could live here.

How often had *that* thought popped into his mind? Typically, he was all about leaving. Hitting the road. Exploring new places. He'd bought the house in Steele Ridge because of his family. In Steele Ridge, he wouldn't become an old man with no one to help him get a pair of glasses.

This place? The water and the views?

The privacy.

Spectacular.

And with the way cash was flying into the business, in another year he'd be able to afford something here. A small weekend home.

#Goals.

"It's nice," he said.

"It is indeed."

"This is where the party was?"

Roni nodded. "Yes. Every summer they'd throw a barbecue. The house is on the lake and his mom would rent extra kayaks and jet skis for everyone to play on. Gosh, that was a great day."

She turned away, facing out the window and pausing for a few long seconds, while she sniffled softly. What was happening? And did she just swipe her right hand under her eyes?

"Roni?"

She popped the glove box open. "Any tissues in here? Oh, good. Napkins."

"Are you okay?"

She wiped her nose, then crumpled the napkin. "Yeah. I just...had a moment, I guess. Two months after that cookout, Jeff was gone. That fast, it was over."

"Hey," Way said. She peeled her gaze from the window and faced him. "I'm sorry we had to come here. You said he wasn't married. His mother inherited everything. She's the one who cleaned out his place. She might know something."

"Like what?"

"I have no idea. That's what we're here for. Maybe she'll let us look through his stuff."

That statement was met with lips pressed so tight it would take a sledgehammer to bust through them. Pissing her off wasn't his intention, but she of all people knew they had to start somewhere. Somewhere being Bernadette Ambrose.

Roni didn't want to believe this guy might be dirty. Whether that made her loyal or a fool didn't matter. Her willingness to protect her friend impressed the hell out of him.

"Last I heard, NSA analysts capped out at 150k a year. How did they afford this place?"

"Jeff's dad. He invented a handheld explosive detection system. He started the company and ran it for a while. They had huge contracts with the DoD. He sold the company five years ago, and he and Jeff's mom moved out here. Between the two of them, they had enough government contacts to start their own country."

"They're both retired?"

"His dad died a year after they moved out here. A shame, isn't it? You work hard all your life, make a bazillion bucks, and wind up throwing a massive stroke."

"What about the wife? She remarried?"

Roni shook her head. "No. Jeff told me his dad was the love of her life. I guess she can't imagine being with anyone else. Which is really sort of sad, because she's not old. Maybe late fifties." She looked over at him. "Loving someone that much has to be a blessing and a curse."

Way wouldn't know. Not that he didn't want that kind of love. In his mind, that might be cool. One person to focus on, to know he'd step in front of any threat for them. Except, that came with expectations and people up his ass all the time.

But waking up to someone each day wouldn't be a horrible thing. "I don't know. Might be nice to have someone like that. A reason to get out of bed every day. A purpose."

"You have a purpose now. You've built a business."

"Yeah, but that's...I don't know. Material."

And look at him getting all mushy. Him. The one whose family made him nuts.

Beside him, Roni stayed silent, but kept her focus on him. Analyzing him, as usual.

"What?" he said. "You don't agree?"

"Material isn't bad." She gestured toward the windows. "Look around. I don't see a whole lot wrong with this."

"Yeah, but Jeff's mom is alone."

Jesus. Was this seriously him having this conversation?

"My mom was the love of my dad's life. Look where it got him. Loving people that much is dangerous."

And he thought he was a cynic? "Where is she now?"

She gawked at him. "My *mother*?"

"Yeah."

"According to her tax return, she lives in Santa Ana with husband number four."

Way let out a whistle. "You don't talk to her?"

"No. Though there's a twisted part of me that likes to know if she's still alive. Every year I run her through the system to keep tabs. Sick, right?"

He shrugged. "Who's to say? I mean, she's your mom. She left you. You have a right to be curious."

He couldn't wait to hear her response. The woman flat out fascinated him. Thinking back on it, Way's parents, busy with Shep and his mom's career, might not have always been available, but when they were, it was all kids all the time.

Always paying attention, always taking the time to listen and offer advice.

For that, he should thank them. Tonight. He'd stop by the house and let them both know.

His GPS chose that moment to kick in and announce he'd reached his destination.

Roni peered straight ahead. "It's the one on the right. And, I don't know."

"Sorry?"

"You said I have a right to be curious. I don't know about that." She pointed out the window. "Turn here."

He pulled in and followed the winding, tree-lined driveway that curved around a three-car garage. The large, multilevel stone home sat at an angle, with two-thirds of it facing the sparkling lake. The builder did this one right because, even from the circular drive in front of the house, Way had a view of the lake. Hell, he could sit here all day.

This was what two million bucks bought.

He'd have to start saving more.

He killed the engine and slid out of the car, inhaling the crisp lake air. He held his arm out, resting his hand on Roni's back for a second as she fell in step beside him. At the brick steps leading to the front door, he held her elbow as they climbed. Ms. Independence shot him a look, but didn't bother pulling away.

"Good breeding," he said. "My mom would kill me if you fell."

"Sure. Blame your mother."

He gave her a smile and rang the doorbell. While they waited, Roni ran a hand over her button-down shirt and hiked the neckline of her tank top a little higher.

The front door opened, revealing a petite woman with short, grayish blond hair. She wore light makeup that, along with cropped bangs, enhanced bright blue eyes and gave her an ethereal quality.

Her fitted black sweater framed a silver peace sign hanging on a leather cord around her neck. Dark jeans hugged her lean body. Way assumed a little yoga might be involved, which would explain the whole Zen, cool vibe.

"Hello, dear," she said, holding her arms to Roni. "It's lovely to see you."

Accepting the hug, Roni stepped inside, wrapping her arms around the woman. "Hi, Bernadette. Thank you so much for seeing us."

"Of course. You know any chance I get to talk about Jeff, I'll take."

The two backed away from the hug, holding eye contact for a few seconds before Roni turned back to Way, her eyes once again moist. Tough day for rock-hard Roni Fenwick.

"Way Kingston, this is Bernadette Ambrose. Jeff's mom."

For such a little thing, the woman had a solid handshake.

"Welcome," she said. "Come in."

She led them down an open marble hallway with a large winding staircase leading to the second floor.

"This is a great house," he said.

"Thank you. My husband designed it. His dream home, I suppose."

They reached an archway that opened to a glass-walled great room with an adjoining kitchen. The giant center island caught his attention. Man, his mom would love that for their family dinners.

Bernadette pointed to the sitting area in the great room. "We'll sit in here. Can I get you anything? Tea, water?"

Both declined, and Way held his arm for Roni to lead the way to the sofa.

"So." Bernadette settled into a deep-cushioned chair across from them. "What can I do for you? I know there hasn't been any status change in my son's case. I call them every week and every week I get the same response: no new leads."

Roni scooted to the edge of her seat. "I know. It's maddening. There's another case that's come up, though. I'm not at liberty to give details, but...well...with your contacts, you can probably find out on your own."

Bernadette pursed her lips. "I'm assuming this is a CIA matter."

"Yes, but there's an odd angle."

"I always love those. What do you have?"

"A gang shooting."

"And this involves the CIA how?"

When Roni paused, Way took over. Outside of the NDA he'd signed, he wasn't a government employee. Still, he'd have to tread carefully here. "It's the ammunition used in the shooting. It's...unique."

Bernadette focused her laser-sharp blue eyes on him. "I'm sorry. Which agency are you with?"

"I'm not, ma'am. I'm a gunsmith."

If that revelation shocked her, she breezed right over it. "I see. So you have an interest in this unique bullet?"

"I do."

"Why?"

He held his hands wide.

"You're not at liberty either." She waved it off. "No worries, young man. As Roni said, I have my own resources. For now, what is it I can help with?"

He'd let Roni take that one.

"One of the dead gang members was being investigated

by the task force Jeff and I were on. I'm wondering if...I hate to ask."

"It's all right, dear. I know how these things work. You want to know if Jeff ever shared anything with me about the case."

Roni nodded.

"I'm sorry to say, he didn't. Frankly, I begged him. I was so bored after I retired and thought, with my background, I might be able to help. He wouldn't hear of it. I suppose I should be proud of him for that. Now I wonder, if he'd confided in me, would we know who killed my only child?"

"I wish I had answers, too."

Way's stomach pitched. The last damned thing he wanted was to distress a grieving woman. But, hell, it had to be done and he wasn't about to make Roni do it. "Mrs. Ambrose," he said, "I'm gonna be really rude here. My mother would skin me if she knew."

The older woman let out a laugh. "A boy afraid of his mother. I do appreciate that. Go ahead and say it. I assure you, it won't be the first time someone has been forward."

"Thank you, ma'am. Did your son leave any case notes we could look at?"

She eyed him for a few seconds, then leaned in. "Let's cut to it, shall we? You think my son is somehow involved with this *unique* bullet? I can assure you, my son was clean. Believe me, I've been through every piece of what he left behind."

Roni cleared her throat and gave Way the stink eye. "No. That's not what he's saying. We're starting with what we know. That's all we can do. And we know one of the men killed with this bullet was a man Jeff was investigating. But Jeff was good, and I think there may be notes or something in his phone or on his laptop. Something that was missed."

Way met the woman's eye. She'd already busted him on his suspicions about her son. Might as well play it out. "Think of it this way," he said. "We're fresh eyes. There might be something we see that'll connect some dots. Maybe help solve your son's murder. If he left notes, we may all get what we want."

Bernadette lifted her chin, giving him a good dose of haughty arrogance.

Yeah, he'd pissed her off.

A few seconds passed while she thought it through. Eventually, she stood and looked down at them. "Fine. I'll give you whatever assistance you need. We have nothing to hide."

WAY OPENED HIS FRONT DOOR AND RONI STEPPED INTO THE living room, setting the banker's box on the floor next to the sofa.

"Coming through," he said from behind her.

She scooted sideways as he dropped two other boxes beside the one she'd carried in from his car. Three boxes. That's what Bernadette had given them. Whether they'd find anything of use in those boxes remained to be seen.

"Have a seat."

He waved her to the giant L-shaped sectional with cushions wide enough for King Kong. In terms of furnishings, he didn't keep much in this room. Only the sectional, a coffee table, and a giant wall-mounted television. Stacked on the coffee table were three books, *Fahrenheit 451, Jurassic Park,* and *One Flew Over the Cuckoo's Nest.* An interesting mix, no doubt.

Beside the books, two remotes sat by side. Everything at perfectly straight angles.

Beyond the living room, the dining room held what looked like a hand-carved table with sturdy legs and squared off chairs.

Everything in Way's home seemed neat. Tidy.

Orderly.

Something she'd taken note of in his workshop, but a man's business could often be different from his home. She plopped down, let her body sink deep, and nearly let out a sigh. All these routine interruptions wore on her, slowing her down.

Closing her eyes wouldn't be a bad idea. Just a few minutes might help.

But...Jeff.

She sat up, ready to get to work.

Way pointed at the boxes. "How do you want to do this? You take a box and I'll take one?"

"That would be the fastest. Maybe pull out anything that looks odd and we'll review it together."

"It's almost dinnertime. Are you hungry?"

She shook her head. "Not yet."

"All right. Give me a half hour notice and I'll make something."

Neat.

Tidy.

Cooks.

She thought back to teasing Maggie about landing the perfect man at the Kingston family dinner. Well, Way would give Jayson Tucker a run for his money.

"I can't cook," she blurted.

Way grinned. "And you're telling me this why?"

"Probably because I'm envious of anyone who can prepare a meal without poisoning people?"

He shrugged. "My mom poisons people. She made this

eggplant bread one time that was so bad even the dog wouldn't eat it."

"Ew. That sounds...different."

"It's different all right. My father is the chef in that house. Total foodie." He paused a second. "No. That's not it. I don't think it's the food so much as the preparation. He likes to taste and figure out how to improve it. His palate is unbelievable. He'll put something in his mouth and the minute it hits his tongue, he knows how it's made. He wastes no time telling you, either."

"Is it annoying?"

"It can be. Sometimes you just want to eat the goddamn food, but he has to give it a dissertation. I suppose that's how I learned. I listened. A lot."

"Do you do that often?"

"Listen? Hell yeah. It made me a good Marine. People are interesting. Even the assholes."

She laughed, but there was truth there. Her life hadn't been easy, yet every setback taught her some new survival trick.

"I'm serious," he said. "Most guys stay away from assholes. I want to know what catastrophic thing happened to make someone that much of a douche."

Pondering it, she rolled her bottom lip out. "Why does it have to be something catastrophic? Why can't someone just be miserable?"

"They can. We all have shit, right? Things that make us who we are."

We sure do. "The way you're talking, I'd think *you* were the psych major."

He shrugged. "I don't know about that. I'm good at figuring shit out, but not at staying put. Me? Sitting in a chair all day? No chance."

"There are plenty of psych careers that don't involve counseling people. I don't sit in a chair all day. I saw enough of the system to know I wanted to help people. Plus, my history—the things I've seen of human nature—makes me a good judge of character." She pointed at the boxes on the floor. "Jeff was not a dirty cop. I'd have known."

He stared at her for a long minute, clearly chewing on a response. He didn't believe her.

We'll see.

She sat forward and held her hands out. "Let's get to it. The sooner we read through this stuff, the sooner we'll eliminate Jeff from the list of potential people who sold you out."

Hours later, after a quick dinner of grilled London broil, leftover sweet potato soufflé, and a salad with the vinaigrette he'd whipped up the other night, Way watched as Roni sat on the floor, legs crossed, with half of a box of notes in front of her.

He liked it. Dinner with her, sitting around in quiet while they pored over files. Unlike a lot of women, Roni didn't need to fill silence. She went about her business, leaving him be.

When she leaned against the sofa and tilted her head to the ceiling, his gaze locked onto the smooth skin of her neck. He wanted his lips there. Yep. Sure did. "You find something?"

She looked back at him. "I don't think so. All this"—she gestured to the stacks of papers, files, and notebooks to her left—"is personal. Everything else is work-related."

The work pile didn't look so big. Which could be a good or a bad thing. "Any bank statements?"

"No, but I found this." She held up a checkbook. "Jeff

was always paranoid about online banking. We teased him unmercifully about it because he still wrote checks to pay his bills. From what I can tell, everything is in order. When he died, he had five thousand dollars in his checkbook. I found reports from his retirement account and another mutual fund account."

"How much?"

"Retirement had forty thousand and the mutual account had fifty-five."

"Not unreasonable amounts," Way said.

She gestured to the stacks in front of him. "What'd you find?"

Before he could answer, her phone buzzed. She checked it, ignored whoever it was, and brought her attention back to him.

Way toed the box in front of him. "This is all mementos. High-school yearbooks, pictures, newspaper clippings from 9/11. I was about to start on the next box."

"We can split that box if you want."

She peered back at him with shadowed eyes and...*no way*. She looked beat. "It's almost midnight. You need a break? I can take you back to the B and B."

"A good listener and observant. You're a dangerous man."

He smiled. "I like to think so."

He stared straight into her lush brown eyes, letting her know that if she wanted a replay of that smoking kiss they'd shared, he wouldn't chase her off.

She let out a long sigh. "Lord, you do tempt me. But no, I'm good. We still have a lot to do here."

Way was afraid she'd say that. He stood and held his hand to her. "Come up here."

When she obliged, he drew her to her feet and squeezed

her hands. "You're tired. How about I make you some warm milk and you take a power nap? In thirty minutes you'll be good as new."

"Be careful, Waylon, I may expect this from you all the time."

"Be careful, Roni, I may want to do it all the time."

When she smiled at him, he dipped his head, testing. She inched closer—a green light if he'd ever seen one—and he closed in, bringing his lips to hers, brushing gently. She slid her arms around his waist, resting them there while he trailed his lips over her jaw to that spot he'd targeted on her neck.

"I've been eyeing this area," he said.

She lifted her head, allowing him better access. "By all means, help yourself."

He just might. He nibbled the spot. Dotted kisses there. Pausing, he inhaled, let the scent of her shampoo— almonds, maybe—ground him. Talk about playing with fire. She was...what? Hard, yet soft. Loyal, yet deceptive.

And for him? Total brain candy. He wanted to crawl into that mind and root around. Figure out what made her tick.

What the hell was he doing?

Depending on what they discovered on this little investigation of theirs, she could wreck him. Did he believe she would? No.

But he definitely had a problem with his dick leading the way.

He drew back, pecked her on the tip of her nose. "Warm milk and a nap coming up. Have a seat."

Ignoring the start of a hard-on, he walked to the kitchen and opened the refrigerator. Way dumped some milk in a pot, put the burner on low, and grabbed the honey and vanilla from the cabinet. A dash of cinnamon wouldn't hurt, so he snatched the bottle, some fresh stuff his dad had gotten at the farmer's market last week.

Eventually, steam rose from the pot. The fragrant aroma of the vanilla couldn't be missed. He dipped a spoon into the mixture, took a taste.

More honey. Two spoons later, he hit pay dirt.

Perfect evening beverage.

Mug in hand, he headed back to Roni and found her curled on his sofa, huddled under the blanket he'd bought on his last trip to Turkey.

Her eyes were closed, her thick lashes resting against skin that wasn't quite olive, but far from creamy.

When awake, Roni Fenwick had an aggressiveness about her. A killer shark, ready to battle. In sleep? Right now?

Peaceful.

As a man who understood the vulnerabilities that came with sleep, particularly for a woman who'd grown up shuffled from one stranger's house to another, he'd take it as compliment that she'd passed out in his home.

He, for damned sure, wasn't gonna disturb her.

Quietly, he moved around to the opposite end of the sofa and set the mug on the coffee table. If she woke up, she'd see it.

Hands now free, he hefted the last box still on the floor and carried it to the kitchen to sort through it without disturbing her.

Way took one last look as she let out a heavy breath. *Bang.* Something kicked him straight in the chest.

Fascinated?

Hell, he was way more than fascinated.

"Well, *shit.*"

.   .   .

IN THE KITCHEN, WAY MOVED THE WOODEN BOWL OF FRUIT from the center of the table and flipped the top open on the box. A stack of manila envelopes greeted him. He hauled those out and found clear plastic shoe bins underneath.

All containing photos. Hundreds of photos. That'd take a while, so he went back to the envelopes, noted the dates handwritten on them. All from the last two years.

Helpful. He chose the most recent one. Dates: May–July.

As much as he wanted to feel bad about digging through a dead man's stuff, he didn't. Not when this guy might have a connection to how Way's design got to the street. Was it a coincidence that Ambrose investigated members of the Street Dragons? One of whom was subsequently killed with Way's bullet? Or at least the design?

The curiosity nut in Way didn't think so. In fact, the curiosity nut thought Jeff Ambrose, by way of his father's DoD contacts, introduced some people to some people who'd made a deal for Way's design. Hell, maybe Jeff made the deal.

Except nothing they'd found in Ambrose's finances indicated wrongdoing. No large deposits, no house in Cayman. Then again, dude was an undercover ATF agent. He'd know to cover his own ass.

Rather than rip the top off the envelope, Way undid the clasp and dumped the contents on the table.

A few photos and three thumb drives slid out. How he loved thumb drives. All kinds of interesting stuff on those. He scooped up the drives and headed to the laptop he kept on the counter in the corner nook.

Firing up the laptop, he stuck the thumb drive in, took a seat in the ladder-back chair, and waited for the pain in the ass spinning wheel to stop. A few clicks later, thumbnails of photos popped up.

Click, click, click. He scrolled photos.

A kid's birthday party—probably a friend, since Jeff was an only child.

At least he thought the guy was an only child. He grabbed the small notepad he kept by the phone and jotted a note to check that.

Click, click, click. More photos. A boat on a lake. He studied the photo. Looked like the area where Ambrose's mother lived.

Click.

Click

Click.

On and on it went until he got to a group photo. Five people standing on a lawn, all holding glasses up in toast.

He checked the date. Last July.

Whoa. Could this be *the* party? The one where Roni met her boss.

He enlarged the photo, studied the faces. No one he recognized. Next photo. A group of kayakers. *Click.* An old guy with a young woman in a low-cut halter top that barely covered her tits. Damn, that was a banging body, though.

He let out a soft snort and clicked. A picnic table with folks talking. Three men—one with his head turned—and two women. He clicked again and...

Wait, was that—?

He clicked back. Zoomed in. Studied the photo.

No good.

The man's head was turned too far for Way to know. He clicked again, then again and again, searching for the man in a red golf shirt. Five clicks later, red flashed on his screen and Way's gut dropped clear to his feet.

14

WAY GRABBED HIS PHONE, CHECKED THE TIME. NEARLY eleven. Clay might—or might not—still be awake.

The sickness rolling in his stomach could be dispatched with one phone call.

Sorry, buddy. Waking your ass up.

He tapped the screen, found Clay's number, and punched the video button. Friends or not, on video, he'd spot any facial tells.

While waiting for the line to connect, Way leaned back in his chair and peered down the hallway where he'd left Roni snoozing away.

From what he could see, still no movement. A good thing, since he didn't necessarily want to clue her in to the Clay connection. At least until he knew what he was dealing with.

Clay's face popped up on screen, his eyes half closed and his short hair stuck to his head on one side. Definitely sleeping. And, yow, Way tried to ignore what looked like a female head in the background.

"Dude," Clay said, "fucking late."

"Uh, yeah. Sorry. You, um, got company?"

Clay peered over his shoulder, then back at the phone. "She's asleep. Hang on."

The picture jerked and then swung as Clay got out of bed.

"Christ," Way said, "I hope you're not naked."

The thought alone made his eyes fry.

"It'd serve you right for calling me so late." Clay waggled his eyebrows. "Now I may have to wake her up for round three."

"You're an asshole."

Way wasn't sure if his friend was an asshole for bragging about getting laid—something that hadn't been on Way's regular list of activities lately—or making comments, any comments, about the woman. In Way's mind, that was a total douche move.

Whatever. Some guys got off on it.

"*You* just woke me up and *I'm* the asshole?"

"It's important."

"I assumed. What's up?"

"I'm looking into this thing with my bullet design."

Clay sighed. "I'm on it. I told you not to worry about it."

"Yeah, you did. But it's my ass on the line."

"I hear you. But it takes a delicate touch. I can't walk into Langley and demand answers."

Understandable, but Way needed answers on something else. "Jeff Ambrose," he shot.

Clay's gaze narrowed as he stared straight at the screen. "Who?"

"Ambrose. The dead ATF agent?"

Clay's eyebrows came together. "What are you talking about? I don't know about any dead ATF agent."

Apparently his friend was still half asleep. "Hey. Focus

here. I know I woke you up, but get your shit together. This is important. Jeff Ambrose. You went to his mother's barbecue last summer. Bernadette Ambrose. She worked for the NSA. Now retired."

A few seconds passed while Clay continued to stare at him. "Oh. *Jeff.* Right. Sorry. I...wasn't thinking. Tired. What about him?"

"There were a couple of agency guys at that party. Don Harding for sure. I saw him in photos."

Again the stunned staring. *Come on, Clay, dial in here.*

"Wait," he said. "You have photos? From *Bernadette's*? Tell me what the fuck you're doing."

In their last conversation, Way had only told him there'd been a shooting. Of course, the guy was lost. "Sorry. When we talked the other day, I told you about the murdered gangbanger."

"Yeah. I poked around. The ammo you sent to Langley is accounted for. No strays. It's confirmed."

Way let out a long breath and dropped his chin for a second while the elephant jumped from his back. At least the bullet wasn't one of the ones he'd created.

Still, the design...

"You okay?" Clay pressed.

Way went back to the phone. "Yeah. I'm good. Something is fucked up, though. Jeff Ambrose, the now very dead Jeff Ambrose, was on an interagency task force, which, by the way, was run by my sister."

"Shit."

"No kidding." He waved it off. "The shooting I told you about? The victim was being investigated by Ambrose and this task force."

"What's the task force?"

"Cigarette smuggling. Huge black market business. We're talking millions."

"And?"

His buddy was getting impatient. Clay wasn't the only one. "A month after I sent my design to Langley, the head of science and development was at a party with Jeff Ambrose."

Clay gave him a massive eyeroll. "Seriously? You think Don Harding, with the crazy tech stuff he sees on the daily, gave Ambrose top-secret info about your design? Dude, if he was gonna sell a design, he'd do it a lot quieter than this."

Way sat back in his chair. Nothing made sense. This whole time he'd been thinking Ambrose somehow got hold of his design and sold it.

However, given the friendship between Harding and Bernadette Ambrose, what if Harding himself had leaked the intel? But then why send Roni to investigate Way?

Easy. The agency needed a scapegoat. Who better than the guy who designed the bullet? If they intended on framing him, they'd send an agent to plant damning evidence.

"Someone might be setting me up. I need whatever intel I can get on Don Harding and who he told about that design."

A thump came from the other room and Way shot a look down the hall. From the sound of it, Roni had woken up.

He went back to Clay. "And I need it fast."

THE SOUND OF WAY TALKING TO SOMEONE ROUSED RONI FROM her nap. Who the hell would he be talking to at this hour?

Straining to hear, she'd stayed curled up on that giant sofa, refusing to move just in case he came back.

In the spirit of partnership, she shouldn't be eavesdropping. Or attempting to eavesdrop. Then again, if the conversation were private, he should have gone outside.

When a good two minutes passed without a sound from the kitchen, she got to her feet, gave her hair a finger comb, and moved down the hallway.

She found him sitting in the corner at the counter space he'd made into a desk. "Hi," she said.

He shut his laptop and looked over at her, eyebrows slightly raised. "Hi, yourself. How was the nap?"

"Good." She pointed at the phone sitting next to the computer. "Sorry to interrupt."

"You didn't."

Oh, now they were going to play this game? The one where she pretended she didn't just hear him tell someone he thought he might be getting set up. No doubt by the CIA.

Who could blame him for thinking that, given her timely appearance in Steele Ridge?

Still casually leaning on the doorframe, she tilted her head. Considered her options. Balls to the wall. At this point, she had nothing to lose. She'd been ignoring Karl's calls all day, so she was probably already screwed. Why not take it all the way. "Way?"

"Yeah?"

"Don't fuck with me."

That got his attention. He slid his chair back and turned sideways, fully facing her. "You think *I'm* fucking with *you*." He let out a sarcastic grunt. "Priceless."

"I heard you mention Don Harding."

"Yeah. So?"

"Who were you talking to?"

"I told you on day one, I have contacts. I'm using them."

"Ah. Your State Department friend."

His lack of response confirmed it. "Are you going to tell me about it? Since we're partners and all."

Way stood and walked toward her, his confident and determined stride suddenly unnerving her, tempting her to step back.

When he closed in, she lifted her hand, pressing it against the soft cotton of his T-shirt and stopped him barely a foot away. Him dominating her space wouldn't keep her on point.

"You mentioned daily calls with your boss," he said. "Did you speak with him today? I don't remember you sharing the details."

"That's because I ignored him. All three times."

Eventually, she'd pay for that. Karl had asked—no, demanded—daily reports. Since striking her deal with Way the day before, she'd avoided the need to explain her newly formed strategy to her superiors.

Karl would want answers and they hadn't found anything incriminating yet. Plus, her assignment was to ascertain if Waylon Kingston had violated his agreement with the CIA.

She didn't believe he had. Not with the effort being put forth to prove otherwise. Which left Jeff's connections with government officials.

Way loomed over her in the classic power move a first-year psych student would call him out on. *Nice try, pal.*

She lifted her chin and gave him a smirk sure to piss him off. She'd grown up in a system that, more times than not, made warriors out of the children within it. No matter how much she liked Way, his attempts to intimidate her were useless.

Taking a tiny step closer, she peered up at him, leaned in just a wee bit so he'd catch her scent. His breath was warm on her cheek, drawing her even closer, reminding her of the internal combustion that occurred every time he put his hands on her.

He tilted his head, gave her a half smile that told her he knew exactly where her mind had gone.

He leaned in another millimeter and ran one finger along the underside of her chin. "What is it you want from me, Roni?"

"That's a loaded question at the moment."

"Ah," he said. "You want to fuck me? Distract me from this conversation? Because, yeah, I'm a guy and"—he stared down at her body, dragging his gaze from her chest back to her face—"and guys like fucking, right?"

His words, clearly meant to sting, hit their mark. Damned if she'd give him the satisfaction. Later, in private, she'd allow herself to feel the hurt. Right now? Survival.

And Veronica Fenwick had that down.

In response to his leering, she did her own visual inspection of his body, lingering in the crotch area before smiling back at him. "I'm guessing it's not unusual. You're an attractive guy. You've got an...edge... that women find appealing."

"I don't get you."

"Join the club."

"You want to fuck me *and* frame me, is that it?"

"No. I only want to fuck you."

She smacked her hand over the back of his neck and dragged his lips to hers. Tongues clashed, lips battled for more, pressing hard as he grabbed her hips, grinding them into his engorged erection.

My God.

She arched into him, loving the roughness, the all-out mind snap consuming her. This man made her want things she never wanted before.

Not just passion. But love. The security to lose her mind and do wicked things to him without worrying about the betrayal sure to come.

Freedom. That's what she wanted.

She pushed away from the kiss. "I'm not framing you. I swear, I'm not."

He ground his hips into her again, closing his eyes as tension hardened his perfect jawline. "Why should I believe you?"

Easy. She wasn't a whore. He couldn't know that, though. "I don't lie when sex is involved. And I sure as hell don't use it as a bargaining chip."

"You lie other times, though."

"Sure. So do you. Down deep, we're both trying to find justice. Our methods might be different."

"And what? You want me to shove you against the wall, fuck you blind, and then go back to business as usual?"

Ew. *That* certainly didn't appeal. Even the mention of it, the cold, distant tone in his voice, doused whatever fire simmered inside her.

Too bad, really. She rather enjoyed the insanity of it all. She patted her hand against his chest. "Well, I suppose when you put it that way, it sounds rather unpleasant."

He took two full steps back, then added a third. The bulge of his erection couldn't be missed, but she kept her eyes up.

Propping his hands on his hips, Way shook his head. "I don't know what the hell you want from me."

"I've been honest with you. I've admitted to everything. My boss sending me here, using Maggie for an introduction, all of it. You asked me what I want from you."

"You haven't answered."

"I want you to help me prove my friend isn't dirty. That he didn't somehow get hold of your design and sell it."

Way nodded. "Fine. How?"

"As much as I don't want to go out on this unstable limb with you, I believe you're right. It's too much of a coincidence that Don Harding was at that party and now your design—or a similar one—is killing Street Dragons." She reached out, ran one hand down the front of his T-shirt, felt the rock hard abs beneath, and nearly purred. She patted his belly, lifted herself to tiptoes and kissed him slowly, letting her lips brush against his. "I'm going to find out if Don Harding played me."

As soon as Way made the turn to drop Roni off at the B&B, she spotted the oversized black SUV that screamed federal vehicle.

"Company," Way said.

Given his life experiences, he was no fool. Plus, strange vehicles in Steele Ridge more than likely weren't difficult to identify.

"Looks like."

"You know who it is?"

Oh, she had a good guess. Karl Quigley didn't get to be the CIA's associate deputy director of administration because he was an idiot. In Roni's short tenure she'd learned three things. One, Karl knew the seedy, backroom ways of politics. Two, he wasn't afraid to use his position to get things done. Three, he didn't like to wait. On anything. Or anyone.

And she'd ignored him all day.

Something, she imagined, he'd make her pay for. Thus,

the surprise visit. One clearly intended to prove she wasn't as out-of-reach as she wanted.

She'd have to tread carefully, considering his friendship with Don Harding.

Way pulled into the driveway, shifted the car to park, and killed his headlights. "What do you want to do?"

She rested her head against the seat and closed her eyes for a few seconds. *Girl, you're in trouble.*

It wasn't just navigating her assignment on behalf of the agency. This thing with Way, the lust had screwed up her thinking. In her professional career, she'd never experienced this. She had, in fact, prided herself on her ability to focus on the job. Being someone who found it hard to trust helped. She'd become so accustomed to not having faith in people that the risk of getting involved on a personal level had never been an issue.

Until she put her hands on Way.

She admired his determination, the flat-out doggedness for justice. Throw in his dark hair, the day-old scruff, the lean, coiled muscle she liked running her hands over, and what was a girl to do?

She opened her eyes. "I think that's Karl Quigley waiting for me. Once I get out of this car, you need to take off. Fast. Hopefully he didn't grab your plate number before you turned the lights off."

Thank goodness for dark streets.

"Uh, I don't like that. I need to make sure you get inside."

"Uh, no. That won't work. How am I supposed to explain that?"

He gave her a pissy look. "Compromise. You get out and haul ass to that door. I'll back out, but face south so they can't see who's driving. Besides, they probably already grabbed my tag number. Just go. Once you're inside, wave or something so I know you're okay."

Men.

"Fine. I'll wave." She gave him a faux-cheery smile. "Don't take offense if I don't kiss you good night."

At that, he snorted. "You're funny."

"Thank you. I'll call you tomorrow."

The second she hopped out, Way was on the move, backing out of the driveway and facing the opposite direction from the parked SUV.

Before she made it halfway to the house, the rear door of the SUV opened, the interior lights illuminating—as suspected—Karl Quigley.

Roni angled back to Way, threw up a hand letting him know it wasn't a serial killer and that he should leave.

Fast.

He hit the gas, leaving his headlights off until he reached the end of the block.

Karl approached, his strides swift as he walked straight across Mrs. Tasky's pristine lawn. "Where the hell have you been?"

Alrighty. This was how it would go.

Still, the nasty tone she could live without. Roni pushed her shoulders back and tilted her head up to the much-taller man. "Right here. In Steele Ridge. Where you sent me."

Being aggressive might not be her best move, but, well...

Winging it here.

When he reached the edge of the walkway, maybe two feet from her, the glow of the porch lamp shined down on him, revealing a scowl and cheeks so hard they could have been carved stone. Then he moved in, crowding the air around her and getting way too close for her comfort and bringing a blast of negative energy with him

Whoa. He was *pissed.*

He stopped, propped his hands on his hips. "I told you to check in every day."

Refusing to back down, she nodded. "I apologize. I was on the move all day and didn't have a private moment."

"Meaning?"

"Meaning, I was with Way Kingston, trying to get information."

His head snapped back. Yeah, that did the trick.

Still, she'd have to be careful here. Whether or not Karl had expected her to actually make contact with Way directly didn't matter anymore. That horse had already left the barn.

"You were *with* him?"

"I was. I'm working on the fly here. Maggie introduced me and he's not stupid. He knows how to gather intel."

"And?"

"It turns out one of his contacts is a hacker. A damned good one that the agency should seriously look at hiring, because Kingston had a full dossier on me in a matter of hours."

This time, Karl nearly gawked. "He knows you work for us?"

"He sure does."

"Goddammit."

She waved a hand. "Relax, sir. It wound up working in our favor. I made a deal with him."

Roni had seen all sorts of anger in her day. Drunken anger. Emotionally damaging passive-aggressive anger. And full-on apoplectic, nose-flaring, vein-swelling, I-will-hurt-you aggression. That vein swelling? Yep. Right here on Karl's neck. "What did you do? I didn't authorize any deals."

Well, chief, too bad. "Did you want me to tell him to hold on while I called my boss at the CIA and asked how to proceed?"

"Watch your tone or I'll put your ass out of work."

He'd put her...*ohmygod.* This bastard sent her on an off-the-books assignment and now he wanted to threaten her?

Nuh-uh. Her days of being made to feel weak were long gone. She'd teach high-school psychology before she let that happen.

"You know, *sir,* it seems to me the agency is in a tenuous position here." She circled one hand in the air. "What with the leaked bullet design. And then there's the fact that you've sent me here on the downlow. I mean, you might want to give me some wiggle room before you threaten to fire me, since I could possibly save all of your butts."

More nostril flaring ensued and Roni felt that surge of pleasure that came with victory.

At least until the front door opened. Roni spun around. Mrs. Tasky stood in the doorway, a bathrobe pulled tight and her hair in sponge curlers Roni hadn't seen in years.

"Is everything all right?"

Roni bobbed her head. "Yes, Mrs. Tasky. I'm sorry to have disturbed you." She angled sideways. "This is...Karl. My friend from work. He stopped by to give me something I left at a meeting."

Eeekk. That was bad. Really bad. Blame it on the late hour and lack of sleep.

"Hello, ma'am," Karl said in his best choir boy voice. "I'm sorry for the intrusion."

Mrs. Tasky eyed him, then went back to Roni. "It's not a bother. I was watching a movie. Thought I'd heard something, though. As long as you're all right..."

"I'm fine, ma'am. Thank you. I'll be in shortly."

Mrs. Tasky retreated, closing the door as she went. Roni faced Karl again. "Just so you know, half this town will know a man named Karl visited me tonight. Maggie used to talk about the gossip mill here all the time."

"Forget that. What's this deal you made?" Karl asked, his voice low and steady, but much softer on attitude.

"Kingston." Using his last name rather than the much-too-familiar Way couldn't hurt. "He got wind of the shootings through Maggie. She took autopsy photos to him and asked his opinion. He figured out fairly quickly that the bullets being used in these shootings were a similar, if not the same, design as his. He wants to clear himself of any suspicion."

"Do you believe him?"

Yes.

Tricky question, though. Her personal involvement with Maggie—and the fact her body was in a state of lust over Way—could, to her absolute horror, be clouding her judgment.

So much for being a killer shark who trusted no one.

"I'm not sure," she said. "As I mentioned, he's experienced in reconnaissance. He could be lying. I don't have enough yet to know."

"What do you have?"

"I overheard part of a conversation. A phone call he had with someone named Clay."

"As in Clayton Bartles?"

Karl knew him. Now this was getting interesting. "I don't know. I only caught the end of it, but he definitely called the person Clay. Kingston also mentioned that he knew someone at State. Does Clay Bartles work at State?"

"Affirmative."

Affirmative? That's all? He sent her here, with zero backup, and intended on filtering information?

Um, *negative.*

"Sir, you've given me an assignment. A solo one that affords me no administrative support. No backup. At *all.* And people are dying, by means of a bullet that may or may not have gotten out of Langley. Let me add that Way Kingston, in my limited experience with him, will not sit around and wait to see if he's going to be sacrificed by the CIA. We need to get ahead of him."

A bird swooped low, nearly walloping Karl on the head. The man flinched, instinctively angling away while the bird settled on an overhead tree branch.

Good, birdie.

Karl peered up, searching for his kamikaze nemesis. All this weird distraction might be a side benefit.

Roni cleared her throat, drawing Karl's gaze. "What does Clay Bartles do at State?"

"He's an aide. You may have seen him before."

"Me?"

"Yes. He was at the cookout where you and I met."

What now? She cocked her head, stood there for a second, not exactly sure if she'd heard him right. "He was...Wait. Who invited him?"

The bird flew off. Karl glanced up again, then back at her. "Bernadette, via her husband, has a lot of contacts. Her knowing someone at State isn't out of the realm of possibility. All I know is he was there the year before."

"How do you know that?"

"I met him. Don also."

Terrific. "All due respect, sir, it would have been nice to know this."

He gave her another hard look. "Watch your tone. I'm

telling you now. Months later, Clay called Don. Said he had a friend with a bullet design the agency should look at."

These people. All their damned secrets. They sent her here with limited information and expected results. Unbelievable. Roni stepped away for a second. Had to. Shaking her head, she inhaled, took refuge in the cool night air. Calm. That's what she needed.

But, dammit, she was tired.

She turned back, held out a hand. "And you didn't think this was information you should give me? A connection between Ambrose, the agency, and Kingston? Are we even looking at Bartles as a suspect?"

And, oh, the full weight of this suddenly came clear. Jeff may have indeed known about the bullets. "Did Don tell Jeff about the bullet design?"

"He says no."

"Do you believe him?"

"I want to."

Not exactly the confirmation she'd hoped for. But things were becoming clearer to her fatigued brain. "This little expedition you've sent me on is to make sure Don hasn't fucked up?"

More silence. Well, screw him. "Karl, I need you to start talking or I'm walking on this assignment. Fire me if you need to, but I'm not about to help the agency blame Way Kingston for something he may not have any control over. Do you think Don has something to do with this? Yes or no."

"I don't know."

Bastard. She balled her fingers, gritted her teeth so hard they might snap. Anything to keep her from releasing the venom she wanted to spew. "Well, what *do* you know? Tell me everything or I swear to God I'll blow this thing wide open. Jeff was my friend. If I'm going to find out what's going on, I need everything you can give me before more people wind up dead. Start talking."

For the first time, Karl let out a frustrated huff. Here they were, two people concerned that their friends might be dirty, or at least mildly soiled.

"Most of it you know."

"Well, tell me the rest."

"Don came to me about the Roy Jackson shooting. As part of their review of the Kingston design, one of Don's people researched frangible ammo and found the news brief."

"That's when you and Don cooked up this investigation?"

"Yes. Don said he wanted to make sure no one on his team leaked it."

"You don't believe him?"

"Again, I want to."

"But?"

"A few weeks after Jeff's death, Bernadette contacted me. Obviously, she was in a state of grief. Angry and searching for answers. She thought I might be able to help her access the investigation into Jeff's death."

When Karl paused, Roni decided she was done screwing around. "And what? You looked into it?"

"I requested information from ATF, which I received."

"And that *information* told you Jeff was on a task force investigating Roy Jackson."

"Yes. At the time, Jackson's name didn't stand out. When Don came to me about getting you involved, I read the report again and spotted it."

A whooshing noise filled her head. Plenty of tentacles on this thing. All of them somehow leading back to Jeff. Her heart sunk. *God, Jeff, what did you do?*

Roni couldn't get ahead of herself. Not until she had all the facts. *Time to ask the dreaded question.* "Do you think Don told Jeff about the design and Jeff sold it?"

"I do."

Dammit. "So I'm not really trying to figure out if Way Kingston double-crossed the CIA, am I?"

When he didn't answer, she continued. "Fine. I'll tell you what I think is happening here. You want to eliminate the possibility that the CIA's head of science and development leaked a top-secret design to a now-dead ATF agent." She threw her hands up, waved them in true drama queen fashion. "An agent who, more than likely, sold the design to a street gang. And whose mother, by the way, is a former NSA analyst."

Karl gave her his best steely bored look, complete with an eye roll. "If you're done," he said, "I'll explain. It's a twofold mission. Kingston double-dipping wouldn't be out of the question."

Roni grunted.

"But, yes, that about sums it up."

"Excellent. At least I know what I'm dealing with."

You lying sack of shit.

IT'S 5:00 A.M. THE MORNING MIST IS THICK AS I SIT TUCKED behind a clump of bushes adjusting my scope.

I have to give myself credit for this location. With over four thousand species of plants, fungi, and mosses inhabiting this park, there is no lack of places to hide while waiting for Petra Cheevers to finish the last lap of her five-mile jog.

Good for her.

She's thirty-five and unwilling to lose her girlish figure.

Maybe her husband is a freak about that. Me? I don't get why any man would want a bag of bones.

This one is a workhorse. Almost every morning she runs in this park, five acres of trails and woods plunked into the middle of a neighborhood. If she's not running, it's either yoga at the studio near one of the small markets her family owns or weight lifting at the gym half a mile from her house. On those days, she runs to the gym and back.

Movement from the northwest corner of the trail draws my eye. A quick look through my scope tells me it's a male. Middle-aged and about to piss me off if he doesn't clear out of my target area.

I'm not leaving any witnesses, so he'd best move on.

He makes his way toward me and I hunker down, out of sight, until I hear the huff and puff of heavy breathing. The sound gets louder, then gradually softer. I take a peek.

The interloper moves around the path, heading toward the exit Petra usually uses.

Usually.

Today she won't be leaving this park. It's too bad, really.

All in all, she's made this way too easy for me.

For people like me, creatures of habit are a godsend.

So easy to kill.

I'm starting to feel the pressure, though. That incessant needling at the back of my neck. With each job comes media attention. Attention brings law enforcement. Sooner or later, someone will make the connection.

While I wait for Petra to make that last turn, I check my scope and put thoughts of media attention out of my mind. I can't worry about tomorrow. Worry, my mother used to say, is a debt paid in advance.

Petra comes into view and the needling in my neck turns

to a hungry burst of excitement. It's not time yet. Twenty more yards.

Let her get closer.

Another piece of scum will be removed from society.

This is my goal. My mission.

You can thank me later.

MUG IN HAND, WAY STOOD AT HIS WORKSHOP'S COFFEEPOT inhaling the nutty smell of his Aunt Joan's favorite pecan coffee.

This early, he needed a jolt.

A big one.

Aunt Joan's brew was a special blend he swore she mixed herself, because he'd been to every coffeehouse within thirty miles of Steele Ridge and none of the varieties matched Aunt Joanie's. He'd even tried himself and failed miserably.

Bribery.

That's what he'd do. Bribe Aunt Joan for the blend's particulars and see if he could recreate it. When he got this current mess cleared up, he'd take some downtime. Hit the road on his bike and maybe, after, mess with pecan coffee.

On television, Shelly Radcliffe droned on about Petra Cheevers, a woman who owned several convenience stores throughout Buncombe County.

Found dead in a park from a gunshot wound.

Mug midway to his lips, Way paused and glanced up at the wall-mounted television. A photo of the victim, a willowy blonde, dominated the screen. His pulse kicked up and a rancid feeling assaulted his empty stomach.

What the hell was wrong with him? Plenty of people got shot. Didn't mean it had anything to do with him.

The workshop door flew open and Hurricane Roni roared in, her compact, sultry body moving fast. She wore her typical outfit of tight jeans, ankle boots, and a low-cut V-neck T-shirt. Even with her leather jacket on, he saw enough of her cleavage to want a whole lot more.

Her long hair fell over her shoulders, a few strands flying as she stormed toward him. "Who the *hell* is Petra Cheevers?"

Whoa.

Way slapped his coffee mug on the worktable, sloshing the steaming brew over the rim onto his knuckles, searing the skin.

Ow. "Shit."

He whipped his hand away, rubbing it against his jeans.

"I just saw the story on the news." He shook his hand out. "Goddamn, that burns."

She reached for his hand, held it so she could inspect the damage, then puckered those pretty lips and...blew. On his hand. Right there in his workshop.

The things he wanted those lips to do suddenly included blowing on other parts of his body.

Talk about hot.

"That's what I'm asking."

What? He gave his head a quick shake. "Sorry?"

"Focus here. Karl called me an hour ago, screaming his head off, after Don Harding called him. Don has an alert out for any shootings involving frangible ammo."

Frangible ammo. The weight of those two little words forced Way's shoulders to dip. "Don't even tell me."

"Oh, I'm telling you. Petra Cheevers died from a bullet that ate a hole through her heart."

Not again. Way closed his eyes, fought the rancidness in

his gut and the bile it shoved into his throat. After a second, he opened his eyes again. "Mine?"

"If it wasn't yours, it's the same design. Do you know her? She's not a client or anything?"

"No. I've never heard of her." He gestured at the television. "They said she owns a bunch of convenience stores in the next county."

"Yes. And she has no affiliations to the Street Dragons."

Fuck. "You're sure? She's not married to or has kids with one of 'em?"

Roni shook her head. "No. She's married to a plumber. They have three young boys. She inherited the stores from her father and has been running them for three years. From what I can find, she's clean."

He leaned in. "And what? There was a giant sign near her body saying my bullet killed her?"

"I did *not* say that and you know it."

"Wasn't Jeff posing as a convenience store owner while he was on the task force? Maybe *he's* the connection? All this shit points to your buddy Jeff as much as me, but you don't want to believe that do you? That your *friend* is dirty. Because"—he threw his hands up—"God forbid that you, a woman who's sworn off trusting anyone, should be duped. Betrayed by someone you believed in."

She poked her finger at him. "Knock it off. Right now."

"No. Guess what, Roni? You're human. Like the rest of us. People get screwed and you, babe, got screwed."

"You don't know half the shit I've seen."

Screaming at Roni wouldn't help him. And he sure as hell didn't want to fight with her. Not with another victim dead from one of his bullets. He held his hands up. "You're right. I was way off out of line. I apologize."

She peered up at him, her eyes tiny slits.

"Seriously," he said. "I was wrong. You didn't deserve that."

Slowly, her features softened, her narrowed eyes relaxing. "Thank you. Apology accepted."

"Good. Petra Cheevers."

"We have to figure out if there's a connection to your bullet design."

"I know. And there's only one way to do that."

"How?"

"We're going to the source. I'm calling Don Harding."

15

WAY HAD TO BE OUT OF HIS MIND. STONE COLD CRAZY.

He didn't give a shit either.

"You cannot call him," Roni said.

Sure he could. "Why? My State Department guy isn't giving me anything. He's probably terrified to get into the middle of it, and I need answers."

"He got you the CIA deal."

Well, well, she'd been busy. "You know about that?"

"I overheard you say his name and asked Karl about him last night. By the way, he wasn't too happy with me. I had to tell him about our alliance."

Ballsy chick. Damn, he enjoyed a fearless woman. "How'd that go?"

"Could have been worse. Even he's not completely sold that this design didn't come out of Langley. Honestly, I think he wants to know as much as we do."

Way shrugged. He didn't trust any of the suits right now. "What'd he say?"

"He told me he met Clay at Bernadette's party."

"Yeah. Clay knew I had a design I was testing. Suggested we run it by the powers that be. See if the spec ops guys could use ammo that destructed on impact. Plausible deniability and all that. Within a couple of weeks, I had a meeting at Langley."

"With Don?"

Way nodded. "Yes, ma'am. He had some others in the meeting. I handed over twenty-five test bullets. Two weeks later, they came back and asked me to tweak the design. Which I did. I sent them another small batch and they requested more. We did the same routine a few times, and they've been testing them ever since."

"Total of a hundred?"

"Yeah. According to Clay, they're all accounted for."

Roni made a humming noise, then ran her top teeth over her bottom lip—and distracted the hell out of him—while she mulled the thing over. "Would he tell you the truth?" she finally asked.

"I hope so."

"But you're not positive."

Way tilted his head. "I'm kinda like you, Roni. I want to believe my old friend isn't dirty. We served together. Did things for our country most aren't capable of. I'd trust him with my life."

"What about with your bullet design?"

"Right now, I'm not sure who I trust." He picked up his cell, punched at the screen. "Let's call Don Harding. See what he knows about my bullets."

HARDING'S SECRETARY—OH, EXCUSE ME, HIS ADMINISTRATIVE assistant. God help Way if he called someone a secretary. A few months back, Maggie chewed him out royally for calling her assistant a secretary. Apparently, it was majorly un-PC to do so.

Lesson learned. The hard way.

"Good morning," he said to Harding's assistant. "This is Waylon Kingston for Mr. Harding. Is he available?"

"One moment please."

Hold music filled his ear and he grinned at Roni. "I'm on hold."

"I can't believe you're doing this."

He waved it away. "Let's poke this bear. See how mad he gets."

"You're aware bears maul people?"

"Oh, I'm aware." The music stopped and he held up a finger.

"Please hold for Mr. Harding," the assistant said.

Way cut his gaze to Roni and nodded. "Thank you."

More hold music sounded and then abruptly stopped. "Don Harding," the gruff voice boomed through the phone line.

"Way Kingston here."

"Mr. Kingston," Don said, his voice smoother. Not so rushed. "What can I do for you?"

There were two options for Way. The delicate way, easing into a conversation about the status of the CIA's testing of his design, or the not-so-delicate way.

He considered it for half a second.

People were dying.

Fuck delicate.

"Petra Cheevers. Run her name. And then tell me how the hell my bullets got out of Langley."

In front of him, Roni's jaw flopped open, her cute little nose scrunching at the same time. Damned cute look.

He'd have to be careful. Keep her out of this as much as possible.

"You must be mistaken," Harding said. "Every sample you sent us is accounted for. Bet on it."

Ha. When it came to the CIA, he wouldn't bet on anything. "Only an idiot makes that bet when people are dying from my bullets. I'm not an idiot."

"You should know, we're currently tearing your finances apart. If one of your deposits is off by a penny, I'll be on you. You sold that design to a murderer. I hope you can live with it."

Nice ploy at baiting him. Way forced a smile, willed his mind to stay focused, keep it light, and not lose his temper. "I sleep fine at night. Why would I be dumb enough to double-dip on a deal with the CIA, an organization more than willing to eliminate anyone in its way? I have nothing to gain."

"Money."

He wasn't exactly living a luxurious life. Sure, he had a nice income—all of it with the proper paper trail. "Check my finances all you want. You won't find anything. If these bullets are my design, they didn't come from me. Which means you have a mole in your department. You'll want to get that cleaned up before it leaks that the CIA lost track of acid-filled ammunition."

The line went quiet and Way's heart rate exploded. The *thump, thump, thump* whacked against the inside of his chest. He swallowed, trying to control his breathing, because, yeah, he'd just threatened the CIA.

"Are you threatening to go to the press?"

Way considered it for a moment. Even if it bankrupted him, he wouldn't allow his design to be used on civilians.

"Find out who leaked my design, Harding. I'm done fucking around."

Before the man could respond, Way poked at the screen, made sure it disconnected, and let out a hard breath.

"Wow," Roni said.

Way tossed the phone on his workbench, watched as it clattered against the wood, then met Roni's gaze. "No kidding. Let's see what he does."

THIS MIGHT BE ABOVE RONI'S PAY GRADE.

Memories of lying on a lumpy mattress, huddled under the covers, praying for peaceful sleep and no pervs peeking in her bedroom door, assailed her.

That feeling, that lack of control devoured her, making her stomach pitch.

Before she did anything, she needed a second to regroup, think the situation through. She settled onto the stool by Way's workbench and closed her eyes.

His warm fingers touched her skin. Childhood instincts roared back and she flinched, snapping her arm away before popping her eyes open.

He lifted his hand, held them both up. "I'm sorry. I shouldn't sneak up on you. You okay?"

Not even close. Somehow, her simple assignment to investigate Way Kingston had turned into a...thing. A thing that left her wondering if the CIA might be setting her target up.

Or if Way might be playing her. Slowly convincing her of his innocence just to get the agency off his tail.

Who to trust?

She shook her head and faced Way, gazing into intense dark eyes that might be holding all sorts of secrets. "You think threatening the CIA with the release of top-secret information is the way to go?"

"Part of this game is getting the killer's attention. If someone in Harding's department—maybe Harding himself —sold my design, I want them to know I'm not afraid of a public fight."

"Even if it gets you killed?"

He waved that off like she was some fool woman. Well, this fool woman had seen enough criminal activity to know certain people had no soul. Zero conscience. And whoever was running around shooting acid bullets was driven by something. Something deep and angry and ferocious. Way Kingston shooting off his mouth would only fuel that anger.

A person capable of this kind of violence would have no issue with adding one more kill to their roster.

"I can take care of myself," he said.

Idiot. As if any of this measured his ability to protect himself. "I'm sure, but taking on the CIA isn't exactly the way to make friends in Washington."

He shrugged. "I don't care about friends in Washington. I won't have my reputation destroyed because the CIA screwed me."

She didn't want to believe it. That the agency would so willingly sacrifice a contractor. But, she supposed, this was politics. Most times, politics stunk.

Her own phone rang. No doubt who this was. In her short time with the agency, she'd learned how fast information traveled. She pulled the phone from her back pocket and saw Karl Quigley's cell phone number light up her screen.

She held it for Way to see. "Karl."

He grinned. "See? That didn't take long."

At least someone was entertained. Roni? She had a hole

burning through her stomach. After Karl's impromptu visit last night, who the hell knew where he might be. He'd hopped into the rear passenger seat of the SUV and left.

Her best guess was he'd flown back to Langley after checking on her.

Might as well face this new round of wrath and get it over with. "I have to take this."

Roni headed toward the back door for privacy. Way might eavesdrop, but there wasn't a whole hell of a lot she could do about that.

She pushed through the door, stepping out into cool morning air and bright sunshine. "Hello, sir."

"Don't give me that bullshit. How does Kingston know how Petra Cheevers died? You *told* him?"

Roni blew out a long breath. Her years in the system taught her many hard lessons. The art of deflection being one of them. "I've told you he has his own contacts. He doesn't need me."

"I'm on Clay Bartles," Karl said, his voice loud enough to be heard in the next county. "Who else? I want their heads on a spit!"

A vision of her head mounted on a spike filled Roni's mind. She glanced back at the door that had swung closed behind her.

"I don't know," she said.

In the grand scheme, it wasn't a lie. How would she know who Way's friends were? He certainly hadn't offered her a list of their names.

"Sir, this latest shooting is still unfolding. Let me reach out to people. See what I can dig up. We may have a bigger problem."

"What's that?"

"The FBI, sir."

"What the fuck do they have to do with this?"

"These murders were all carried out in the same manner."

Karl didn't get to his position by being a dope, so Roni let the silence play out while he absorbed her statement.

"Shit," he said.

"Yes, sir. The common characteristics—the frangible bullets—suggest the possibility that these acts were committed by the same person. Which means—"

"Serial killer."

Bingo. *You've just won a microwave!* "Yes, sir."

Given the Bureau's expertise in behavioral analysis, all a local law enforcement agency had to do was indicate they might have a serial killer running loose and the FBI could intervene.

Which meant more investigators searching for a top-secret frangible bullet. And if that bullet was found in a CIA lab?

"Political shitstorm," Karl said.

"Yes, sir. I believe you are correct."

The line went dead.

"Hello?"

Roni pulled the phone from her ear and checked the screen. Call ended. She tipped her head back, peering up at a sky so blue she couldn't imagine one single bad thing happening under it.

But, oh, bad things had most definitely happened.

Stowing her phone in her back pocket, she walked to the door leading into Way's workshop. He'd shot a rocket-propelled grenade into an investigation involving a dead ATF agent and two CIA executives. And, somehow, she'd wound up in the middle.

Worse, she didn't know who the liars were. Professional

suicide. That's what this assignment was. She'd come to Steele Ridge fully aware that she'd have to use her friendship with Maggie to get to Way. To prove he had double-dipped on his design.

Except nothing pointed that way. The man's finances were clean, his reputation even more so. Which shouldn't have surprised her, considering his sister's honorable qualities.

Which left what?

Karl Quigley.

In his attempt to protect Don Harding, Karl had misled her about someone on Don's staff possibly leaking Way's design. And, well, making sure Don hadn't done anything illegal.

Stuck. That's what she was. Caught in what could turn into one hell of a nasty scandal.

No way out.

Nuh-uh. She hadn't survived foster care with that kind of fatalist thinking.

She could do this. Even if it meant taking on the CIA.

DITCHING WAY WASN'T AS EASY AS RONI WOULD HAVE LIKED, but she'd give the man credit for his persistence.

He'd peppered her with questions for ten minutes until she admitted she wanted to speak with her contacts regarding the case, but wasn't at liberty to share and would fill him in later.

Scout's honor.

Eventually, he'd agreed. Only after Sam arrived, distracting him with a business issue.

Thank you, Sam.

Now, Roni pulled into a vacant parking space on Main

Street across from Blues, Brews, and Books, affectionately known to locals as the Triple B. Unless things had changed in the last six months, the Triple B, a combination bar, coffee shop, and bookstore was owned by Miranda Shepherd, significant other to Britt Steele, Maggie and Way's cousin.

At this hour, the morning rush would be in full swing, giving locals plenty of opportunity to catch up on town gossip.

And ignore Roni, who'd phoned Maggie and asked her to meet at the B for coffee so they could compare notes on Petra Cheevers.

After dodging an older woman driving an ancient Lincoln, Roni scooted across the street and spotted Maggie, in full uniform, her hair up in the requisite ponytail and her eyes hidden behind a pair of sleek, dark sunglasses that had Jayson Tucker written all over them. Maggie strode along the sidewalk, her gait even, but not rushed. All command presence like they'd been taught in their respective training.

"Girl," Maggie said, "you take your life into your hands jumping in front of Mrs. Royce. She and that Lincoln would crush you like a bug."

"No kidding." Roni jerked her thumb. "She had to be speeding."

"Please. Don't get me started. Remind me to tell you the story about the great duck rescue. My cousin Reid almost became a pancake."

Small-town drama. Had to love it.

An older man pulled into a reserved parking space, and Maggie grabbed Roni's arm. "Let's walk. That's Mr. Greene. When it comes to gossip, he hears everything."

Maggie led her away from the B, heading past a cute little boutique that hadn't yet opened.

"So," Maggie said, "what's up?"

With Maggie being a no-nonsense woman, Roni cut right to it. "Petra Cheevers."

"The murder last night? It's not my jurisdiction, you know."

"I'm aware."

Maggie halted on the sidewalk, checked behind them for busybodies, then cocked her head. "Then why are we talking about this?"

"Because Petra was killed with a frangible bullet similar to the one that blew away Roy Jackson."

From behind the sunglasses, the tops of Maggie's eyebrows hitched up. "And Chad Hopkins. Also out of my jurisdiction."

"Correct."

"Are you telling me it's a serial? That's crossed my mind."

"Sure looks like it. What do you know about Petra Cheevers?"

"I don't know anything. Again, it's not my case."

Roni clucked her tongue. She'd have to be careful. Maggie was unaware of the alliance between Roni and Way. He'd made it clear enough that he didn't want her involved, and Roni respected his intention to keep his sister safe. However, Maggie had access—lots of access—to databases and federal agents and crime labs.

In truth, Roni had that access, too. But it would require her to either come out of the shadows on her secret investigation, or bring Karl and Don up to speed.

Right now, both options stunk.

"Well, Sheriff, how do you feel about making a call and comparing notes with the agency investigating the Cheevers murder? I think this case is connected. And not just by the bullets. It's more than that. At first I thought it was the gang members. But Petra has no gang affiliations."

Maggie dipped her head, peering over her glasses at Roni. "Are you still thinking this has something to do with Jeff and the task force?"

Yes. "What I think is that these murders are connected. The bullets tell us that. We just don't know why."

HERE I AM, ONCE AGAIN SITTING IN A RENTAL CAR, TWO DOORS down from Waylon Kingston's home, pondering my situation. It's dark and the night is unusually warm for February in North Carolina. I inhale the fresh breeze through my half-open window.

I've seen a lot in life, and there are things I constantly question. Terrorism. The intentional deaths of innocent children.

Politics.

Most days, I'm disgusted by the filth wandering this earth. How in hell did we become such a selfish, uncaring society?

Even as I sit here, I feel the weight of my crimes. The deaths I've caused to further my mission.

Guilt? Perhaps.

Sadness.

Absolutely.

It's more than that, though. I'm unable to satisfy the rage that gnaws and scrapes at me from inside, desperate for relief—for freedom—that never comes.

What it'll take, I'm not sure. With each kill, there's another reason to move to the next. I'm not stupid. I know my time will run out. I can live with that.

What I can't live with is the idea that this hateful need

inside me will go unfulfilled. That, undoubtedly, will drive me insane.

A motorcycle engine roars, cracking the silence that comes with evening.

I check my watch: 9:30. Apparently, Way likes an evening ride. I jot that in the notebook next to me, then return my gaze to the windshield.

On a night like this, I can't blame a man for getting out. I myself enjoy long rides in the country.

A motorcycle. Open road, fresh air, being in control.

That's what I need. I make a mental note to research the best motorcycles for beginning riders and feel...hopeful.

Maybe there's an answer. A quenching to this awful thirst.

Two doors down, a lone rider reaches the end of Kingston's driveway. The rider—Kingston, I assume, based on the long, jean-clad legs—pauses and checks traffic.

Did he spot me?

I hunch down, wait for the roar of the engine, and do a quick-peek as he hooks a left, speeding off in the other direction.

The minimal streetlamps on the quiet mountain road works in my favor. Even if Kingston saw the car, he wouldn't have seen me.

I consider whether to follow.

Mountain roads, darkness.

It doesn't take long to decide.

Way Kingston may have just made my life a little easier.

THIS WAS WHAT WAY CRAVED. A LONG RIDE TO CLEAR HIS head and figure out his next steps. Plus, he needed to distract himself from a certain petite brunette who kept creeping into his thoughts.

He didn't know what the hell to do with Roni. Well, he knew what he *wanted* to do with her. He wanted to bury himself inside her and give her multiple orgasms. Over and over and over. All day long he imagined what she'd sound like as she came. Would it be a hard exhalation? Or maybe a sigh.

A long moan.

That one was a killer and, even now, the stir of an erection took his thoughts to places other than the winding road in front of him.

Damn the woman.

What was she doing now? Alone at the B&B only a few blocks west.

At the stop sign, he set his feet on the ground and flipped the visor of his helmet up while contemplating his direction. A light breeze blew across his cheeks and he closed his eyes a second, let the fresh air settle his thoughts. When this mess got cleared up, he'd take off for a couple weeks. Get some downtime.

He loved being on this bike.

But first, the CIA. And how the hell they lost track of his bullets.

He opened his eyes.

Right. He should definitely go right, away from Main Street and the heart of Steele Ridge.

Away from Roni.

Except, on his way out, he'd strapped the extra helmet—the much smaller one for a woman—to the bike. And even as he did it, he knew why.

As if maybe, by his blessed luck, he'd run into her somewhere in this sleepy little town at this hour.

Behind him, a car's headlights swung around the curve, reflecting off the road signs.

Right.

Definitely.

He slapped his visor back in place and made the turn just as his phone rang, the sound coming through his Bluetooth system.

"Hello?"

"Hi."

Roni's voice. She must be psychic. He accelerated, felt the vibration of the engine and the whip of wind against his neck. "Hi."

"Oh," she said. "Sorry. Wind noise. Are you on your bike?"

"I am. Just left. Needed a ride."

"No prob. Do you want to call me back? I have a question about the bullets."

The bullets. Of course. What did he think? That she'd call him up and announce she was butt-naked, waiting for him? Not with his luck. "What's your question?"

"The capsule the acid is in. I'm assuming you bulk order them?"

"I ordered two hundred right before I sent the revised batch to Langley. I test-fired twenty-eight, I used a hundred on the samples now at Langley and I still have the remaining seventy-two. I counted them all to make sure. Why?"

"I was able to get a copy of Roy Jackson's autopsy report."

Please let her tell me something good. Anything that might clear him of any involvement. "And?"

"There's a fragment of the capsule. I don't have photos— yet—but the report says there's part of a number on it."

The manufacturer's lot numbers. Brilliant. He hit the

throttle again and his mood lifted. "You're thinking we might be able to match the lot numbers with my stash?"

"It's a stretch, but..."

"It's worth a try."

"Do you have records of the lot numbers?"

Every goddamned one of them. He wasn't about to release the samples without recording all identifying features.

"I absolutely do. They're in my safe."

"Excellent. Where are you riding to?"

"Not sure yet. Figured fresh air would help me on our next move. You've done it for me." He eased to a stop at the next corner. An image of Roni in one of her tight tank tops filled his mind. "Wanna come for a ride?"

Well, shit. Inviting the woman to hop on the back of his bike, her curvy body snug against him, wouldn't exactly help the semi hard-on he sported.

So much for going right, asshole.

"Now?" she asked.

"I'm eight blocks from you. Throw on boots and a jacket. I got a helmet on the bike."

"Really?"

The raised pitch in her voice indicated a certain level of interest. "Roni, get out of your own head for two seconds. Don't think this to death. Take a break, get some air, and we'll go back to my place and check lot numbers."

Even as he said it, he made a U-turn in the street, passing a black sedan with a lone driver as he doubled back toward Tasky's B&B. "I'm on my way. Jacket and boots, Roni. Be there in two."

16

DON'T RUN WITH SCISSORS.

When Roni was seven, her father had given her that sage advice. Now, at thirty-two, that's all she could think about.

Because, make no mistake, climbing on the back of a motorcycle with the hotness known as Way Kingston wasn't just running with scissors. It was running with a multitude of scissors.

Fistfuls of scissors.

Recently sharpened ones.

And yet, here she was, in her suite, sliding into the only low-heeled rubber-soled boots she'd thrown into her suitcase before heading to Steele Ridge.

For so long, she'd been determined to control her surroundings. Stick to a routine. Limit new people. All of it an effort to reduce the chances of spontaneous events—good or bad—disrupting her life.

Maybe she might even enjoy it.

Outside, the not-so-distant roar of an accelerating engine drew her to the street-facing window. She pushed back the heavy curtain.

One flight below, Way came to a stop at the curb. For a few seconds, she stood in the window, watching him climb off the bike with that easy confidence she'd noted the first time they'd met.

All long legs and lean muscle, Way had...something. An innate calmness that drew her to him. He'd become the change that made her behave differently. Her own personal Chaos Theory.

Not only was she breaking routine by heading out on a motorcycle—*deathtrap, anyone?*—she'd been canoodling with the target of her investigation.

Complicated.

But not enough to keep her from fluffing her hair and grabbing her leather jacket from the wall hook. As soon she opened the door, she heard Mrs. Tasky's voice.

"Well, Waylon Kingston, as I live and breathe. Aren't you a sight for sore eyes?"

Mrs. Tasky had no shortage of clichés.

"I could say the same about you, ma'am," Way said, his voice light and playful.

Lord, Roni liked him.

She reached the base of the stairs and met Way's eye, but quickly broke the contact before the eagle-eyed B&B owner got any ideas about churning the Steele Ridge gossip mill. This late-night visit alone would get the town criers going.

When Way glanced at Roni on the stairs, Mrs. Tasky angled back, eyeing her boots and jeans and jacket.

"Hello, Miss Roni. Y'all going out?"

"Yes, ma'am. I'm sorry we disturbed you."

At least tonight Mrs. T hadn't made it into curlers and a bathrobe yet.

"Oh, nonsense. I was just watching my shows and doing a little needlepoint before bed. Where are you two off to?"

Residents of small towns had no shortage of nerve.

"It's a nice night. I thought we'd go for a ride." Way nodded at Mrs. Tasky and swung the front door open. "Shall we?"

"We shall," Roni said. "Good night, Mrs. Tasky."

"Y'all be careful now."

Advice that, in this case, came too late. Being careful would have meant Roni never leaving her suite.

"We will, ma'am. You be sure to lock this door after us."

Waylon Kingston, Steele Ridge born and bred, had managed to end the conversation without being rude.

Clearly, the man understood people. Whether that came from navigating small-town politics or his time as a Marine —probably both—he was skilled in the art of maneuvering.

Something she'd be wise to remember.

Way led her outside, closing the door behind them. Before Roni's feet left the porch, Way glanced over at her. "You do realize that by eight a.m. the Triple B'll be buzzing about us."

"I was afraid you'd say something like that."

He paused on the walkway and smiled at her. "Small towns, babe. Nothing stays private."

She peered back at the giant farmhouse where Mrs. Tasky peeped out the front window and held a hand up.

"Lord," Roni muttered.

He laughed. "Eight a.m. Count on it. We can skip this, if you want."

"What good will that do? Everyone will still know you were here. If they're going to gossip about me, I might as well not miss out on the fun of the ride, right?"

He pursed his lips, and she assumed some smartass sexual innuendo might be in play.

She smacked his arm. "Don't say it. Not one word."

The two of them broke out laughing and, wow—that little zing of affection felt...good.

Amazing even.

For just those few seconds, she'd let it happen, let herself feel the rush of enjoyment without analyzing the ramifications. One light-hearted moment without worrying about giving herself over to a man and losing him.

Her breath caught. Trapped. Right in her chest. She sucked in her stomach, held it for a moment as she swallowed.

Put it away.

She imagined holding a shovel, filling a hole, packing her sadness and anger away and stomping on the dirt to make sure the ache never came free. Stomp, stomp, stomp.

But, *ohmygod*, he made her want to ditch the shovel. To stop isolating herself and chasing away good people in a twisted attempt to self-protect.

When her eyes filled with tears—*oh, just terrific*—she blinked. Then blinked again. How much humiliation did she have to take?

He tilted his head. "Talk to me."

"I'm so sor—"

"No. Do *not* apologize for how you feel. Ever."

"Is everything all right?" Mrs. Tasky asked from the now open door.

Humiliation complete.

Way squeezed Roni's arm and faced Mrs. Tasky. "Yes, ma'am. Thank you. Roni had to...uh...sneeze."

Sneeze?

Now, that was ridiculous. Ridiculous enough that the tickle in Roni's throat crawled all the way up and somehow turned into a laugh. A good solid one that had her slapping a hand over her mouth.

Way looked at her, a bright smile lighting his face.

"Are y'all *drunk*?" Mrs. Tasky asked, her voice heavy with disapproval.

"No, ma'am. I can promise you that. We're just..." He looked down at Roni. "Well, ma'am. I think we're having some fun here."

Wouldn't *that* make the busybodies euphoric?

Well, screw it.

She'd dealt with a lot of nonsense in her lifetime. Somehow, people gossiping about her seemed...okay. Better than okay. At least, in an odd way, it made her part of something. Something bigger than her isolated world.

She peered back at Mrs. Tasky, who stood one hand on the door, more than ready to close it and get on the phone with her friends.

"Eight a.m.," Way muttered, reminding Roni that by morning the whole town would know about them.

She moved closer to him and bit her lip. "As the song says, let's give them something to talk about."

She went up on tiptoes—how she loved a tall man— wrapped one hand around the back of his neck, and dragged him to her. Their lips met. Unlike the last time they'd kissed, this one was...soft. Slow, even brushes of skin against skin that made Roni's heart pump and swell and —*God*—when had she felt that before? Never. This was everything. Passion and safety and...calm.

Zero chaos in this kiss.

Setting her free hand on his chest, she patted the soft leather of his jacket. "You have a problem, Way Kingston."

"Honey, I have more than one."

She snorted. "True. But now you have another."

"And what's that?"

"I think I'm crazy and I really like kissing you."

His lips twisted as he leaned in, resting his forehead on hers. "First of all, I like crazy. It's never boring. And the kissing? If that's what you consider a problem, it's one I'd like a whole lot more of." Then he smacked her on the ass. "Now, get on this bike before the phone lines combust."

IN WAY'S MIND, THIS WAS WHAT RIDES SHOULD BE. A NICE night, the churn of heat raging in his body, an insanely sexy woman snug up against him while they enjoyed fresh air.

He came to a stop sign and dropped one hand, setting it on her calf and giving her a pat. He loved touching her. Putting his hands against the soft curves of her body. And the places he'd yet to explore? Those haunted him. Kept him up at night.

He checked both directions, then hit the throttle, his mind firmly on Roni. He'd take his time with her. Let it last. Because one thing was for sure, Roni Fenwick had no plans on staying. Based on the file Micki had put together, Roni was a runner.

Her style of running differed from his. He disappeared when his family decided to get up in his business. With Roni it was deeper. Probably because the people she was supposed to be able to depend on had disappointed her.

Abandoned her.

He couldn't blame her father for getting sick. Shitty luck. But her mother? What the fuck? Who walks out on their kid and doesn't come back when she becomes orphaned?

Best he could tell, opening up to people, allowing them to connect, wasn't Roni's thing. Too risky. He couldn't blame her. With all the losses she'd suffered, why should she trust that people wouldn't hurt her?

Behind him, she shifted, tucking her thighs flush against

him and tightening her hold on his waist. "You okay?" he asked.

"Yep," she responded via the Bluetooth system in the helmet. "Just getting comfortable."

Good. He liked her close like this. His body liked it, too. He pictured her, butt-naked and stretched across his bed, that unbelievable body of hers right there for him to feast on. An erection started to stir. Lord, if he didn't do something with that tonight, he'd go fucking insane.

"It's fun being out here with you," she said.

"I had a feeling you'd like the bike."

"Why?"

"It's a solitary thing. I sense you like being alone sometimes."

"I do. Being alone is easy. I'm used to it."

Of all the things she might have said, that one hit him right in the gut. For whatever reason, he didn't want her alone anymore. No matter where this thing with them went, he intended to share his pain in the ass family with her.

"Well"—he let out a soft laugh—"welcome to Steele Ridge, where no one ever leaves you alone."

He made a left.

"Where are we going?"

"Figured I'd take you up the mountain. There's a spot up there I like to stop at. You can see the town. It's cool at night."

He hit the first curve, accelerating through it as Roni leaned with him, instinctively knowing not to knock them off balance as he navigated a series of switchbacks. As usual, the rush of roaring through the mountain's curves brought a sense of euphoria, an absolute high he'd never get tired of.

In short, he loved this. Loved it even more with Roni along for the ride.

Headlights suddenly reflected in his mirror. Which, yeah, kinda pissed him off. Not that he owned the road, but he didn't want to deal with people while having fun with Roni.

The headlights flashed again, drawing his eye to the mirror. The car picked up speed, bearing down on them as he entered the next switchback.

"Hang on," he said to Roni via the Bluetooth. "I'm gonna put some distance between us and that idiot."

God help him if the asshole was drunk. With all these damned switchbacks, he'd run them all clear off the mountain.

The dark mountain road closed in. He inhaled, then slowly released the air, focusing his mind. He'd ridden these roads hundreds, if not thousands, of times in the dark. Trees on his right dipped into a steep wooded drop-off that, if they went over, would kill them.

No going over.

That was for sure.

On his left, a sheet of rock face climbed high into the air, the road literally wrapping around it for miles. Any escape would be straight on this road or roughly a mile and a half ahead, where a small patch of graveled shoulder served as an emergency area. If he could get there, he'd slide right in and let the asshole blow on by.

Behind them, the asshole came out of the S curve they'd just maneuvered through and hit the gas. The sound of his engine gunning bounced off the rock face on the quiet mountain road.

The front grill of the car reflected in Way's mirror. *Holy shit*. This guy was nuts getting that close on these roads.

Had to be drunk. Wasted or sober, he was too damned close.

Way hit the throttle and the bike came alive, easily leaping forward, handling the curves like a champ. He shot through the next turn, the bike leaning far to the left, and Roni let out a gasp.

"We're good," he said. "Stay with me."

Headlights reflected again as the car, unable to react as fast to the tricky road, came around the turn. He pushed the bike harder, increasing speed again.

Way envisioned the next switchback. Hard left and a straightaway for maybe five hundred yards. And then, the emergency cutoff.

He navigated the sharp turn with Roni glued to him. Once clear, he hit the throttle, shooting through the darkness and putting enough distance between them and the car to give him time to pull off.

There it was. The sign for the emergency area.

"I'm pulling over up here. We'll let him go by."

"Thank God. He's freaking me out."

"Yeah. Too dangerous on these roads. I can't believe he hasn't gone off the side."

The car's headlights flashed as the guy came around the curve, but Way cruised into the cutoff, coming to a stop next to the six feet of guardrail at the edge of the cliff.

He spun back, looking over Roni's shoulder as the sedan barreled straight for them.

Jesus. "Run!" he shouted into the Bluetooth.

"What?"

"Move it. Now!"

They made a mess of tangling legs as they hopped off the bike. Roni's foot caught on the seat, sending her stumbling, and Way's pulse exploded. Panic surged. *Shit, shit, shit.* They had to move.

He latched on to her arm, kept her from hitting the

ground. She scrambled, her feet slipping against the loose gravel as Way damn near pulled her arm from the socket.

He glanced around, his head swiveling, searching for shelter.

The guardrail wouldn't help. Nothing but a drop-off on the other side.

A clump of trees behind where he'd pulled in.

Only option.

"Go!" he shouted. "To those trees!"

The car's gunning engine drew closer, the lights ricocheting off the guardrail. *Fuck*. This guy was about to take them all over the edge.

"Jump!"

Chest heaving, Way went airborne, dragging Roni through the air with him as he twisted around, hoping to take the brunt of the fall and cushion her.

A bush clawed his face and something warm—blood—oozed down his left cheek. He landed on his side, the impact whipping his neck as Roni landed half on top of him.

Ugh. Pain tore at his ribs, sending paralyzing shocks in all directions. Damn, that hurt.

At least he'd taken the majority of the hit.

He peered back at the road. The oncoming car.

His bike.

"No!"

The driver slammed his brakes, ramming into Way's bike, the one he'd rebuilt—tip-to tail—

himself.

No.

Momentum carried it forward, pushing it toward the end of the guardrail. The horrendous screech of metal against metal echoed as the bike scraped against the guardrail.

And then—gone. The bike tipped over the edge and, from the sound of crunching steel, crashed against rock, tumbling to the base of the mountain.

Way leaped to his feet and sprinted straight for the car. The driver, submerged in the dark interior, stomped the gas and shot backward.

Before Way reached the road, the driver stopped and the clunk of shifting gears sounded again.

Tires spun, searching for traction and Way sprinted toward the car, catching up and grabbing hold of the door handle.

Locked.

Goddamnit. He banged his fist against the glass, trying to peer inside. Hat. The driver wore a black hat or something.

The tires finally caught and the car lurched forward. Way pumped his feet.

He couldn't do it. Couldn't run fast enough, and hanging on wasn't worth the injuries he'd suffer.

He let go, tripped and stumbled two, maybe three, feet.

Going down.

No doubt. Protecting his already banged-up ribs, he twisted his body, landing hard on his elbow.

"Ach! Goddamnit!"

A shock of pain lanced straight up his arm, smothering his shoulder and neck. He'd be lucky if he didn't dislocate something.

"Way?"

Taillights rounded the descending curve and disappeared.

Son of a bitch.

Way sat up, found Roni charging toward him.

"I'm okay," he called. "Are you alright?"

She halted in front of him and squatted. "You're sure? Oh my God! That guy was crazy."

She reached for him. "Ow. Easy on the arm. My elbow is screaming. Fucker could have killed us. You sure you're all right?"

"I'm okay. I'll be sore tomorrow, but okay." She stood and held his good arm. "You should get up before another car comes around."

She helped him to his feet and dug into her jacket pocket, holding up her phone. "I'll call for help."

"You didn't happen to get the plate number did you?"

"I sure did. I looked when he first pulled up behind us. He's toast."

17

"WAY!"

Ah, shit. The last voice he wanted to hear right now was that of his overbearing sister. He shot a look at Blaine—Deputy Do-Right, as Reid called him.

"I didn't call her," Do-Right said. "Probably heard it on the scanner."

"Uh-oh," Roni said. "She won't be happy."

Way let out a sigh, then turned and found his sister, backlit by the spotlight the road crew had set up, in full-on charging bull mode. She wore workout tights and an oversized T-shirt he suspected was Jayson's. Her hair was clipped back, the ponytail bobbing as she approached. Given her early morning workouts, she may have rolled out of bed for this event.

Before she got close enough to blast him, he held up a hand. "Don't freak. We're fine."

Maggie, being Maggie, kept on walking, hurdling straight for him. This would not be fun.

Bracing himself, he took three steps, ready to intercept and shut her the hell up the minute she started yelling.

Instead, she plowed right into him, wrapping him in a hug that sent a fresh batch of pain through his ribs.

"Ach."

"Oh my God," she said. "You're okay."

As much as she liked to tangle with him, lecture him on what he should be doing and when, his sister had a protective streak bigger than the county in her care. By the way she held on to him, she was half out of her mind with worry.

He slid his arms around her, patting her back and pressing his lips against the side of her head. "I'm okay. We're good. I promise."

She stepped backward, holding him at arm's length, and, yeah, that hurt a little, too.

"You're sure? Nothing is broken? You've got a cut. Blaine, get those EMTs over here. He needs to go to the hospital and get checked for a head injury."

"Mags, stop. I'm okay. A little sore."

She turned to Roni. "Are you hurt? What do you need?"

"Nothing. I'm good. I'll have some bruises, but I'm fine."

"Mags," Way said again, "shut up a minute."

She smacked her mouth closed and drew her eyebrows together, deepening the crease enough to bury a body in there.

She cocked her head. "Pardon? You almost get yourself killed and you tell me to shut up? What were the two of you doing out here? Are you insane?"

"He must be," Do-Right muttered.

Maggie sucked in a breath and turned to Do-Right. "Blaine, give us a second. Please."

She waited for the deputy to wander off before facing them down. "What happened?"

Way took that one. "Car ran us off the road."

"What car? Did you recognize it?"

He shook his head. "No. Black sedan. A Nissan, I think. Roni got the plate."

"Good. I swear, Waylon, how many times have I warned you about riding that damned bike on these roads at night? It's too dangerous."

"Hey," he said, "what the hell are you yelling at me for? It's not my fault some asshole tried to run us down." He jerked his thumb toward the guardrail. "And did you notice my bike is gone?"

She scanned the emergency area. "What?"

"I put years into that thing and it's...gone. Over the goddamned side. That fucker better pray I don't find him."

"Oh, my God. Waylon! You're lucky that bike was all you lost." Maggie shook her head. "I can't believe someone would do this. Roni, give me that plate number. We'll take care of this right now."

That quickly, his sister went from anxious family member to determined sheriff.

Roni recited the plate number to Maggie, who tapped it into her phone. "You're positive about this?"

"I'm sure. The car had a light over the plate."

"Excellent. Give me a couple of minutes to run this down. Sit tight."

She hustled off, leaving Way and Roni standing on the side of the road while deputies and various other folks analyzed the scene.

The full weight of the situation descended again. Way gritted his teeth. *Fucker, fucker, fucker.* Both he and Roni could have been killed.

Mind spinning with visions of the two of them tumbling over a cliff, he ran his hand over his face while his gut seized.

"Are you okay?" Roni asked, gently touching his good arm.

"It's...hitting me. What could have happened out here."

She glanced over at the emergency flares in the road. "It could have been bad, no doubt. It's not your fault, though."

Wasn't it? He'd been on these roads thousands of times without incident. As soon as he threatened to go public about a CIA breach, someone tried to run them off the road.

Could they have... "Shit."

"What?"

He peered down at Roni, studied her beautiful face and dark eyes that kept his mind firmly in the gutter. Sexual fantasies sure beat the thoughts currently shredding him.

"I don't know. I'm thinking crazy, right now."

"Why?"

She worked for the agency. If he said it, she'd laugh at him.

She stepped closer, getting into his space, and the smell of her soap, something musky, fired his senses.

"You think the agency set this up."

Maybe he wasn't crazy. "It's nuts, right?"

"Honestly? I don't know. The timing, considering your call with Don, makes me wonder. But, the CIA taking out American citizens? I don't want to believe that."

"Yeah, well, they're thinking about the bigger picture. I'm a pain in the ass they can sacrifice."

"Let's see what Maggie says about the plate number. This could be random. Some drunk kid screwing with us."

The plate number. She was right. Once they had the tag info, they'd move to the next step of tracking this fucker.

"Damn," Way said. "You're good. I can't believe you caught that tag."

"My Quantico training is hard to shake."

Right now, that training might be saving them.

At the edge of the road, Maggie exited her cruiser and marched back to them. "Well, kids, we've got a problem. Plates don't match the car."

Of course. "They were stolen?"

Maggie shrugged. "Probably. I'll contact the owner of the plates and see what I can find out."

"So now what? We sit around and wait? He could have killed us."

Not to mention that he destroyed Way's prized possession.

"Waylon, relax."

He gawked at her. Relax? Seriously? He knew his sister, knew this to be her way of trying to remain calm in a toxic situation. Even if this was Maggie's way of dealing with stress—after all, her little brother almost went careening off a mountain—her attitude pissed him off.

"No, Mags."

"No what?"

"I won't relax." He jabbed his finger to the spot where his beloved bike went over. "That was my bike!"

"I know. Believe me. But, hey, better the bike than you, right?"

She didn't get it. And, yeah, logically, he understood she was trying to get him focused. To wrap his mind around the fact that he wasn't lying at the base of a mountain in a broken heap for his parents to bury.

But goddammit...his bike.

"I know what you're doing here," he said, "but back off."

His sister sighed.

"And quit that sighing. That was a 1985 Sportster! A 1985, Mags."

"I know what it means to you."

"Do you?"

She slid a gaze to Roni, then back to Way. "Don't yell at me. And, yes. I do."

"Then you'd know that this is killing me right now." He balled his fists, squeezing so tight the tips of his fingers should have snapped clear off.

He had to move. Get away from her and burn off the aggravation. He walked away, his steps quick and merciless as his feet pounded gravel.

Good old, dependable Maggie. Everyone's savior, ready to fix every damned thing whether he wanted her to or not.

All.

The.

Time.

Way couldn't deal with her trying to be the calm in the storm when he wanted to fucking *pummel* something. Just put his hands around the neck of that driver and squeeze.

His bike...

He reached the guardrail and stopped. Halted on the edge of the cliff.

Jesus. Nowhere to go. He turned, found Maggie and Roni, backlit by the emergency spotlight.

Great. Now they thought he was nuts. He turned, headed back to the road, and shoved his hands in his pockets just to have something to do with them. He sure as hell couldn't hit anyone.

Punching a guardrail would just be fucking stupid.

Focus here.

First, his bullets hit the street and now this? The bullets —why did he even do it? After ten years in the military he knew the risks of getting into bed with the government.

And now...his bike. He reached the edge of the road, his toes hitting blacktop. Walking there would be yet another stupid idea. Even lit up like this, a car could run him down.

Nowhere to go.

Shit.

He whipped back. Paced the gravel, stopping at the guardrail. Trapped. That's what he was.

He tipped his head back, stared at a starlit sky.

All that open space and peace.

He'd rebuild the bike.

Way lifted his head, looking out into the blackness over the cliff. His brother Shep, the expert climber. That's who he'd call.

He'd know how to rappel down and collect the pieces.

Behind Way, the crunch of rocks underfoot brought him from his thoughts. His sister couldn't help herself. Just had to get into it with him.

"Mags, you need to give me a second."

"It's me."

Roni.

Excellent. The full fucked-up-ness of the situation descended like the crash of his bike against the mountain. Roni had witnessed the whole thing. His words with Maggie, his meltdown, his storming off.

Yeah, real mature, pal.

He turned away from the guardrail and spotted her closing the last few feet between them. God, she could have been killed. Maggie was right. The two of them could be dead right now, and he was whining about a motorcycle?

"I'm sorry," he said.

"About what?"

He pulled his hand from his pocket, waved it above the rail. "My shit-fit over the bike. It's a hunk of metal."

"Something tells me it's a hunk of metal that was important to you."

"Yeah. A little bit."

"I get that."

He gazed at her, but in the darkness couldn't read any facial cues. "Roni?"

"Yes?"

"Are you head-shrinking me, right now?"

She snorted. "No. Truly. I had a sweater once."

A sweater story. *Yeah, totally head-shrinking me.*

"It was my dad's," she said. "I had it until I was fifteen. I was in yet another foster home. They were okay people, super religious. They had a rebellious son. He was sixteen and he'd spy on me, do little things to annoy me. Throw my stuff in the yard, bang on the bathroom door when I was in there. Stupid stuff."

"What an ass."

"He had issues, for sure. Anyway, I came home from school one day and the sweater was gone."

Come on? Seriously? "He took your *sweater*?"

She shrugged. "I could never prove it, but I went nuts. I stormed into his room demanding he give it back. One thing led to another and I slugged him." She made a fist and threw a punch. "Bam! Just let him have it right on that hateful mouth of his."

At that, Way smiled. Tough little Roni Fenwick. "No way."

"Yep. Within two hours, they removed me from that home. I didn't care either. He'd tormented me. Now, knowing what I know about psychological behaviors, I recognize that he was a predator. When I was in college, I did an Internet search on him. He's in prison now. Rape."

Oh, man. She'd seen some nastiness. "I'm sorry."

"Don't be. I don't regret punching him. I regret the violence, but, for every woman he violated, he deserved that punch. And then, on the flip side, I wonder if I fueled his rage. Did my punch make him even angrier at women?"

Hell no. Way wasn't gonna stand there and let her take responsibility for that sicko. "You can't take that on. You know that, don't you? That whatever was going on in that guy's mind wasn't your fault."

"Intellectually, I know, but I wonder." Facing the road, she sat down on the guardrail, hooked her hands over the top and kicked at the stones at her feet. "My point is, I get how material possessions can matter beyond reason. Tell me about the motorcycle. What's its story?"

Definitely head-shrinking him.

Or maybe not.

He was no expert on vulnerability, but he knew enough to recognize she'd just shared something intensely personal.

In return, he'd do the same. And maybe showing her that vulnerability didn't mean weakness.

He sat down next to her and glanced over at the police cruisers. The swirling red lights bounced off the rock face on the opposite side of the road.

"I have," he said, "well, *had* two bikes. The one we just lost was the first bike I ever owned. A 1985 Harley Sportster. I bought it off a high-school buddy's dad for two thousand bucks."

She let out a whistle. "You were in *high school*? How did you afford it?"

"He let me make payments until I paid it off. Took me two years. Besides, when I bought it, it didn't run and had a ton of rust on it. Back then, I knew a little about engines, but not a lot."

"And yet, you bought a bike that didn't run."

He laughed. "Yeah. I saw the potential. Plus, I needed something to love."

"I'm sorry?"

"I've mentioned I was alone a lot when I was a kid. At times, I liked the freedom of being on my own. I'd hop on my mountain bike and disappear for a few hours. Ride some trails and explore."

"You entertained yourself. I know all about it."

"Yeah." He smiled at her. "And, well, when I got to high school, porn may have been involved."

"Oh my God." She laughed. "Thanks for oversharing."

If she thought that was oversharing, Way wouldn't tell her about going online and showing Shep his first set of tits. Older brothers. Gotta take care of the younger ones.

He bumped her with his shoulder. "I'd been mountain biking, but as I got older, I wanted more. The rusty motorcycle was the next step. My dad isn't exactly handy with an engine, but my cousin Reid is. Reid helped me get that bike going and then Dad helped me with the cosmetic stuff. Adding chrome, that sort of thing."

"It was more than a bike to you."

He nodded. "Yeah. It gave me something to do. Kept me out of trouble. Over the years, I've spent a ton of time customizing it." He glanced behind him to where his beloved bike tumbled to its demise. "I love that bike. It's a classic."

In the darkness, he met her eye and something in his brain snicked.

He'd devoted years of attention to a motorcycle because, well, it didn't expect anything from him. No questions about where he spent his time, who he was with. Yet, it had always been there on a bad day or when his family made him nuts. He'd hop on the bike and disappear.

The bike, in short, became his lover.

And how fucking twisted was that? That he'd let an object fulfill what he'd been missing on an emotional level.

It had to stop. This kingdom of one.

Roni Fenwick.

Headshrinker.

"You'll rebuild it," Roni said.

He blew air through his lips, then jerked his head. "I'll rebuild it. For fun. Because it's a cool toy."

She smiled at him. "You don't *need* it, Way. Just like I didn't need the sweater. I liked having it, but it didn't make me who I was. I made me who I am. I suspect the same about you. You're a good man, Waylon Kingston. You don't need a motorcycle to prove it."

Roni followed Maggie to her cruiser with Way lagging a step behind. She glanced to her right where, ninety minutes earlier, Way's motorcycle had gone hurtling over the banged-up guardrail.

Lord, it had been a wild night. Adding Maggie and her curious glances wasn't helping. The woman wasn't stupid. Her brother and her friend—a CIA agent who'd shown up in town unexpectedly—had almost been killed.

Yes, Maggie had questions. She was also too much of a professional to ask them. But Roni had to handle it or wind up alienating one of her few trusted friends.

Except, Roni had no answers. Zip, nada, zero. Add her attraction to Way and things got...complicated.

An assignment.

That's all this should have been. A damned investigation into secret ammunition with a distant tie to Jeff Ambrose's unsolved murder.

That was a few days ago. Now? She still intended to solve both crimes.

She also wanted to bang the hell out of her supposed prime suspect.

Who was she kidding? With Way, it was more than sex. From the second she'd seen him, she'd been curious. Looks aside, the man had an edge. A charming, sort-of-rough edge that didn't allow him to get spooked by an expert at pushing men away.

The absolute pull of him, that down deep attraction to his determination and lack of fear in taking on the CIA, might literally destroy her.

Corny as it sounded, this was a man of honor.

And she sure as hell hadn't had many of those in her life.

As they reached the car, Maggie shot her a look before sliding into the driver's side.

Complicated.

"You take the front," Way said to Roni.

She nodded and joined Maggie in the front seat of the cruiser.

When Way settled into his seat, Maggie met his eye in the rearview mirror. "I'll take Roni back to Mrs. Tasky's first."

Roni didn't know Steele Ridge all that well, but she knew it would be more efficient to drop Way off and then head into town.

Which only meant big sister intended on having some sort of talk with her brother. *Not happening.* Roni was done with people in power excluding her from conversations. If Maggie wanted to talk about her, she'd do it in front of her.

No discussion.

"Seems to me," Roni said, "it would be easier to drop Way off first."

"I don't mind the extra driving." Maggie shifted the cruiser into gear, punching the gas with the confidence of someone all-too-familiar with the winding road.

"Maggie," Roni said, "what's on your mind?"

Her friend kept her eyes on the road, shooting through darkness and roaring around a curve. "I have a lot on my mind. Guessing you know that. I'm not sure this is the time."

"Well, when is the time?"

"Christ," Way said from the backseat. "Someone kill me."

Maggie glanced in the mirror. "After what just happened, not funny, Waylon."

"Bad timing. Sorry. How's about we all just shut up?"

Ha. Good luck there.

Roni twisted around, the pressure of the seatbelt tugging on her. She gripped it, gave it a good yank for maneuvering room, then peered at Way over the seat. "You know what she's doing. She's dropping me off first so she can grill you about why we were together."

"Of course I know that."

"I do *not* like people talking about me when I'm not around. It involves me. I should be included."

The pressure of the seatbelt irritated her—or maybe it was the situation. Roni turned front again and stared out the windshield into the darkness while the tension in the car nearly strangled her.

"Fine," Maggie said, her voice a little too snappy for Roni's taste. "Let's talk. What's going on with you two? And don't try to deny it. I've got a county to oversee and you two are up to something."

MAGGIE TOOK THE NEXT TURN A LITTLE TOO HARD AND

momentum shifted Way left. After years of driving this mountain, his sister knew it well enough that he didn't worry about her crashing. But she was keyed up right now and that, mixed with blackness and an unforgiving mountain, didn't necessarily make for comfort.

"Mags, all due respect, take it easy. It's been a long night."

She hit a straightaway and gave him another second of hard eye contact via the rearview. His sister had questions.

Lots of them.

And he might or might not answer them. Time would tell.

Way shut up and focused on the back of Roni's head. If they were smart, they'd all get some sleep and discuss this in the morning.

On his best day, his family's meddling taxed him. Never mind after someone nearly knocked him off a mountain.

"Waylon," Maggie said, "start talking."

"About?"

"Please. Don't be an ass. You almost got yourself killed tonight. And worse, you brought Roni along for the ride. Literally."

Roni put up a hand. "Oh, now, hold on, Maggie."

Mags? Hold on? Please. That was the dead last thing she'd do.

"I will not hold on. My brother—a gunsmith—called me two days ago with questions regarding the type of bullet used in a murder." Maggie took another glance at him in the rearview, then went back to the road. She ripped through a hairpin turn, cutting it way too close to the gravel edge.

Jesus, she might kill them yet. "Maggie, slow down."

She eased off the accelerator. "Since when are you, of all people, afraid of fast driving? Or maybe you're changing the subject, because God forbid Waylon Kingston should have to explain himself."

Yep. *Here we go.*

Except she lifted one hand from the wheel and waved it off. "Forget it. I'm not fighting with you about that. This is a police matter and I'm a cop. I ask questions. Deal with it."

A police matter. This thing was starting to unravel, and the one thing he didn't want was Maggie involved. And yet, here they were with her square in the middle. He owed her at least a partial explanation. "So, ask your questions."

"Fine. Let me tell you how this looks. My friend, who works for the CIA, shows up unannounced inquiring about a gang shooting that may or may not be connected to the unsolved murder of a colleague. A few days later, my brother, who builds and modifies weapons and ammunition for a living, asks me questions regarding yet another murder committed with the same frangible bullets. Now we've had two more murders committed with highly specialized bullets that, in the whole of my career, I've never seen. And both murders were in fairly close proximity to my county and you, the ammunition expert."

Hidden in darkness, Way flinched. When she laid it out that way, it did look bad.

He leaned forward. "You came to me first, remember? You asked my advice. Why shouldn't I be curious about that second shooting? I'm a gun guy."

"Gang members slaughter each other all the time and you never asked. It's been driving me crazy since you called me, but heaven help me if I ask you about it. You'll just jump on me about butting into your business. As if I'm not allowed to be concerned about my brother. Well, guess what? Too fucking bad."

Oh, wow. His sister dropping an f bomb.

"I want to know," she ranted, "why you care about these shootings. If it's idle curiosity, fine, I'd be thrilled. But if it's more, you better tell me right now so I can help you."

To that, he had no answer. Other than the obvious one... that he was indirectly involved in the whole godforsaken mess.

Roni swung around and faced him.

"We should tell her."

It took every bit of his control to stay silent. Why in hell would he want to tell her? From the beginning, he'd wanted to avoid getting Maggie involved. Bad enough there was some twisted connection with a member of her task force. An extremely dead one.

Throw in the CIA and he had a class-A shitshow on his hands.

Mags navigated the last of the switchbacks leading down the mountain. "Now we're getting somewhere. Tell me what?"

When they stayed silent, Maggie eased the car to a stop at a stop sign and shot them both an I-will-hurt-you look. "That's how we're doing this? Fine. Allow me to be direct." Her foot still on the brake, she angled back to face Way. "Tell me you didn't build these bullets."

Which he couldn't do. Not if the agency could be lying about the test bullets.

Roni swung back and, even in the dark, he saw the desperation in her wide eyes. She didn't like keeping information from her friend.

He loved the loyalty, hated forcing her to choose.

"We have to tell her," Roni said. "Please."

We.

Not you.

With the shit hitting the fan, Roni Fenwick, CIA employee, stepped up to help take the heat.

He peered back at his sister's tight-lipped expression that could have been hurt, worry, or anger. Maybe all.

He'd wanted to shield her from this when, in fact, he probably should have done the exact fucking opposite.

Damn. Way to royally screw the whole thing up.

He held up two hands. "Okay. But you have to listen. Let me finish and then you can ask questions."

He paused for a few seconds and waited for her to nod. Jesus. Maggie silent? He couldn't believe it. They'd see how long it lasted.

"The short of it is," he said, "I designed a frangible bullet that the CIA has been testing."

Her mouth fell open. "The *CIA*? Oh, my God. Let me pull over so I can focus."

She hit the gas again, drove half a block to the now-closed convenience store, and pulled into the empty lot, choosing the first parking space. His sister, had to love her. She had the whole damned lot to herself and made sure to pull into a spot. After shifting to park, she unbuckled her seat belt and spun sideways.

"Okay. Go ahead. The CIA."

"When you came to me with the autopsy photos from that first gang shooting, I, well, I lost my shit a little bit. I mean, how often do you see an acid-filled bullet? Not to mention one that looks a whole lot like one I designed. Anyway, I sent the agency an initial batch over the summer. They asked for some tweaks, which I made. I then sent another batch. They have one hundred total."

She raised her hand. "Can I ask a question? Just for clarification?"

Good old Mags. "Go ahead."

"It's the obvious one—"

"According to the agency," Roni said, "they still have them all."

Maggie faced her, cocking her head one way, then the other. "Oh my God. That's why you're here."

18

SHAME, IN THE FORM OF BILE, CRAWLED UP RONI'S THROAT. She'd known Maggie would eventually figure out she'd been used. By her supposed friend. Roni had hoped it would be after the case wrapped and she could explain how secrecy was a matter of national importance. That the CIA could have been compromised, yada, yada.

None of that happened and any rational explanation, in Roni's mind, fell flat.

"Before you get mad—"

"Oh, I'm already there. You misled me."

No sense denying it. "I did. I tried to avoid it."

"That's what you're going with? Don't patronize me."

"I'm not. Honestly. I've been conflicted about your involvement from the beginning. I thought if I could get you to introduce me to Way, that would be the end of it. That I could keep you out of it."

"She's telling the truth," Way said. "She didn't want to mix you up in this. Neither of us did. This involves the agency's head of science and development and the associate deputy director of administration. They're guys with connections. None of us want to fuck with them."

Maggie faced Roni. "The associate deputy director is your boss, isn't he?"

"He's a couple levels above me, but yes. When the first murder occurred he came to me, along with Don Harding from science and development. Asked me to use my friendship with you to investigate Way. They think he sold the design to someone else. That he's double-dipping."

"He wouldn't do that." Maggie looked at him over the seat. "Tell me you signed an NDA."

"Yeah. I'm clean as a whistle."

"Then where are these bullets coming from?"

They took the next ten minutes to bring Maggie up to speed. As they talked, her ever-efficient friend jotted notes on a dome-light-illuminated notepad she'd pulled from her glove box.

When Way finished, Maggie checked her notes. "You're sure the agency has all one hundred bullets accounted for."

"As far as I can tell."

"And it's not as if the CIA has never lied."

"Maggie—"

Mags pointed at Roni. "You're not innocent in all this. Not by a long shot. The two of you have been running around doing your little investigation—an investigation within my county"—she jabbed her finger into her own chest—"that includes information about a task force I created. And you didn't even bother to tell me? Are you *kidding* me? Give me one good reason why I shouldn't be royally pissed at both of you."

Behind her, the swish of clothing drew her gaze. Way shifting around in his seat. "Are you all right?"

"I'm fine."

What a night. Lord, Roni had blown this. Risked one of the few relationships she truly never wanted to be without. She had to say something, anything, to knock Maggie's rage to a ten rather than a forty.

But she was right. About all of it. Roni let out a sigh, rubbed both hands over her face and let them drop. "You're right. I'm sorry."

"That makes two of us," Way added.

Maggie cocked her head, cupped a hand over her ear. "Come again? Way, did you really just apologize?"

"I know you're pissed."

"Pissed? What I am is worse than that. I'm disappointed, Waylon. Roni is one thing. She had a job to do. I get that. But you're my brother. You should have come to me!"

"He couldn't."

They both swung to Roni, who, as tough as she was, considered staying out of the family squabble. But her role had contributed to this mess.

"Roni," Maggie said, "I'm talking to my brother."

"I know. But this involves me. And, all due respect, Mags, if you'd listen for two minutes, he'd tell you he didn't want to involve you because he knew it would be a conflict for you. Plus, he was worried about you."

"Worried about me? Why?"

"He's dealing with the CIA. Do you think they give a crap about collateral damage? If it meant national security, they'd take both of you out."

He reached over the seat and touched Roni's shoulder. Which only drew his sister's stunned gaze.

"Roni," he said, "we're good here. You don't need to—"

"Yes, I do. This is partially my fault, and I won't sit here and let her tear into you."

Maggie's mouth dropped open and the car filled with an awkward silence that made Roni's skin itch.

"The two of you," Way said. "Shut it. Mags, we screwed up. We're both sorry, but believe me, it was in your best interest. You and I? We don't always agree, but you're my sister and I'll be goddamned if I'm going to put you in harm's way. I don't care if you are the sheriff."

His sister held his stare for a solid ten seconds that could have been ten minutes. Formidable. That was Maggie.

She finally broke eye contact and shook her head.

"Damn you, Waylon."

"I am sorry," he said. "If it means keeping you safe, I'd lie to you ten times over."

After a prolonged and intense study of the convenience store sign, she waved a hand. "You're a pain in the rear, but apology accepted."

Roni leaned back and rested her head against the seat. "I promise you, I'd never intentionally do anything—*anything* —to jeopardize our friendship. God knows, not many people can put up with me. I can't risk losing the ones who can. When I was assigned this case, I wanted to get you out of it while we determined if Way was double-dealing." She stole a glance at him. "Now I know he's not. Together, we're trying to figure this out."

Maggie puckered her lips. "The two of you are enough to kill me."

When they both snickered, Maggie hit them with another of her deadly stares. "I'm not kidding. I almost lost my brother and my friend in one swoop. If you're not going to be careful for yourselves, do it for the people who care about you."

People who care. The words wrapped around Roni, gave her a sense of inclusion she didn't often feel. With that, came guilt. And, wow, she could live without that. But...they *had* deceived Maggie. Straight up kept her out of the loop. And Steele Ridge's sheriff hated not being briefed.

"Message received," Way said. He glanced at Roni. "Right?"

"Absolutely."

Still, clearly agitated, Maggie pointed at Roni. "Are you carrying?"

"Not currently. I have my personal sidearm locked in a lockbox at Mrs. Tasky's."

"Start carrying it."

"You know I will. Besides, I'm in no hurry to piss you off again by defying you."

Way barked out a laugh. "Not so tough now, are you?"

"Everyone's a smart mouth," Maggie muttered.

Roni smiled. "Right now I'm a scared smart mouth. You've never yelled at me. You're kind of a badass."

"Well, this badass wants to know who the hell was driving that car. After what you've just told me, I'm afraid it wasn't a drunk teenager."

AFTER BEING DROPPED OFF AT MRS. TASKY'S, RONI HEADED to her suite. This entire assignment had been one cluster after another. She wasn't even sure it was fair to Mrs. Tasky to have Roni under her roof.

Someone had tried to kill her. Her or Way, maybe both. What if the killer came here, where Mrs. Tasky, a bystander, might get hurt?

Roni sat on the edge of her bed, ran her hands through her long hair and tugged to release the tension.

"I don't know what to do," she muttered.

Certainly not the first time that had occurred, but at the moment, she felt more alone than ever.

She couldn't stay here, though. Couldn't bring danger to this house.

Her phone buzzed and rattled against the bedside table. A text.

After the last few hours, who knew what this could be? She scooped it up, spotted Way's name.

Of course he'd reach out now. At the exact moment when she felt alone.

Vulnerable.

And, for the first time, all too willing to give in to it.

Damn him.

She tapped on the message.

You okay? I'm here if you need something.

Alone, confused, and wondering who the hell tried to run them off a mountain, she had a slew of emotions churning inside her. And now he sends her a text asking if she's okay?

No. Totally not okay.

Desperate to move, to do *something,* she got to her feet and paced the barely fifteen by fifteen room. Too confining. That's what this was.

What a night. Death had never scared her. Before this week anyway. Now? After spending time with Maggie's family, being welcomed into their home and witnessing the small-town workings of Steele Ridge, her life played in her mind like a bad B movie.

She had nothing. No family, no home.

No *roots.*

Worse, she'd spent a good chunk of her life ignoring that fact. Until tonight when some psycho thought it a good idea to run her and Way off the road. Now, her lack of connections came into sharp focus. If the psycho had succeeded, if she'd died on that mountain, who'd bury her? Would anyone even mourn her?

No roots.

And being alone, pacing in her suite, was a giant exclamation point on the fact.

Start over. That's all she needed to do. Maybe take a chance. Open up to the possibility that she could have her own home and family.

So what if she had no roots? She'd grow her own.

She reached the far wall and spun around, completing another lap. If she was in her apartment, she'd head down to the gym. Run a couple of miles on the treadmill, pound the heavy bag, battering it with kicks and punches. A good physical workout always helped clear her mind.

Except, no gym at Mrs. Tasky's.

She glanced down at Way's message again. He'd almost been killed tonight and he was checking on *her*? What about what *he* needed? Or wanted?

If the kisses they'd shared were any indication, she might know *one* thing he wanted. Physical attraction, she was sure, would never be a problem. She wanted more than lust, though. She needed rock-solid support. A man who'd stand by her and give her...

Hope.

Something to believe in.

Ignoring Way's message, she scooped up her phone, wallet, and keys and headed for the door.

WHAT AM I DOING?

Even as Roni pulled into Way's driveway, the question

lingered. She'd been sent to Steele Ridge to do a job. An important job.

And what she had on her mind definitely didn't fall under her job description.

But, hey. Where was the CIA when she'd almost gotten catapulted off a mountain? Roni's eyes snapped to the rearview mirror. Nothing but darkness behind her. She'd spent the ride over checking—and rechecking—that mirror. The lone car that had pulled behind her on Main Street had turned down a side road. Beyond that? No suspicious cars.

Excellent.

She turned the engine off. Way's SUV and his remaining motorcycle sat parked in front of the barn, the overhead spotlight shining down on them.

What am I doing?

She could leave right now. Forget the whole thing.

She lifted her phone from the cupholder, tapped on Way's message and read it.

Four times.

At the very least, she should respond. Let him know she was okay. Relatively speaking.

Why couldn't Steele Ridge have a twenty-four-hour gym?

Finally, she poked at her screen and tapped out a quick response.

Not okay. In your driveway.

Ten seconds, then twenty more passed. What if he was inside, figuring out how to get rid of her?

Rejecting her.

To her own mortification, she actually liked Way Kingston.

A lot.

And for someone who'd spent her life perfecting the art of isolation, all this liking the man created issues.

Still, she had to smile.

Strike up the band, I like this guy.

Her phone vibrated. *Way.* She frantically poked at the screen. Schoolgirl crushes and the silly excitement they brought were kinda fun. And a completely new experience.

She tapped his message.

Girl, what are you doing? Get in here. Back door.

She let out a breath, laughing at herself as relief took hold.

By the time she exited the car, he stood on the small back porch, backlit by the lone sconce. His T-shirt was half untucked, his jeans riding low on his hips—oh, baby—and his feet bare.

The bare feet?

Killer.

Without a doubt, Way and his lean muscles did something to her. Brought out a hunger she'd shoved away for years. Experiencing him in his own space where he'd probably had those bare feet kicked up while he watched sports or read one of those books on his coffee table, triggered long-dormant memories of home. Her home. Before her father passed and they'd had "chill" nights. Just the two of them. Completely at ease despite her mother's absence.

God, I want that again.

As she approached, Way shook his head. "Are you insane? Someone tried to kill us. You should have called me."

Lovely way to obliterate her little fantasy. "Nobody tailed me. I made sure. Can I come in?"

He stepped back and waved her inside. "Of course. What's wrong? Did something else happen? Talk to me."

Oh, something happened all right.

"There's no twenty-four-hour gym in this town. You know that, right?"

The look he gave her, that cross between she's-totally-whacked and someone-must-have-hit-her-on-the-head made her laugh. Which didn't necessarily help convince Way she hadn't lost her mind.

She crossed the threshold into his kitchen. "A gym. My building has one. In times of extreme stress, I like to go there. Burn off some steam."

"O-kay. If it's that important, I can call my cousin Reid. See if he'll let you use the gym at the training center. If, you know, that's the thing you really need."

Now he's getting it.

She spun around, met his gaze, holding the stare long enough to communicate, unless he was a complete moron, that she wanted him. Naked. On his bed and—wow—a blast of heat, an absolute volcano, erupted inside her.

Fanning herself wouldn't exactly be appropriate.

"That's not what I want," she said. "I think you know that."

His lips, those amazing lips she'd like to devour, lifted into a smile and she rushed him. Barreled right into him and smacked her hand over the back of his neck, dragging him to her, mashing her lips against his.

He wasted no time sweeping his tongue into her mouth, then retreating. In and out, in and out—*wow, wow, wow*—. The teasing motion snapped her mind to his bed again. The two of them naked, their bodies entwined and doing... things. Really fun things.

Rather than break the kiss, he lifted her straight up, clamped his hands on her ass and oh, that felt good. She wrapped her legs around him, hanging on as he carried her through the house. And, hello, that whole carrying thing took her to another supremely lovely level. When did Roni Fenwick ever allow anyone to get her off her feet?

He turned into a darkened room and flipped the light switch.

She backed away from the kiss, her chest rising and falling. "Lights on?"

"Oh, yeah. I've been thinking about this for days. I want to see you."

He tossed her on the bed and ripped his T-shirt off, revealing one hell of a set of six-pack abs and ropey muscles she'd spend the night curled up with.

Propping herself on her elbows, she lifted one foot and pointed it at the bulge in his pants. "Lucky me."

"One thing," he said.

"Do tell."

"If I do anything you don't like, you have to say something. I want you happy." He flashed a smile. "And highly satisfied."

WAY COULD NOT BELIEVE HIS LUCK.

If nearly getting pushed off a mountain got Roni into his bed, he'd deal with it. Every night if possible.

Damn, she drove him wild. In the best possible way.

He reached out, grabbed her foot and slowly slid her boot off. "Is that a deal?"

"Me being highly satisfied?"

He laughed. "Yeah."

"I'm all about satisfaction. Particularly when it involves hot guys."

He tossed her boot over his shoulder, then her sock before repeating the exercise with her other foot. This would be fun. *She* was fun. In a twisted, fucked-up sort of way.

He stood for a second, just looking. Enjoying the view of her on his bed, her long, dark hair spilling across his comforter. He itched to get his hands there. Grab hold and get lost in the silky strands, maybe run his fingers over her sculpted cheeks.

Too many clothes.

Both of them.

He wanted her bare-assed naked. Free of her requisite tank top and unbuttoned overshirt. Skin to skin. That's what he liked.

"You are so damned beautiful."

She sat up, hooked her finger into his belt loop, and pulled him forward, popping the button on his jeans and slow-oh-oh-oh-ly dragging his zipper down.

He dropped his head back, focused on the feel of her fingers, that light touch through the fabric. "You're killing me."

Then her hands were inside his pants, moving around his hips into his boxer briefs. She guided his underwear and jeans down. His erection sprang free.

She ran the tip of her finger over him and his brain fried. Just zzzzppp. Done. He lifted his head, found her grinning up at him, those devastating dark eyes connecting with his. *Can't take it.*

He kicked out of his pants and underwear. "You're not getting any sleep tonight," he said.

"I'm not a great sleeper anyway."

She jerked her overshirt off and he shoved her back on the bed, got right to work unfastening her jeans. He needed to see her. All of her. Working her pants over her hips, he ran his hands over her toned legs.

Red thong.

God help me.

He tugged the jeans free and stroked his hand back up her leg, pausing at her inner thigh, then rubbing one thumb over the crotch of her panties. Her wet heat seeped through the cotton and he met her gaze. "All mine."

She bolted to a sitting position, whipping her tank top over her head, revealing—thank you, sweet baby Jesus—a red bra that matched her panties. Hard nipples poked through lace. *Can't stand it.*

Had to touch.

He reached right into the bra, pressing his palms against her nipples and cupping his fingers over the soft flesh.

Latching on to his wrists to keep them in place, she closed her eyes and let out a little moan. Banging her all night wouldn't be good enough. Not for him.

Reaching behind, she unhooked her bra. He slid his hands away, moving them up to her shoulders. For the fun of it, he inched the straps down, revealing more and more and more until—oh yeah—the bra was completely off.

Roni was more than his imagination had conjured. All full breasts and curvy hips that made him think of bombshell pinup models.

So damned beautiful.

I want her.

She lifted her hand, wrapping her fingers around him, gently stroking. The friction, combined with the sight of her hard nipples, forced him to lock his jaw, pretend that he wasn't about to blow all over her hand.

Speaking of. He reached for her, cupping his hand under her chin. "I love how that feels."

"Good. Please tell me you have condoms."

Bet your sweet ass I do. "Yep."

But, hell on earth, he didn't want to move. Not with how good her fingers felt on him. Reluctantly, he eased away from her and walked to his dresser and the stash of rubbers he kept there. When he swung back, she'd rolled to her side, staring as he ripped the package open and worked the condom on. "You like watching?" he asked.

"I like watching you. Now get over here and get inside me before I lose my mind."

He moved back to the side of the bed, dragged her panties off, and stuck one finger inside her. Just...bam. She let out a gasp, ground her hips against him and slammed her hand against the bed. "Oh, that's fantastic."

Stroking inside her, he watched her eyes roll back in her head and—wow—too much. He'd give her an orgasm she'd never forget. First thing. Totally blow her mind and then he'd get inside her and give her another one.

That was the goal. Orgasm after orgasm after orgasm.

WAY KINGSTON'S FINGERS SHOULD BE INSURED. THAT'S ALL Roni could think. A million bucks. Ten million maybe. He drove his middle finger farther inside her, then stroked and stroked again and Roni's lower core caught fire. Pressure built and swirled, layer after layer creating a euphoric sensation.

"So good," she moaned.

So, so, good. He was going to do it. Make her come first. Not that she minded, but...no. She wanted him inside her when it happened. So deep she'd forget her stone-cold heart and let herself, for the first time, be free. Free to enjoy whatever he wanted to give her.

To let him in.

Way stroked inside her again, murmuring something

filthy that she couldn't quite understand, but somehow wanted to hear more of.

He kept stroking and stroking, kicking that pressure up and up and up.

"Stop."

His finger stilled and—dammit—she was so close.

"Wait," he said. "You want me to stop?"

She rocked her hips, urging him on. "No." He stroked again. "Yes!" She grabbed his shoulders, her nails digging into his skin and he withdrew his finger. She pulled him to her. "I want you inside me. Right. Fucking. Now!"

She dropped to her back and opened her legs. In one swift move, he pulled her to the edge and—yes!—plunged into her, the movement hard and fast and so incredibly deep she cried out.

"So good," she said, just in case he got any crazy ideas of stopping.

"My girl knows what she wants," he said.

His girl. She liked the sound of that.

And, yes, she knew. More, more, more. She lifted her hips, nearly bucking under him, urging him on. Faster, harder, faster, harder.

Never enough. Never.

"Don't stop. Please," she said. "Harder."

He pushed inside her again, his hips like pistons, pushing her closer and closer to that edge. "Go," he said. "Just let go."

He kept talking, telling her every place he'd lick and touch and lick and touch. If only she'd come for him. Way Kingston? Filthy mouth.

But she kinda loved it.

Who knew?

"So close," she muttered.

And then he did it. Rammed himself into her, holding her hips in place as he ground into her, creating a whole other type of friction that—ohmygod. She squeezed her eyes closed and flashes of color—red, pink, blue—exploded.

She gripped Way's wrists and moaned as her body convulsed.

Still, he pumped his hips. Again and again and again.

She opened her eyes again and the sight of him, all taut muscles and sculpted jaw, indicated she wasn't the only one going over that fantastic edge.

"Look at me," she said.

He locked his dark eyes on her and a piece of her heart broke free. Just sliced right off. One night with Way and she crumbled.

After one last plunge inside her, Way threw his head back. His grip tightened and he held her there, their bodies rammed together, his fingers digging into her skin.

He cried out, the sound like heaven to her. Letting go, he braced his hands on either side of her, their bodies still joined.

She could stay like this awhile. Easy-peasy. His warm breath tickled her ear and she snuggled against him, loving the simple pleasure of it. Intimacy. So powerful.

He lifted his head, smiled down at her, and dipped his head closer. The kiss was gentle, a soft brush of his lips and so utterly perfect that Roni thought maybe, just maybe, Way Kingston might make her believe in love again.

THE BUZZ OF HER PHONE JOLTED RONI FROM THE BEST SLEEP she'd had in months. Maybe years.

Something about Way let her decompress. Let her feel safe.

Rest.

A beautiful thing she'd never realized had been lacking. At least until now.

Bzzz, bzzz, bzzz.

The phone again. She pried her eyes open and blinked against the early glow of sunshine slipping between the cracks in the blinds.

Slowly, she eased from under Way's arm draped over her shoulder and rolled to her side. His arm dropped to the bed and she glanced up at him. No movement. The man slept like the dead. He must have been as tired as she'd been.

Not a surprise. Between the hell they'd been through on the mountain the night before and the ensuing round of crazy good sex, a month of sleep might not be enough.

Mmm, mmm, mmm, the man knew the way around a woman's body. A thought that didn't make her all that happy, since he'd clearly had plenty of practice.

Roni Fenwick, jealous. Go figure.

The bling of her voice mail notification replaced the buzzing, and Roni scooped the phone from the hunk of tree trunk Way had modified into a nightstand. Talented guy, for sure.

She tapped the screen, noted the time—7:03—and found Maggie's name attached to the voice mail. Rather than risk waking Way up with more noise, instead of listening to the message, she read the transcript.

Call me. ASAP.

Short and to the point. Typical Maggie.

Beside her, Way rolled to his side, dropping a kiss on her shoulder. "What's up?"

"Maggie called. She wants to talk to me."

"You need privacy?"

"I don't think so. But maybe we shouldn't announce that we just spent the night together."

He grinned. "You don't want my sister to know I gave you three orgasms last night?"

She flipped over and faced him, worming her leg between his and sliding it against him. "Seems to me, you got as good as you gave."

"Absolutely. And if you keep that up with your leg, you're gonna get as good as *you* gave again."

Promises. Promises.

"After I call your sister, I'll take you up on that."

He kissed her, long and slow, morning breath and all. Neither of them seemed to mind. He pulled back from the kiss. "I had fun last night. Well, after we almost got thrown off that damned mountain."

"I knew what you meant. I had fun, too. I think we're..."

Good together. No. Couldn't say it. Too soon. Wasn't it? For both of them. They'd just met. Obviously, they had chemistry, but the situation was highly charged. She'd been in enough bad relationships—sexual and platonic—to know that charged incidents often brought on feelings that wouldn't survive the mundane trappings of everyday life.

"Yeah," Way said. "We're good together."

"Wow. You just read my mind."

He ran one finger down her cheek. "I feel it, too. I'm not sure what the hell to do about it. Eventually, you're gonna leave."

Maybe.

What was wrong with her? Lust had fried every working brain cell. She had a career in DC. The perfect job, for her anyway, and now all of a sudden small towns and picket fences seemed mighty appealing. Women like her didn't get that particular fairy tale.

Or did they?

Maybe the fairy tale needed to be tweaked. Small towns, picket fences, and commuting on weekends.

Getting ahead of herself. That's what she was doing right now.

She tapped Maggie's name and waited for the phone to connect while Way's hands explored her naked body.

"Hey," Maggie said.

Roni smacked at Way's hand, now firmly cupped around her left breast. "Hey."

When Way didn't budge, she helped her own cause by whipping the sheet off and sliding out of bed. She made her way to the open bedroom door and across the hallway to the bathroom, where she locked herself in and leaned against the sink. "What's happening?"

"Where are you? I stopped at Mrs. Tasky's, but you weren't there."

"I'm...out. Couldn't sleep so I ran for breakfast."

"Are you at the B? I'll come by."

Oh, boy. "Um, no. You need something?"

"I need to see you and my brother. He didn't answer his cell."

Because he'd left it in the living room last night.

Roni blew out a silent breath. Messy, messy, messy, all this lying to her friend.

But, this early, Maggie must have something interesting to tell them if she wanted a face-to-face meeting. "I can come to your office," Roni said. "Now?"

"That works."

"Mags? What is it?"

"I talked to the owner of those license plates. One Joe Brady. The plates were stolen yesterday and placed on a vehicle—also stolen—that was discovered twenty miles from here at two a.m."

"In other words, a dead end."

"Exactly. Now that you've brought me up to speed, though, I got to thinking. I may have information that will help."

That was all Roni needed to hear. "I'll get a hold of Way and be right there."

She swung the door open and found Way sitting on the edge of his bed.

"That was Maggie. Get dressed. We're going to her office."

19

Upon arriving at Maggie's office, they found the reception desk empty. Shari, the sheriff's department's executive assistant and one-woman miracle organizer, must've had the day off.

"Mags?" Way called.

"My office!"

Way held his hand out to Roni, ushering her ahead of him. Anything less than proper manners would mortify his parents.

He fell into step beside her as her boot heels clicked against the tile and filled his mind with visions of her in high-heels. And only high-heels.

Yeah, they'd have to experiment with that some. Damn, he couldn't wait to get his hands on her again.

He glanced down at her, all freshly showered and carrying her messenger bag over her shoulder. He'd swung her by the bed-and-breakfast so she could, as she put it, avoid smelling like she'd gotten laid all night. Now she wore her leather jacket over skintight jeans, a snug T-shirt, and those high-heeled boots that gave her wicked sexy frame an additional few inches. The .38 tucked into a holster at her waist was the finishing touch.

Roni made the turn into Maggie's office, knocking lightly as they entered. His sister sat behind her desk, her sheriff's uniform pressed sharply enough to slice wood.

She glanced up from the document she'd been reading. Dark half-moons and puffy skin under her eyes indicated a lack of sleep. All due to Way nearly getting blown off the side of the mountain last night.

"Hey." Maggie pointed to the two guest chairs in front of her desk. "Sit."

At best, his sister's office could be described as no-frills efficiency. As a responsible administrator, Maggie didn't spend county money recklessly. When it came to running her department she could squeeze a nickel so tight, the head would pop off.

Something Mags took great pride in. She didn't need an over-the-top office. She needed a good staff.

Roni took the chair on the left and Way dropped in next to her.

Maggie leaned in, resting her arms against the desk. "I'm assuming Roni told you about the plates?"

She sure did. And it kept his mind spinning endless theories about the CIA trying to take him out and who might be responsible for the shootings. Don Harding? Karl Quigley?

All possibilities Way couldn't eliminate.

"She did," he said.

"Which," Maggie said, "makes me believe that it definitely wasn't some drunk teenager looking to mess with you last night."

Roni nodded. "I agree. Someone stole those plates and

put them on another vehicle to keep from being discovered."

"Given what you told me about your off-the-books investigation, I think you've rattled someone."

"It has to be the CIA," Way said. "Someone leaked my design and now they're trying to cover their asses."

Maggie made a humming noise. "Possibly."

Over the years, he'd learned to hate that noise. With *that* noise came disagreement. But after what they'd all been through last night, he wouldn't launch into his usual full-scale-defensive maneuvers. "What are you thinking?"

"I'm not discounting the CIA, but one of those bullets being used in the murder of a Street Dragon, a gang my task force had been investigating, intrigues me. It's another angle is all."

"Which is why we talked to Bernadette Ambrose," Roni said. "She gave us boxes of Jeff's belongings. I was hoping we'd find something about the Street Dragons, but so far, there's nothing."

Maggie met her gaze. "His mother knows a lot of people, Roni."

"I know. Think about the people who attended those annual barbecues at her house. I don't want to think Jeff is at the root of this."

Way held up his hand. "Hang on. Why are we so sure Harding is clean?"

"Think about it," Roni said. "He's in charge of the CIA's science and development department. No offense, Way, but if he wanted to betray his country, he'd do it with something a whole hell of a lot bigger than bullets."

Oh, Way had been thinking about it. Nothing but for the last six damned days. "You think? The bullets are literally small enough to keep off the radar. If I'm him and thinking about cashing in, I'm keeping it low-key with a small project. Less likely to get caught that way."

Maggie picked up a pen sitting on her desk and tapped it. "He has a point. I was up half the night thinking that exact thing."

Well, look at that. He and Mags agreed on something. "And?"

She peered over at Roni. "As much as I don't want to say this, I think we need to focus on Jeff. As the head of the task force, I have access to all his evidence."

The skin on Way's arms puckered. Man, oh, man he'd like to get his mitts on some of that evidence. "Anything you can share?"

Maggie looked back at him and lifted a shoulder. "I don't know. But when Jeff died, in an effort to aid in the investigation, I went through everything I had and sorted it. Anything he gave me, I turned over to the ATF and FBI."

"Please tell me you made a copy."

Maggie hit him with a smugass grin. "Do you think I'd be dumb enough to turn over the only copies I had? Of course I made copies." She pointed to two file boxes sitting in the corner. "That would be them."

Moisture filled Way's mouth and he sat forward, literally salivating. "Did you find something in there?"

"Don't know yet. I haven't had a chance to look. And before you ask, I can't allow you to look either. That's evidence."

"Roni was on the task force," he shot, hoping his straight-arrow sister would see his logic.

God forbid Mags would bend the fucking rules once in a while.

She stared at him like his last working brain cell had died.

"Right," Way said, putting enough boredom in his tone to put everyone to sleep. "What are we doing here, then?"

Maggie stood. "I wanted to make sure you were all right. And, well, to see if you might like to help me carry these boxes into the conference room."

What the fuck? She wouldn't let them see what was in there, but now she wanted them to move them?

He gave his head a hard shake. "Mags, are you wasted or something?"

Roni snorted. "She's not wasted. If I know your sister, I think she wants us to carry those boxes into her conference room and, while we're there, definitely *not* look through them without her knowledge."

"I have no idea what you're talking about."

"Ha!" Roni smacked both hands on the chair's armrests. "Maggie, I adore you."

"I bet you do." His sister wagged a finger at the boxes. "You've got one hour while I run out to do a well-check. I swear to God, if anything goes missing from those files, I'll arrest you both."

ONE HOUR TO GET THROUGH TWO LEGAL-SIZED BANKER'S boxes stuffed with notes.

Sure we can.

Roni stood in the conference room, gloved hands frantically pulling files and spreading them across the table. The gloves protected everyone, Maggie included. She'd taken a risk allowing them to view these files, and Roni wasn't about to let her get nailed over something as simple as leaving prints behind.

Maggie's generosity only extended so far. How the heck would they get through all this in one hour?

She checked the tab on the folder in her hand. "Some of these are dated and some are labeled with names. Let's start alphabetized piles and see what's what."

Because, God help them, she had no idea what they were looking for.

"Good idea." Way set a folder in the middle of the long table. "This is an M folder. Start the As at this end and we'll work our way down."

Quickly, she set the folder she held just above the one Way had placed. "And this is a dated one. June. Put anything earlier in chronological order above the As. That way we'll have a timeline."

It took them seven precious minutes to unload the boxes, but the result was neat stacks of folders, all containing information regarding Jeff Ambrose's investigations and his death.

Way ran a hand over his face. "No idea where to start. There's a ton of stuff to photograph here."

Roni had to agree. The information, when faced with such a short time to absorb it, overwhelmed her. "Let's break it down. We're looking for a connection between Jeff, your bullet design, and anyone who might want a Street Dragon dead. Right?"

"You make it sound simple. A ton of people want gang-bangers dead."

Roni swung around the table, perusing the folders as she went. *July.* She snatched the folder in front and flipped it open. "Work with me here. You sent the first batch of bullets to the CIA in July. Let's assume anything relating to the leak of your design starts there. We'll go through the July folder and, if we don't find anything, we'll go to June and then August and September."

Nodding, Way grabbed two additional folders. "That

works. But we don't have time to read all this stuff. Spread everything out and we'll take photos. Make sure you grab a shot of the name on the folder so we know time frames."

The two of them worked in silence, side by side, spreading documents along Maggie's conference room table and snapping photos.

Twenty minutes into the chaotic process, they'd cleared six folders, three each.

"Just finished August," Way said.

"Good." Roni took a picture of some handwritten notes and flipped the page.

Snap, snap. She flipped the page, *snap,* flipped the page. The methodical rhythm kicked in, getting her through several pages until...*hello.*

"Huh."

She scanned the photo of what looked like a journal page with more of Jeff's handwritten notes. Her mind ticked back to the antique leather journal with leather cords binding the pages. She'd always admired it. Jeff had told her it belonged to his father.

"Don't read," Way said. "It wastes time. Take the pictures and we'll print everything later."

She flipped back one page. Another journal page. In the photo, the leather cords that bound the pages were visible.

"Roni, keep going. Tick tock."

She flipped two pages. More journal notes. Another page. Another journal note.

"When we were going through Jeff's stuff the other night, did you see a leather notebook? It has a metal C clasp on the front."

"No." Way took pictures of four documents spread in front of him. "Why?" He pointed at the open folder in front of her. "Keep going. We've got thirty minutes."

"Jeff kept a notebook. It was his father's. He carried it with him and kept case notes in it. It must have gotten turned over to the ATF after he died."

"And what?"

She held up a page. "See the leather cords holding the pages in place? Those are from the journal."

"Okay." He jerked his phone at the file. "Keep going. Maybe there's something in there."

Right. *Snap,* new page, *snap,* new page.

Whoa. A list of names.

"Way?"

He let out a sigh. "Roni, for Chrissake, stop reading. We've gotta get through all this stuff."

Ignoring him, she focused on the list. Four names down, one caught her eye.

Roy Jackson.

Right after Jackson's murder, she'd been tasked with investigating Way and his bullet design. Using her finger, she moved to the next name on the list.

Chad Hopkins.

Next name.

Petra Cheevers.

Petra who owned convenience stores that probably sold cigarettes. *Hmmm.*

Roni tipped her head back and stared at the ceiling. The other names. The three before Roy Jackson. She'd seen them in Way's files. What was the order though? "Oh my God."

"What?"

She looked at him. "In your files. There were three cases before Roy Jackson. I can't remember the order."

"Ben Abrams, Jim Hayes, and Roberto Cortez."

No. Something was...off. She went back to the notes.

"Was that the order, though?"

"What do you mean the order?"

"When they were killed. Was that the order?"

He met her gaze. "No. Hayes was first. Then Abrams and Cortez."

"You're sure?"

"Absolutely. I studied that file. When men are killed with a bullet you created, you remember that shit."

She smacked a hand on the page in front of her and held it up. Way grabbed it. "What's this?"

"Read the names. Roy Jackson is the fourth name down, followed by Chad Hopkins and Petra Cheevers."

"No way." His gaze shot to the document and the muscle in his jaw flexed and released, flexed and released, as he read.

Jim Hayes.

Ben Abrams.

Roberto Cortez.

"Jesus."

She flicked her finger against the page, sending a *fffttt* sound into the air. "Are you thinking what I'm thinking?"

He peered back at her, his eyes darkening with some emotion she couldn't quite identify. Excitement, anger, horror?

He nodded. "This is a kill list."

FROM THE HALLWAY, THE SOUND OF SOMEONE—MAGGIE— clearing her throat penetrated the conference room door.

Way glanced up from the list in front of him and met Roni's eye. "She's back."

"I hear that. We have to tell her about this list. It's in *her* files."

Tell her?

No chance. Telling Maggie, without a doubt, meant bringing in the feds. They'd been part of the original task force and Jeff's superiors would insist on being involved. Never mind whoever was investigating his murder. Of that, Way was sure.

"I don't want her involved. It's a damned miracle she hasn't found this list in the first place."

Roni shrugged. "Back then, the people noted were suspects Jeff had targeted in the cigarette smuggling operation." She waved at the boxes. "When Maggie turned everything over to the feds, she made her copies and filed them."

"The list didn't mean anything then."

"Oh, it meant something. It gave them a suspect list for Jeff's murder. Once they were cleared, though..." She shrugged.

Someone knocked on the door. "Hey," Maggie said. "I'm back."

Knowing her, in about ten seconds she'd open the door.

Continuing the plausible deniability charade for Mags meant getting the crap strewn across the table back in the boxes.

Roni hustled to the door, cracking it open. "Hi. You're early. Can you give us a few minutes?"

"Sixty seconds," Maggie said.

Before Roni had even closed the door, Way began reassembling the files and storing them.

Roni joined him, the two of them leaving the file containing the journal notes—the kill list—on the table between them.

"I'll put away these other files," he said keeping his voice low so Miss Big Ears on the other side of the door wouldn't hear him. "Make sure you get photos of that entire file."

"On it."

Quickly she laid the pages out in a long row and went to work snapping shots.

"Got 'em." She tucked her phone in her pocket, then reassembled the file and held it up. "We have to tell her," Roni whispered. "I know you don't like it, but it's for her protection. If anyone knows she has this..."

"What?"

She shook her head. "I don't know. But she needs to know. For her own protection. Professionally and personally. I love that you want to protect her, I really do, but your sister prides herself on her professional reputation. Having this information sitting in a box while people are being murdered is, at the very least, negligent. And what if the killer figures out she has this list? Does her name go on it?"

"Shit."

Way hadn't considered that. His first reaction was to protect Maggie. Keep her out of this mess. Even if it got him his head handed to him. Again.

He pushed his shoulders back, closed his eyes for a second to organize his thoughts. Murders, his bullets, Maggie.

Right now, the only thing that mattered was keeping his sister safe.

He opened his eyes, met Roni's gaze, and nodded. "Mags! Get in here."

Voilà. The door swung open and in stepped Maggie. "Quit screaming. What's up?"

"Sorry. I...Never mind." He waved her in. "We found something you need to see."

20

Maggie's gaze shot from Way to Roni and back. For a second, a spurt of panic caved in Way's chest. He considered backpedaling and glanced across the table at Roni.

Two formidable women. Combined, their law enforcement knowledge trumped whatever experience he brought to this mess.

Roni reached across the table, handing Maggie the folder. "Remember the leather journal Jeff carried?"

"Of course. He wrote case notes in there. He always gave me copies. He thought they might be helpful, since it's my county."

Copies. All she'd ever had was copies. For whatever reason, the tension locking up Way's air, released. "You didn't have the actual journal?"

"No. I'd see him with it in meetings, but as far as him actually showing it to me? Never. I'm not even sure he gave me everything."

"Why?"

"Some of it was disjointed. Like there were pages missing. I assumed he gave me what pertained to my jurisdiction."

"Where's the journal now?" Way asked. "Do you know?"

"My guess is the FBI has it. After Jeff's murder, a new set of agents showed up. They specialized in law enforcement murders. They probably have everything related to Jeff's investigation. Not that it's helping, because his case is an absolute iceberg."

An iceberg. Good old Mags. "Who do *you* think killed him?"

"No idea. I do have a theory."

As he knew she would. "Which is?"

"Jeff was undercover, working a case that included a cigarette manufacturer and a distributor making millions from illegal sales. Jeff found a warehouse—"

Roni's hands shot up. "Full disclosure. I told him about the warehouse and the cigarettes being stored there."

Maggie gave her a look.

"Hey, I know," Roni said. "But we agreed to work together, so I told him what I knew." She grinned. "In the spirit of partnership."

"You two are killing me. I can't believe you kept all this from me."

Whoa, now. He'd been to this party enough times to know he should redirect the conversation before big sister went into full lecture mode. "We'll talk about that later. What's your theory on Ambrose's murder?"

She faced him again. "Easy. Someone figured out he was ATF. How his cover got blown, I don't know, but I think that's what happened. He knew where all those illegal cigarettes—ones that made the manufacturer and distributor millions—were stored. He also knew how the operation worked."

"You think someone from the manufacturer or distributor killed him?"

"They'd be the obvious suspects."

"Makes sense," Way said. "Did the feds clear them?"

"Don't know. The FBI doesn't exactly keep me in the loop."

The resentment in his sister's tone wasn't lost on him. She hated being excluded. And this? The murder of her friend? The lack of information had to be destroying her.

For the first time, the weight of Maggie's job hit him. She didn't only have to deal with ornery residents, she had federal agencies to contend with. The politics alone would be a total pain in the ass.

"The owners of the manufacturing plant and the distributor are still persons of interest," Roni said.

Both Way and Maggie looked at her. "Your FBI buds?" Maggie asked.

Roni nodded. "They don't tell me a lot, but I check in on the case."

"Good to know. But we're getting off track here. If the journal doesn't have anything to do with Jeff's murder, what are we talking about?"

Roni pointed at the folder. "We found a list of people Jeff made notes on. The pages are in order in there. Take a look at page four or five."

Doing as she was told, Maggie set the folder on the table and flipped pages until she reached the list. "This one?"

Leaning in, Roni checked the page. "That's it. "

Maggie read the names, her eyes narrowing as she moved down the list. "Wait. Am I seeing this right?"

"You are," Way said. "I think we found a kill list."

· · ·

RONI WATCHED AS MAGGIE RESTED BOTH HANDS ON THE TABLE and leaned in, her head dipping low for a second.

"This," she said, "has been in those files the whole time?"

Way moved to her side—God help him if he tried that consoling thing. Maggie would skin him.

Women like Maggie—like Roni, too—didn't want to be coddled when they thought they'd screwed up.

Look at that, he tucked his hands in his pockets.

Smart man.

"Mags," he said, "we just hashed this thing out. Before this week, there'd be no reason for you to think that was a kill list. Hell, when we saw it, it took us a second to realize what we had."

"He's right, Maggie. What we have to do now is figure out who else has copies of this list."

Maggie lifted her head. "They might be our killer. Stands to reason that it's someone in law enforcement."

"Could be. If all of Jeff's files were turned over, it's either someone who was on the task force or whoever has access at the ATF and FBI."

Lord, the idea of a federal agent being a serial killer sat like cement in her stomach.

"The bullets," Way said. "Whoever has this list also has access to the bullets."

Roni jabbed a finger at him and rushed over to the poster-sized tear-away sticky notepad mounted on the far wall.

"Let's break it down."

She grabbed a marker from the bowl on top of the credenza, uncapped it, and went to work.

"We have the ATF." She wrote the initials on the page,

tore it off, and pasted it to the wall. "Next is FBI." She wrote it down and placed the page beside the ATF one.

"The task force," Maggie added.

"And the CIA." Her own damned agency.

It didn't stop there either. As a former FBI agent and a task force member, her name could go on three of the four pages.

All around, this sucked.

"Put Harding and Quigley on the CIA list," Way said. "And, shit, if we're being brutal, add Clay Bartles."

"Interesting," Maggie said.

"I don't want to go there, but he's in the middle of this thing."

Roni added Clay's name. "And how do you plan on ruling him out?"

"No clue. I'll deal with that next." He gestured to the list. "We'll finish this and see what we have."

"Well, if we're adding him, we need to add all of the science and development department."

"And all the task force members," Maggie added. "Along with anyone at the ATF and FBI who had access to Jeff's notes. That's a lot of people."

Way walked to where Roni stood and leaned against the table, arms folded. "We're getting too wide here, ladies. Focus on the tangibles." He held up one finger. "Who saw or knew about Jeff's notes *and* had access to my bullets."

Maggie joined them at the end of the table. "He's right."

Roni tapped the page with the CIA names. "It's got to be here, then. Karl, Don, and Clay all knew Jeff. They were at the barbecue when Don and Clay talked about Way the first time."

"Stands to reason someone could have overheard the conversation," Way said.

"Really? You think the two of them are going to sit amongst a group and have an open conversation about acid-filled bullets?"

"No. What I'm saying, smartass, is from what you've told me about that party, there were big shots there. Who's to say Clay or Don didn't tell someone else?"

"I'll buy that," Maggie said. "I was there, too. Between Roni and I, we can make a list of the people we knew."

"Good."

Roni made a humming noise. "It won't be enough. This is high-level stuff. Some of the people there were above our pay grade."

"Okay," Way said. "We need the invite list."

Ha. As if it were that easy. "His mother already gave us two boxes of files. Are we supposed to ask her for the invitation list now?"

"No. Not if we can help it anyway. How were you invited to this shindig?"

"What do you mean, how? He told us about it."

Maggie snapped her fingers. "Yes. But he e-mailed an invitation so we'd have the particulars. Address, date, et cetera. It came from one of those online invitation sites. Oh, Waylon, I know where you're going with this."

He pulled his phone from his front pocket and tapped the screen.

Maggie stepped closer, peeking at the screen. "Who're you calling?"

"Micki."

"Oh, my God."

"Sorry, Mags. You can leave if you want, but I'm about to break any number of federal laws."

Maggie met Roni's eye with a what-are-we-doing look.

Roni lifted a shoulder. "In for a penny..."

"You two. Killing me."

"Good morning." A woman's voice filled the room by way of speakerphone.

"Hey, Mick."

"Second time this week. Jonah's going to have a fit when he sees how far ahead I'm getting."

He grinned. "How do you know it's not a social call?"

"I see you all the time at family events. How often do you call me for social reasons?"

"She's got a point there." Maggie said.

Not bothering with an argument, Way launched into his spiel. "Remember Jeff Ambrose?"

"Ambrose? Dead ATF guy, right?"

"That's him. I think he's involved with something."

She responded with a resigned sigh. "Should I even ask?"

"For your purposes, it doesn't matter. Maggie says he used one of those online invitation sites for a party he threw in July. I need the invite list."

"Well, this just gets curiouser and curiouser. Got some bad men at this party or what?"

"We're not sure. Maybe. Do you think you can get into his e-mail and figure out which online site he used for the invitations?"

"Waylon," Micki drawled as if Way had leveled the most heinous insult.

"Sorry," he said. "Dumb question."

"Give me to the end of the day. My brother wants a draft of my new cyber warfare course by noon. And, since he's my employer, I should probably oblige."

"No problem. I have other calls to make."

He disconnected and set the phone on the table. "While

she's doing that, I'll see what I can dig up from Clay. Feel him out a little."

"And," Roni said, "we need to check the lot numbers on the capsules. We never did that last night."

They'd been...busy.

Way waved her to the door. "Let's go to my workshop. We'll do that now."

Maggie wandered back to where she'd left the folder on the table, flipped the cover closed, and held it up. "I'm calling the agent in charge of Jeff's murder investigation. If they're not aware of this list already, they need to be briefed." She met Way's eye. "Sorry, little brother. Your bullet fiasco is about to get leaked."

OUTSIDE THE SHERIFF'S OFFICE, MORNING SUNSHINE SPRAYED quaint Main Street buildings with glimmering light. Steele Ridge's epicenter held classic charm that lent itself to window-shopping and grabbing a coffee or a doughnut at the Mad Batter bakery.

Passing the bakery earlier, Roni had spied the sidewalk chalkboard with the anonymous quote warning her that trust didn't come with a refill. Once it was gone, it would never come back.

Words to live by, for sure.

In many ways, Steele Ridge was totally foreign to Roni.

Her life had been spent in suburban sprawl with strip malls and big box stores less than a mile away.

This place?

It gave her...space. Room to breathe and think and slow down. Even while working.

Way headed to the driver's side of his vehicle, so she paused on the sidewalk and glanced up at a bright blue sky.

"You okay?" he asked.

"I'm good. Thinking about small-town living."

"It's different."

"But nice."

He shrugged. "If you want privacy, this isn't the place. Everyone knows everyone's business. But you also can't go three feet without running into a friend."

Considering she didn't have many of those, there'd be an odd sort of comfort with such familiarity. "I think I'd like that. Not the nosiness, but the friendships."

"Maybe you should visit more often." He gifted her with a smile that sent a ribbon of heat fluttering from her core.

"Careful what you wish for, Waylon."

A large black SUV made the turn from Main Street, heading straight for them and...shoot.

Quickly, she looked away. "This might be a problem," she told Way. "I think this is Karl again."

She checked her phone. The one she'd silenced to avoid distractions while rummaging through files. Three missed calls. All Karl.

"He's looking for me," she said.

"Why?"

"Probably because I haven't been checking in regularly. Why don't you head over to your place? I'll get rid of him and walk back to Mrs. Tasky's for my car. Meet you at your house in a few."

"No."

Um, pardon? Since when did anyone who wasn't her boss tell her what to do?

"No?"

Way closed the car door and met her on the sidewalk. "I'm done avoiding these guys."

Yeah, well, welcome to my world. But, considering Way was

tops on the CIA's suspect list, confronting Karl wouldn't be wise. "No," she said. "No. No. *No.*"

"Sorry, babe. This is my life they're fucking with. I'm not about to lie down and let them set me up for murder."

The SUV rolled to a stop and the rear passenger window slid down. As expected, Karl, all well-groomed and pocket square in place, eyed her.

"Get in."

He kept his gaze on hers, avoiding Way.

"Quigley," Way said.

Finally, the man faced him. What choice did he have?

"I'm not talking to you," Karl said.

"Way," Roni said, "please, let me handle this."

Except Way headed straight for the vehicle, his strides long, determined, while Roni hustled beside him.

Whatever foolishness he was about to get into, she'd have to derail it.

But Way had a look about him. That locked jaw aggressiveness that gave her a blood rush. How she loved a man with an iron spine.

Bad, bad, bad. All of it. Getting fired for canoodling with her target would look great on her résumé.

Way pointed at Karl as he walked. "What are you doing to fix this mess?"

"Stop right there," Karl said.

Roni set her hand on Way's arm, which only drew her boss's gaze. *Yep, getting fired here.*

Karl let out a snort and waved a dismissive hand. "Are you fucking kidding me? I send you out here to do a job and you're getting cozy?"

"Watch it, Quigley," Way said. "You talk to her with respect. She's busting her ass for you people when you've fucked this whole thing up."

"Sir?" Karl's driver said, clearly wondering if he should intervene.

And, oh, Lord, this could get seriously, epically ugly. "Stand down," Karl said to the driver. "I'm getting out. Pull over to the side and wait for me."

Getting *out*?

Now the three of them would linger in the street having a chat?

The car door opened and Karl exited, leaving his suit jacket behind. He closed the door and the driver pulled forward to an open spot near the curb.

Karl pointed to the side of the building where they'd have at least a smattering of shelter from curious residents.

After this, half the town would be jawing about the suit in the black government vehicle.

If they only knew.

Roni and Way followed as Karl found shade on the side of the building. He crossed his arms, peering down at the much shorter Roni. "I gave you orders to check in."

"I'm sorry, sir, but..."

"What?" He jerked his chin to Way. "How can you justify this...*alliance*? And, before you lie to me, you left your phone on last night."

Oh, God. He knew.

When she didn't respond, Karl snorted. "A tip for you? If you're going to stay all night at the home of someone you're investigating, shut your goddamn phone off. At least give us a challenge when it comes to tracking you."

"Sir, it's not..."

What? Not what he thought? The man hadn't survived the rigors of Langley by being stupid.

Or foolish.

She cut a sideways glance at Way, then back to her boss.

"The bullets. Way—Mr. Kingston—hasn't sold them. I'm convinced."

"You're convinced? How nice."

Way mirrored Karl's stance, folding his arms across his chest and taking one step closer, which only magnified the fact that he had an additional inch on the man. "Knock it off with the sarcasm, Quigley. You know as well as anyone I didn't double-dip on this thing. Why would I do that?"

"Money."

"Please. You're the goddamn CIA. You know I don't need money. Think about it. I have zero to gain by double-crossing the agency. You assholes would take me out in a second."

A definite point there.

Unfazed by Way, Karl focused on Roni. "What do you have for me?"

"Sir?"

"Information. I sent you here to do a job. What do you have for me?"

"Someone tried to kill us last night."

He cocked his head. "And?"

And? As if an attempted murder were a common occurrence.

"Someone tried to run us off the mountain."

"You were together?"

"Yes, sir. I managed to get a copy of Roy Jackson's autopsy report. The capsules inside the frangible bullets have lot numbers on them. We were headed to Mr. Kingston's workshop to see if the numbers were close to the stash of capsules he has. The ones he used to make the samples for the agency."

Before he could ask more questions, she continued. "A car ran us off the road. We managed to get to safety before the car crashed into Way's motorcycle and pushed it off the side of the mountain."

"Did you get the tag number on the car?"

"Yes. The plates were stolen from another vehicle."

Karl swung his head to Way. "Did you recognize the driver, the car, anything?"

"No. Too dark."

"Of course." Karl huffed out a laugh, then pinned Roni with hard eyes. "I expected better from you."

"I'm sorry?"

"Damned fool."

Way stepped closer, getting way too close to Karl for Roni's comfort. "Last warning, Quigley. Watch your tone."

Ignoring Way, Karl shook his head. "This is a disaster. You came here with one job and now what? Your hormones are in a goddamned twist to the point that you can't see what's going on? He wants you to think someone tried to kill you last night. You think he didn't set that up? That he's not using you? Please."

Quick movement beside her drew her attention. Way cocked his arm back and—*no.*

Stop him. Roni jumped, literally leaping, inserting herself between the two men.

"Don't." She threw her full body weight against Way, pushing on his chest. "You can't do this. It'll only make it worse. Please."

"Go ahead," Karl taunted. "Hit me. Give me a reason to have your ass locked up. I don't give a goddamn if your sister is the sheriff."

Damned Karl, knew exactly what he was doing. In the intelligence community, research was king. He'd know what buttons to press on Way.

And he'd done it. Just jammed his finger against the family button and held it.

A spurt of something fierce and wild scorched Roni's skin. Some weapons should never be fired. Family being one of them.

She whirled on Karl, curling her fingers in tight fists, squeezing so hard pain shot straight to her knuckles.

Karl had accused her of being used by Way when the CIA had done the same damned thing. They'd sent her here, expecting her to be a good little soldier by leveraging her friendship with Maggie to pin these murders on Way.

Civil duty or not, she didn't like being a pawn.

Or misled.

This entire situation stunk, and the cynical, streetwise part of her itched to believe Karl and Don Harding had orchestrated one hell of a cover-up.

Another thing that pissed her off.

"Pack your stuff," Karl said. "Get your ass back to Langley. I'll deal with you there."

He'll *deal* with her? As if nearly getting killed was her fault?

I'm so done.

With Way behind her, so close that their bodies bumped and the scent of his soap lingered, she lifted her chin, pushed her shoulders back.

"I'm not going anywhere. Not until I figure out how those bullets got out of Langley." She stepped even closer, propping her hands on her hips. "Because one thing is for sure. Way Kingston is innocent in all this. Either you can't face that or you're trying to save Don Harding's rear. I won't stop until I know what happened."

She moved away from Karl, tossing a glance over her

shoulder at Way, who wore a happy, satisfied grin. "I'm done here. Let's go."

"Hey," Karl called, his voice sharper than a guillotine blade. "The only place you're going is Langley. Right fucking now."

Way by her side, Roni kept walking. "Sorry, Karl. No can do. If I were you, I'd get my ducks in a row."

"You realize what you're doing? Your career is over. You'll never work again."

"Keep walking," Way said. "He's full of shit. He doesn't have that kind of power."

She breathed in, lifted her chin. She could do this. Walk away. No matter what the consequences.

"I'll wreck you," Karl said with such ease Roni shivered.

Pawns.

Everyone.

She thought back to her father dying. To the subsequent homes, some good, some not-so-good.

She'd survived. Made something of herself.

And she'd do it again.

She halted and turned back. "Go ahead and try. I've dealt with way worse than you."

After arriving at Way's and exchanging greetings with Sam, Way and Roni locked themselves in his workshop. Literally bolting the door.

At the floor safe, he placed his finger on the keypad and punched in his code. Might be time to update the code. Just in case.

"You keep the capsules in the safe?"

"With the CIA involved? You know it. Anything regarding this project is locked up."

Whether he'd had a sixth sense—or straight paranoia—he wasn't sure, but somehow he'd known to take precautions.

And yet his bullets might still be taking out civilians.

He lifted a small plastic storage container from the top shelf along with the typed list of numbers and then relocked the safe.

"This is them."

At his workbench, he popped the lid and gently dumped out the contents.

Roni set her messenger bag on the stool next to the bench and stared down at the pile of tiny capsules that could have been used for any number of medications. "This is everything that's left from the batch you did?"

"Yeah." He held up the list. "This is every number. The ones I sent to Langley are marked with an L next to it." He set the list between them and flattened the pile of capsules, shoving half toward Roni. "I triple-checked the list, but let's do it again. You check this pile, I'll do this one. You have that autopsy report showing the capsule fragment?"

She nodded as she retrieved her phone from her messenger bag. "Yes. On my phone."

Way grabbed his spiral notebook and unclipped the pen he always made sure to attach. Nothing sucked more than having a brainstorm—an absolute honey of an idea—and not having a pen handy.

"Read off the number."

She dictated the lot number from the autopsy report. Way jotted it down, placed the notebook between them and checked his list. None of the ones he sent to Langley matched.

Not even close. A good sign, but, at this point, he wouldn't take anything for granted. They'd still go through each capsule to make sure he'd recorded the numbers correctly.

He scooped up one of the empty capsules, held it between his fingers, and studied the stamped number on the outside. Lot numbers, depending on the manufacturer, tended to be a combination of dates and facility codes that enabled management to quickly identify where the product came from and when. The system came in handy during recalls.

In terms of Way's stock, if they got a match or even a close number, they'd know the CIA had lost track of one of his test bullets.

Even then, this wasn't foolproof. The distributor could have repackaged the capsules, mixing the lots. Until they found the shooter, Way wouldn't know if his bullets were the ones shredding these people.

He eyed the number, comparing it to the one he'd written down.

Side by side, they worked quickly, checking the numbers, placing an x next to the number on his list and then tossing the empty capsules back in the container. The work was oddly therapeutic and reminded him of being at the shooting range, focused on a singular task, shutting out all distraction and mental noise.

He glanced over at Roni, took in her straight nose, the softness of her cheek, her long hair that curled gently over one shoulder.

His mind tripped back to all that hair spread across his bed pillow and, damn, he wanted her again.

This thing was friggin' complicated.

Obviously sensing his stare, she met his gaze. "Got anything?"

"No. Everything matches the list."

"Me too. Which is good."

Sure was.

By the time he reached the last capsule, Roni had completed her pile.

Way watched as she placed her last capsule back in the container. "Nothing," she said.

He checked the number on his capsule. Perfect match to the last unmarked number on his list.

Relief, mixed with an odd sense of frustration, lingered. At this point, he didn't know what the hell he should be feeling.

Gently, he set the capsule on top of the pile inside the box. "Total bust. Nothing even close."

"Well, that's good. It's one more thing to help clear you."

"I keep thinking there's an answer, right in front of me. Instead, wall after wall after wall."

He scrubbed both hands over his face.

Roni gently squeezed the upper part of his arm. "Don't lose hope. You know it's a process. We'll keep eliminating things as we go."

Right. Excellent advice. Giving up wasn't an option. Given the personal nature of this project, he needed that reminder.

He dropped his hands and faced her. "Thank you."

"I haven't done anything."

"Yeah, you have. Your boss pretty much just threatened to vaporize your career and you're taking a chance on a guy you barely know."

She slid her hand down his arm, sending sparks to his brain. And maybe other parts of his anatomy.

When she reached his wrist, he turned his hand and hooked his fingers around hers.

"I know enough," she said. "Your sister trusts you. That alone is a badge of honor."

Maggie. He'd been hard on her over the years. Constantly on edge, ready for her to stick her nose where he didn't think it belonged.

In short, he'd been a critical shithead because his over-protective sister cared.

"I owe her an apology."

"Maggie?"

"Yeah. I'm a defensive prick around her."

"Well, alright then." Roni smiled. "Good to know."

"It's true. Every time I see her coming, my ass tightens up. I assume she's about to piss me off with her meddling. I shouldn't do that."

She made a humming noise that he was sure would be followed by some sort of female know-it-all lecture.

"Let's take a second," she said. "Maggie isn't innocent in all this."

Wait. What? No lecture? What was that about? On alert for some kind of headshrinker trick, he eyed her. "What do you mean?"

"I worked with her for months. At her worst, she's a control freak. At times, even micro-managing. It can be frustrating. It's also what makes her thorough. Yes, she's a buttinski, but she's fierce and capable and means well. On a personal level, I'd imagine it's, well, difficult to tolerate. Confining even. Have you talked to her? Actually sat her down and told her why you get defensive. No screaming, no accusations."

Over the last few months, he and Mags had had some royal blowouts.

He shook his head. "It always turns into a screaming match."

"Then I think you should initiate a conversation. My guess is she's usually the one to come to you, and you've just said you're ready for battle upon seeing her. You're constantly in a reactive state."

He hooked his index finger around hers and tugged gently. "If I initiate it, I won't be defensive."

"Exactly. Tell her at the start you're not interested in fighting and let her know—*calmly*—why you act poorly. Maggie is reasonable. And she loves you. She'll listen. In fact, she might be the ambassador we discussed. If you can talk to her reasonably about your issues with her, it's the perfect segue to asking for her help with your family."

Way leaned in, got right next to her ear, and didn't argue when she nudged closer to him, her body damn near molding to his.

"No offense," he whispered, "but for a girl who grew up in the system, you know a lot about family."

"I was exposed to different parenting styles. Not all good. I learned from everyone."

She eased back, tipping her head up at him. In his mind? Open invitation. Plus, he hadn't kissed her since this morning and...well...way too long.

He lowered his head, moving slow, letting her meet him halfway by going up on her tiptoes. He brushed his lips against hers, taking in the minty taste of her breath, and his pulse slammed.

Never enough of her. For sure.

Parting her lips, she deepened the kiss, pressing her curvy little body into him, making him want so much more.

Later.

When they weren't in his office with his assistant right outside the door.

He slipped his hand around her waist to her back, where he patted the upper part of her ass.

Roni pulled back from the kiss and he gently tapped her lips with his own. "I like kissing you."

"Couldn't agree more. But we have work to do."

Regretting every second he couldn't be kissing her, Way nodded. "And you've convinced me. About Maggie. Thank you."

"You're welcome." She eased away from him and pointed at the container of capsules. "Now that we're done there, how are you doing chasing down your friend Clay?"

Way retrieved his phone from his pocket and tapped it. "I texted him, but nothing yet. I'll leave him a voice mail. Then we'll see how Mags did with the FBI."

21

DC IN WINTER HAS NEVER BEEN ONE OF MY FAVORITE PLACES. If I wanted snow, I'd move north where communities know how to deal with slick roads and plowing.

Here? The newscaster announces an inch of the pesky white stuff and panic ensues. Markets clear of basic food supplies—bread, water, canned goods—and the all-important batteries. Schools announce closures while working parents scramble to find sitters. Even the government temporarily shuts down.

Typically, before I even finish my breakfast, the snow has melted and all goes back to normal.

It's nothing but a hassle.

In a rental car—obtained using a stolen identity, of course—parked two doors down from Clay Bartles's home, I watch white flakes float from the sky. A dusting covers roofs, cars, and tree branches along the city street.

I check my watch, an old analog one I've had for years. I like the simplicity of analog, but even more I like that its data can't be tracked.

Simplicity, indeed.

8:54 p.m.

I've been waiting for Clay to arrive home for over an hour. Normally, I'd surveil my target for a week or two, learn his habits. This time, I haven't had the luxury.

I'm winging it. Never recommended, but I've learned a few things.

Clay is single. His girlfriend of four years ended the relationship eight months ago. Since then, he's dated occasionally, but has had no ongoing relationships.

In short, he's pining over the woman he should have married long before she got fed up with his schedule and the constant call of the United States government.

I like Clay. I really do. Unfortunately, he's become a liability and I can't risk his continued interference. I need to clear the decks, so to speak, and continue my mission.

If that means eliminating Clay, well, that's that.

A car—Audi convertible—cruises by me, slowing as it nears the Tudor style row homes toward the end of the block.

Near Clay's home.

And seeing as he drives an Audi convertible, my pulse kicks up.

The mission continues...

At this hour, there are still spaces on the street and a quick flash of brake lights illuminates the damp road. The driver stops, then deftly hurtles back into a space, his hard-fought parallel parking skills on full display.

I glance around, doing a perimeter search for any nosey bystanders. I don't see anyone—*thank you, Mr. Weatherman*—and slip from the rental with my Colt .45 in hand.

Crossing the street, I pick up my pace, my gaze darting left and right. All clear. Three doors down, a porch light glimmers. Clay's home. Out of my peripheral vision, I check the Audi again as the interior light shines.

Definitely Clay. Still sitting in the car, more than likely checking his phone. He's a workhorse this one. Constantly brings the office home. Even on a Saturday night.

The car door opens and he exits the vehicle, reaching into his backseat for something.

This might be it. My chance. A tree and a Buick block my shot, so I hustle forward, my feet silently pounding the sidewalk as I clear the offending Buick. My head throbs from gushing adrenaline and I focus on lifting my weapon. On the shot.

But...no.

He stands upright, wrecking my opportunity by shouldering a briefcase and heading across the street.

I lower the gun, keep moving along the sidewalk.

A streetlamp shines down on his strawberry blond hair. I slow to a casual, not-so-determined walk.

The man was a recon Marine and I have to assume his senses are still laser sharp. Like parallel parking, his military skills would be hard to forget.

Ten feet in front of me, he reaches the sidewalk and pauses, digging through the outer pocket of his messenger bag for something. Keys perhaps.

Tsk-tsk-tsk. He should know better. Don't all the so-called safety experts warn to always have your keys at the ready?

Now.

Weapon at my side, I increase my pace only enough to resemble a resident ready to escape the falling snow that will turn this city into a chaotic mess.

The street light. I'll have to walk under it, the glare sure to light me up like fireworks on inauguration night.

Keys jangling, Clay glances up, peering straight at me. "Oh," he says, smiling at me. "Hey."

Even in the dark I see his gaze drift from my face down to my raised hand.

To the gun.

I slide my finger to the trigger, draw a breath in and let it out slow.

His eyes widen, the whites so clear that my blood roars. "What—"

Bang.

Bang-bang.

The suppressor does its job, masking the fierce power of the .45.

Clay's body bucks backward and he gasps. His eyes bulge with disbelief and...fear.

I've seen this look before. It's the one people wear right before they die. Clay Bartles has it.

He will die.

He knows it.

Before he hits the ground, I turn and head back to my vehicle, casually checking my perimeter—my six, as they say. Clay's body settles onto the sidewalk, his blood marring the fresh, pristine bed of snow.

Across the street, a curtain parts and light spills from inside, but it's too dark and too far for them to see me. I snap my coat collar up and hunch against the falling snow.

Another mission complete.

JUST AFTER DAWN ON SUNDAY MORNING, WAY SLID OUT OF bed, leaving Roni sleeping peacefully.

After another extremely excellent night of sex, waking up like this would be something he could get used to.

He stood on his side of the bed—*whoa, now they had sides?*—memorizing the sight of her dark eyelashes resting against her almost-but-not-quite olive skin. Damn, he loved her skin. Soft and touchable and...lush.

In sleep, she retained a calmness that in no way represented the fully awake tiger known as Roni Fenwick.

Puzzle, this woman.

Bare-assed naked, he scooped his phone from the bedside table and walked to the hallway, pausing a second as the aroma of brewing coffee brought his senses to high-alert. *Thank God for automatic coffeemakers.*

Shower first. Then caffeine.

No sooner had he dropped the phone on the bathroom vanity than the screen lit up. Hopefully Micki telling him she'd hacked Ambrose's e-mail and managed to find his party invitations. As of last night, she hadn't found anything, but her project for Reid had run long and she needed more time.

He glanced at the screen. Blocked DC number.

Definitely not Micki.

Clay?

In an effort to let Roni sleep, he shut the bathroom door, grabbed his robe from the hook and slipped it on before the call went to voice mail.

"Hello?"

"Waylon Kingston?"

"Speaking."

"Good morning, sir. This is Special Agent Terrence Holbrath. FBI."

Feds. On a Sunday. Interesting. Maybe one of Maggie's contacts. She'd said she'd reached out to a few people, but hadn't heard back.

"What can I do for you, special agent?"

"I'm calling regarding Clayton Bartles."

Clay? What the hell was this about now? Roni had told him to keep an open mind about all suspects, even Clay.

Clay?

Really?

But, shit. If this guy told him his old military buddy had been arrested for selling Way's bullets, he'd lose his goddamned mind.

"What about him?"

"I'm sorry to inform you, but Mr. Bartles was murdered last night."

Mur...Way shook his head. A sharp burn tore up his spine. Did he say murdered?

Way squeezed his eyes closed, held one hand up. "Hang on. I'm sorry. Can you repeat that?"

"Clayton Bartles," the agent said, his voice steady, direct. "He was found shot in front of his home around nine o'clock last night."

Shot.

Jesus.

Way blew out a hard breath as the information penetrated his tired mind.

Holbrath, clearly a pro at this, gave him a few seconds to get his shit together.

"Mr. Kingston, are you all right?"

All right? He was far from fucking all right. His buddy was dead. Shot after Way had asked him to look into the CIA's mishandling of his bullets.

Still holding the phone to his ear, he leaned back against the sink, bent at the waist, and forced himself to breathe. *One, two, three.* Slow, even exhalations.

Clay dead.

Focus.

"Mr. Kingston?"

"I'm here." He straightened up, tipped his head back and then to both sides, breaking up the tension. "Clay was my friend. Military buddy. How can I help?"

"We found his phone in his briefcase. There was a voice mail from you and a couple of texts."

"Yes, sir. We were working together. On a project."

"I see. And what project was that?"

Sticky business right there. Way had signed a nondisclosure agreement that basically forced him to keep his fucking mouth shut in regard to frangible bullets.

Did his NDA with the CIA cover murders?

"Special agent, since the FBI is handling this rather than the DC police, I'm assuming you're aware Clay worked for the State Department."

"Yes, sir," Holbrath said. "Given Mr. Bartles's job, his case has been assigned to the FBI."

Not a shock, since the attorney general or the head of a government agency could request the FBI investigate when an employee was involved in a criminal offense. In this case, a murder.

Upon hearing of Clay's death, his boss had probably called the FBI.

"Mr. Kingston, is there anything you can tell us that may help?"

"I'm a government contractor. I've signed a nondisclosure agreement."

"This is a murder investigation."

"I'm aware. But I'm also legally bound by an agreement."

No matter how much he wanted to help find Clay's killer, violating that agreement might put him in the crosshairs of the CIA. And no one would convince him Clay's death wasn't connected to this mess.

Zero doubt.

If the agency took out Clay, a State Department employee, they sure as shit wouldn't mind ridding the earth of Waylon Kingston.

"Look," Way said, "let me talk to my lawyer. See what I can tell you that's not going to violate the NDA."

"We can protect you," Holbrath said. "No one needs to know you violated the agreement. We'll bring you in quietly."

Sure. Right. Clay said he'd ask around on the QT and look where it got him? On ice at the morgue.

"I'll call you back," Way said. "And Holbrath, you said Clay was shot. I know you can't give me any details, but I gotta ask about the bullets."

"What about them?"

"Were they frangible?"

Please say no.

When the only response was silence, Way squatted down, dipped his head, and tried to concentrate through the throb behind his eyes.

God almighty, what the hell was going on?

"Mr. Kingston, I'm urging you to help us out here. We'll do whatever we can to keep you out of trouble."

"I'll talk to my lawyer," Way said. "And call you back."

He poked at the screen, rose to his full height, and braced one hand against the sink. He needed a plan here.

Talking to the feds might get him killed. Hell, someone had already tried taking him out. Now with Clay gone, who'd be next? Maggie? And what about Roni? She'd basically told her boss to go fuck himself.

A soft knock brought him from his reeling thoughts. Roni. Awake.

Way looked up, checked his face in the mirror, found

nothing but dark circles under spooked eyes. *Get it together, man.*

He cracked his neck again, let out a long breath to slow the cortisol explosion in his brain, and swung the door open. "Hey."

Roni stood in the hallway in his T-shirt, her hair a healthy sleep-riddled mess. She studied him for a few long seconds and then reached for him, clasping his forearms. "What happened? You look terrible."

So much for getting it together. "Clay was murdered last night. In front of his house."

Her mouth opened partway and her eyes narrowed. "Murdered? How?"

"Shot." He held up his phone. "I just got a call from the FBI. They found the message I left for Clay last night."

"They want to question you."

"They sure do."

"What'd you say?"

He huffed out a laugh. "What could I say? I told them I was working with Clay on a project. That I'd signed an NDA and would have to consult an attorney. Which is code for me stalling so I can figure out what to do. And, get this, the bullet?"

"Don't tell me."

"Frangible."

"He *told* you that?"

"Not in so many words. I asked. He didn't respond." Way shrugged. "It's enough confirmation for me."

"What was the agent's name?"

"Holbrath. You know him?"

"No. But let me look into this. See what I can dig up."

She spun away from him, heading back to the bedroom.

"No," he said.

She scooped her phone from the bedside table. "What are you talking about? *No?* We have to get ahead of this."

"I don't want you asking questions. That's what Clay did and look where it got him."

"And what? We sit around and let people continue to die? That's not okay with me."

Oh, they'd do something, but she wouldn't like it.

Not one bit.

22

Roni could not believe what she was hearing.

She held up both hands, pushing them through the air in an attempt to halt the barrage of insanity coming her way. "Just...stop. I think you're in shock or something."

Had to be. The man just told her he intended on calling the CIA to inform them of his intention to violate his nondisclosure agreement. One that kept confidential the details of ammunition capable of horrific results.

Way set his hands on her arms, gently moved her to the side, and walked by her, heading to the bedroom. "I'm not in shock. Pretty much, this is the clearest I've been since this started. I call Harding, tell him the FBI is on me, wanting to know why I communicated with a man right before his murder. I'll say I have no choice. The last thing Harding wants is for this to get out. Ultimately, he was in charge of those bullets. His ass is on the line as much as mine."

"And if they're setting you up?"

He took a pair of jeans from the shelf in his closet and tossed them on the bed. If he whipped that robe off, she'd be in big trouble. His body? All that lean, coiled muscle that immediately made her nipples hard would do her in.

Shake it off.

She followed him into the bedroom, keeping her distance. If he touched her again, she might throw him down on that bed and do seriously naughty things with him.

Next he moved to the dresser, pulling a T-shirt from the second drawer. "We already know that's a possibility," he said. "I'm done playing. Clay's dead. Makes me think they're going after the people I've talked to. Who's next? You, *Maggie*?"

"You can't do this. It's crazy. You're about to make an enemy of the CIA."

"Maybe. But I'm not gonna live this way. Constantly worried about the people I care about. I'm done fucking around. I'm going at this guy. They already tried to kill me, how much worse can it get?"

"Um, maybe they'll succeed?" Roni flapped her arms. "And we have no proof that Don and Karl are behind this."

He waved her off. "Come on. You're being naive."

Naive? Her? *Ha*. She wanted a day where she felt naive. It'd be a whole lot better than her usual cynicism. "Be careful, Waylon. You're dangerously close to pissing me off. I'm not above believing Don and Karl are involved, but I'd like proof."

He locked his eyes on her, the intensity nearly blowing her back a step. Well, too bad. If he wanted to wreck his life, fine, but she wouldn't let him insult her.

"You know it's them," he said. "You *know* it."

"I want proof!"

He gawked at her, let out a little huff. "What more do you need? I sent them the only samples I have. Outside of Clay and the CIA's science and development department, no one else knew about my design. I keep the specs locked in my safe on a laptop I purchased for the sole purpose of storing confidential data. I've never even hooked the damned thing up to wi-fi. That's how fucking paranoid I am. You tell me how anyone besides the CIA is responsible for that design getting leaked."

When no answer materialized, she went with the only thing she could. "I don't know."

"Exactly. Someone at Langley screwed the pooch. You don't want to face it."

Of course she didn't. She worked there—well, maybe not anymore. This assignment, from the beginning, had her teetering on a high wire between loyalty to her friend and loyalty to her job. To her country.

The idea of someone within the agency selling or even reverse engineering that design...

Her stomach pinched and released. *Pinch, release, pinch, release.*

Betrayed, once again, by people she should have been able to trust.

Trust doesn't come with a refill.

The Mad Batter bakery sign sure nailed that one.

"If you call Harding," she said, "it'll be a mistake. On many levels. You're way off here."

"I don't think so."

"I'm asking you to give me time to call my friends at the Bureau. Let me see what I can dig up on Clay's murder."

"No."

Frustration and lack of patience slammed together, pinching her stomach again. Way Kingston. So stubborn. What did she have to do to make him understand?

She lifted her hands and shook her fists at him. "You're going to screw this whole thing up. If you talk to the FBI, or anyone else for that matter, it'll get leaked. I know how these things work. Do you know the chaos that will create? The CIA losing track of ammunition designed to leave no evidence? Are you *kidding* me? They'll be crucified."

"As they should be. Civilians are dying. That's what you should focus on. Take your government employee hat off for one second and think logically."

Oh, no, he didn't. She cocked her head. "Think logically? Please, tell me you did not just say that."

HELL, YES, HE'D SAID IT. HE WOULDN'T APOLOGIZE EITHER. Not when she talked nonsense to him.

Jesus.

What was with the people in his life? Everyone wanted to shove themselves straight up his ass and tell him what he should do.

When he didn't answer, she huffed out a laugh. "I see talking to you will get me nowhere."

Slowly, Roni turned, picked up her jeans from the floor, and slid them on under the T-shirt she'd worn to bed. His T-shirt.

Too quiet. Her movements too were...calm. Definitive. Defeated. A niggling panic pebbled the skin on his arms.

"Now you're leaving?"

"Damn right I am."

"Come on, Roni."

She breezed by him on her way to the door. "No. You come on. You have no interest in listening to me. You'll do what you want anyway, so why should I bother trying to reason with you."

Now it was his fault. Another typical reaction he should

be used to. He should take a cue from his Uncle Eddy and hole up in a secluded cabin for years.

Isolating? Sure. But at least no one bugged him.

What a miserable existence, though.

Way stepped into the hallway, following her. He wanted angry Roni back. Sick bastard that he was, angry Roni got him hard. All that fire and energy? Total turn-on.

Quiet Roni? She scared the crap out of him. *Head-shrinker*. Totally screwing with him.

And manipulation wasn't his bag.

She opened the door and something in his chest twisted. *Bolting.*

Maybe permanently.

Did he want that? After what they'd shared? The way she'd crawled inside him and wedged herself there? When she wasn't driving him crazy, challenging him on so many levels, he'd enjoyed her. And waking up next to her would never get old.

At what cost, though?

Way Kingston would never be marriage material. Not with his need to be on his own. Self-absorbed? Possibly. At least he owned it.

What the hell was the point of pretending it could be different with Roni?

From the threshold, she turned back, staring at him for a few long seconds.

Stop her.

If for no other reason than to keep her safe. He should do it.

Ah, hell. Might as well suck up the damned foolish pride and tell her he was wrong. It'd be so simple. The words were there, pushing their way out, tearing up his throat.

Say it.

But, goddamn, his jaw wouldn't open. Stubbornness that let him survive ten years in the military kept it locked shut.

It should be so simple. To just...stop her.

"I...can't believe you're going to let it just die," she finally said.

The raw, clipped control of her voice gave him a stab of guilt. His favorite weapon of choice from women.

Say it.

No.

Saying it meant giving in. Giving up on the life he wanted. The one that let him hop on his motorcycle and disappear for weeks.

Because Roni?

High-maintenance.

She needed way more than he could give and the resentment would build.

And build.

And build.

Yeah, better to let her go now than deal with the pain-in-the-ass hassle of losing the relationship later.

He shoved his hands in his robe pockets, his gaze locked on hers as he stood there, unmoving, shoulders back, head high.

Let her go.

It might be over between them, but he wasn't about to let her leave by herself. Not after someone tried running them off the side of a mountain.

"I'll take you back to town."

"No. I'll call a car."

That wasn't happening. "You're pissed at me, but don't be reckless. Someone tried to kill us. Close that door and don't move while I throw clothes on."

. . .

RONI FOLLOWED WAY TO HIS SUV, HER GAZE FOCUSED ON THE barn doors just beyond the vehicle. The pressure in her head grew and grew and grew. An overfilled tube ready to burst.

Don't.

She couldn't do this, couldn't let him break her heart, absolutely wreck her this way.

She sucked a vicious breath through her nose, held it for a few seconds, then punched it out.

Pressure, pressure, pressure.

Such a fool.

Way Kingston? How did she ever think that man might be right for her?

All he wanted was to be alone and all she wanted was to belong. Two more incompatible people couldn't be found. But that was her, all the way back to losing her dad, she continually wanted the man she couldn't have.

"You'll never learn," she muttered.

She bit down on her bottom lip, dug her teeth in enough to pull the pain from her collapsing chest, but...no good.

Dammit. She needed a release. A full-blown tantrum, just wailing and crying until exhaustion hit. Until her body emptied itself of anger and hurt.

Not yet. Not here. Definitely not in front of him.

She'd learned a long time ago not to give away her power. Even to Way Kingston. Make no mistake, he had enough power. Somehow, the man had quietly convinced her to partner with him and risk her assignment.

To trust him.

The pressure in her head pounded at her, reminding her of her failures. The minute she'd put eyes on Way Kingston, felt that little pull, she should have run.

And yet, here she was. Pissed off and...heartbroken. Because she wanted him.

Foolish, foolish girl.

Paralyzing pressure clawed at her, filling her throat and...*Please, no.*

Still following Way, her feet crunched over gravel, the sound—*crunch, crunch, crunch*—scraping at her nerves. She stared at the back of his head and the short dark hair she'd spent half the night digging her fingers into.

She opened her mouth, tried to force out a breath.

Pressure.

Too much.

She couldn't do this. Couldn't contain the hurt. Waylon Kingston would not bring her to her knees.

Her eyes throbbed and...*shit*. Moisture bubbled up.

Crying? Really?

He didn't deserve her tears. Not for one second.

She lifted her chin, swiped at her eyes, but the horrific pressure refused to quit and sent more tears streaming down her cheeks.

Way reached his car, but she couldn't get in yet. Not like this. Not when he could see.

She spun away, taking a few steps. Yes, she'd look nuts, but what else was knew?

A police cruiser pulled into the driveway.

"Really?" she gasped.

Just her luck. Total emotional collapse and Maggie shows up?

Once again, she wiped her cheeks and ran her wet hands over her shirt.

Way's shirt. *My God.*

She let out a caustic laugh. "Terrific. My walk of shame."

"Well," Way said, closing his car door. "This gets better and better."

On that, they agreed.

She tipped her head up, shook off the negativity, while Maggie exited her car. Lord, showing weakness in front of Maggie, the strongest, most capable woman Roni knew, only added to the humiliation.

Worse, Maggie was in full, pristine uniform. Buttoned up to the fucking teeth, complete with gun belt hanging on her hips. All while Roni stood in a wrinkled T-shirt smelling like sex. Another fresh wave of humiliation toppled her.

On her approach, Maggie eyed Roni's outfit, then shifted to her brother's bedhead. Didn't take a genius to figure this one out.

"Morning," she said, keeping her gaze firmly off of the Harley Davidson T-shirt belonging to her brother.

"Hi." Roni gestured to Way's SUV. "I was...um..."

Why bother? Maggie had eyes and she sure as hell wasn't stupid.

"Just leaving?" Maggie, ever-so-helpful, suggested.

"Yep. Heading back to town."

Where Roni would attempt to keep Mrs. Tasky out of harm's way by clearing out and finding somewhere to hunker down until she figured something out.

Make a plan.

That's what she'd do. Determine how to keep her bosses happy while getting Way Kingston out of her mind and heart.

Maggie cocked her head. "Are you upset? Your eyes are red."

Oh, honey. I'm more than upset.

Explaining to Maggie meant revealing weakness. She'd

broken one of her cardinal rules of law enforcement by becoming personally involved with a suspect.

"I'm fine," Roni said. "Tired."

Ach. Nothing like insinuating she'd been up all night. Having sex.

With Maggie's brother.

But, Maggie, being the pro she was, breezed right over that. "It's been a rough few days. But I need a word with you both." She peered over Roni's shoulder to where Way stood. "How about I drive Roni back to town and then come back to see you."

"I'll take her," he said. "I'll make sure she's safe."

"Waylon, I'm a sheriff." Maggie patted her sidearm. "I think she'll be fine with me."

When Way didn't respond, Roni angled back to him. Time to put them both out of misery. "Maggie will take me back."

He didn't like it. She saw that clearly enough by his granite cheeks and hard stare.

Pissy.

Well, too bad. She knew what she needed and it was distance from him. Enough that she'd have her little meltdown and be done.

"All right," he drawled. "No chance of me winning this one. Both of you be careful. And text me when you get to town so I know you're okay. Mags, I'll see you when you get back."

Maggie waited for him to get inside, then turned back to Roni, rolling her bottom lip out. "You know, my brother can be a challenge. On many levels."

Ya think? "I'm learning that. Thank you for the tip."

"You're welcome. I definitely don't want to be in the

middle of you two, but I'm here if you want to talk. You're still my friend and I don't like seeing you cry."

"I wasn't—"

"Don't lie to me. I'm a woman, I understand disappointment when it comes to men."

No denying it. She'd already misled Maggie once. Doing it again might dissolve their relationship completely.

Trust doesn't come with a refill.

"I'm sorry. I don't want you in the middle either." Roni circled her hand in front of her chest. "I'm...churned up. This case. It's complicated."

"It is. Which is why I'm telling you I'm here if you want to talk. I know what this feels like."

"What?"

"Getting too close to a case. I fell in love with Jay when I was supposed to be protecting him. Talk about questioning your competence. Women like us don't allow ourselves the frivolity of love."

Women like us. Before this week, Roni might have considered herself worthy of Maggie's respect. Now? She didn't belong in the same town, never mind on the same level. "Not when we let it screw with our objectivity we don't."

"Is that what you did?"

She shrugged. "I was sent here to do a job."

"And you're doing it."

"I also crawled into bed with your brother."

Maggie's head snapped back and she blew a long breath through her lips. "Maybe you could have censored that last bit. But, hey, since you didn't and here we are, I will reiterate, he's a challenge. He's stubborn and opinionated. At times, he has a temper and says things he immediately regrets. As his sibling, I've learned this the hard way."

All of this would have been handy to know a few days ago. Now it only reinforced Roni's idiocy.

"But," Maggie continued, "he's also generous and caring. Did you know he drops supplies off at area shelters after every trip he makes to the grocery store? Homeless, pet, battered women. Any shelter he can find, he goes in, dumps a load of stuff and leaves. Last summer, some drunk butthead drove his car across the baseball diamond in the middle of the night and tore that sucker to shreds. The league did a fundraiser to raise money for the repairs. Way matched the funds. Ten thousand dollars. Just handed it over. His heart, Roni, despite his tendency to be a moron, is huge."

Hearing these things, amazingly good things, only confused her. She'd known about the animal shelter, but the rest of it? That was new information.

She had no doubt that underneath the obstinance was a good man. But Way was a lone wolf.

"The problem is, Mags, I need more. I want to be someone's partner. To share my opinions." She smiled. "Set him straight when he's making catastrophic mistakes."

"Oh, boy. He loves that."

"Exactly. I think we can chalk this one up to a misstep. Plain and simple. I wanted to keep you out of the personal aspects of it. You're important to me, Maggie."

Maggie waved that off. "This has nothing to do with us. I'm a neutral party."

Thank God. Roni didn't deserve Maggie, but she'd continue to be grateful. "Thank you." She glanced at the cruiser. "I need to go. Calls to make. Did you hear about Clay Bartles?"

"I did. I've been pulling frangible bullet shootings every day and saw it in my report."

"That's why you're here."

"Yeah. But not about the case. I thought I'd check on my brother. He's a nuisance sometimes, but his friend was just murdered. Possibly by a bullet he designed. Can you imagine?"

No. She couldn't. She'd been so busy trying to work the problem, she'd forgotten Way would be grieving his friend. Reacting to the devastating news.

Something that might make him irrational.

How many ways could she mess this up? Roni ran her palms up over her forehead. "I didn't even ask him. I'm such a jerk."

"Nah. You're in get-'er-done mode, trying to keep him from responding out of emotion."

"And you're too kind. I've made a mess of things."

"I think you both need a few hours to settle in with this information. Figure out the next steps. I'll take you back to Mrs. Tasky's so you can get some rest."

"I'm going to a hotel. After what happened on the mountain, if someone is after me, I don't want Mrs. Tasky hurt."

"Understood. But you're not going to a hotel. You'll stay with Jay and me. Our place is a fortress, and he left yesterday for a magazine shoot in New York. The company would be nice and maybe we can compare notes. Try and figure this out."

Before Roni could respond, Maggie waved her keys. "Let's go. You can soak in the tub in my room. Borrow whatever you need from the closet. We'll get your stuff from Mrs. Tasky's later." She turned toward the house, then paused, looking back over her shoulder. "And don't worry about Way. He'll come around."

Somehow, after this last exchange, Roni didn't think so.

23

Maggie.

Terrific.

Way stood in his kitchen waiting on brewing coffee while the aroma of Miss Joan's pecan blend kept the last of his patience from going completely bust.

Everything good could be found in Miss Joan's coffee. And with this pisser of a day—not even 8:00 yet—he needed the caffeine, because holy hell, how many strong-willed women did a man have to deal with in one morning?

Well, if Maggie thought she'd come in here and poke at him, she could hop back into that cruiser and leave.

She knocked once on the back door, spotted him through the glass, and came in.

"Hey," she said.

As the coffeepot gurgled beside him, Way turned to face her. "Hey. Coffee is on. And fair warning, I'm in a mood."

His sister held her hands up. "I come in peace."

Thank you, sweet baby Jesus. He blew out a breath. "Excellent. Is Roni settled?"

"Yeah. I took her to my house."

Perfect. Security at Maggie's included a gated entrance and surveillance cameras in every available place. No one would get near the house without an alarm going off.

Maggie pointed at the coffeepot. "Can I get a cup of that?"

He pulled another mug from the cabinet, poured two cups, and handed one off to Maggie before heading to the fridge for creamer.

"I'll drink it black," she said.

"No milk?"

"No. Jay cut back on dairy, so I'm being supportive. Sucks to be me sometimes." She sipped the steaming brew and winced. "Lord, I don't know how you drink it so strong."

"Easy. I like it."

And, hello? His sister giving up dairy? The cheese deprivation alone could kill her. "What's that like?"

"What?"

He shrugged. "Caring enough to give up something you love."

"Cheese limitations aside, it's pretty freaking awesome. He loves me, so it doesn't feel like a hardship. Plus, he's given me a most excellent life. If he wants to try different diets, I'll do it. No question." Maggie held up the mug in toast. "Even if it does take a bit of adjusting."

Adjusting. Something he wasn't particularly good at. Maybe it was a control thing with him. The need to have his world operating on his terms. No surprises.

The military had given him too many surprises. Roadside bombs that blew off limbs, foreigners spitting on him just for being American, terrorists that beheaded people to make some unknown point Way would never comprehend.

But then there were good surprises, too. Like the kids

who'd squeal when he handed them lollipops. Talk about tragic. A kid who'd never had a lollipop?

"Mags, you may have noticed, I suck at adjusting."

"Correction, Waylon. You suck at adjusting to certain things. Relationships being one of them."

He nodded toward the driveway. "Did she tell you?"

"About crawling into bed with you? She sure did."

Way winced. "Damn, you women. Is there anything you don't talk about?"

"For the record, I could have done without the specifics. I don't care if you get involved with my friend. We're all adults. As long as you respect each other and don't make me a go-between, I'm all good. What I care about is the two of you shredding each other."

"I wouldn't do that to you. Frankly, it's none of your business."

"Ha. There's the Waylon I know and love."

He snorted. "I'll tell you this, though; I like her spunk. She's..."

What? Smart. Beautiful. Persistent.

Maddening.

All of the above?

"Aggressive," Maggie offered.

"Yeah. Most of the time, in a good way."

"Except when you don't want to be challenged. When you want it your way." She held up her hand. "Before you start yelling, I get it. We come from the same DNA, and we know when we're right. To our very core, we know it. The problem with relationships, and trust me, I had to learn this with Jay because we're both alphas—"

"That's an understatement."

"Funny man. Shut up a minute."

Way whipped off a smile. Maggie. Maggie. Maggie.

"Anyway," Maggie said, "the problem with relationships is this little thing called compromise. And when you have two stubborn people, that can be downright painful. An absolute bloodbath."

"Exactly. I'm not into pain, Mags."

"Well, baby brother, welcome to life. It's filled with pain. Paralyzing, mind-numbing pain that you can't escape."

"Sounds terrific."

"Actually, when you love someone, it is. You don't mind the pain because you know you'd step in front of a bus—or worse—for that person. And vice versa. Jay and I have blowouts. It's not paradise every day. We're independent people with major hang-ups. Honestly, our relationship works because he travels so much. It gives us time to miss the other. When he retires, there will be major adjusting to do."

"You realize how twisted that sounds, right?"

She waggled her hand. "Maybe it's twisted. Maybe not. He left yesterday for New York. Last night, I curled up on my couch with Riley and had girl time. Then I soaked in the giant tub and had the bed to myself. Total peace. No phones ringing. No agents demanding his time. It was great, Waylon. I mean, off the charts."

"Where's the but?"

"I woke up four times last night. He wasn't next to me and I hate that. The push-pull of relationships defies logic."

"And this is fun?"

"Oh my God, yes. It's more than fun. It's harmony."

"So what are you telling me? I have to give up the life I want."

"Not at all. But you have to make room in your life, Way, or you're going to spend it alone."

Alone. Like the old guy in Guam.

Before Roni Fenwick showed up, alone didn't seem so bad.

Now? He couldn't stop thinking about her. About her drive and determination. Her balls-to-the-wall attitude.

He set the mug on the counter. "She makes me nuts sometimes. I mean, how is it possible to love and despise the same thing about someone?"

"Silly boy. Welcome to the world of relationships."

Running his hands over his face, Way sighed. "It's so complicated."

Maggie walked to the sink and dumped her coffee out. "I can't drink this. Sorry."

"Whatever."

Beside him, she propped one hip against the counter. "Look, take it slow. You and Roni just met. You're figuring each other out. When it comes to her—and I'm not talking behind her back here, she admits it—she has abandonment issues."

"I know."

"So, you being you, wanting to hit the road on a whim, will need to be dealt with."

"I can't give that up."

"I'm not saying you need to. But you'll have to figure out the compromise. Respect what she's survived and make sure she knows, without question, that you're coming back to her."

He cocked his head. Thought about it. Didn't seem so hard. "I could do that. No problem."

"And, when she tells you what to do, be aware it's about controlling her environment. You, of all people, should understand that. She thinks if she can control everything, she won't get hurt."

"She's vulnerable."

Maggie poked a finger at him. "Precisely! Believe it or not, underneath all that piss and vinegar, she's terrified. And, if you ask me, your heart is big enough to help her with that. You have an amazing capacity to love."

Jesus H. Christ, now she was pouring it on.

Heat stormed his cheeks. He looked down at his boots, spotted a smidge of dirt on the floor, and swung one foot back and forth over it.

Maggie laughed. "I'm embarrassing you?"

"Uh, yeah. I mean, it's weird, Mags."

"No it's not. You show people all the time how good you are. That's what drew Roni to you. Embrace it. If you enjoy spending time with her, talk to her. But if this is some kind of adrenaline-fueled attraction due to crisis, you need to end it. It's not fair to her."

Talking. His favorite thing.

Not.

But, his sister had a point.

And while they were at it...

"Mags, can I ask a favor?"

Her eyebrows hitched up. "Always. You know that."

He'd have to handle this carefully. Not say something that would trip one of Maggie's triggers, something he seemed to be good at. "When I left the Marines, I wanted to come home. Back to my family."

"And we're incredibly happy you did. We missed you."

"Which makes me really thankful. It does."

"Oh, wow. I hear a but coming. Are you leaving?"

"Noooo. No way."

"Phew. You scared me. Mom would freak."

Didn't he know it? "That's part of what I need help with. My phone rings all day long."

"Your business is growing, that's good."

"It is growing, but it's not the clients calling. It's you guys. Either calling or texting. All day long."

"We don't call you all day."

Careful. If he didn't approach this rationally, it would end up with them at war. He took a second, lined up his thoughts. Then he slid his phone from his front pocket and held it up. "You guys don't realize it, but you do. The proof is right here." He lowered the phone, dropping it on the counter. "Usually what happens is one of you calls. If I don't return the call in a few minutes, then you guys start calling each other wondering where I am and it's a domino effect. My phone blows up and I have to return everyone's calls. Mags, that's a lot of friggin' calls. I can't take it anymore. I need some...space, I guess."

Maggie narrowed her eyes, studying him while she processed his words.

"Don't scream at me," he said.

"I won't. I'm just...stunned. I didn't realize we did that, but I can see it. I mean, it's not intentional. We just start calling around to see if anyone knows where you are."

"I know it comes from a good place. That's why I've never said anything. I didn't want to sound like a douche complaining because my family cared about me. I've hit my limit, though." He whipped off a smile. "You'll love this. I need your help."

"What do you need me to do?"

Bam. Just that simple. No sarcasm. No extended harassment or teasing. Dang, this turned out to be way easier than he thought. "Talk to everyone for me. Please. Just come up with a system that gives me space, but satisfies you all. I promise I'll call back that day, but I might be in the middle of something, so unless it's an emergency, don't hunt me down."

His sister nodded. One solid jerk of her head. "How about we agree that you don't have to call back until after your work is done?"

"Unless it's an emergency."

"Right."

"Yeah. That works."

She swiped her hands together. "Easy. I'll take care of it today. And I'm sorry. I honestly didn't realize."

"It's okay. I should have said something sooner."

"Eh. I could see why it would be hard. No worries, little brother, I'm on it." She turned back to the sink, rinsed out her mug, and shoved it in the dishwasher. "But, listen, none of this is why I came here. I heard about your friend Clay. I'm sorry. Is there anything I can do?"

Now this topic, he'd openly discuss. "The FBI called this morning. They found my messages on his phone. They wanna talk to me."

Maggie's eyebrows hiked nearly to her hairline. "Not without a lawyer you won't."

"I stalled. Told them about my NDA and that I had to talk to my lawyer."

"Good. That criminal guy Jonah knows is excellent." She whipped her phone from her back pocket. "I'll get his number for you."

Good old, Mags. He reached over, folded his hand over hers. "It's okay. I'll take care of it."

She peered up at him, all wide-eyed and wounded. "You're sure?"

A few weeks ago—heck, a few days ago—he would have made some snarky comment about her butting out. In turn, she'd have responded that he should be grateful she cared, yada, yada. Round and round they'd go until one of them walked away pissed off and yelling.

Now, he'd take a different approach.

Women like Maggie and Roni were problem-solvers. In short, they needed to be fixing shit. Why it took him so long to figure that out about his sister was a mystery, but he suspected one Roni Fenwick had something to do with it.

He smiled at Maggie. "Some things I need to do myself. This is most definitely one of them. I do appreciate you wanting to help, though."

She angled her head, narrowing her eyes in dramatic fashion. "Who are you and what have you done with my brother?"

With that, he gave her a playful shove. "There are limits to this newfound patience."

"Too much?"

He held up his thumb and index finger, pinching them close. "Little bit. Now go. Let me talk to Roni. See if I can clean up my mess."

THE DRIVE UP THE MOUNTAIN GAVE WAY TIME TO SUCK IN fresh air and clear his mind. In no particular hurry, he ignored the gray pickup passing on the left of the straight-away. Looked like a woman driving, but it was hard to tell with the baseball cap.

Either way, passing on a mountain road wasn't exactly brilliance at work. Everybody was in a hurry. *Go ahead, dumbass.*

Normally on a sunny Sunday morning he'd hop on his bike and take a long ride, stopping for lunch at some dive bar along the way.

Today? Minus one well-loved motorcycle and unwilling to risk the second, he drove his Tahoe along the curving road leading to his sister and Jay's place. In his mind, the place was a mansion. Ten thousand square feet with decks and oversized windows on all sides giving kick-ass views from any spot.

Way didn't envy a lot, but when it came to his sister's new residence, yeah, he sure envied that view.

He slowed down, maneuvered through the hairpin turn, and lowered his visor when glaring sun blinded him.

Warm rays shined down and—*shit*—he missed that damned bike. The years he'd spent searching for parts, perfecting the engine and handlebars, ticked through his memory. Sent a surge of fresh anger streaming.

Dwelling on it wouldn't help. Besides, Shep had already promised to help him retrieve as much of it as they could. How they'd do that Way had no idea. He'd leave it to his mountain-climbing brother to figure out.

Up ahead the gray pickup had pulled into an emergency area on the side of the road, hazards blinking.

What the hell? The woman had blown right past him and now sat, possibly disabled.

With all the crazy bullshit he'd dealt with this week, he should drive on by. Call Maggie and tell her to send a deputy up to handle it.

Café owner.

There was the old guy from Guam, flashing in his mind. No matter what Roni had said, despite it making a lot of sense, when it came down to it, Way had let that old man down.

The distance between Way and the pickup narrowed.

Call Maggie.

But he was right here. And it was a woman, he thought, driving.

What if she needed medical attention? Having a seizure

or something. By the time an ambulance got all the way up here, she'd be dead.

"Son of a bitch."

He couldn't do it. Couldn't drive by and risk something happening to the driver.

Easing to a stop behind the truck, he grabbed his .45 from the steering column holster that kept his weapon in reach at all times. Damned handy, that.

He might be playing good Samaritan, but after the week he'd had? No risks. If whoever drove the pickup intended to set him up, Way wouldn't make it easy.

Before exiting the Tahoe, he grabbed his extra holster from the glove box and secured it to his waistband, draping his T-shirt over it. If this was a woman in distress, freaking her out by approaching with a weapon wasn't exactly neighborly.

He shot Maggie a text, letting her know there was a disabled vehicle on the road and to send a deputy ASAP.

If it turned out to be a false alarm, he'd text her again, but for now, he had shit to do and couldn't get too caught up here.

Keeping his gaze on the driver's side door, he tucked his phone in his front pocket and strode toward the truck, hands at the ready.

"Hello?" he called.

No response.

Through the back window he spotted short hair under a black baseball cap. The truck dwarfed the driver. Woman. Had to be.

She rested her head against the rear glass of the cab. Sleeping? If so, she was crazier than he'd originally thought when she'd passed him on the road.

He approached the driver's side. The window had been

lowered. Any other day, it wouldn't have struck him as odd. Today? After his friend being shot and his fight with Roni, nothing seemed ordinary.

And that bugged him enough to send an icy stab straight up his neck.

"Ma'am?" Another two steps and he'd be at the door. No movement from the driver.

What the fuck?

Something's off.

He angled sideways in front of the door. "Ma'am?"

No response. His pulse ratcheted up, the buh-bum-buh-bum whooshing in his ears.

Paranoid. That's what he was. And damned tired from the late night with Roni.

Relax, dude.

He inhaled through his nose, let the cool mountain air refocus him.

"Ma'am, are you all right?"

Finally she moved, turning her head toward him. *Holy shit.*

Bernadette Andrews sat in the pickup, her short hair covered by the baseball cap. She looked different now. Gone was the ethereal quality he remembered. The eyes. Something had changed. The laser-sharp blue had turned stormy. Feral.

He shook his head, focused on the woman behind the wheel and what the hell might be going on.

"Bernadette?"

Her arm came up.

Gun.

Shit.

Way lunged sideways. *Boom!* She fired off a round, the bullet whizzing past him.

He dropped, his body hitting the hard pavement with a thwack. He rolled under the truck. Exhaust pipe heat blasted down on him and the engine clunked into gear.

Shit.

Inches above his face, the driveshaft whirled as he worked his gun from his holster and reached up. Boom. He fired through the floorboard.

Bernadette's piercing scream cracked the quiet morning air. Another clunk sounded and then—nothing. Zero movement.

Did the bullet connect? Was she injured?

Dead?

The driver's side door popped open—definitely not dead —and two small sneaker clad feet hit the pavement. Another cry—the whine of an injured animal—scraped at Way's nerves and Bernadette dropped to one knee. The woman peered at him under the truck, baring her teeth.

Feral.

"I'll kill you," she said, as if she were reciting a shopping list.

She aimed the gun.

Boom!

The round exploded inches from Way's face and ricocheted off the pavement sending bits of hot oil-soaked concrete skittering into his mouth. He spat them out, hoping to hell he hadn't lost any teeth in the mix.

Beyond Bernadette's shoulder, an SUV with glossy black wheels came around the curve. Hell no. He didn't need his sister's superstar boyfriend driving into this goatfuck.

He shifted the gun to his left hand. Twenty yards away, the Rover slid sideways and halted, the horn blaring.

Bernadette rolled to her side—*boom*—and fired at the Rover.

Go.

Way's heart banged against his chest wall, the pounding bringing him to focus. *Take her out.* He fired. The gunpowder's familiar smell of burnt plastic rose and he inhaled, let it snap him back to his training.

Bernadette wailed again and reached back, grabbing her ass cheek. *Got her.*

A dark patch soaked one side of her jeans.

But, Jesus, for a wounded woman, she wouldn't stop. *Adrenaline.* She scrambled to her knees.

He peeked at the Rover and no.

No.

Roni kicked the door open, leaping out, gun in hand. Using the door for cover, she fired at Bernadette. *Boom. Boom-boom.*

Way took aim at one of Berndatte's ankles, pulled the trigger and...*click.*

Jammed. *Goddamnit.*

He racked the slide and cleared the jam.

Boom, boom, boom. Bullets flew from Bernadette's gun, the sound bouncing off rock and echoing.

At the Rover, Roni's piercing swear reached him. Way whipped his head around. She flapped her hand. Shot? Too far away to see blood. Maybe grazed.

He scanned the ground. Roni's gun had skittered beyond the cover of the Range Rover's door, landing near the side of the road. Out of her reach.

If she tried to retrieve it, Bernadette would plug her full of holes.

She'd better not move. "Stay there!"

Bernadette peeked under the truck, checking on him, and Roni charged toward the front of the pickup. Of course. Damned stubborn woman. Why should she listen to him?

The truck suddenly sagged. Bernadette. Crawling back into the pickup.

Go. He scooted to the passenger side, slid out from under the truck and hopped up at the window just as Bernadette slammed a fresh magazine into her gun.

He raised his weapon, but Bernadette was quicker.

Way ducked.

Boom. Glass shattered and shards blew out over his head. *Move.*

He duckwalked to the rear of the truck. Rising, he did a quick peek. Bernadette lunged from the cab, firing off two rounds in Roni's direction. She spun back and—*duck*— blasted another round at Way.

Shit.

The bullet careened off the truck bed. Metal chips and paint flew, smacking into Way's forehead. Warmth oozed near his eyebrow and his eye stung. He closed his eyes, opened them to a kaleidoscope of red.

Dammit. Bernadette would be on him in seconds. He wiped his eyes, trying to clear the blood. *No good.*

He wiped again. And blinked. Better.

At least until the barrel of a gun pressed against his temple. "You're done."

Bernadette's breath was hot on his ear. Way's mind exploded, sending blasts of panic, one after another, firing into his bloodstream, making his head pound as he gritted his teeth.

And waited for the bullet to rip into him.

"Bernadette!"

Roni's voice.

Thunk.

Way flinched at what had to be the sound of something hard connecting with Bernadette's skull. The gun barrel fell away and Way spun, ready to pounce. Roni stood with a large hunk of rock in one hand. He peered down to where an open gash on Bernadette's head chugged, covering her short grayish blond hair with oily blood.

The rock. Roni must have whacked her with it. Fearless woman.

My girl.

Sirens wailed, stabbing at Way's already fried nerves. He spun, found Maggie's cruiser bearing down on them. The car came to a screeching halt as the door flew open and Mags jumped out, drawing down on them. All in seemingly fluid motion.

For all the grief he gave his sister, she was damned good at her job.

Way put his hands up. "We're fine."

"What the hell's happening?"

He glanced down at Bernadette and blew out a hard breath. "I think we found our shooter."

24

RONI SAT ON THE BACK STEP OF THE OPEN AMBULANCE, sunlight blazing down on her, while Cash Kingston wrapped her bleeding hand. Behind her, another medic jotted notes on a clipboard.

"You're lucky it only grazed you," Cash said.

Truer words didn't exist. Particularly if it had been one of the frangible bullets they'd been chasing.

At the time, she'd lost her head, seeing only Way's empty SUV and Bernadette Ambrose on the ground firing under a pickup.

Presumably at Way.

Something had snapped in Roni's brain, obliterating any sense of reason. With her training, she should have known better. But Way needed help. If making herself a target was the cost of saving his life, she had no problem doing it.

Lord, when had she ever gone that far for someone?

Beyond Cash, a second ambulance carrying Bernadette pulled away.

So many questions. Was *Bernadette* their serial killer? The one shooting people with Way's deadly bullets? Given her connections to all the players, it could very well be, but none of it made sense.

"I don't understand," Roni muttered.

"Honey," Cash said, "welcome to the club. I can't figure out half the shit I've seen."

Given his job, Roni didn't doubt it.

Beyond Cash, Way strode toward her with Maggie in tow. Between his quick steps and his glaring, Roni didn't need to be a genius to figure out he wasn't happy.

"Roni," he said, his tone sharp enough to carve cement. "What the hell were you thinking?"

Cash secured the last of the medical tape and offered her a movie-star-worthy smile. "My brother. Always a charmer." He straightened up, angling back to Way. "Dude, take it down a notch."

"Fuck off, Cash. Do you even know what she did?"

Alrighty. Apparently Way had no fear when it came to his older brother. Was it wrong that she found it a little, well, hot?

Cash looked back at her with arched eyebrows. She shrugged. "He's right. I stepped into the open to draw her fire. I must have flinched, because there's no way that bullet should have missed me."

He shook his head and sighed. "In that case, his beef with you is legit. Women are just straight-up crazy sometimes."

With that, he turned away, facing the storm known as Way Kingston. "Go easy on her. She was trying to save your ass."

Way halted. Just...*bam*. Who knew it was that easy to deter him?

Cash stepped aside, giving Roni a helping hand up from her seat on the back of the ambulance. "Thanks, Cash."

"You're welcome. I'll put together some stuff for you to take care of the wound." He jerked his head at Way and Maggie. "Good luck with these two."

Maggie edged around Way, holding one arm to block him. "Before anyone starts yelling, are you all right?"

Had to love Maggie. Roni nodded. "I'm good. It's just a graze." She gestured to Jay's SUV. "Did it get hit?"

"Two shots to the door."

"Oh, ouch. I'm so sorry."

Maggie waved the apology off. "Don't you dare apologize. You just saved my brother's life. Besides, Jay won't care. Knowing him, he'll buy another one."

Way propped his hands on his hips. "What the hell were you doing here?" he said to Roni.

"I didn't like the way we left things. I was literally pulling out of the gate when Maggie called me. She said she heard shots."

"Come again?"

"You pocket-dialed me," Maggie said.

"I...Hang on." He plucked his phone from his front pocket, checked the screen. "I sent you a text."

"Which I got. I was still on my way to my office, so I turned around and headed back up the mountain. On my way here, you called me. Or, your pocket did. That's when I heard gunshots. When you didn't respond, I freaked and called Roni on my work phone."

Roni glanced back at Bernadette's pickup, then back to Jay's wounded SUV. If she had waited another minute, what would she have found on this mountain road? All she knew was that she'd roared around the curve and found Way under fire.

He met Roni's gaze, the heat from a minute ago now cooling. "You could have gotten killed."

Did his voice just crack a teensy bit? Probably, but they didn't have time to argue over her actions. "But I didn't. So let's skip the lecture about the stupidity of jumping in front of a bullet. I did it because I wouldn't have been able to stand it if you died. Believe me, I wasn't being heroic. It was actually quite selfish. So"—she waggled her hand—"spare me your derision."

Way straightened up, drawing his eyebrows together, then faced Maggie.

Did he expect *her* to help him?

He'd likely be waiting a long time. Certain things were a girl code violation and this one was rated a Class A felony.

Maggie put up two hands. "I'm not getting into this with you. Personal issues aside, we've got chaos here. I already have calls in to ATF and the Bureau. They're on their way to the hospital to question Bernadette."

"Was she even conscious?" Roni wanted to know.

Maggie gave a quick nod. "Responding to commands. Which is fairly unbelievable, considering her injuries. She has a nasty laceration and probably a concussion from you clocking her, and she'll need surgery for the gunshot wounds. Total mess."

Roni blew out a burst of air, letting her shoulders drop with the release. She refused to feel guilt. Not after what Bernadette had put them through.

She tilted her head back, letting the sun's warm rays wash over her as she tried to make sense of it all. The few times she'd met Bernadette, the woman had always been welcoming and kind. Anyone friendly with her son, she'd say, was always welcome.

Without question, she adored Jeff, as any mother should. But to what end?

Roni gave up on the sun and met Maggie's eyes. "I'm so

confused. I mean, we've been in Bernadette's presence. Did you ever think she'd be capable of"—she turned, gestured to the police cruisers and flashing lights behind them —"*this?*"

"God no. I'm as stunned as you are. I'm sure ATF and the Bureau are already hunting down judges for search warrants. They'll want to go through everything in her house."

Roni thought about the grand house on the lake she'd so admired. Who knew what Bernadette, former government analyst, had hidden in there. "Think about all of her contacts. Don Harding, Karl. Clay. She might be our common denominator."

"I don't know," Way said. "Even if she got the design, it takes skill to build that bullet. And what's the connection between my bullets and avenging Jeff's death?"

"I guess that's what we need to find out," Roni said.

She gazed at the techs processing the crime scene. County employees. All of them. She bit down on her bottom lip. *Haywood* County.

Ohmygod.

She whipped her head to Maggie. "This is a crime scene. In your county."

Maggie smiled and nodded. "I like the way you think. Let's go."

"Wait," Way said. "What?"

Maggie started toward her cruiser. "We need our own warrant. I'll find my favorite judge. Tell him there's been a shooting and I need to search Bernadette's house. If we work quickly, we'll beat the feds there."

MAGGIE DROPPED RONI AND WAY OFF AT HIS WORKSHOP.

After their fight, the last place Roni wanted to be was alone with him. Her emotions were too churned up. Too clogged with visions of his bullet-hole-riddled body. The man was too stubborn, too focused on doing everything his own damned way. She couldn't live like that. She'd worked too hard to build a life of independence. To have control of her world.

And she couldn't give it up.

Besides, she had a call to make. To Langley. Where she'd clue in Karl Quigley and Don Harding about their friend going psycho.

Way handed her a burner he'd retrieved from his safe. Only she would fall for a guy who kept a stash of new, untraceable phones.

Shaking her head, she texted Karl from her own phone, letting him know she was about to call him from a different line and that he should, without question, answer.

She waited a few seconds for her phone to flash the lovely word *read*.

"He got my message." She grabbed the burner phone and dialed.

On the first ring, he picked up. "Karl Quigley."

"It's Roni. Call me back from a secure line. We'll need Don on the call also."

"You don't order me around. I call the shots."

"Fine. But while you're calling the shots Bernadette Ambrose is getting two bullets pulled out of her ass."

Heavy silence filled the phone line. Good. She'd shocked him.

"What?"

"You heard me. Now, if you'd like, I can go into great detail on this call or you can call me back—with Don present—from an unmonitored line."

"I'll call you back."

Excellent. The egomaniac wasn't a complete loss. She punched the end call button on the phone and held it up. "He's calling me back."

"Good. Can we talk?"

Now he wanted to talk? No way. Maybe tomorrow or next week or three months from now, but right now she couldn't do it. Not when every inch of her was exposed and vulnerable. All he'd have to do was apologize. Hold his arms out and she'd give in. All because she wanted to be held, by him, and given a little comfort after a firefight.

Can't do it. If Way Kingston wanted to be part of her life, he'd have to learn to compromise. To listen once in a while.

"No talking," she said.

"Roni—"

The burn phone rang. Literally saved by the bell. She hit the speaker button. "Hello?"

"It's Karl."

His voice filled the room and Roni glanced behind her, making sure the door to the outer office was closed. Even with the door shut, she lowered the volume on the phone.

"Do you have Don?"

"Patching him in now. Don?"

"I'm here." The words came in a rush. "What's this about Bernadette getting shot?"

"Waylon Kingston was ambushed by Bernadette Ambrose on a mountain road."

"What the hell, Fenwick?"

"Bullshit!"

Ignoring them, she continued. "It's true. I was there. Saw the entire thing. She took multiple shots at him, and subsequently at me, with a Colt .45. The same caliber weapon used for the frangible bullet shootings."

"What the hell?" Karl thundered.

Roni held her wounded hand up as if they could see it. "We don't have a lot of time. Let me finish and then ask your questions. If you don't believe me, I'm happy to send you a photo of my bandaged hand to show you where the bullet grazed me."

"What about Kingston?" Don asked.

She glanced over at Way and put her finger to her lips to keep him silent. "Alive and well. Unharmed. Although it was his two bullets that wound up firmly ensconced in Bernadette's rear. She is, as we speak, in surgery."

"My God." Don let out a harsh breath.

If he thought he was stunned now, he should keep listening.

"By the time she's out of surgery," Roni said, "the Bureau and ATF will be waiting for her. They'll have questions, I'm certain, as to why the mother of a murdered ATF agent chose to shoot at a CIA employee and the creator of an insanely catastrophic frangible bullet the agency is now testing. See what I'm saying here? If the feds pull on that string, who knows what might be revealed? If I were a betting woman, I'd say someone shared that bullet design with Bernadette."

"It sure as hell wasn't me," Don said.

Way waved a hand, drawing her attention. "Ask about Clay," he mouthed.

She nodded. "What about Clay Bartles? What was his involvement in the deal with Kingston?"

"Yes," Karl said much too quickly. "It had to be him. We don't have 24/7 access to Bernadette's or Bartles's conversations, but he was intimately involved with the deal. They could be working together."

Oh, these fuckers. Already she could sense the spin

doctors at work. Roni glanced at Way, who gritted his teeth so hard a muscle in his jaw jumped. He'd better not say one word. She pointed at him, then slashed her hand across her throat.

When he nodded, she nearly gawked. Good for him. "We have one problem with that, fellas," she said.

"What's that?"

"From what I understand about this bullet, it takes a certain amount of skill to recreate it."

"Bernadette was a field agent," Don chimed in. "She knows how to use a weapon. She went through the Farm, for God's sake."

"She obviously has firearms training. Based on what we saw today, I can't comment on her marksmanship skills. It was a...stressful...situation. I think we had her scattered enough that she plugged a lot of holes in two vehicles rather than damned near killing us both. That being said, just because she knows her way around a handgun doesn't mean she knows how to create a bullet like this. I have to believe the same of Clay Bartles."

That last part about Clay? A total reach. She didn't know diddly about his gunsmithing skills. She peered up at Way and held her hands palm up, silently asking the question. Way shook his head indicating Clay wouldn't have the necessary knowledge to reverse engineer the bullet.

"In fact," she said, "according to Way Kingston, Clay did *not* have that level of experience. So, gentlemen, I'm asking you, before the feds pull on that thread, is it possible someone from science and development helped Bernadette? Because it sure is looking like she had help."

When the line went quiet, Roni closed her eyes for a second, centering her thoughts. *Containment.* That's what they wanted. She reopened her eyes. "Tick, tock," she said. "If we don't get ahead of the feds, this thing will go viral."

"No," Don said. "It didn't come from me or my people. Frankly, I wish it had. We'd at least have an answer."

"We need to button this up," Karl said. "I'll reach out to ATF and the Bureau, see what they have."

Whether he'd be honest with her about what they said, was anyone's guess. Somewhere in this process, Roni had lost sight of who to trust inside Langley.

She glanced over at Way. The person she came here to dig up dirt on had wound up being the one most honorable. "While you're at it," she said into the phone, "figure out how to keep Waylon Kingston's name out of this. Or I swear to you, I'll call the news networks myself. Keep me posted."

She clicked off and tossed the phone on Way's workbench.

"Thank you."

"Don't thank me yet. Your ass is still in a sling here, pal. It'll be a miracle if we keep your involvement under wraps."

"Still. Thank you for trying."

"I'm pissed at you, but you were innocent. A contractor doing work for your country. Plus, I like your family. I'm not about to let you go down for this."

He studied her through narrowed eyes. "You like my family."

The comment came as a simple statement and it nearly gutted her. Yes, she liked his family. Too much. She should have known better. Being surrounded by loving people who allowed her into their warm fold wasn't the norm in Roni's world.

"I do," she said. "They don't deserve to see you dragged through a scandal. Or worse."

"I agree. That wasn't my point, though. I'm wondering

where *I* stand in all this. You like my family, but what about me?"

Question of the day. She felt...something. Something big and powerful and unlike anything she'd experienced before. It held an edge of desperation that equally terrified and thrilled her.

And she wanted more of it. Plenty more. Based on what she'd seen, Way couldn't give it to her. She didn't need—or want—him to completely give up the Kingdom of Way, but there had to be room for her.

That, she knew.

"Way, I've been alone a long time. This last week with you made me realize that. Which, I suppose, is a good thing."

"Okay." He shrugged. "I think."

His rich, dark eyes made her think of warm fires and... home. She might be completely dreaming now. Total wishful thinking.

She slid onto the counter-height stool beside Way's workbench, fiddled with the tip of her fingernail where a rough edge needed filing. When this was over, she'd treat herself to a manicure.

"I have no family. I've spent years convincing myself that I'm fine without it. It's the insanity of self-protecting—as if *that* really works. Then you come along and, as maddening as you are, I feel, I don't know, safe, I guess. Like I want the family I've been denying myself. With you, I can suddenly picture a future I never allowed myself to hope for."

A punch of emotion blocked her throat, trapping her air.

He stepped toward her. Way to the rescue. If he touched her, she'd be a goner.

She held up her hand. "I'm fine. Again. This is all good. I'm finally being honest with myself."

"I don't understand. Isn't feeling safe the whole point of being in a relationship? How is that a deal-breaker?"

"It's not. The deal-breaker is you being accustomed to life your way. You're entitled to live it how you want. Unfortunately, I'm just as stubborn, so for us to be together, we'll both have to bend. I'm not sure you're ready for that."

He let out a long sigh. Closed his eyes for a second. Poor guy.

"It's all right," she said. "We're in the middle of a mess right now. Let's not pile on. Besides, I'll be heading back to DC soon. I don't even know if I still have a job. I'll need to deal with that."

Her phone rang. Her personal one. Not the burner. She slid it from her back pocket. Maggie. She tapped the screen. "Hi. What's up?"

"I got the warrant. I have a team heading to Bernadette's."

Roni hopped off the stool, her heels clapping against the tile. "We'll meet you there."

"Uh. No."

Given that the home was part of a criminal investigation, Roni knew there'd be no way Maggie would let them inside. "We'll wait outside. I promise."

"I don't want either one of you on the property. The feds will eventually show up, and I want that scene pristine."

Meaning no civilians trampling through.

"Fine. We'll stay across the street. But we'll be there. Just in case something comes up."

Before Maggie could protest, Roni hung up. "Let's go," she said to Way. "Maggie got us a warrant."

25

THIRTY MINUTES INTO THE DRIVE TO BERNADETTE'S, RONI'S phone rang. A local number. T. Holbrath.

Holbrath.

She knew *that* name.

She tapped the screen and put the phone to her ear. "Roni Fenwick."

"Ms. Fenwick, this is Special Agent Terence Holbrath."

Special Agent. The one who'd phoned Way regarding Clay's murder. She'd wanted to check him out, which led to their argument this morning. She should just blame the whole thing on this guy. It would be so much easier than thinking about her and Way's useless attempt to deal with each other.

"Agent Holbrath, how can I help you?"

Way's head snapped sideways. She pointed at the road, reminding him he had precious cargo on board. Namely her.

"Ms. Fenwick, I understand you're acquainted with Bernadette Ambrose."

"I am. Her son was a colleague."

"Yes. I'm sorry for your loss. I'm also aware of the incident this morning. Are you all right?"

She glanced down at her bandaged hand, thankful that was the only injury suffered. "I'm fine. What can I do for you?"

"I need for you to come to the hospital."

Ha. He needed? She had an entire list of things *she* needed and nobody seemed in a great rush to provide them.

Now she wanted a pity party?

Nuh-uh. Not going there. She'd left pity parties behind after her last foster home. "I'm in the middle of something. What's the problem?"

"Bernadette Ambrose. She's out of surgery and would like to speak with you."

Roni gawked. She couldn't have heard that right. "Excuse me? Did you just say Bernadette wants to speak with *me*?"

At that, Way whipped his head at her again, this time swerving a little, then going back to the road. "Sorry," he said. "But what the hell?"

"Yes." Holbrath spoke over Way's apology. "She's refusing to give a statement until she sees you."

Gobsmacked, Roni stared out the windshield at the giant oak trees lining the four-lane road. This was a new one. "Any idea what she wants to speak to me about?"

"No, ma'am. But she claims she'll tell us everything if she speaks to you first."

"You're not doing it," Way grumbled. "No way."

Another thing they'd be forced to disagree on. Because, yes, she was most definitely doing this. Curiosity alone was enough to get her there. "Is her lawyer present?"

"On the way. All we need is you."

"Well, then, I guess I'll be there shortly." She poked at

the phone and tossed it into the cupholder. "Change of plans."

"You can't be serious," Way said.

"You'd better believe I am. Take me to the hospital. Bernadette has something to say."

THREE HOURS LATER, AFTER BERNADETTE WAS TRANSPORTED from recovery and doctors cleared Roni for a visit, Roni entered Bernadette's hospital room. The closed-in, antiseptic-laced staleness released an assault of memories. Her father wincing in pain as his body, literally loose skin over bone, fell deeper and deeper into unconsciousness.

The heart rate monitor. She'd stood there, grasping her father's hand, wanting so much to just hang on. *Please, Daddy, please.*

Even then, at such a young age, somehow she knew. So she squeezed his hand tighter, trying not to cry—*brave girl*—as the bright green number on the heart rate monitor went lower.

And lower.

And lower.

Right in front of her.

Just one time, she wanted to enter a hospital and not think of the night her life changed forever.

She eased out a breath and nodded at a man with short graying hair sitting by Bernadette. He stood. He wore a navy suit that must have been high quality, because there wasn't a wrinkle to be found and they were already at midday.

"Hello," Roni said.

He set the leather portfolio he'd been holding on the bed and approached.

"Hello. I'm Rhyne Ingrams. Ms. Ambrose's attorney."

"Criminal or private?"

"Criminal."

"Well, okay then."

She glanced over to the bed where the color on Bernadette's face resembled freshly poured cement. Part of her head was wrapped in gauze and a sheet covered her up to her chest, but her arms lay on top revealing the wrist restraints securing her to the bed. More than likely, her ankles met the same fate. Beside her, a monitor beeped once, then went quiet, and another rush of memories flashed.

Focus.

Right here. Right now.

A whooshing sounded and the blood pressure cuff around Bernadette's arm went into action.

She winced at the tightening wrap and waited for it to release. "Thank you...for...coming."

The words came slowly, obviously the effects of anesthesia. Roni was no lawyer, but letting Bernadette—and her drug-addled mind—speak to anyone was insanity.

"You're welcome. Are you sure you want to talk right now?"

"I've already spoken with her," Ingrams said. "She's determined to do this." He pointed to the chair he'd vacated. "Please. Have a seat."

Ingrams was probably already planning his appeal. Well, good for him. He moved to the open space by the wall, leaning back on it, arms folded. "I'll be right here, Bernadette."

"Thank you, Rhyne." She angled her head to Roni. "I'm sure you have questions."

"Plenty."

"You should know, it was a just mission."

A just *mission*.

What that even meant, Roni hadn't a clue. "Forgive me, Bernadette, but I fail to see how shooting me or Way Kingston is a just mission. Were you driving the car the other night? The one that nearly sent us flying off a mountain? Was that part of the mission, too?"

"The list was twelve people."

Roni knew of only one list with twelve people on it. The thought of it made her stomach twist. She closed her eyes, let out a long sigh. "You have Jeff's journal."

Why hadn't they even considered that? They'd assumed the ATF or FBI had taken the journal as evidence when they should have simply asked if either department had it.

Bernadette looked off toward the window where a bright blue sky teased anyone locked inside the building. "I found it in his apartment. The night he died, I went there. Laid down in his bed. Just to smell him. My baby. They'd killed him. Left him to die in the street like an animal."

As angry as Roni was, her heart kicked. Grief, she understood. Particularly when the loss vaporized the lives of loved ones.

Setting aside the fact that Bernadette had tried to kill her, Roni touched her hand. "Jeff was a good man and a great friend. Be proud of that."

A lazy half smile tugged at Bernadette's lips. "You're kind. I can see why he enjoyed you. You know, he had...feelings...for you. He never admitted it, but I knew my son. He spoke of you in a way that made me think you were special. Which is why I asked to see you. He'd want me to tell you the truth."

Jeff? Roni sat for a second, thinking back on the dinners and phone calls they'd shared after a hard day. Friends. That's all she'd sensed back then. If he'd thrown her signals of anything more, she never caught them. Or maybe she hadn't wanted to. "I never knew. I wish I had."

"I suppose he didn't want to ruin anything. One thing about my boy, he knew how to hide his emotions." Bernadette cleared her throat and her eyes drifted closed. "I found the journal in his bedside table. By the time investigators got to his apartment, I'd tucked it in my purse."

"That was evidence."

Bernadette's eyes snapped open again and she met Roni's stare. "My son was dead, and I intended to deal with whomever caused it. I wasn't worried about evidence."

Grief-induced rage wasn't uncommon, but this wholesale slaughter of suspects? Bonkers. "How do you even know the people in that journal are responsible?"

"Who else could it be?"

Plenty of people. But Roni didn't think it worth arguing. The woman had gone on a full-blown vigilante bender. Nothing rational would make sense to her.

"Bernadette, did you shoot those people?"

Part of Roni hoped she'd say no. That perhaps, with her deep pockets, she'd hired someone.

"Bernadette," her lawyer said, "I'll caution you here."

"Thank you, Rhyne, but I know what I'm doing. I want those bastards—the remaining ones—on the list to know it was me." She locked her gaze on Roni's. "I shot them. I was a field agent early in my career. I learned how to shoot and steal cars and stay under the radar. All these years later, I still enjoy practicing my shooting. I'm good, too."

Oh, God.

From his spot on the wall, the lawyer sighed.

"Where did you get the bullets?"

"Jeff had them."

Of all the things she'd expected to hear—wooing the

design out of Don, bribing a member of Don's staff or Clay Bartles—Roni hadn't anticipated Jeff's involvement.

Oh, Jeff. What did you do?

Stealing herself for disappointment she sat forward, giving Bernadette her full attention. "Jeff?"

She nodded. "He kept a workshop at my house. In the basement."

By now, Maggie would be well into her search of Bernadette's home. As soon as this conversation ended, Roni would call her, direct her to the basement.

"He liked to tinker with rifles," Bernadette continued. "Sometimes handguns, but mostly rifles. He'd come out to the house and take his guns into the woods for target practice."

"How did he get the bullets?"

"At the time, I didn't know. He had them in the safe. He'd given me the combination. Just in case. When I opened that safe, there were eighteen bullets. He'd drawn a sketch that I found on the shelf beside them. A blueprint."

"Did Don Harding tell him how to do it?"

"I don't know."

"Oh, Bernadette. Please. You've come this far. Tell me the damned truth."

She rested her head back, closing her eyes again. *Dammit.* Hell of a time for the aftereffects of anesthesia to silence her. "Bernadette? Do you need a break?"

Please say no.

Bernadette shook her head and opened her eyes. "At the time, all I knew was he'd built bullets with acid in them. Months went by, and then last Tuesday I got a call from Clay Bartles. I'd introduced him to Jeff at one of the barbecues. They'd become friendly. Clay asked me about the bullets. Knowing Jeff liked guns, he'd shared Mr. Kingston's project idea with him. After the reports of gang members dying from the same type of bullet, he was concerned that perhaps Jeff had leaked the idea."

Roni dipped her head. Way would be devastated by this news. Still, Way had never shared the exact design. "How did Clay know the specs?"

"He swore to me that he never told Jeff the exact design. Just how the bullet worked. He never even saw it. I believed him. I know Don Harding. He'd be protective of information such as that."

Don's ability to keep secrets wouldn't matter. Jeff was a gun guy. Loved tinkering with them and had even made suggestions to Roni about certain triggers that might work better for her. Given his knowledge of firearms, it wasn't a stretch to think he could recreate the bullet.

As suspected, Way's bullets had been reverse engineered.

"Jeff figured it out on his own," Roni said.

"I believe so."

"Is that why you killed Clay?"

Bernadette paused, but didn't bother looking at her lawyer. Everyone knew where he stood on this matter.

Finally, Bernadette met Roni's gaze. "I didn't want to. He called me again. Getting nervous and asking questions. Wanting to know if Jeff could have built the bullets himself. He wouldn't say it, but I know he was asking if my son sold that ammunition. Clay became...messy."

As much as she wanted to fight it, gravity took hold and Roni's mouth slid open. How had she not sensed any of this on the visit to Bernadette's? "Oh, God. Why? He was doing the right thing."

"Saving a bunch of lowlifes and implicating my dead son? Not while I'm alive. Jeff was everything to me. I couldn't have it. But I also wasn't done. Clayton Bartles was in the way."

"Collateral damage. Like Way and me."

Bernadette gave her a hard look. "You can't understand. He was my son."

The woman was insane. Whether it was grief-inflicted or her years in the spec ops world—possibly both—she'd become a full-fledged sociopath.

Roni leaned forward, clasped Bernadette's hand. "You're right. I'm not a mother. I can't understand. But I don't see how murdering twelve people would make up for losing Jeff. Still, I'm very sorry for your loss."

Roni stood and met the lawyer's gaze. Before he could say anything, she headed for the door.

"I had to," Bernadette called. "You don't think the world is better off without those people? Without criminals? I spent *years* dealing with garbage like them. What makes this different?"

Unbelievable. If years of serving her country would do this to Roni, she didn't want it. Not one bit. She turned back. "Proof makes it different. You had no proof any of those people murdered Jeff. Maybe they weren't angels, but you don't get to play judge and jury. That's not what our government trained you for. Somewhere along the way, you lost sight of that."

With that, she turned and walked out the door, leaving a silent Bernadette behind.

In the hallway, Way leaned against the far wall talking to Agent Holbrath. Lord, Way was easy on the eyes and just the thing she needed after a conversation that left her...gutted.

Gutted and grimy.

A four-hour shower wouldn't wipe that filth off.

Way broke free of Holbrath, boosting himself off the wall and falling in step beside her.

"Ms. Fenwick," Holbrath called. "I need a word."

"No," she muttered to Way. "I can't."

He gave her arm a gentle squeeze. "I'll talk to him. Meet me outside."

When had she turned into a helpless female? But at the moment, she said a silent thanks for having Way beside her.

She kept moving, her gaze on the door ahead. *Get there.* That's all she had to do. Get out of this hospital with its nasty, confining air. At the double doors, she smacked at the button on the wall. *Come on, come on.* A beep sounded and ever so slowly the doors inched open.

Before they stopped moving, she squeezed through, spotting a stairwell sign. Perfect. She'd take the stairs down, run off some of this rancid energy.

Roni bolted down the stairs, her boot heels banging against the steps and echoing throughout the enclosed space. She hung on to the metal rail as she pounded down the first flight, then the second.

Fresh air.

That's all she needed.

First floor. Finally.

She swung that door open, stopped in the hallway, and peered left. Dead end. She went right, passing a gift shop and a coffee bar near the front entrance.

Right there.

Fresh air.

Through the revolving door, she went into sunshine and oxygen and a cool breeze that immediately eased her mind. Mountain air. Who knew?

"Excuse me," an older man said, angling around her to the revolving door.

Quickly, she moved to the side, propping one shoulder against the building's edge while inhaling and exhaling, letting her body do the work of settling itself. God, what a mess.

Talk about a political firestorm. NSA, CIA, FBI, ATF. All of them involved.

"Hey."

Way stood just outside the revolving door. "You okay?"

She shook her head, a spastic snapping back and forth. He strode toward her, arms out. "Talk to me."

No. She couldn't let him put his hands on her. As much as she wanted the comfort of being held, the heartbreak wouldn't be worth it. She had to free herself before she became any more attached to Way and his stubbornness.

She held her hands up, halting him. "She did it," Roni said. "Murdered all those people. She told me she shot them. And then she tried to kill *us*. She nearly knocked us off that mountain."

Then he did it. He reached for her, wrapping one arm around her, bringing her close and crushing her against him. She didn't fight it. Just settled her cheek against his chest, breathing in the faded scent of his laundry soap and wanting...more. Of this.

Of him.

Dammit.

They'd never work. She knew it. And yet, she stayed in his arms, taking in every ounce of whatever he gave.

He dropped a kiss on top of her head. "You're okay. I promise. You're okay."

"What's worse is I feel sorry for her. I know what it's like to be alone. To suffer a devastating loss like that. It's horrible. What she did is *horrible*."

"Y'all all right over there?"

Still snuggled against Way, Roni turned her head. A nurse leaving the building. Great. Nothing like a public meltdown.

"Yes, ma'am," Way said. "Thank you."

The nurse stood, obviously waiting for Roni to answer. "Yes," she said. "I'm fine."

Then she backed away from Way, looking up at him and nodding. "I'm good. Thank you."

The nurse moved on and Roni shook her head. "I have to call Maggie."

"Why?"

Roni slid her phone from her back pocket. "The rest of the bullets are in Bernadette's basement. In a safe."

"She's already there," Way said. "The feds beat her to it. Sounds like they took over the scene."

"Dammit." She poked Maggie's name on the screen. "I'm still calling her. She can tell them where to look."

BY THE TIME WAY GOT RONI BACK TO MRS. TASKY'S, MAGGIE had alerted the feds to the bullets and they were scouring the workshop.

For now, there was nothing to do but wait until Maggie and the feds sorted the mess out.

At least they were safe. But holy hell, Bernadette Ambrose was a fucked-up woman.

Way pulled to the curb, sliding his SUV into park, more than ready to walk Roni inside.

"No," she said. "I'll go myself."

"I can walk you in."

She shook her head. Damned hardheaded woman. "Come on. Let me at least make sure you get in there okay."

"I don't want you to. I need...space."

Ah, shit. He hated the *space* line. Typically, he was the one giving it and suddenly the healthy weight of it pressed in on him. Quite the weapon that one.

Plus, she wouldn't even make eye contact and that never turned out well.

"*Space,*" he said. "What does that mean exactly?"

"I need time to think. About you. About what went on this week." She circled her hand around her head. "I'm a mess."

"So, what are you gonna do?" He jerked his head toward Mrs. Tasky's B&B. "Sit inside alone?"

She faced him, meeting his gaze dead on. "I'm going back to DC. I have a job, Way. At least, I think I still have a job. The rest of this is for people way above my pay grade to figure out. I've done my part."

He forced himself to not react. To not scoff or shake his head or any other damned form of body language that would piss her off. But, really? She couldn't be serious. Not after what they'd been through. "You're going?"

"We both knew this wasn't forever."

For a solid five seconds he absorbed it. Took stock of that punch to the chest, which, in his mind, might be heartbreak. Sure, he'd had women drop-kick him, but none of it ever felt like...this. Like his world changing.

Whatever it was, it sucked. "Oh, hell no," he said. "Don't put this on me. You're going because *you* want to."

She let out a sigh, then broke eye contact, staring straight ahead out the windshield. "I suppose that's true."

She lifted the door handle—wait. She was going? Just walking away?

Apparently, because she hopped to the curb, started to close the door, then turned back. Her dark eyes shimmered under the waning afternoon sun. Tears. Damn, he hated making women cry.

"Goodbye, Way. Thank you for everything."

"Roni, wait!"

She shut the door, waving him off. *Not happening.* She wasn't walking away like that.

He shoved at his door, stepped out onto the running board and peering at her over the open door. "Seriously? You're leaving like this?"

She didn't turn. Kept on moving, maybe even speeding up, trying to put distance between them.

He watched her go, watched her climb the steps and reach the door. Her name was right there on his tongue. *Stop her.*

Way opened his mouth, but...nothing. He couldn't do it. Couldn't beg her to stop. Without bothering to glance back, she closed the front door and was gone.

"Well, shit."

His pulse hammered and a throbbing pain nearly split his skull open.

Women.

Always a challenge.

What did he need with her making his life hell? He'd done all right without her all these years. He'd just move the fuck on.

Right?

How hard could it be?

26

Two days later, under a cloudless blue sky, Way leaned over the guardrail where his beloved motorcycle had tumbled to its demise.

His head spun, either from the height or the shots of whisky he and Reid had consumed the night before.

Wasn't his fault he'd stopped into the B for a beer—or twelve—and Reid saw his car out front. The two of them wound up sitting there amongst a crowd of regulars, getting wasted and complaining about everything from global warming to late mail deliveries.

Goddamn, he couldn't drink like he used to.

All he knew was someone had called Maggie. Being the good sister and cousin she was, she'd loaded the two of them into her cruiser and got them home so they could sleep it off.

Only problem for Way was that Shep, being an early riser, knocked on his door at 7 a.m. and now stood beside him, peering straight down the rock face at hunks of scattered metal.

"That is a fucking mess," Shep said.

He wasn't kidding. Engine here, handlebars there, one tire hung up on a branch, the other at least a hundred feet below that.

Remnants of his motorcycle everywhere.

"What do you think? Can you retrieve it?"

Shep pulled a face that lacked any form of encouragement. "No."

Damn. If his brother said they couldn't get it back, that was the end of it. "Well, *that* sucks. It's a classic. I wanted it back."

"I can get parts of it. Not everything. To get to that tire—" Shep pointed at the one hanging on the branch, "—I would have to work my way along the rock face." He pointed to a jutting ledge covered with loose rock. "That loose rock is there for a reason. It's falling from above."

A guy didn't have to be an expert climber to know that looked dangerous. Even for Shep, the best damned climber around. Hell, the guy met his girlfriend while saving the lives a bunch of numbnut novices who thought surviving the wilderness for days would be easy.

What am I doing?

Shep smacked his hand on the guardrail. "I will attach my rope here and rappel over that ledge. I cannot see what's below, but if I—"

Way held his hands up. "Stop."

His mind skipped ahead to a vision of Shep's broken body swinging alongside the mountain after being pummeled by boulders the size of Mars.

All for a hunk of metal.

What kind of man sends his little brother into a situation like that?

"I could—"

"Stop," Way said.

"Why? I'm not done speaking yet."

Way let out a frustrated laugh. Good old Shep. He set his hand on his little brother's shoulder and squeezed. "I know. But I don't want you to do this. Forget it."

"Why? You said you wanted the motorcycle back."

"I do. But not enough to let you do this."

His brother gritted his teeth. "I *can* do it."

He'd have to handle this carefully. One surefire way to piss off Shep—a guy on the spectrum—was to question his ability. Particularly when it came to climbing.

"I *know* you can do it. You're the best climber in three counties. It's not about whether you can or not."

"Then what is it?"

"You could get hurt."

Shep shrugged. "It's always dangerous."

"Yeah, but you have Joss now. And"—Way waved a hand —"it's a motorcycle. If it was a person down there, it'd be different."

"I thought you loved the motorcycle."

He had no idea. "I do."

"Okay. I can do it then."

Seriously, hangover notwithstanding, a shot of scotch would do a world of good right now. "No, Shep. I don't want you to. I can live without the motorcycle. What I can't live without is you. Got it?"

And that fast it hit him. Way didn't need the damned bike. All the jokes about that motorcycle being his one true love?

His head snapped back. An absolute slap upside his head.

He'd managed to detach himself so much that his family accused him of only loving a machine. How pathetic?

No wonder Roni questioned his ability to commit.

He tugged on Shep's sleeve. "We're leaving."

"What about the bike?"

"Fuck the bike. I don't need it."

What he needed was a petite spitfire named Roni Fenwick.

AFTER TWO DAYS OF SELF-IMPOSED SOLITARY CONFINEMENT, Roni headed back to work.

She flipped the lights on in her office, took in the bland gray walls and equally bland tweed carpet, and missed...trees.

Steele Ridge trees.

And mountain views backlit by a sky so blue it had to be sent straight from heaven.

"Dammit."

Three days ago she'd left Steele Ridge. Left Way Kingston, a man unafraid of her independence and ballsy attitude. Most men ran screaming.

Way?

He liked it.

But she had a life in DC. An apartment and a job.

Well, she thought she had a job. After the fight with Karl outside of Maggie's office, she wasn't quite sure if she'd come in today and be terminated. Somehow that didn't feel like such a bad thing.

And what was that about?

A single woman faced with losing her job and she didn't mind it? Who the hell would pay her rent? And car payment? Not to mention the other myriad of bills.

She walked to the desk, dumped her messenger bag on top. The desk phone rang and she scooped it up without even checking the ID. "Roni Fenwick."

She tucked the handset on her shoulder while she unloaded her bag. Lunch sack, notepad, water jug.

"Hi. It's Maggie."

Oh, Maggie. Thank God. She needed a friendly voice on her first day back. "Hey, you."

"I tried your cell, but figured you were in your office."

"You figured right. My first day back."

"You must be happy to be back to your routine."

Not by a long shot. Once again, Roni glanced at the bland walls. She could lie to Maggie, pretend like it was business as usual but why bother? "I'm..." She shook her head. "I don't know, Mags. Something feels different now. After the things Karl said to me—and the situation in general—I'm dissatisfied, I guess. And coming back here? I feel...nothing. I don't even have a window."

"Well, you're used to being in the field. When have you ever sat in an office all day?"

"Never. But I'm also good at this training job."

"So, be a trainer somewhere else. Have you even looked around to see what's out there? What about the private sector? Heck, you could develop a class for Reid's training center. I bet he'd love something like that. It might not be full-time, but I know he pays well. Part-time in the private sector might equal your full-time government salary."

Not working full-time? She'd been working since she was sixteen. Work, school, work, school. Anything to avoid thinking about her lack of roots.

I want roots.

When Roni didn't respond, Maggie sighed. "Look, I'm not making light of it. After what you went through last week, I could see why you're feeling this way. You've always been passionate about your work. I don't see you being happy in something that doesn't satisfy that passion."

"Exactly. Knowing what I know now, about Bernadette—everything really—I just don't know if this job is the one for me. Frankly, I'm pissed that I felt compelled to use my friendship with you to clear a case. That's not right."

"It's the job, though. I get it. It doesn't make me feel any differently about you."

And this, right here, would be why she'd latched on to Maggie Kingston. A realist to her core, Maggie didn't hold grudges. She might be the kindest person Roni knew. "This, my friend, is one of the reasons I love you."

Whoa. Where did that come from? Fascinating how easy that one little word was. *Love.*

Maggie laughed. "Now you're sucking up. But you know I feel the same about you. We girls need to stick together."

Roni smiled, dropped into her desk chair in her windowless office, and stared at the crappy wall. Right now she could use a good dose of fresh mountain air, sunshine, and gossiping residents.

And with it, some Way Kingston. Had she been foolish to walk away from him? Then again, he hadn't tried all that hard to stop her.

Tears bubbled and she blinked them away. She could call him. Maybe they could still see each other. Grab a meal every once in a while.

I need more.

She needed him to let her into his life and make her an equal in the relationship. It couldn't always be him calling the shots. That wouldn't happen.

"How's Way?" *Ach.* "I'm sorry. Forget it. I'm not putting you in the middle."

"Oh, please," Maggie said. "It's fine. He's...Way. Keeping to himself. He did actually invite us all over for a cookout the night before last."

"Wait. Way?"

"Shocking. I know. But he's trying to not be such a grouch when we take an interest in him. Although," Maggie snorted, "we may have been too much for him. He took off on his motorcycle yesterday."

Of course he did. Still, the cookout, for Way was a major step. Could there be hope? She shook her head. Couldn't think that way. Couldn't get her hopes up.

"Did Shep recover the other bike?"

"Nope."

Damn. Roni sat forward. "He couldn't get to it?"

"From what I heard, he could. Way didn't want him to. Said it was too dangerous."

Seriously, had someone cracked Way on the head? Because this was just too much. "It must have killed him to leave that bike there."

"Honestly, I don't think it did. I spoke to him before he left yesterday and he shrugged it off. Said he'd build another one."

When Roni didn't answer, Maggie laughed. "That was my reaction, too. So, here I am, calling you to say I think something has changed with him. I wanted you to know that."

Oh, Maggie. Roni made a humming noise while she pondered Maggie's intentions. "Mags, are you meddling? You know he hates that."

"Which would be why I'm talking to you."

Now Roni flat-out laughed. A good belly laugh that made her feel light and happy and ready to move on to whatever could let her feel this way continually. "You are something else, sister."

"I love my brother. Sue me. Besides, that's as far as I'm taking it. I really just wanted to check on you. I know the week was nuts, but I was sorry to see you go. I miss our talks. But hey, it's your first day back after a stressful week. See how you feel. After a few days, if you're still not happy, we'll talk to Reid."

We. How awesome was that?

"Thank you, Maggie."

"I didn't do anything."

"Yes, you did. You absolutely did. Let me think about it. I'll call you in a couple of days."

"Whatever you want. I'm always here for you."

After saying goodbye, Roni set the phone back in the cradle and sat back. *We.* That's what Maggie had said. Such a lovely inclusive word that meant support and connecting and having each other's back.

Safety.

Maggie might not be family in the biological sense, but thinking on it now, Roni didn't need that. What she needed was to create her own little tribe. Family but not.

Her phone rang again, displaying Karl's number. He wasn't wasting any time.

She hit the speaker button. "Roni Fenwick."

"My office," he snapped. "Right now."

Fuck you.

That's what she'd like to say. The man sent her on a goose chase, insisted she risk a cherished friendship, withheld information, and nearly got her killed. Now he wanted to order her around.

No, sir.

Nuh-uh.

She stood, opened her messenger bag and shoved her lunch sack back in. The notepad and water jug went next.

"No." She opened the top desk drawer and pulled out the few personal items.

"Excuse me?"

"I'm not coming to your office. I'm in the middle of something."

A gurgling noise drifted through the phone line. The associate deputy director of administration was clearly not accustomed to being defied.

"Let me make this easy on you, sir. I quit."

"*Excuse* me?" he repeated.

"My job. I'm quitting. I'm cleaning out my desk as we speak. I busted my ass last week while you assholes nearly got me killed and did you even *think* to say thank you?"

"You had a job to do."

Lord, what was she doing? Chasing happiness. That's what. "I did my job. You may not have agreed with my methods, but I saved the CIA from one hell of a scandal. And, oh, by the way, we stopped a whole slew of people from being murdered. You're welcome. Where are we with Way Kingston?"

"All clear on that," Karl said. "We spoke with the FBI. Given Bernadette Ambrose's connection with Clayton Bartles, there's no need to bring the agency into it. The Bureau will simply put in a report that Bartles gave Jeff Ambrose the idea for the bullets. That's where it'll stay."

"Good. Way is innocent in all of this. Be sure to let him know that. He deserves that much from you."

With that, she poked the button, disconnecting the call. "Dumbass," she muttered.

The phone immediately rang. Karl again. *Sorry.* No can do. As the phone rang and rang, she double-checked the desk drawers and glanced around the office.

She'd brought minimal personal items to her office, blaming it on building security and it not being worth having her personal items searched.

Should have known.

Shouldering her bag, she headed to the door. On her way out she'd drop off her ID, make arrangements for her final paycheck and be done with all of this.

She waited for the panic to hit. The telltale don't-do-it sign, but...nothing.

Only a bizarre sense of calm. She gripped the strap of her messenger bag, lifted her chin, and headed for the door.

FINDING RONI'S ADDRESS, WITH MICKI'S HELP, TURNED OUT to be insanely simple.

Something that didn't sit well with Way at all. A single woman living alone shouldn't be that easy to find.

He rode the elevator of her apartment building and with each passing floor felt more and more confined. Somehow, he hadn't pictured her living in the enormous brick complex that probably held more people than all of Steele Ridge. But, hey, it was close to her office.

The doors slid open and he stepped off the elevator, following the signs for apartment 1114. As he walked, he counted the doors, checking the numbers as he passed. 1104, 1106, 1108. The further he moved into the bowels of the building, the more the hallway seemed to narrow, trapping him inside the concrete.

1110. Two more to go.

If he had to live here, he'd shoot himself. Simple as that.

And that revelation had him rethinking this whole thing. If she was happy here, in this prison of a dwelling, did they even belong together? Could they find the compromise? If it meant having Roni in his life, he'd give a little, absolutely. But he couldn't live like this.

1114.

There it was. He checked his watch one last time: 6:30. He'd intended on waiting until later, ensuring she'd be home after a long day at work, but he'd wheeled into town three hours ago and couldn't stand the pressure anymore.

He needed to see her.

Fast.

He rapped on the door and stepped back so she'd get a clear view of him through the peephole. After the way they'd left things, maybe he should hide. He wouldn't blame her if she didn't answer, but he wouldn't give up. Not until they at least talked. Then, after she'd heard him out, she could send him on his way.

He wouldn't be happy, but he'd do what she asked.

Except the door swung open. She stood there, one hand on the inside knob—ready to fire it closed probably—and her eyes a little wide. She wore her signature tight jeans and a low-cut tank top that gave him a nice view of her lush breasts. Man, he was a goner.

The heavy silence between them was enough to drown him.

"Uh...hi," he said.

"Hi. What are you doing here?"

No leaps of joy, that was for sure. He couldn't get hung up on that. She'd opened the door. It was a start.

He hit her with the so-called Kingston smile. The one that supposedly slayed people. "I was in the neighborhood?"

That got him an amused eye roll. "I'm surprised to see you."

"That was my intention." He pointed inside. "Can I come in? Talk for a few minutes."

"Of course, yes. I'm sorry. You just...stunned me."

She waved him inside, gesturing down a short hallway that led to a living room with a white leather sofa and glass coffee table. A lattice screen partitioned the room, giving a decorative flair to hiding the bed.

Studio apartment.

How the hell did she stand living in barely five hundred square feet?

Two suitcases sat open on the sofa, clothes neatly stacked inside. Something akin to panic poked at him. She'd just gotten back, where the hell was she going?

He pointed at the cases. "You going somewhere?"

"I am."

Shit. "Taking a trip?"

"Sort of. I quit my job today."

Holy crap. The panic gave way to a burst of hope. If she quit her job, maybe he'd get lucky enough to convince her to come back to Steele Ridge.

She walked to the sofa, made like she wanted to move the suitcases so he could sit down.

"Leave them." He pointed to the small bistro table with two chairs. "Here is fine. Where are you going?"

"I'm not sure. Maybe to find you?"

Mid-step to the bistro table, he paused. Did she just say what he thought? He faced her, met her gaze, and...nothing. The woman was an expert at masking her emotions. Which he supposed was part of this twisted attraction to her. Underneath all the spark and fire, she kept him guessing. He adored her for that. "You were coming back to Steele Ridge?"

She nodded. "I feel like we need to talk."

"I'd love that."

She cocked her head, gave him a sly grin. "A man wanting to talk. Fascinating."

"Well, no. I don't *want* to. I'd rather bash my head in

with a hammer. But I agree with you that we should. That way I can tell you I'm an ass."

"I like the start of this conversation."

Okay. He'd give her that one. So far so good. He stepped closer, but left a good two feet between them. "I'm used to being on my own," he said. "I thought I liked it. After time with you, even though how we came together sucked, I liked it. Loved it, in fact. Having someone to bounce ideas off of and go riding with. It was"—he shrugged—"I don't know, nice, I guess. You know?"

"I do know. I felt the same way. And speaking of, Maggie told me about the bike. I'm sorry. I know what it meant to you."

He waved it off. "Thanks, but after all the bullcrap from last week, I'm seeing things differently. I mean, we were standing there—me and Shep—and I'm hanging on to the metal guardrail, staring down at all this loose rock that could crumble and cave my little brother's head in. I couldn't do it. Not for a motorcycle. Nothing is worth that. It made me realize how much energy I put into a hunk of metal." He shook his head. "What kind of man does that?"

Roni stepped closer and set her hands on his arms. That same old bolt of heat shot through him. He wanted her. He knew it.

"Maybe the bike was a way to love something without risking getting hurt. Believe me, I'm an ace at it. I think you like living in the Kingdom of Way. If you let someone else in, they get a say in what happens. A hunk of metal doesn't speak."

At that, he smiled and squeezed another inch closer, just in case she took pity on him and let him do wicked things to her.

"It's not your fault," she said, clearly in headshrinker

mode. "As a kid you were used to being on your own and as you got older you took refuge in it. There's nothing wrong with that."

"There is if it keeps you from what you want."

Go ahead. Ask me. She wanted to. Way sensed it in the way her eyes narrowed. "Please, ask me what I want." He stepped even closer, fully in her space now and close enough to feel her warm breath on his neck. Slowly, his insides came apart. "I'll tell you what I want if you ask."

She tipped her head up, met his direct gaze. "What do you want?"

"I want you. You challenge me and make me think. And, hell, I like having you close."

She stared up at him, her eyes big and so insanely dark he couldn't anticipate what she might say.

Which probably wasn't a good thing for him.

Then she blinked.

Twice.

I've got a shot.

That brief hesitation, he'd learned, sometimes meant weakening. He didn't want her weak, though. He wanted strong, pushy Roni Fenwick.

"What are you thinking?" he asked.

"I don't know."

He laughed. "I guess it's not a no. That's good."

She glanced around the apartment, waved her hand. "This is my home. I thought it was, anyway. Now, without a job here, I'm not sure." She faced him again. "I enjoyed Steele Ridge. Maybe not everyone knowing everyone else's business, but there was comfort there, too. Like something I'd been missing. I never felt that before."

"Why do you think I take off on my motorcycle for weeks at a time? It's a pain in the ass sometimes with everybody up in your grill all the time. Going to the post office turns into a two-hour trip. You see twelve freaking people who ask a billion questions."

"But that's what I've never had. I kinda like that."

God help her, then, because if she moved to Steele Ridge, she'd have a truckload of it. "So, what are you saying? You want to move to Steele Ridge?"

"I don't know. I could try it, but if things don't work out with us, I'd have to move."

"Who says things won't work out?"

"First of all, if you haven't noticed, things don't necessarily go my way when it comes to relationships. And you brought it up so we might as well talk about it."

Here it comes. All the reasons it won't work. He'd tackle them one by one. "Okay." He waggled his fingers. "Give it to me."

"I've been alone pretty much my whole life. Spending time with you and your family makes me want more of it. I want the bond you all share and to, well, belong."

He shrugged. "I want that, too. Let me prove it to you. I think we'd be good together."

"But you like to leave for weeks at a time. I'm not okay with that. A few days maybe, but if we're going to be together, I want us *together*."

"You want the picket fence?"

"No. I want company and conversation." She gestured to the room again. "I don't want this anymore. Every night I come home to an empty apartment. I'm done being alone all the time. And I think that's a deal-breaker for you."

On the way here, Way had prepped for this. Hours on his motorcycle gave him plenty of time to think. About her, what she'd need.

What he'd need.

As independent as she was, he'd anticipated her wanting more than he'd ever given. After the life she'd had, she deserved that.

Which meant stepping up. Leaving behind the resentment that'd built up regarding his family.

"I hear what you're saying. I think I have a compromise."

"What?"

He grinned. God help him if she didn't go for it. He'd be toast. Absolutely charred.

"I have an extra helmet," he said.

"Pardon?"

"For road trips. I have an extra helmet. You could come with me. I think that would be...fun. Just the two of us. The open road. No plan. What do you say, Roni? Wanna take a chance?"

SHE SURE DID.

Roni stood in front of Way, her heart slamming hard enough that he might have felt the blast from where he stood.

Could she do this? Give up everything here in DC and take a chance on Steele Ridge? Small-town life versus the chaos of DC.

Why not?

Darn, her heart. Always wanting something just out of her reach.

Do it.

She closed her eyes, fought the confusion fogging her brain. At this point, she wasn't sure if her heart or her brain was sending the messages.

Maybe both?

Wouldn't that be a dream? Finally, her world coming together.

She held his gaze. Even if she said yes, threw herself into his arms and agreed, could he actually do it? Give up that privacy he craved so much?

"Are you sure about this?" *Please let him be sure.* "Because this would be huge for me. To take a chance and then have you decide you can't do it would devastate me. And...and what if I want kids one day?"

The second the words burst free, she regretted it. Too much. She'd thrown too much at him at once. But, well, it was what it was. If he couldn't handle it, better to know now.

"I love kids," he said.

Hope, a truckload full, exploded in her chest. "Kids require stability. If this progresses and we have kids, we can't be taking off on a motorcycle."

"But we can load kids into a car." He held up his hand. "They're not in school all year. We'll make it work. We can both get what we want."

Oh, Way. An answer for everything.

"You have to be sure. That's all I'm asking. Sure you can deal with having someone new in the Kingdom of Way."

He dipped his head, hovering just over her lips. "Do you hear that?"

"What?"

"That squeak."

What the hell was he talking about? But, oh, his lips were right there. So close to hers. "What squeak?"

"Listen hard. It's the gates to my kingdom opening."

She kissed him. Just slammed her lips against his and threw her arms around his neck, pulling him closer, loving the feel of him against her.

He angled his head and parted his lips, slipping his

tongue against hers in a gentle movement that made her previously frozen heart overheat.

She could love him. If he'd let her, she could do it.

She slid her mouth from his and hugged him, pressing against him and hanging on while she propped her chin on his shoulder and squeezed her eyes closed, fighting a spurt of happy tears.

New man. New life.

Fresh start.

He'd offered her the life she'd dreamed of. A version of it anyway. A compromise.

If he could do it, so could she.

He patted her lower back. "Roni? You okay?"

More than okay. Roni Fenwick, the practiced cynic was...hopeful.

She eased back. For this, she wanted to be looking straight at him.

At her future.

"I'm great," she said. "You make me think I can have things I've always dreamed of. That's a gift I will always love you for. Thank you."

He leaned down, resting his forehead against hers. "Don't thank *me*. Everything feels right when I'm with you. You make me happy and I didn't realize how long it'd been since I felt that. So, thank *you*. Now, what do you say? Wanna take a road trip?"

Yes.

She let out a laugh. "I don't have a job and I'm apparently moving to Steele Ridge, so why not?"

He smacked her on the rear. "We'll hit the road for a week, then come back and move you out of here. How's that sound?"

She smiled at him, so handsome and...hers. "It sounds great."

"Good, because I have to bring Hugo and Boss home with me by next week."

"Hugo? *And Boss?* You're taking *both* of them?"

He gave her a mile-wide smile. "They're too damned cute. And they've been through a lot. How can I split them up? Plus, it turns out my cousins have a shitload of land where the pups can hang out when I'm on the road. Or they can ride in the car for roadtrips. It'll be us and the dogs."

The Kingdom of Way. Her, his family and the dogs. How far they'd come.

She threw her arms around him, smacking a kiss on his cheek. "I'm so proud of you. I can't wait to see you with them."

Finally, she was home.

THE STEELE RIDGE SERIES

Steele Ridge: The Kingstons

Steele Ridge: The Steeles

ACKNOWLEDGMENTS

One of the things I love most about being an author is the people I'm fortunate enough to meet along the way. Ten years ago, I crossed paths with Milton and Rhonda Grasle. What started as a professional relationship has grown to a friendship I will always be grateful for. When my *Burning Ache* plot fell apart, I e-mailed Milton and Rhonda and invited myself over.

For two days.

With little notice, they opened their home to me and helped me come up with new plot ideas and a kick-butt heroine for Way. I wish I could find adequate words to express my gratitude. To Milton and Rhonda, thank you for your friendship and for caring. Muhwah!

Tracey Devlyn and Kelsey Browning, thank you for the amazing ride, not to mention your patience while I figured out Way Kingston. He drove me crazy, but has a special place in my heart.

Thank you also to one of my other go-to guys, John Leach. No matter what I throw at you, you have an answer. I keep trying to stump you and it never works!

Tony Iacullo, I so appreciate you helping me weed through the continuous legal questions that arise. Thanks also to Dianna Love for schooling me on the use of a cell phone while riding a motorcycle. I hope to try it myself sometime. To my beta readers, Amy Remus and Liz Semkiu, I know how valuable your time is and I'm honored you spend it with my books.

To Team Steele Ridge, Leiha Mann, Sandy Modesitt, Gina Bernal, and Martha Trachtenberg, this giant fuzzy panda known as Steele Ridge wouldn't grow without your support. It really does take a village.

Finally, as usual, thank you to "my guys" who always make me smile at the end of the day. I love you.

ABOUT THE AUTHOR

 **Adrienne Giordano** is a *USA Today* bestselling author of over thirty romantic suspense and mystery novels. She is a Jersey girl at heart, but now lives in the Midwest with her ultimate supporter of a husband, sports-obsessed son and Elliot, a snuggle-happy rescue. Having grown up near the ocean, Adrienne enjoys paddle-boarding, a nice float in a kayak and lounging on the beach with a good book.

For more information on Adrienne's books, please visit www.AdrienneGiordano.com.

Adrienne can also be found at:
    Facebook.com/AdrienneGiordanoAuthor
    Twitter.com/AdriennGiordano
    Goodreads.com/AdrienneGiordano
    Sign up for Adrienne's newsletter at:
    https://adriennegiordano.com/newsletter

Printed in Great
Britain
by Amazon

31789401R00212